# This
# Child
# Is
# Mine

# Also by Henry Denker

NOVELS

I'll Be Right Home, Ma
My Son, the Lawyer
Salome: Princess of Galilee
The First Easter
The Director
The Kingmaker
A Place for the Mighty
The Physicians
The Experiment
The Starmaker
The Scofield Diagnosis
The Actress
Error of Judgment
Horowitz and Mrs. Washington

The Warfield Syndrome
Outrage
The Healers
Kincaid
Robert, My Son
Judge Spencer Dissents
The Choice
The Retreat
A Gift of Life
Payment in Full
Doctor on Trial
Mrs. Washington and Horowitz, Too
Labyrinth

PLAYS

Time Limit
A Far Country
A Case of Libel
What Did We Do Wrong
Venus at Large

Second Time Around
Horowitz and Mrs. Washington
The Headhunters
Outrage!

# This Child Is Mine

A N O V E L

❧ Henry Denker

WILLIAM MORROW AND COMPANY, INC.

New York

75130

It is the policy of William Morrow and Company, Inc., and its imprints and affiliates, recognizing the importance of preserving what has been written, to print the books we publish on acid-free paper, and we exert our best efforts to that end.

**Library of Congress Cataloging-in-Publication Data**

Denker, Henry.
This child is mine : a novel / by Henry Denker.
p.   cm.
ISBN 0-688-14125-0
1. Custody of children—United States—Fiction.   2. Mother and child—United States—Fiction.   I. Title.
PS3507.E5475T47   1995
813'.54—dc20                                                          94-32360
                                                                               CIP

Printed in the United States of America

First Edition

1  2  3  4  5  6  7  8  9  10
BOOK DESIGN BY PATRICE SHERIDAN

To Edith, my wife

# Chapter 1

It had been a warmer than usual day for a midwestern June. The heat hung heavy even after the sun went down. Bill and Christine Salem had discussed keeping the air conditioner on all night. Bill said it was not only efficient to do so but certainly could not harm Billy. Christie questioned that, especially when she recalled, "This afternoon, each time I picked him up from his bassinette, the little folds at the back of his neck were very damp."

"So were mine, darling. It's been one hell of a hot day."

"Exactly what I mean. What if he turns his head in his sleep? Suppose his damp skin is suddenly exposed to the cool air?"

"Okay, okay," Bill conceded. "I will close the air-conditioning vents in the nursery."

They went to bed immediately after the ten o'clock news. Bill had an early-morning meeting to discuss an annual computer-maintenance contract with a large company. Since this was the first deal of such size his young business was ready to undertake, he wanted to be fresh and sharp for the negotiations.

Having decided that the most convincing argument he could make was that a maintenance contract was more economical than the emergency service calls he had been making on the company in the last few months, Bill drifted off to sleep.

Christine fell asleep more easily. But she woke with a start.

She wondered, had Bill wakened her? No, from his breathing she knew he was finally asleep. What had wakened her? She glanced at the clock on the night table. By its dim light she could make out the time. Four twenty-six.

It had been more than six hours since she had nursed little Billy. Long past his usual feeding. Yet he was not crying. Strange. Unless fed on time, Billy always cried. She sprang from the bed and raced across the hall into his room. He was asleep. She reached out, touched his soft cheek. Cold. Very cold. Unnaturally cold. She touched him gently. He did not react. She lifted him into her arms. He was limp. *Limp.*

"Bill!" she cried out, then began to breathe into her son's open mouth in a desperate attempt to administer her improvised version of mouth-to-mouth resuscitation. By that time Bill was racing into the room demanding, "Chris! What is it? Chris!"

She held out their son to him.

"Billy! He's not breathing!"

"Give him to me!" Bill demanded, seizing the child from her arms. He, too, tried to breathe life into the infant's mouth.

"The hospital!" Chris cried in desperation.

They raced down the stairs, into the garage. Bill handed her the tiny limp body as he started up the station wagon, backed out, and turned in the direction of the hospital.

Horn blaring at the cross streets, wheels screaming on the turns, within seven minutes the Salem family arrived at Mercy Hospital's Emergency Entrance.

With Chris at his side, Bill Salem, his infant son in his arms, raced to the entrance, pushed through the door, shouting, "A doctor! We need a doctor!"

A nurse in white rushed out to meet them. One look and she directed them to an examining room. Within moments a doctor entered, took the infant from Bill's arms, carefully applied his stethoscope to the infant's chest and back, glanced at the tearful mother, then at the father.

"Mr. . . . ?" The doctor was asking for the name.

"Salem."

"Mr. Salem . . . Mrs. Salem . . . I'm sorry, but your baby is dead. Has been for some time. Several hours, maybe."

"That's impossible!" Christine shouted, and hurled herself at the doctor. Pushing him aside, she gathered her son into her arms. "I want to see another doctor!"

When neither the doctor nor the nurse moved, she demanded, "I insist on seeing another doctor! One who knows what he's doing."

"Chris . . . Christie . . . darling," Bill pleaded, trying to take his son from her arms. She refused to surrender him. "Honey . . ." he pleaded.

Still she refused, tears streaming down her cheeks.

"Nobody wants to do anything . . . nobody wants to do anything . . . nobody. Not even you!" she accused.

"Christie, please . . ."

"Not even you," she continued to accuse her husband.

Finally, her eyes turning upward, she fainted. Fortunately Bill was able to catch her before she fell. Gently he removed the infant from her hold and passed him to the nurse.

"I'd better give her a shot before she comes to," the doctor said. "She'll need it, for what's coming."

"Mr. Salem!" Dr. Grissom, in charge of the Emergency Service, summoned Bill.

Torn between Christie's pain and the doctor's pointed request, Bill glared at him as if to say, *Damn it, man, have you no respect for my wife's suffering?*

Nevertheless, the doctor persisted. "Mr. Salem, please!"

Another comforting hug to Christie, to keep her until he returned, Bill crossed the empty lobby to confer with the doctor.

"Mr. Salem, I can appreciate your shock, your wife's shock, at the sudden death of your infant son. But there are things to be done. . . ."

"I will make all the arrangements. We'll have little Billy removed as soon as possible."

"I'm afraid you misunderstand," the doctor replied. "I want your permission for the autopsy."

"Autopsy? What for?" Bill Salem demanded, outraged.

"To find the cause of your son's sudden death, if possible."

"What the hell good will that do now?" Bill demanded in a voice so loud it brought Christine to his side.

"Bill?" she asked through her tears.

"It's nothing, hon. Nothing," Bill said, glaring at the doctor as if to warn him: *Don't mention autopsy to her. Not now.*

The doctor was forced to insist, "Mr. Salem, we would *like* your permission. But we can proceed without it. It's the law."

"Law? What's the law got to do with this?" Christie demanded.

With an apologetic look to Bill, in as calm and professional manner as he could, the doctor said, "Mrs. Salem, whenever a death occurs without a history of illness or some other cause, the law insists on an autopsy."

"Autopsy?" Christie repeated. She turned to Bill, demanding that he intervene to prevent it. When Bill did not, she turned on the doctor.

"You mean you want to take my son's . . . my baby's . . . take his soft little body and just . . . no! No! I won't let you! I won't!"

She raced to the examining table and clutched her tiny son in her arms, ready to defy the world.

The doctor appealed to Bill to intercede.

He moved to his wife, tried to take their dead child from her arms. She was adamant, a woman defiant, protecting her only child from what she considered a barbarous ritual.

Bill pleaded, "Christie . . . darling . . . it's the law. There is nothing we can do to stop it. They have to do it. To find the cause."

She turned to confront the doctor.

"The cause? You want to find the cause? Oh, I see now. You've been watching too much television," she accused him. "These days anything happens to an infant, it becomes child abuse. You think we *did* something. *I* did something. To cause his death. I love him! He's everything to me, everything!"

She broke down. Bill embraced her, pressing her wet face comfortingly against his shoulder.

In a soft and respectful voice the doctor used the moment to say, "Mrs. Salem, there are many causes of infant death. Brain hemorrhage. Meningitis. Myocarditis. *And* Sudden Infant Death Syndrome. For the record and for the advancement of medical knowledge so that such deaths may one day be prevented, it is crucial that we know the cause in all cases. We would like your permission."

"It can't help Billy!" she challenged him.

"Mrs. Salem, if you could spare just one mother the pain you are now going through, would you do it?"

"This would . . . could . . ." Christie started to ask, then, more calmly because she needed to make sure the doctor was being truthful, she stared into his eyes. "You mean this could one day help other little ones like Billy?"

"The more we know, the better our chance to prevent such tragedies."

Christie Salem considered his words. Then, slowly, she held out her arms, permitting the doctor to take her son.

# Chapter 2

❧

Bill Salem shepherded his wife along the empty early-hours corridor of the Emergency Service. Though she was fairly tall, protected by her big, muscular husband, Christie Salem appeared quite small. Her loose black hair, in disarray, distracted from her neatly featured face, which was now stained with tears that dried to leave a light white salt stain.

Just before they reached the exit, the doors swung open. A young nurse, reporting for duty on the six o'clock shift, took one look at Christie Salem's face and drew back to hold the doors open for them. She had seen that look before.

Bill led Christie out into the humid but cool air of the summer dawn. The light was breaking far to the east, just beyond the river that split this small midwestern town in two.

With great tenderness he guided his benumbed wife to their station wagon. Fastening her seat belt for her, he climbed in alongside, then started the car toward the exit gate.

He drove slowly, very slowly, in great contrast to the reckless speed at which he had driven only a few hours ago, when he thought there was still a chance of saving his infant son.

He anticipated every traffic light, slowing down long before necessary. He wondered, *Am I trying to put off bringing Christie home? Because it will be so empty now? The nursery, the first place I rush to when I get home every evening, am I trying to avoid it now?*

*And Christie, since she handed Billy over to that doctor, she hasn't said a word. Not a word. I know one thing. No matter how deep my own pain, I don't dare cry. Not now.*

He drove on in silence. Christie stared. Straight ahead. With eyes that seemed to see nothing. When he arrived at their corner, about to make the turn onto their street, she spoke for the first time.

"No," she said.

"No?"

"Just keep driving," she said.

"Where?"

"Doesn't matter."

Because of her strange and unaccustomed manner, he continued driving straight ahead.

They had left the city and were out on the state highway. Perhaps it was the open country, the freedom from the city, that enabled her to talk.

Her first words were, "Me. It was me."

"You?" he asked, puzzled.

"If I just woke up at the time I was supposed to . . . if I hadn't overslept . . ." she said.

"It couldn't have made any difference. The doctor said no one knows how it happens."

"If I'd been there when Billy was fighting for breath . . ."

"Hon, please, stop tormenting yourself," Bill tried to console her, while he counted the ways he himself might have changed this tragic outcome.

Suddenly Christine asked, "Do you think he knew? I mean, did he feel anything? Pain? Did he struggle? Try to fight to stay alive?"

"Christie, darling, no one knows. So you can't go on blaming yourself. It was no one's fault. No one's fault."

Suddenly, with great conviction, she blurted out, "He felt he'd been abandoned."

"By whom?"

"By me."

"Abandoned?" Bill replied. "God, honey, there's never been a more devoted mother! Never!"

"I left him," she said, with the conviction of one who had spent considerable time pondering a situation and had arrived at what she believed was the only answer.

"When?" Bill challenged. "*When* did you leave him?"

"I went back to work," she said.

"But we hired Mrs. Baines. The best baby nurse we could find. Everybody said she was terrific. And she was. You can't blame yourself for that. You were home every four hours to nurse him. How can you say he was abandoned?" Bill demanded.

"Never should have done it," was all she would say, and fell silent once more.

In a while he granted, "If you really think that's what did it, then put the blame where it belongs. On me!"

"Not your fault. Mine."

"Who was it asked you to go back to work?" he demanded.

"Doesn't matter," she said, persisting in self-guilt.

"But it does. If I hadn't needed the extra income to expand the business . . . If the business wasn't growing . . . If, if, if! If the computer plant hadn't moved south, I'd still have my job. I wouldn't be in my own business . . . wouldn't need capital to expand. Of course, if my business didn't do so well, we wouldn't have had Billy. Not yet. Don't you see, Christie, it's all built on ifs. There's only one thing sure. You were a terrific mother. Always. From the very first moment."

"Then why did he die?" she asked.

He had no answer to that.

They drove on in silence. Seeking answers, he performed a silent accounting of his own. It all started with his layoff from the computer plant. For months thereafter, almost a year, he had searched for a new position that would allow him to use his technical expertise. He had gone several hundred miles out of town applying for jobs. He had sent out what seemed an endless number of résumés. With no more response than two interviews and no job.

Things had grown so bad that their savings and his termination pay had dwindled to the point where Christie's income alone no longer was able to stave off the loss of their home through foreclosure.

Out of sheer desperation he seized on the idea of opening up a small computer repair and maintenance business, working out of their garage.

Christie had suggested the name: Handyman, Inc. He had fliers printed up, put a few small ads in the local newspaper. It developed that there was a need for the service he had to offer.

The name "Handyman, Inc." was so inclusive that electronic jobs of all sorts were referred to him. After a year and a half the business had prospered to the extent that for the first time they felt comfortable with the idea of having a child. Three months after Billy was born, the business was doing so well that Bill needed a helper to service his accounts. And their garage was no longer large enough.

That was when he broached the idea of Christie returning to her job at the small advertising agency where she had worked when they first met and until she was seven months pregnant with Billy.

To make sure their little son would not suffer from their change in plans, they had found the best baby nurse in town. Christie arranged her own work schedule so she nursed Billy at eight in the morning before she went off to work. She came home for lunch at noon to nurse him again, and left the office at four. All so that his every-four-hour nursing schedule would never be interrupted. At night, she was always up every four hours in anticipation of his feeding. Rarely did he wake before her.

And that first day, Bill thought as he drove aimlessly along the country road, her reluctance, her misgivings, at leaving Billy with Mrs. Baines. She repeated every instruction half a dozen times. And Mrs. Baines, patient and experienced baby nurse, kept nodding and smiling. She had been through these first day jitters with many working mothers before Christie.

Mrs. Baines hadn't even minded that Christie called three times that morning to make sure everything was all right. And that night, he remembered, Christie said to him, "I think he knows."

"Knows what?"

"That I left him. When I came home at four o'clock to nurse him, I think I could feel him sucking even harder. I think he missed me. It did something to his sense of security."

Yet when they brought him in to Dr. Whitmore for his regular checkup, the doctor found weight gain normal, reflexes normal, heart and lungs normal.

Christie asked, "Does he show any signs of being left with a stranger? They say babies can be very sensitive, even at three months."

Whitmore said, "They can indeed. But evidently this young man is secure enough to cope with the change in his daily routine. I wouldn't worry about it, my dear."

Those were his words, "I wouldn't worry about it, my dear."

Yet it had happened. During the night of June 22, 1994, it had happened.

*Now Christie is blaming herself for it. If there's to be blame, if anyone's to blame, it's me. I should have been good enough to succeed on my own. Not have to ask her to leave Billy in the hands of a nurse and go back to work so I could keep the business expanding. My fault.*

They were out into farming country. The narrow rutted road ran between wide fields of newly sprouting corn. It seemed they had been driving for hours.

"Hon . . . ?" he asked. She did not respond.

He reached a small crossroads that afforded him enough room to turn around. He started back.

After a time Christie asked, "Where are we going?"

"Home," Bill said. "We are going home."

This time she did not protest. She stared straight ahead. Dry-eyed.

# Chapter 3

†

Because of the delicate nature of SIDS tragedies, the police commissioner had made it a rule to assign a plainclothes female officer to the compulsory investigation. Detective Dorothy Hendricks was a slight, tidy woman with short brown hair that framed a plain face with sensitive brown eyes. She made a point of appearing ingenuous almost to the point of being inexperienced, though she was actually an acutely aware investigator.

When she appeared at the door of the Salem house, she was admitted by one of the many neighbors who had gathered to lend what aid and comfort they could to the grieving Salems.

Once introduced to Christie, Dorothy Hendricks explained that this was simply a routine visit. She asked Christie to show her little Billy's room. While she carefully examined the room, the bassinette, the toys, she asked Christie to relate all the details she could recall preceding her shocking discovery.

Christie relived the familiar routine. Bathing little Billy, fresh diaper, gown over his diaper.

"Then I fed him again. . . ."

"Bottle or breast?" Dorothy Hendricks asked.

"Breast. Always my breast. I felt it gave him a stronger sense of security to . . . to see him through the night . . . until the next feeding, usually about one o'clock."

"Did you notice anything different about him that particular night? Any difficulty in feeding? Or the way he reacted? Anything like that?"

"If you remember, that was a particularly warm day for June. So he perspired more than usual. But aside from that, nothing. I walked him around after feeding him—I always carry him around a little, to burp him, you know. I always . . ."

She realized that she had lapsed into the present tense. That awareness made her begin to weep self-consciously.

"Feel free, Ms. Salem," Dorothy encouraged softly. "It helps."

Patiently, with great sympathy, the woman led Christie through the detail of the events leading up to placing Billy into his bassinette.

"Now, when you placed him back in here . . ."

"I did exactly what Dr. Whitmore always said to do. Set him on his side, not on his stomach. As an extra precaution, roll up two towels. Put one on each side of him so if he does try to turn during the night, he won't end up on his stomach. Dr. Whitmore said it could happen when an infant sleeps on his stomach."

Dorothy noted that Christine avoided using the term Sudden Infant Death Syndrome. Or SIDS. She could only refer to the sad event as "it."

"Then I covered him with his light blanket. . . ." Christie reached into the bassinette to pick up the fluffy light blue–trimmed white blanket. When her hand began to tremble, Dorothy took it from her and returned it to the bassinette.

"Mrs. Salem, when did you get your first hint that something was wrong?"

"Do you have any children?" Christie asked.

"No, no, I don't," Dorothy admitted.

"Well, if you had, you'd know that when you're nursing, you develop your own personal clock. You know almost to the minute when he's going to wake up hungry. You anticipate it. Even when you're asleep. You just know. So you wake up and, most times, sure enough, he's awake or waking and asking for your breast. But that night . . . when I woke suddenly and didn't hear him, I . . . I sensed there was something wrong. . . ."

"But before that, you had absolutely no sign, no hint?"

"Nothing." Then, feeling accused, Christie added, "They told us the autopsy report said there was absolutely no evidence of neglect or abuse. So if that's what you're thinking . . ."

"Please, Mrs. Salem. It was a clear case of Sudden Infant Death Syndrome with no known cause. Nobody is accusing you. All we are doing is collecting facts. So we can close this case."

"*You* can close it," Christie said. "But I will never be able to close it! Never!"

"I know," Dorothy commiserated. "I think I should prepare you. There will be a social worker who will ask you many of these same questions. Believe me, none of us means you any harm. This is all for the public good."

"So I've been told."

"I can tell you one other thing," Dorothy said. "Based on all the cases I've investigated, I know that while the pain never goes away completely, things do get better. People *do* resume their lives. There *are* other children. So, grieve, but don't despair."

Whatever comfort Christie found in those words slowly dissipated as the day wore on. When evening came, friends and consoling relatives departed. The house was empty except for Bill and herself.

Exhausted by the demands thrust on him to arrange the funeral, contending with well-intentioned mourners, making emergency provisions for his absence from his business, Bill Salem urged, "Come, hon, let's go to bed. Maybe tonight we can get some sleep."

Without a word or a gesture she yielded to him, permitting him to lead her up the stairs. She undressed by habit, slipped on a nightgown, then seemed suddenly fumbling and inept when it came to pulling back the covers. He did that for her. When he slipped into bed, he put his arm around her and drew her close.

Her body had never been so cold. He pressed against her, hoping to share his warmth. So close, they fell asleep.

Not two hours later he woke. He was alone.

"Christie? Hon?" he called softly.

No response. He rolled out of bed, searching and calling at the same time.

"Chris . . . Christie . . ."

He raced to the head of the stairs to see if there was a light on below. It was dark and quiet. He started down to investigate when he heard her voice, coming from Billy's dark room. He went to the door. He found her.

She was at Billy's changing table. Laid out before her in the darkness were one of Billy's fresh diapers, his gown, a fresh, clean white receiving blanket to wrap him in.

His first thought was, *She's broken under the strain.* His voice betrayed his fear as he called, "Christie!"

She turned to find him in the darkness. "Don't worry, I am just going through the steps. . . ."

"Steps?"

"Doing what I did that night. Trying to discover what did I do wrong."

"The autopsy *proved* you did nothing wrong," he insisted. "*Nobody* did anything wrong."

"Something must have been different. I have to find out," she said, quite calmly but with great determination.

He tried to embrace her and lead her back to their bed. She brushed his arms aside with such force that he knew not to try to thwart her.

He watched as she reenacted the procedure she had followed all the days of her young son's life. She went through each stage, slowly, thoughtfully, trying to recall how it went that last time: bath . . . oil . . . fresh diaper . . . gown. She picked up the empty gown, placed it against her shoulder, walked it around, patting it as she used to pat her little son. She wrapped the empty gown in the blanket, carefully forming it into a triangle, folding over one side, then the other, finally folding the bottom up. She placed the blanket in the bassinette and rolled up two towels to serve as buffers to keep the blanket in place.

Throughout she repeated to herself each action and the purpose as she performed it. When she was done, she said, "Everything . . . I did everything right. Then why . . . why?"

She broke down. He held her close, heard her whisper, "Wrong. I must have done something wrong that one time . . . something. . . ."

After Christie had succumbed to the sedative their doctor had prescribed to see her through these first terrible days, Bill Salem slipped out of their bedroom.

He went into Billy's room. Found himself repeating the steps Christie had gone through. Bath . . . oil . . . fresh diaper . . . gown. He himself had done all that for Billy a number of times. They believed in that, Christie and he. Having a child, caring for a child, was a shared experience.

Just as now, alone in this room, in the dead of night, he was able to protest, silently, but protest nevertheless, *losing* a child was a shared experience, too. No longer faced with having to comfort Christie, Bill Salem was able to give way to his own pain.

He had not wept since his own father's funeral, but at his son's empty crib, Bill Salem started to weep. Tears. Hot tears started down his stubbled cheeks. He was gasping when he suddenly heard what he thought was movement in their bedroom. Hastily he brushed his tears away with the backs of his hands. He started for the bedroom. One look and he was relieved to discover that Christie was still in bed, curled up on her side, asleep.

But relief was not able to ease his own pain. He went back into Billy's room. Billy's room. That was no longer Billy's.

Now he felt free to weep with no inhibitions.

# Chapter 4

❧

In the first few days after the simple funeral, men and women from a SIDS support group who had each suffered the same tragedy called at the Salem house to console them. To reassure them they were in no way responsible for what had happened.

But Bill knew his wife well, well enough to suspect that, though she appeared to listen, to absorb and accept their reassurances, she could not fully believe them. After they left, he urged her to consider going back to work.

"You're right. I must resume a normal life," she resolved. "If not for myself, then for you, darling. God knows you've been through as much as I have."

For several days Christie woke early each morning despite a sleepless night. She dressed and set off for work. The relief Bill felt at this new stage in her recovery was shattered when on the fourth morning Mr. Derwent called to inquire when Christie might feel up to coming back to work.

On the fifth morning Bill parked down the street from the house. He waited for her station wagon to pass, trailed her at a discreet distance. He followed her to the city library. There he tracked her down in the Professional Periodicals Room. He observed her poring over the latest issues of various journals devoted to pediatrics. She was reading up on the latest findings concerning Sudden Infant Death Syndrome.

That afternoon Bill went to consult Dr. Whitmore. After reporting his discovery, Bill asked, "Doctor, do you think I should take her to see a psychiatrist?"

"Bill, no two people go through the grieving process in quite the same way. True, men and women both feel pain. But in cases like this there is a difference. Christie, the woman, lived through months of pregnancy in great anticipation of Billy being born. Lived through the travail and joy of giving birth. Now that he is gone, and so suddenly, there is a tremendous void in her life. What she dreamed of during those nine months . . . what she went through the pains of childbirth for, has been taken away. In the worst possible manner. What she needs now is not psychiatry but something to fill that void."

"You mean . . . another baby?" Bill asked.

"Exactly," the doctor affirmed.

"There's nothing I'd love more. But with her feeling the way she does now, I was afraid to even suggest it."

"The mere thought of being pregnant again would give her something to look forward to," Whitmore counseled.

That night when Bill had broached the idea as gently as he could, Christie replied, "Darling, no need for you to feel guilty."

Taken aback by her strange reply, he said, "It's not a matter of feeling guilty, it's what would be best for *us*."

"You mean best for *me*," she corrected.

"No, I mean *us*. Just as Billy was for *us*, so a new baby would be for *us*. We'd be a family again."

She did not respond but lay beside him in their dark bedroom, staring up at the ceiling, seeing nothing.

After a long silence he asked, "What did you mean?"

"About what?"

"Guilty. Why should I feel guilty?" Bill demanded.

"I said no *need* for you to feel guilty," she pointed out.

"Which means that I should be feeling guilty even though there's no need," he insisted. "I demand to know what you meant by that!"

"I don't blame *you*," she insisted, but it was so strong a denial that he was now sure that she did.

He drew her to him, pressed against her, and spoke softly into her ear.

"Christie . . . darling . . . this is no time for us to be drawing apart. We need each other. You need me. And, if anything, I need you even more. I wish I could do and say all the things I would like to at such a time. But I can't . . . for . . . for fear . . . of . . ."

"For fear of what it would do to me," she said softly, part statement, part question.

"Yes," he admitted.

"I know, darling, I know."

He felt her hot tears on his bare chest. He held her close, kissed her, and eventually she responded. Soon, soon, they were making love for the first time since that awful night.

After, and in the quiet of the night, she confessed, "I thought that you felt guilty about my going back to work. That was the one thing that was different. My not being here for him all the time. Maybe he felt unwanted and just decided to . . . to leave."

"No child was ever loved more than we loved Billy," he insisted.

She embraced him and clung to him, and they both fell asleep.

# Chapter 5

✤

In the weeks that followed, Christie and Bill Salem relived the last night of their infant son's life, seeking the elusive clue that might explain despite what all the doctors had told them could not be explained.

Times at the dinner table, or late at night after making love, when Bill sensed that she was at just such a moment, he would say only, "Please, darling . . ."

They both knew those two words were sufficient to plead: *We have to give up this searching. It can only lead to more pain, more frustration for both of us.*

Meantime, work proved some salvation. The challenge of creating new layouts for newspaper ads for the Derwent Agency, the demands on her imagination and creativity, diverted her mind from constant grieving, searching, questioning. It served to restore a sense of discipline to her days.

But there were always the nights.

Five months had passed. Christie had not become pregnant. They began to suspect something was wrong. Before she became pregnant with Billy, there had been such a time, too. But that was explained by her gynecologist as the result of Christie having been on the pill for several years.

This time Dr. Moncrief advised, "Give it another few months."

\* \* \*

Four more months went by. Bill went to consult Dr. Moncrief on his own.

"What about all these new ways that pop up in the newspapers and on television virtually every day? Ways to practically manufacture babies in the laboratory. Shouldn't we try that?"

Again Moncrief urged patience. "Those methods are not for use in all cases. Most times couples go to extraordinary expense and trouble only to be disappointed."

"There's no medication? No fertility drugs?" Bill asked in desperation.

"Bill, I've never seen parents of a SIDS baby who could be completely convinced that in some way they weren't responsible. It is a natural reaction in a highly unnatural situation. Even more true of women than of men.

"Perhaps Christie is suffering an emotional block that, for the time being, keeps her from conceiving. Guilt, perhaps. Or a feeling that she is incapable of being a good mother."

"How is she going to prove otherwise if she doesn't become pregnant?" Bill demanded in frustration.

"Bill," Dr. Moncrief comforted him gently, "you're both young. Both healthy. You have a good sperm count, good motility. Give it time."

"How much time?" he persisted.

"I can't answer that," the doctor said. "No one can."

Seeking some solace, Bill conceded, "At least she doesn't go to the library anymore. And when the SIDS group drops by, she seems more patient about listening. Though once they're gone, she always cries."

A bit reluctantly, but in the interest of truth, he admitted, "I feel the same way. But I don't dare cry. Not when she can see me. It would only make her feel worse."

"Typical, Bill. When one SIDS parent suspects the other might go to pieces, he, or she, becomes stronger. Strong enough for two. And I commend you for it. Keep it up. As for another pregnancy, I still say, give it time."

# Chapter 6

❧

Lori Adams, slender, blonde, looking even younger than her twenty years, stepped out of the street-level offices of the obstetrics-gynecological clinic on West Forty-eighth Street in Manhattan.

She started east toward Eighth Avenue, unaware of the noises of impatient auto and truck horns that were directed at her as she crossed the busy street against the red light.

"Hey, you crazy kid! You blind or something?" a hoarse, angry voice berated her.

But it was the screech of a car stopping suddenly to avoid hitting her that brought her out of her dazed condition. She started to run toward the opposite side of the avenue, only to trip, fall, and cause a wide, unsightly run in her pantyhose, which began to turn pink, then red, from her bloody knee.

A middle-aged black man came to her side to help her to her feet.

"You all right, kid? You need help?"

"No, I'm fine . . . fine. . . ." Lori protested, though by now she had begun to weep silently.

"Can I get you a cab?" the man persisted.

"No, please, just leave me alone," she replied, tearing her arm free.

"Look, if you need—" he continued.

"I don't need anything!" she insisted. "And if you don't leave me alone, I'll scream for help."

In face of that threat the black man backed off and raised his hands, palms facing her to indicate surrender to her threat.

"Sorry, kid. Only wanted to help." He started down the street, turning back once to see if she was safely out of any danger.

*Shouldn't have done that, shouldn't have said that,* Lori reproached herself. *He was only trying to help. Got to find Brett . . . got to find Brett . . .*

She turned south on Eighth Avenue to Forty-sixth Street, then realized that in her distraught haste she had crossed the avenue when she should have remained on the west side. This time she waited impatiently for the light to change and ran across once it had. Then she continued on Forty-sixth to Joe Allen's, the informal, moderate restaurant where many young actors and actresses either worked between jobs or hung out at mealtimes between auditions and interviews.

Her single glance disclosed that Brett was not there. Lori inquired of the cashier, Goldie Levine, "Isn't Brett scheduled for this afternoon?"

"Was. But took two hours off. They're casting a new Sam Shepard play at the Hayes. He's hoping for a chance to read," the cashier said, with an air of sympathetic despair. She had watched a whole generation of young aspiring actors pursue the same futile routine. Like ocean waves dashing against a sea wall, only to fall back each time, until the ocean seemed to surrender out of sheer exhaustion.

One by one, the young aspirants disappeared. To where, she did not know. Only a handful lasted, few succeeded, very few became known. One or two became big movie stars. Later, Goldie would boast, "He worked here, you know. Was a waiter. Now he gets ten million dollars a film."

But most of them, and most likely Brett Mann, too, would go the usual way. Eventually disappear and be forgotten. Yet, despite the odds, young men like Brett Mann and young women like Lori Adams kept thrusting against that high insurmountable bastion called "The Theater."

Jaded though she was, Goldie had never become inured to the troubles of those young people who worked at, or frequented, Joe Allen's.

As now, she realized that Lori was in the throes of some personal problem and desperately needed (tearfully, if Goldie could judge from the red rims of Lori's eyes) the assurance and comfort of Brett Mann.

"Sweetie, sit down," Goldie urged. "Coffee?"

Lori shook her head but began to weep again. Then she nodded, yes, coffee would help.

Goldie led her to the table in the far corner of the large restaurant. On the way, other young actors and actresses called out, "Hi, Lori," and similar salutations. Though she tried, she could not return their well-meant greetings.

She waited almost two hours, and through four cups of coffee that she allowed to turn cold, before she spied Brett entering. Goldie obviously called to the tall blond young actor, for he stopped at the cashier's desk. As soon as Goldie whispered a few words, Brett stared across the room and hurried toward that far table.

"Lori, sweetheart, what is it? What's wrong?"

"How did you make out?" she asked, partly out of genuine interest but mostly because she could not find the courage to answer his question.

"Waited an hour and a half, and then, just before my turn to read, they said the part was cast," he reluctantly reported. "Now, you . . ."

Lori looked across the table at him, fixed on his eyes to read his honest reaction, and his words, when she said softly, "Brett, I am pregnant."

Hoping to find sympathy in his eyes, support, encouragement, she found only fear. Staring into her eyes, he pleaded for a pardon for what he evidently considered a verdict of guilty of the crime.

They both sat still and silent. Watching from her post at the cashier's desk, Goldie Levine had seen this same scene enacted too many times during her years at Allen's not to know what it meant. A young actor and actress living together or loving together. Then the

23

inevitable occurs. How they faced it varied from case to case. But there were two usual outcomes. Either they split up, or else they decided to continue on together. Until they eventually did break up. Goldie had learned that few couples survived this trauma.

Brett remained silent. Lori dared not speak for fear that if she did, she would start weeping. She had promised herself that was the one thing she would not do. She would be strong. She would be mature. So that later he could not accuse her of exacting his loyalty through some feminine trick.

"Lori . . . darling . . . we . . . we have to think about this. I mean, we can't, shouldn't, make any rash decisions that we might later regret," he said, faltering with every phrase.

*Oh, God,* she realized, *he's starting to sweat. He's even more frightened than I. And I was looking forward to his strength . . . so looking forward . . .*

"Look," he said, "let's get out of here. Let's get some air . . . fresh air . . . It's too . . . too close in here, too hot. . . ."

Goldie watched them leave, thinking, *He didn't take it too well. Too bad. Nice young people, both of them. Well, they're not the first, and they won't be the last. Unfortunately.*

They walked east along Forty-fourth Street, passing the marquees of theaters with current hits. Though it was not quite dusk, the marquees were already fully lighted. As Brett and Lori passed beneath them, he glanced at her in the light, a quick, furtive glance. To see if she was crying. He thanked God she was not. He had seen her cry before. Twice. The time when she was one of two finalists for a part in a new Off-Broadway play and was edged out by another young actress who had been imported from California because she was considered "a name."

"A name" being someone who was not a star but who had some audience recognition and who could be used to plug the show in TV interviews.

The name Lori Adams was not "known." The way things were going, it never would be. Still she had persevered. Acting classes, volunteering to take part without pay in readings of new plays, doing anything in the theater that might lead to that one role that would do it for her. Make her "a name." Eventually, possibly even a star.

She was not only beautiful, she had talent. More, she had character. She would be a wonderful wife. Especially for an actor who needed that kind of support.

Yet now she looked so sad, so forlorn, staring straight ahead for fear of confronting him. Because she sensed, as he knew, that he was not prepared to give her the response she so desperately needed.

They reached Times Square. They were surrounded by the garish marquees of movie theaters and huge billboards with moving figures and electronic words that ran on endlessly.

The noises of slowly moving impatient traffic assaulted them. Suddenly Brett seized her hand. "Let's go someplace where we can talk."

"Where?"

He dared not suggest the only place where they could have privacy and quiet, their little apartment. That would be too confining.

He led her in the direction of Bryant Park, just behind the main New York Public Library. There were benches there, new benches, since the park had been redone and the drug dealers had been driven out.

On Sixth Avenue and along Forty-second Street pedestrians hurried on their way. Some headed home. Some to early dinner. Some were working students headed toward the City University on the north side of Forty-second.

Brett selected a bench as remote from the others as possible. They sat down, silent for a time. When they spoke, they both spoke at the same time.

"Look, Brett, you don't have to—" Lori began.

While Brett was saying, "Lori, darling, I'm as much a part of this—"

They both stopped.

"Yes, Brett, what were you going to say?"

"This is as much my responsibility as yours. Besides, I've been thinking, especially today after waiting so long, then never even getting the chance to read, to show them what I could do with the part . . . I thought, what the hell are we doing? Torturing ourselves with false promises. Ambition? Crap! Ambition, perseverance, even talent, don't make it. Sure, we hear stories of young actors who get one break and go on to become stars. But for every one of those, there are hundreds, thousands, like us, who never make it. Who fade away, are never heard from again. Who become door-to-door salesmen. Or sell shoes or men's suits or God knows what in shopping malls. If they're lucky. Well, there comes a time when a man has to face the truth. And this—what's happened to you—to us—may be just the thing I needed to make me face the truth."

*He's doing this, saying this,* Lori thought, *because he thinks I expect it, demand it from him. The other day he said the complete opposite. He was determined and strong and confident. No talk then of quitting. He was looking forward to that reading with confidence. I can't let him do this, or even think it.*

"Lori, honey, remember my cousin Ernie?"

"Runs the tire agency in Newburgh," Lori recalled.

"Right," Brett said. "He's always been after me to give up this rat race. That's what he calls the theater. Wants me to come into the business. Says with my charm and good looks I could sell tires like they've never been sold before. That way . . ."

"No, Brett," Lori interrupted, "I can't let you do that. You can't give up."

"But that's the beauty part, baby. I can be working and at the same time, since it's only an hour away from Broadway, I could drive in for a reading or an interview or a meeting with a director or producer. It's a perfect setup!"

Even in the fading glow of late afternoon she could see that he was trying to convince himself even more than her.

She reached for his hand.

"Brett . . . honey, I know you want to say all the right things. Just don't try so hard."

They were both silent for a time. The street noises, cars, buses, sudden laughter, angry shouts, felt much closer now. Too close, intruding on their privacy.

"Any other time—" Brett said suddenly in a single burst of words, then fell speechless.

"I know, darling, I know."

"God, when did it happen? What night? Do you know?" he asked.

"Does it matter?" Lori asked softly.

"Have you thought about—" he began, then hesitated.

But she read his mind. "First thing I thought. I said to myself, it's so simple these days. Why not? But then, for some reason I can't even explain to myself, I discovered that I couldn't."

"You're not that religious."

"I told you, I don't know why I can't. I just can't," she persisted in her quiet, determined way.

He did not pursue that.

"Let's get something to eat. You must be starving," he suggested.

"I'd rather just go home," she said.

They both had a restless night. He tried to console her by making love. She refused him.

In the early hours just before dawn, knowing he was awake though quiet, she said, "I know."

"What?"

"What I will do," she said.

"You'll do it," he assumed.

"No. But I've made up my mind. I'm leaving."

"Leaving? Where will you go?"

"Back home."

"Home? Back to the Midwest?" Brett asked, taken by surprise. "What about your father? He never liked the idea of your coming to New York. The one time he came to visit, I had to move out that week until he left. What'll he say—'I told you so'? In addition to everything else, you want to face that? I won't let you."

"Brett, darling, you no longer have the right to 'let' me do anything," she said, more firmly than she had said anything since the doctor had spoken those fateful words to her.

"Lori . . . honey?"

"I've been thinking about it all night. If I did have an abortion, I would hold it against you the *rest* of my life. If I made you give up your career, *you'd* hold it against *me* the rest of *your* life. Brett, you are not a tire salesman. You are an actor. A damn good one. One day someone will recognize that, and you'll have the career you deserve."

"And you?"

"I'll go back home. If my father refuses to accept me, I'll find some organization, some charitable institution, that takes girls like me."

"God, don't say that!"

"Say what?"

" 'Girls like me.' You're not like all the other girls who become pregnant. This wasn't a one-night stand. Or something that happened in the back of a car during some rock concert. I love you. We love each other. This is different."

"Is it?" Lori asked. "Here we are. I am pregnant. We are not married."

"I said I'd marry you!" he protested.

"And I said no. This is no longer your problem. It's mine. I'll handle it my way."

"The baby . . . what will you do about the baby?"

"I don't know. Yet," she admitted.

# Chapter 7

⚜

Two days later Lori Adams called home. She told them she was coming. Brett took her down to the squalid bus terminal on Eighth Avenue and Forty-second Street.

She did not board until the last moment, which gave them time to talk.

"You'll write me often?" he asked.

"If you want."

"I want, damn it, I want! I love you, Lori. I always will," he protested. "I told you, we could get married."

"And move up to Newburgh . . . and sell tires?" she countered. "So that five years from now you'd have me *and* the baby to blame."

"Board!" the driver called to them.

Quickly Brett embraced her, holding her face close so he could whisper into her ear.

"I swear, first break I get, I'll come for you. We'll get married."

To hurry them and start on schedule, the driver raced the powerful motor with a roar.

Lori slipped out of Brett's arms to climb the two steps into the bus. She found a seat alongside an elderly woman who seemed pleased to have a companion for the long trip west.

Brett watched the bus pull out and start up the ramp onto Ninth Avenue.

*Lori . . . Lori . . . I'll come for you. Believe me . . . just as soon as I'm able,* he vowed. And meant it.

The bus had just crossed the George Washington Bridge, leaving the Hudson River behind. It was heading west on I-80 when Lori's elderly companion said, "I know how you feel, my dear."

Lori hardly dared glance at her. *Did she know? How could she? Women don't show until the fourth month. Or was there some betrayal on a pregnant woman's face?*

Even without encouragement, the woman rambled on, "Same thing happened to me. Except when I was young, we went by train. I always did like trains better than buses. But I cried all the way home, too."

Pausing only a moment, she continued, "Was he a nice man?"

Lori was at a loss to answer, so she whispered a simple, almost noncommittal, "Uh-huh."

"Mine, too," the woman agreed, with the air of thinking back a long time.

Suddenly she startled Lori by asking, "What did he die from?"

"Die?" Lori asked in astonishment.

"Your father . . . what did he die from? Was it one of those quick things like a heart attack? Or was it the long, slow, lingering kind?"

"Oh, no," Lori replied, "my father didn't die. He's fine. Fine."

"But you've been crying ever since you got on . . ." the woman replied, then stopped suddenly to gasp, "Oh, my!"

In those two syllables she revealed that she suddenly knew everything she needed to know about the young, pretty blond-haired woman who would be her companion for the rest of the journey west.

It was raining when the bus pulled into the station in Caryville. Not a hard rain. Just a depressing, continuous drizzle. Lori started up from her seat. Her newfound, and now newly lost, companion for the last eleven hours reached out to take her hand.

"My dear, I hope all goes well for you. And the little one."

Lori bent down to kiss her on the cheek. Meantime, the driver was calling, "Anyone for Caryville?"

"Got to go," Lori said, hurrying forward to the door.

The driver was waiting at the open luggage hatch. Lori identified her two suitcases, which had been new when she left home almost three years ago.

When she struggled to lift both bags at once and was unable to, the driver helped her to the protected area under the overhang of the modest bus station.

She waited there, looking around for some sign of her father. She did not find him. At once she assumed, *He didn't come. He couldn't face it. Not that I blame him.*

Though she did blame him. She did. Stern though he was, given to strict discipline because of his early military years, she had not expected that he would desert her now.

She was forced to consider her alternatives. There were two friends in her senior class in high school who still lived in Caryville. She might call them. Only they had since married, and she did not remember their new names. Perhaps if she skimmed the very thin Caryville phone book, that would revive her memory. She shoved her bags closer to the wall to protect them from the rain, then started for the booth at the end of the station. She found the phone book hanging by its galvanized link chain. She discovered it had been trashed by some predator. Pages had been ripped out. The ones that remained were mutilated.

She dropped it and turned away. As she did, she heard her name.

"Lori . . ."

She looked in the direction of the voice, to find her father's old Plymouth. The angle of the windshield, and the monotonous sweep of the wipers, made it difficult to identify him at once. As the car moved slowly toward her, she could finally make him out.

In that instant she knew she was trying to read his face. Was he as angry as she expected? Or was he merely grim? Her dad had his moods. Some days you couldn't tell. Was he angry with the world outside? Or was he angry with himself for not fulfilling his

31

own dreams? There were days, too, when he silently suffered the pain of old war wounds and never let on.

He brought the car to a stop and came out to greet her. He put his arms around her, kissed her on her damp cheek. She read it not as a kiss, but a mere brush that spoke more of disapproval than love.

Without a word he hefted her luggage into the backseat of the car.

"They're damp," she started to say, to prevent him from getting the back of his beloved car wet. But she realized that the car was now nine years old, no longer the prized possession it had been when he proudly drove it home on that long-ago day.

They sat side by side, their silence exaggerated by the sound of the wipers, one blade of which made a halting, annoying sound as it slowly stuttered across the wet glass, leaving streaks that interfered with her vision.

They stopped at one of the few traffic lights in Caryville when he spoke for the first time.

"Who was it? Do you know?" he asked, staring grimly ahead to avoid facing her.

The question, his manner of asking it, assumed she had become promiscuous. It hurt. Much as he disapproved of her relationship with Brett, she had never given him cause to believe she had departed so far from the values held dear in his household to have become a slut.

She answered with a single word.

"Brett."

A long silence followed. They were turning the familiar corner of West Elm, their block, when he spoke again. "Man twenty-two, twenty-three, able-bodied, you'd think he'd be man enough to face up to his responsibility."

"He offered. Insisted. I couldn't let him destroy his career."

"Didn't much worry about *your* career, did he?"

"I don't want any man to marry me because I'm pregnant."

"A little late to be having pride."

He said no more. Nor did Lori. They arrived at the house.

From her mother's look, her embrace, Lori knew that ever since her call saying she was coming home, her mother had suffered all the recriminations and accusations of which her father was capable. Lori's predicament had become her mother's fault, her mother having failed to instill the proper values. She was wrong and guilty for every time she disagreed with his strict rules for child rearing. Whatever had gone wrong was her fault, not his. Lori could read it all in that desperate embrace with which her mother clung to her for only a moment. Any longer would have angered him even more.

He carried both heavy bags up the stairs only to discover that the passageway was too narrow. Angrily he set down the lightest one and continued to the top of the stairs, where he turned toward her old room.

Meantime Lori and her mother sat silent in the small living room. Her mother not daring to speak, Lori unable to say anything to relieve the tension so obvious in her mother's red-rimmed eyes.

To make contact with her daughter yet not offend her husband, Sara Adams suggested, "I made a baked dish. Like you always liked."

She was on her way toward the kitchen when he came back down, his arrival announcing that Lori's bags were installed in her old room.

Lori started for the stairs, her mother following, saying, "I'll help you unpack, darling."

Entering the familiar room that had not changed a whit in the past three years, Lori took in the tufted white spread on her bed, the flowered cretonne draperies at the window, maple chair with the cushion of matching fabric. Only her little desk was different. Instead of being cluttered with books and papers, it was totally clear. Faithfully polished and oiled by her mother, but unused.

Sara Adams, never a strong woman since a painful stillbirth years ago, tried to lift the smallest of the two suitcases. Lori took over, swinging the bag onto the neat white bedspread.

"You rest," her mother said. "You've had that long trip. I'll do the unpacking."

"No, Mama, it can wait."

"But you'll be crushing all your lovely things," her mother protested.

"There will be no unpacking," Lori declared.

"Lori . . . sweetheart . . . ?" her mother pleaded.

"I can't stay here," Lori said. "I couldn't stand seven months of his silences, his looks. His . . . accusations."

"Lori, dear, you have to understand. . . . He was always so proud of you, always expected so much from you. . . ."

"And I let him down, betrayed him," Lori completed the thought. "Which is why I can't stay."

"But where will you go? What will you do?" her mother pleaded.

"I don't know. But before this week is out, I will!" she said with great determination.

# Chapter 8

✤

Lori Adams stood outside the private residence and office of Dr. Samuel Burkhardt. She clutched in her hand the Want Ads column of the Caryville *Journal*. The last time she had applied for a job, instead of a role in a play, was her last year in high school, when she sought work at the local Wal-Mart to earn the money to pay for her trip to New York and to sustain her through her first weeks there.

Though the name Burkhardt was known to her, she had never met him. So she would be applying to a total stranger. But she assured herself that this was no different from reading for a part in a play. Except, of course, this time no one would hand her a script and give her time to familiarize herself with her lines before she was called on to speak them.

She had never worked in a doctor's office. But she had done volunteer secretarial work at the office of Actors Equity when there was a strike impending. So she could truthfully say that she had some office experience.

Thus armed, assuring herself that she was applying for the role of office helper, she started up the redbrick path to the white porch. She pushed the bell and heard a brief but pronounced chime. A recorded voice responded, "Please come in and make yourself comfortable in the waiting room."

Lori did as she was told. She found two patients already waiting. She took a chair, picked up a magazine, and pretended to browse through it. But she felt too ill at ease to be able to concentrate. Soon a third patient left the doctor's inner office. Lori heard him call, "Next!" His voice was firm, brisk, almost impatient.

Twice more that procedure was repeated. Each time the voice was the same. Crisp, efficient. The last patient was inside for a long time. When she finally left, that voice followed her: "And do not take liberties with that medication, young lady! Next!"

Lori put aside the frayed magazine she had been skimming and started toward the doctor's consultation room. She was at the threshold when she caught her first sight of him. He was older than she had expected, closer to sixty than fifty. He had bushy hair that seemed almost white at the sideburns and a brush mustache that was gray and a bit unruly. Which, she later discovered, resulted from his tugging on it when he was thoughtful or troubled.

"Ah," the doctor exclaimed, "a new patient. What a relief from hearing the same old complaints from the same old patients. What seems to be your problem? Or are you here for a blood test?"

"Blood test?" Lori asked.

"A young woman as pretty as you, looking like the essence of good health, would only come to a doctor's office for a blood test to secure a marriage license," the doctor said.

"No, sir, I'm here about the job," Lori said, almost apologetic by now.

"The job . . . the job . . ." Burkhardt repeated, as if the idea were unfamiliar to him. A tug on his mustache, and he seemed to recall. "The job. Of course." He shook his head, a single distressed gesture. "I'm afraid that has been filled."

"Oh," Lori said, trying to conceal the depth of her disappointment.

"I told them to discontinue that ad. But they said if I paid for a two-week run, a two-week run was what I was going to get. Sorry, my dear."

"Of course," Lori said, starting to rise with the appearance of decorum and pride that belied her desperate need.

She started for the door when Burkhardt called, "Miss . . . Miss . . ." He realized that he did not know her name.

"Adams. Lori Adams."

"Miss Adams . . . Lori . . . tell me, what are you doing here?"

"Caryville is my home. I was born here. Went through school here," she protested.

"That wasn't what I meant," the doctor replied. "What are you doing *back* here?"

"What am I doing—" Lori repeated, to make time to summon up any explanation but the true one.

"I remember you, child. I had a son in your graduating class."

"Dennis Burkhardt?"

"Yes, Dennis," the doctor confirmed. "I managed to catch the last half of class night during your graduating week. I saw you in the play. Everybody said, 'That girl is going to become a great actress. She's going to New York.' "

Lori began to blush.

"Did you? Go to New York?" he asked. When she nodded, he remarked, "And came back? Gave up?"

"No, not exactly."

"Didn't give up. Just came back," he commented on the anomaly.

Lori felt a sudden impulse to turn and flee. Yet she felt rooted to the spot. Until Burkhardt beckoned her back. She hesitated, then started toward him. She stopped at the chair but did not sit down.

"Tell me, Lori, how long?"

"How long what?" she parried.

"How long since you first felt your breasts become fuller. Engorged, as we physicians say." When she did not respond, he continued, "And mornings, the nausea and the occasional vomiting . . . how long?" the doctor insisted.

She felt a rush of tears to her eyes but managed to contain them.

"Two months," she was finally able to admit.

"Two months . . ." He seemed to evaluate. "Have you been under a doctor's care ever since the diagnosis?"

"No."

"You should be," he said, motioning her to be seated. Once she was, he asked, "Have you made any decision?"

"I am not going to force him to marry me," she declared. "I am going to take charge of my own life!"

"I meant, are you going to have the baby or not?" he asked.

"I am going to have it," she replied firmly.

"Good. It is a natural process of which I approve. Provided the sacrifice demanded of the mother and the infant is not too great," Burkhardt declared. "Now, that settled, let us make some plans. First, I will find you an obstetrician who insists on regular and frequent checkups. Second, we must try to find you a job. Any kind of work that will keep you active and involved. Will you need a place to live?"

She hesitated, then replied with a nod.

"Mother understood but father did not," he assumed. It was not necessary for Lori to confirm that. "Rough as things have been in this community the last few years, there must be some business that needs a bright, presentable young woman. We must both keep looking. Now, you check with me in two days!"

"Yes, sir . . . I mean, Doctor."

In two days there were no signs of a job. Not from among the ads that Lori pursued, nor among Burkhardt's associates and acquaintances.

Brett called four times during those two days. Only once was Lori home. Despite his pleas and his insistence, she refused to come back to New York. Nor did she offer him any encouragement when he continued to insist on getting married.

To put him off, she invented a scenario that included a great job, an apartment of her own, a good obstetrician to see her through her pregnancy, of which only the last was true.

She could not admit her fears and uncertainties, else he would come after her whether she wanted it or not. Meantime, at home, her father grew more silent and at the same time more hostile. Though her mother comforted her with her eyes, she dared not speak within his hearing.

The situation had become so intolerable that Lori began to give serious thought to applying for welfare and seeking refuge at the town center for the homeless. Pride, pride alone, made her refuse to yield to that alternative.

Under Burkhardt's urging, she applied to do volunteer work at the hospital. At least it would provide her with a decent diet during her working hours. If she guarded her little money, it might last until she found a paying job.

After a succession of disheartening days and nights her concern about Brett gradually turned into resentment. Her situation was as much his fault as her own. True, he had made gallant offers to marry her and go to work as a tire salesman to provide for her. A sham, she decided. He knew she would not permit him to do it. So he could make his bold offers without any risk.

Twice during those days she determined to go back to New York. Force him to do what people used to call "the right thing." But early next morning, still awake, she realized, no, no, he did mean it. He did love her. He would marry her. Even if it meant sacrificing his career. She loved him, believed him, and believed *in* him. She would see this through. Somehow.

From the end of the second week on, she began to receive notes from him, with little amounts of cash. Ten dollars. Five. Twenty-five. She suspected he was working longer hours waiting on tables. Or else had picked up some new kind of work in addition. Brett had a friend, Jimmy Hawkins, also a young aspiring actor, who maintained himself by doing housework. He had a regular list of clients whose apartments he dusted, cleaned, changed the bed linens, did all the things a housemaid would do. Did it well. With no sense of shame or loss of status.

Perhaps Brett had gone into business with Jimmy. Or had Jimmy gotten a role in an Off-Off-Broadway play and had to be free for matinees twice a week, so Brett took over for him to earn that extra money that he was sending her?

Small as the amounts were, Lori regarded them as a deposit. A deposit on his intentions for the future. He was not running and hiding as many young men in similar circumstances did.

At the end of the fifth week the administrator of Caryville

Medical Center (which was the pretentious name by which the sixty-bed hospital was known) had begun to notice the young blond woman who had lately been serving as a volunteer. And who was doing exceptional work. The administrator came on the floor of the reception area one afternoon to interview her.

"Ms. Adams . . . Lori . . . I've been noticing your work since you started on a volunteer basis. Very efficient. Very dependable. Trouble with many volunteers, since they are donating their time, they are not regularly available. I was wondering, if your other personal duties allow, would you be available to do a regular eight-hour shift, six days a week? It doesn't pay too well, but these days the fact that it pays at all is something."

"Why—why, yes, I'd be quite able, very willing in fact," Lori was delighted to reply.

With great relief, and despite her mother's tears, Lori Adams moved out of the home that had become a prison to her. She found a small one-bedroom flat over the garage of a friend of Dr. Burkhardt's.

That her new place was so small proved a blessing. It needed very little furniture to fill it. It was a warm place on cold nights. A secure place against rain and snow. Except in the most inclement weather, it was close enough to the hospital to walk.

It would serve well for the months during which the baby inside her was growing and developing. She had found a place where she could feel at peace with herself and her resolve to have a sound, healthy infant.

# Chapter 9

Christie and Bill Salem sat patiently and silently in Dr. Moncrief's consultation room. Their appointment had been set for two-thirty, but the doctor had been delayed at the hospital.

When she did arrive, Dr. Moncrief greeted the Salems so warmly that it caused Bill to suspect the doctor deliberately assumed such an optimistic attitude because she sensed Christie's troubled state of mind.

"Well, let's have a look," Moncrief said, sending Christie off to the examining room to disrobe.

As soon as Christie closed the door, Moncrief lowered her voice to ask, "Well, Bill?"

"Not good, Doctor. Times late at night I still find her in the nursery. Redoing everything she did that night. Bathing Billy, nursing him, walking him around. Still looking for the cause."

"How about your sex life? Does she seem eager for that?"

"Yes. But it's not making love. It's clinical. I'm simply the instrument through which she hopes to become pregnant again."

"Fear," Moncreif said. "Desperately as she wants another child, she fears having one. Afraid the same thing will happen again."

"Doctor, you've got to *do* something!"

Moncrief prolonged her usual gynecological examination to make an assessment of Christie's emotional condition. Her observations confirmed what Bill had said. Once Christie had dressed and joined them in the consultation room, Moncrief began:

"Christie, you know even better than I that once again you are not pregnant. Since there is no physical impairment that prevents it, I must conclude that it is purely emotional. So I suggest, as a first step, that perhaps you can surmount by dealing with an infant firsthand."

"But if there's no infant—" Christie protested at once.

"I would like you to volunteer at the hospital to serve as a substitute parent. Take care of little ones who, for one reason or another, are deprived of the closeness of their natural mothers."

Bill sought some response in Christie's eyes. Instead of a glow of enthusiasm he found only increased tension and fear. Quick to make the same observation, Moncrief changed course.

"Of course, there is another way. A more direct way to overcome your difficulty." She wrote a name and address on her prescription pad. "Call this woman. Go see her."

"Who is she?" Christie asked gingerly.

"Dr. Dornan. A psychiatrist."

"You think I'm going insane, don't you?" Christie accused.

"Of course not. But I do think you are going through a particularly rough time. You need some help to get over it. We all do from time to time," Moncrief declared firmly. Then she softened her attitude to ask, "Christie, have I ever given you any but my best advice?"

"No," Christie was forced to admit.

"Then do this for me. And for Bill," Moncrief urged.

Christie Salem considered her plea, and glanced at Bill, who encouraged her with a slight reaffirming nod. Finally she conceded very softly, "All right, Doctor."

Bill reached for Dr. Dornan's address, but Moncrief handed it to Christie.

Dr. Lorene Dornan was a woman in her mid-forties, small, dark, not at all imposing. She used those qualities to entice her patients into trusting her as they would a close friend. The same in her professional discourse as well, she was not given to arch terminology but used everyday language. In that way the mystery with which some professionals chose to surround their treatment gave way to a relaxed intimacy that encouraged patients to open up more fully and freely. Thus she achieved a high percentage of favorable outcomes.

Her first few sessions with Christie Salem were devoted to a slow penetration of the wall she had built up around herself.

Dornan pointed out that this was a time when Bill, too, needed to grieve and to be consoled. A time to be closer rather than driven apart. At that Christie began to cry. Silently, not sobbing, but with a slow but steady flow of tears, accented from time to time by a slight gasp and a sniffle.

Dr. Dornan passed a box of tissues to her. At the same time she asked, "What has Bill done that you deny him your compassion? What are you blaming him for?"

"I'm not blaming him. If he would just stop blaming me . . ." Christie blurted out in defense of herself.

"I've spoken to Bill. I can assure you, he does *not* say Billy was your fault."

"Because he's too considerate of my feelings. Sometimes I wish he would let loose and say what he really thinks," Christie exclaimed.

"Why? Because you need confirmation of your guilt?"

Christie shook her head, a feeble attempt at denial.

"Christie," Dr. Dornan resumed, in a voice even softer than usual. "I'm afraid you're a victim of our times. In olden days, long ago, when some such unexplained tragedy occurred, people would blame God or fate. Always something outside their control. But in our age we think it is the height of intellectual honesty to assign blame to our parents, to society in general, or, failing that, to ourselves. We cannot accept the fact that something happened simply because it happened. Bill is not to blame. You are not to blame. There is absolutely nothing anyone can do to reverse what happened. We have to consign that to the past."

"But . . ." Christie started to protest.

"I did not say forget it, or forget little Billy. I say only, recognize that is all past. We have to deal with the present. And the future."

"I would like to." Christie began to weep once more. "If only for Bill's sake. If ever a man was born to be a father, Bill was. You should have seen him with little Billy. And yet . . ."

"And yet, for some reason, now you can't conceive," Dornan said it for her. "Could that be what you really feel guilty about? That in addition to being a bad mother for Billy, you are being a bad wife to his father?"

"I wish, I try. . . . But sometimes I think that whatever causes the seed and the egg to join together no longer works in me. There's that biblical word. They used it for Sarah in the Old Testament and for Elizabeth in the New—*barren*. I think I have become barren. That's my punishment for what happened to Billy—barrenness. I don't know . . . I don't know."

Dornan handed her the box of tissues again.

After conferring with Dr. Moncrief, Dornan invited both the Salems to a joint session.

More tormented by his wife's condition than he had allowed her to suspect, Bill Salem tried to give Dr. Dornan the impression that he was totally in control of himself, prepared to listen to her report soberly and with compassion. Christie sat stiffly upright in her chair, betraying her conflicts only by the flexing of the fingers of her left hand, which clutched a damp, wrinkled handkerchief.

"Bill, Christie and I have now had eight sessions. But talking alone has not produced the desired result. So I feel compelled to suggest a step which I think will have more direct benefits."

Without intending to, Bill Salem betrayed the depth of his anxiety by coming to what he thought was his wife's defense.

"Doctor, if you are about to suggest that Christie be committed, I won't hear of it! Absolutely not! Whatever you think, Christie and I will see this through together. Won't we, darling?"

Christie was stunned by this sudden revelation of her husband's state of anxiety, too stunned to respond.

"Bill, I was not about to suggest any such thing. Far from it. I want Christie to come out of herself by herself. Instead of brooding on what cannot be changed, I want her to become more involved with the life around her. Christie has much love to give and the need to give it. I want her to have that opportunity."

"God knows, we've tried," Bill protested. "Every suggestion Dr. Moncrief has come up with. Sex at the time of month, the time of week, the time of day. Taking temperature before sex to make sure conditions are favorable. But nothing. Nothing! However, if *you* have any suggestions, we will try. Believe me, we will try."

"It is my opinion," Dornan replied, "that as an addition to trying to conceive, Christie and you take another step. Consider adopting. There are healthy infants who need exactly the love and caring two people like you can give them."

Bill looked toward Christie, waiting for her to respond.

Haltingly she admitted, "We . . . we've discussed that."

"And?" Dornan prodded.

Christie looked at her husband, begging to be relieved of the need to explain.

"Chris, honey, this is just among us. You trust me, you trust Dr. Dornan. . . ."

Christie Salem nodded, then faced the doctor. "Bill brought it up first, but I'd thought about it even before."

"But failed to mention it to *him*?" Dornan asked skeptically.

"Not 'failed.' Refused."

"Why?" Dornan asked.

Christie did not reply at once until Bill urged, "Christie! Now is the time! Tell her!"

"I . . . I was afraid."

"Afraid you wouldn't be able to take care of an infant? I thought we worked all that out," Dornan said.

"We did," Christie admitted. "But maybe it wouldn't be good enough for *them*."

"*Them?*" Dornan asked, disturbed that she had missed something important in her conduct of these sessions.

"*Them*," Christie iterated. When Dornan's puzzlement became even more obvious, she explained, "The adoption agencies. The people who have babies to give."

"What about the agencies?"

"I would never want to get a baby under false pretenses. One should not lie about something of such lifetime consequence," Christie replied staunchly.

"Two decent young people, hardworking, with excellent reputations. Why would you have to lie?" Dornan asked.

Christie steeled herself before replying, "We would have to tell them."

"Tell them what?" Dornan was puzzled.

"About . . . about Billy . . ."

"Of course," Dornan agreed.

"Then they will say, 'She killed one, can we trust her with another innocent, helpless infant?' "

"Christie," Dornan explained, "nobody blames you except you. Adoption agencies understand. You won't be the first mother they've met who has suffered a SIDS experience. In fact, they might think that makes you and Bill preferred applicants. That you will be even more devoted and careful of an infant. And if you need any recommendations or references, list Dr. Moncrief. List me."

Christie looked at her husband, who urged her on with a firm nod and eyes that pleaded, *Let's do it, Christie, let's say yes!*

With considerable relief Christie Salem nodded.

"I have here a list of all adoption agencies in this area of the country," Dornan said, handing it to her.

# Chapter 10

✤

Lori Adams stood naked before her mirror, turning left, then right, to examine her body profile. She realized there was no disguising it now. In her fifth month she was definitely beginning to show. If she were of fuller figure, carrying more weight, she might have been able to conceal her condition for another month or two as an ordinary weight gain.

Reluctantly she came to the conclusion that in fairness to Ms. Berryman, her supervisor, who had been most kind and caring, she must reveal her condition. It would give Berryman the opportunity to find and train a replacement. As to her own situation, Lori might manage to scrape by on what little she had been able to put aside until now. When those funds ran out, she would then be forced to appeal to one of the state or local agencies that were equipped to assist unmarried pregnant women.

She waited until the end of the day when Ms. Berryman was free and then knocked on the door to her private office.

"Yes?" Ms. Berryman called back in a preoccupied voice. "Come in, come in." It was a familiar tone of address to Lori. One that Berryman often was forced to resort to when she was burdened by some difficult administrative problem.

Lori's instant reaction was, *She's too busy to have patience with personal problems now.* She turned to run, but Berryman's commanding voice insisted, "Come in!"

Lori pushed the door open, hesitated, then, gathering her courage, entered.

Berryman was on her feet, poised over her desk, in the process of arranging personnel slips to figure out how to manage her human inventory to staff the hospital, while at the same time giving as many as possible the opportunity to celebrate Christmas with their families.

Without interrupting that work, Berryman asked, a bit impatiently, "Yes, Lori, what is it?"

"Ms. Berryman, I can come back. It isn't an emergency."

"Not yet," Berryman said. "Sit down, child, sit down."

Lori perched gingerly on the edge of the visitors' chair, while Berryman continued moving personnel slips around on her desk, every once in a while removing one of those who could be spared for the holiday.

Suddenly, without prologue, she asked, "When does your doctor say you'll be expecting?"

Caught by surprise, Lori began to repeat, "When does my doctor . . . ?"

Berryman glanced at her across the lighted desk area. "Good God, child, this is a hospital. I'm a trained health professional. Did you think I hadn't noticed? A girl as slender as you. Reminds me of that joke men used to tell. About the young woman who was so skinny that when she swallowed an olive pit, six men left town. Your hips have become more, shall we say, shapely. And there is that nice bulge to your belly. What is more, attractive as you are, you look even more so, reflecting that inner happiness pregnant women radiate!"

Lori felt a bit sheepish that what she considered a closely guarded secret had been so apparent to the professional eye of Ms. Berryman.

"Will you be able to work through the holidays?" Ms. Berryman continued matter-of-factly.

"Yes, yes, of course," Lori was quick to agree.

"Good," the supervisor said, with a finality that brought the interview to a close.

"Aren't you going to ask . . ." Lori started to say, but could not quite bring herself to say it.

"Ask what?" her supervisor replied, a bit impatiently.

"Well, for one thing, what's going to happen? How long I'll be able to carry on?" Lori replied.

Ms. Berryman abandoned her work to look up at Lori. "Child, we're not living in the Dark Ages. You will work as long as you are able. Which I should judge would be at least into your eighth month."

"But the patients—"

"They'll love it," Berryman assured. "They'll begin to follow the progress of your pregnancy. First thing every morning they'll be expecting a report from you. It'll be a tonic for them. Take their minds off their own problems. There is something about the continuity of life that inspires us all. Don't worry about it, child."

With considerable relief Lori started from the office. As she was opening the door, Berryman called to her, "And after that?"

Lori turned back.

"Have you given that any thought? Made any plans?"

"I've thought about it . . . thought a lot. But plans . . . No, no plans," Lori confessed.

"Any time you want to talk about it, feel free," Ms. Berryman invited.

Six weeks later, again in the early evening hours of a cold late January day, Lori Adams knocked on her supervisor's door.

This time Ms. Berryman seemed to be expecting her. She gestured her to a chair and offered, "A cup of tea, dear?"

"No, thanks. But if you have a little time . . ."

"A little or a lot, as much as you need," Berryman assured her. "What have you decided?"

"That's my problem. I *haven't* decided," Lori admitted.

"Have you been in touch with the father?"

"He keeps writing, even sending what little he can from time to time," Lori admitted.

"Is there any chance of getting back together?" Ms. Berryman asked.

"He'd like to. But it wouldn't work."

"You're no longer in love," Berryman assumed.

"No, we are. . . ."

"Then what's the problem?"

"He'd have to give up his career," Lori explained.

"Lots of actors and actresses have children, and it doesn't seem to affect their careers," Berryman commented.

"That's because they *have* careers," Lori explained.

"Ah, I see," Berryman realized. "He'd have to give up his ambition and get some job. Any job."

"I never want him to feel that I—or the baby—robbed him of what he wants to do more than anything in the world," Lori said.

"You realize, Lori, that you may be depriving him of the right to assume his burden as a father and a man. He may not appreciate that."

Lori hesitated before she could confess for the first time to anyone, "When I said I didn't want to be—didn't want the baby to be a burden to him—I thought, I hoped, that he would insist. That after I left New York he . . . he would follow me and bring me back. . . ."

"But he didn't," Berryman pointed out.

"Don't blame him!" Lori rushed to his defense. "You have no idea what it's like for a young actor these days. One chance, just one chance, can mean a lifetime. And if you're not there when that chance comes along, you can wind up selling tires or insurance or something. Then, for the rest of your life, whenever you watch a film or see a play or a television show, you sit there and say to yourself, 'I could have played that part. Even better than that guy. I could have . . . except for Lori, except for the baby.' Ms. Berryman, you have no idea what a bitter poison such resentment can bring to a marriage."

Respectful of Lori's tearful revelation, Berryman realized, *She really still loves him.*

# Chapter 11

Lori Adams caught herself twisting a strand of her blond hair. Remembering that Brett had always chided her about that, instead she picked up one of the old frayed magazines from the reception-room table, only to discover that she had seen it months ago on her first visit to the prenatal clinic of the hospital.

Soon, though to Lori not soon enough, Dr. Wahl's door opened. The gray-haired woman, who always reminded Lori of her own grandmother, beckoned her into the examining room.

During the routine examination, as all patients do, Lori tried to read the doctor's reactions.

*What did she find? Was it good? Was it bad? Was she satisfied with what she found?*

It seemed more important to please the doctor than to experience good health, or for her unborn baby to experience good health.

Finally Dr. Wahl spoke: "Lori, are you keeping up with your exercises?"

"Yes, Doctor," she replied at once, and defensively, "Is there something wrong?"

"No, no, nothing wrong at all," Wahl reassured her. "In fact, everything is fine for eight months. Better than fine. Which does raise one question."

"Yes, Doctor. I've been thinking, too," Lori admitted.

"A month from now you'll have to face it," Wahl pointed out. "Any chance at all of going back home?"

"My mother, yes. But . . ."

"Yes. Fathers do seem to be more unforgiving. As if becoming pregnant was a hostile act against them. So what *will* you do?"

"I . . . I've been thinking, doing a lot of figuring."

"How far two-hundred-and-twenty-seven dollars a week will go?" Wahl asked, betraying how deeply the doctor had delved into the economics of Lori's situation. When Lori failed to respond, Wahl continued, "Rent, infant care while you're at work, food, baby needs, medications and supplies. Not very encouraging mathematics."

"I could apply for welfare . . . food stamps," Lori said. "But even that wouldn't be enough. What do you think I should do, Doctor?"

"Lori, my dear, I give patients all kinds of advice: medical, sometimes psychiatric, and even just plain personal advice. But I have never advised a woman on what to do about adoption. Advice is easy. Living with the consequences is hard. This is a decision you have to make for yourself."

"Dr. Wahl, what would *you* do?"

Wahl smiled, deepening the usual wrinkles in her aging face. "Answering that would be the same as giving advice. Lori, over the last six months I've come to know you. You are a bright young woman. I'm confident you will come to a sound decision."

In the days that followed, during her free moments between hospital chores, Lori played out every possible scenario she might follow once her infant was born.

She would call Brett and say, "Brett, congratulations! You're a father!" *No*, she decided, *bad joke.*

*Why am I being so cruel to him? So unfair. What did I expect him to say when I told him? A heroic speech from a play? An immediate declaration of undying love and loyalty? No, first he looked scared. Like a frightened teenager ready to run away. It was only later he spoke of taking a job, supporting me and a baby.*

*If I can't make it on my own, it isn't fair now to blame Brett. He did offer. I was the one who refused. Too fast.*

*Well, I won't be too fast now. Not about adoption. I will be very, very careful.*

*Of course, before I even consider adoption seriously, I could just gather my things, pick my baby up in my arms, and arrive at my family's front door.*

*What could my father do? Refuse to take us in? No. That would create more talk in town than if he did take us in. But what kind of life would that lead to? For me. For my child. No. No solution there.*

Eleven days after her last visit with Dr. Wahl, Lori called her. "Doctor, I am not saying I would do it, but if I decided I wanted to, who should I talk to?"

"I would talk to Ms. Heckinger, counselor in Social Services," Wahl said.

The appointment with Rose Heckinger was set for the end of Lori's workday. Since the late-afternoon sun shone through the window behind Heckinger's desk chair, Lori was forced to squint, preventing her from reading the reactions in the counselor's eyes. Realizing that, and of the importance of putting Lori at ease, Heckinger suggested, "Why don't we get comfortable?" She moved to the couch, causing Lori to turn in her direction away from the direct rays of the strong sun.

"Now, then," Rose Heckinger began, "eighth month? Or early ninth?"

"Beginning of the ninth," Lori said, studying Heckinger's face. She seemed so young. Perhaps not even thirty. Plain brown hair, hanging loose. Nice face. Good strong features though. Giving one a sense of confidence that overcame Lori's reservations about the counselor's youth.

"Since you've come to see me, I assume you are seriously considering the matter of adoption," Heckinger said.

"I . . . I have thought about it," Lori admitted.

"You realize how important a step that is?"

"Yes," Lori replied, surprised, since she expected that Heckinger would encourage her.

"Have you considered all other possibilities? All the people you might rely on at such a time?"

"Yes," Lori replied.

"And there is no one? Not the baby's father? Not your family? Not any close friends?" Heckinger enumerated.

"No one," Lori replied, yet felt compelled to come to Brett's defense and explain, "It's not that he didn't want to. I couldn't let him ruin his career."

"You understand that if you *did* decide to give your baby up for adoption, he would have to be notified," Heckinger pointed out. "The natural father has certain legal rights."

Lori had never considered that possibility.

"Perhaps you might contact him," Heckinger urged, as if the interview would be suspended until she had done so.

But Lori persisted. "Would . . . would the authorities be able to *do* anything to him?"

"He could be liable for support. But the important thing is to see that his rights are protected."

"But it's *my* baby," Lori protested.

"Still, it's the law."

"What happens when they can't find the father, or don't know for sure who he is?"

"Then, in this state, the mother's permission will suffice," Heckinger replied.

Lori nodded thoughtfully.

Shyly, as if the question itself were deemed a commitment to adoption, Lori asked, "Is it possible . . . I mean, is it ever done that the mother is allowed to see . . . can meet . . . can see . . ."

"Approve?" Heckinger supplied the word Lori groped for.

"I do not want my child to become just another file! Just another case in the hands of some social worker or some agency. He is not going to be 'just another.' He is *my* son. And if *I* can't give him the best, I still want the best for him."

Of course you do," Heckinger agreed. "If we can find 'the best,' would that reassure you?"

"It doesn't matter what anyone else finds, *I* would have to be sure. I would have to see them for *myself*."

"Approve," Heckinger reiterated, to define what Lori was asking for.

"Yes . . . I would feel better if I could see them. Especially the woman. I think if I could see her, her face, her eyes . . . I would know if she is the kind of woman I could trust my baby to."

"Adoption agencies don't like the mother who is giving up a child to know who the adoptive parents are. You can understand that."

"Yes. But I promise I would never go find them. Or try to find my baby. I just want to be sure, that's all. There's so much in the papers and on TV about babies being adopted and abused. . . . I just have to be sure . . . sure. . . ."

Lori broke off before she might begin to weep.

"Lori," Heckinger asked, "what if I could arrange for you to meet a possible adoptive couple? Ask any questions you wish. Except two. Their names. And the city in which they live." Lori was about to answer when Heckinger forbid it. "Don't answer now. Think about it. Then come back in a day or two and tell me."

Two days later Lori asked for an appointment with Counselor Rose Heckinger.

"I would like to meet some couples you think would make good adoptive parents for my son," Lori announced.

"With complete anonymity?" Heckinger wanted to make sure.

"I just want to know what kind of people they are. Will they be good, kind, loving parents to my son?"

On the day arranged, Lori Adams, bulging with pregnancy in her ninth month, arrived at the office of Counselor Heckinger prepared to meet some total strangers.

# Chapter 12

❧

Social-services counselor Rose Heckinger sat at her desk considering what to do with the file she held. It was one of the number of files recommended to her by the Tri-State Social Services Department on Adoptions. Those files she decided to return to the department she placed on the left side of her desk. The files on the right she considered good potential adoptive parents.

The file she now held involved one of the couples Lori Adams had rejected. Three times in the last ten days, couples anxious to adopt an infant had been interviewed by Lori.

Three times she had decided against them. The first couple did not impress her as well matched. The wife appeared too tentative, too shy. As if she were subservient to a domineering husband. Which could mean he would be a domineering father as well.

*Not for my child,* Lori protested silently. *I had enough of that in my own life.*

She had disapproved of the second couple because she sensed that the husband was less eager than his wife to adopt. He appeared to be indulging her, as if buying for her some luxury she craved. Despite proof that he was wealthy enough to guarantee her baby a lavish lifestyle, and sympathetic as Lori felt toward his wife, she had decided against them.

The third couple, whose file Rose Heckinger had been debating over, Lori had rejected on the basis of what she could only describe as: "A feeling . . . a feeling I have. I can't explain it. I just didn't . . . didn't feel comfortable giving my baby to them."

Which caused Heckinger to remark, "My dear, you are not casting a play. You can't expect perfection. You are trying to find two good, decent people who want a child to love. Your child."

Lori had replied in kind, "Ms. Heckinger, please don't misunderstand. But if we were casting a play and made a mistake, we would fire the actor and hire a new one. I don't have that privilege."

Now, sitting at her desk, pondering that experience, Heckinger wondered if there would ever be a couple Lori Adams would approve.

Heckinger opened the next file on the center of her desk.

DONNER, HAROLD & CYNTHIA: Ages, 34, 29. Childless due to defect in husband's sperm production. Resident in small town in southern part of adjoining state. Own their own home. Husband, independent businessman. Operates number of launderettes which provide steady fairly substantial income. Home and backgrounds carefully investigated. Met all state criteria for adoptive couples. Excellent references. Longtime church affiliation.

Heckinger decided to arrange for them to meet Lori.

The Donners' instant impression of Lori was of a very pretty, very blond, very pregnant young woman. The Donners glanced at each other, sharing their approval.

*What a beautiful child this young woman would provide us.*

Lori's instant reaction was, *This man could not be the father of my child. Too short, too dark, too heavy. Even strangers would know at once my child was adopted. I need a family in which my child belongs . . . that's the best word for it . . . the only word for it . . . belongs as if he were born into it.*

The interview went awkwardly. The Donners sensed from the outset that Lori disapproved of them.

As they were leaving, Donner whispered, "Young lady, I only ask, think it over. You won't find two people who want a child to love more than Cynthia and me. We would do the best for him. Or her. We're not particular that way. Just a child. Any child."

Lori had great difficulty explaining her reasons to Rose Heckinger.

She could only say, "I didn't want to hurt their feelings. They were actually two very nice people. But they just . . . just didn't look like they . . . they wouldn't have looked like a family. And I want my child to be part of a family. Look like them. So when you saw a photograph of them, you wouldn't say, 'Uh-oh, that child is not theirs. It's adopted.' "

"Lori," Rose Heckinger asked, "are you looking for an adoptive parent who looks like your baby's father?"

"No!" Lori protested so strongly that Heckinger knew her surmise was correct.

*She is still in love with him,* Heckinger reasoned.

"I don't know if we can fulfill that particular requirement, my dear. Perhaps I made a mistake agreeing to these interviews in the first place."

"No, please, please," Lori begged, "I'll know the right couple when I see them. I'm sure I will!"

"Well," Heckinger considered, "we'll . . . we'll see."

But she held out no more promise than that.

By the beginning of the following week half a dozen new files arrived on Ms. Heckinger's desk. She studied them carefully. For, though Lori's standards had proved a problem, Rose Heckinger was forced to admire the fact that this young mother-to-be was stalwart in her convictions.

Among the half-dozen files was one that recommended itself to Heckinger for special consideration.

SALEM, WILLIAM, CHRISTINE: AGES 32, 28. From a small city at the westernmost corner of the neighboring state. Husband owns new but profitable service business. Wife, advertising, small agency, willing to forego career for sake of adoption. Good character references. Good financial picture. Excellent community. Fine schools and medical facilities available. No other children.

Aware of Lori's criteria, Rose Heckinger decided to meet this couple herself before subjecting them to an interview.

Her first impression was: husband tall and thin. And light-haired. Based on what Lori had said, the opposite physical type of the man she had last rejected. Perhaps there was a possibility here.

Heckinger also noticed that Ms. Salem had subtly reached under the table to her husband's hand. He grasped it, for mutual reassurance. They were both obviously equally tense and eager for this meeting to go well.

To put them at ease, Heckinger began, "I'm sorry to ask you to attend such a meeting. But in this case it is necessary."

"Please, Ms. Heckinger, no need to apologize or even explain," Bill Salem replied.

Christie joined in, "After the months we've been trying to find a baby . . . did I say months? It's been almost two years. And I can't even count how many agencies and hospitals. So this meeting doesn't faze us. Does it, Bill?"

"Ms. Heckinger," Bill asked, "what do you think the mother might be looking for? I mean, why does she want to see us . . . meet us face-to-face . . . what is she likely to ask? What should we say?"

"That's important, Ms. Heckinger," Christie pleaded. "This is as close as we've come to getting a baby. We would hate to spoil our chances. So what should we say? Or avoid saying?"

"Just be yourselves. Be truthful," Ms. Heckinger counseled.

In the small reception room adjoining Heckinger's private office, Christie and Bill Salem waited patiently. The meeting had been arranged for two o'clock. It was now twenty past the hour. Though Bill felt as anxious as his wife, he tried to endow the situation with a sense of calm by remaining seated. Christie continued to pace back and forth from the window to the bookshelves at the far wall.

"Christie, honey, simmer down. In fact, come here." He beckoned to her. As she approached, he reached for her hand. Cold. As cold now as in those terrible days after little Billy's death.

He tried to gently coax her to sit beside him. She refused and resumed pacing. Suddenly she turned, and in a strained whisper said, "She changed her mind!"

"Hon, please," Bill whispered.

"Then why isn't she here?"

"Maybe there are last-minute things . . . papers to sign. Or advice or—I don't know—something," he ended up lamely.

At that moment there was a faint knock on the door. Christie froze, then turned slowly in that direction. Bill moved to her side to support her. They both watched as the door opened slowly.

Ms. Heckinger smiled at them, then stood aside to urge pale, blond, very pregnant Lori Adams into the room.

"I'll leave you folks alone," Heckinger said, "for as long as you like. When you're done, pick up that phone and let me know."

She withdrew, closing the door quietly behind her.

They stared at each other. Lori, the mother, stared at the woman who desired to become her child's mother for the rest of its life. Christie, the woman eager to become that infant's mother, stared at the birth mother. Each with a hundred questions, many of which she would never be allowed to ask according to the protocol of this meeting.

Bill studied the young blond woman with questions all his own. He glanced at his wife, knowing she wanted to please this young woman and earn her approval as desperately as he did.

"Shall we . . . shall we all sit down?" he suggested.

Lori took the small armchair, which almost dictated that the Salems would have to sit together on the couch facing her. It served to delineate the difference between them. A woman alone against a couple, husband and wife.

Christie sought to break the tension by saying, "I want you to know that I understand how you feel."

"You can't!" Lori disputed.

*Oh, God, I said the wrong thing,* Christie reproached herself. *I hope she won't hold it against us.*

Lori meantime suffered her own self-reproach. *I shouldn't have been so sharp with her. It isn't her fault I have to give up my baby. The poor woman is so tense, as tense as I am.*

To ease the moment, Bill Salem felt compelled to intervene, asking, "Did they tell you anything about us?"

"They said you seem like fine people, respectable people. With a good home and a great desire to adopt a baby," Lori said.

"Did they tell you about . . . ?" Christie started to ask, then faltered.

"Christie." Bill realized that in his anxiety to make this meeting succeed he had broken one of the rules by using her name. He was as nervous as Christie, possibly even more so.

Christie assumed command of the situation. "What I was trying to say, we had a child, a little boy, three months old. Actually two months and twenty-seven days . . . and we lost him."

"Lost him?" Lori asked. *How does one "lose" something as precious as a baby?*

Christie could read the question in her eyes. "SIDS. Sudden Infant Death Syndrome. No cause. No reason."

She felt the surge of tears but was determined to control them.

"Oh, I'm sorry," Lori replied. "They never told me. What a terrible thing that must be."

"Yes, quite terrible," Christie agreed. "But, I want to assure you that Billy, that was his name—Billy—had the best care in the world. I mean, no baby had more love, more . . ." She began to falter.

Bill came to her assistance. "What my wife is saying is true."

"Please, dear, I know what you're trying to do, but this is between two mothers." Christie turned to Lori. "My dear, I think I know the questions that must be racing through your mind. So I will do my best to save you the trouble of asking them.

"We are pretty middle class. We own our own home. With a small mortgage. We live in a relatively quiet town. Not large. But large enough to have a good hospital and some good doctors. So your, our—the baby—will always have the best of care. We live a quiet life. My husband is busy all day, and some nights, too, the kind of business he is in."

61

A look from Bill warned her not to become too specific about details.

"We are members of a church. Though maybe we don't attend as often as we should. But we will attend more often now, I promise you. And—and the schools—yes, about the schools. From kindergarten on up through high school our schools rank in the top ten percent in our state. So you don't have to worry about how well prepared your—the baby—will be when he grows up. Or she. As for college, we started a fund the day that Billy was . . . was born."

The determination to be simple, straightforward, and factual deserted her. Slowly tears began to trace down her cheeks. Without a word Lori reached out to clasp Christie's hand to comfort her.

The moment of sympathy encouraged Christie. She wiped her eyes with her fingertips, then smiled and said, "Ask, ask anything you want to know. We have nothing to hide, nothing to be ashamed of."

"Would you *tell* him?" Lori asked.

"Tell him what?" Christie asked, glancing at Bill in puzzlement.

"About being adopted," Lori said.

"We would have to. After all, everyone would know—our family, all our friends. It would be dangerous *not* to tell him. To have a child discover such an important part of its life by accident could be very traumatic."

"Exactly," Lori agreed. "He should know. But what I meant was, would you tell him about *me*?"

"If you want."

"It's very important that he know, and believe, that I love him. It's because I love him that I am giving him up. It's for his own good. Her own good."

Now Lori began to weep. Christie held out her own handkerchief to her.

While she dabbed at her eyes, Lori said, "There's so much I would want my child to know. It wasn't just, just a thing that happened. His father and I were committed to each other, deeply committed. If the circumstances were different . . . if he . . . doesn't matter. It wasn't meant to be, that's all. But I want my child to know that it was cared for and well loved even before it was born. Him or her. I want them to think of me as a woman who will always love them. Wherever they are."

"I promise, when the child is old enough to understand, we will tell him," Christie assured her.

"Is there anything *you* want to ask *me*?" Lori replied. "Anything about his father? He is a young man. Healthy. Decent. Working hard at his profession. Though lots of people wouldn't choose to call it that. You see, he is an actor. And a good one. Someday they'll see—they'll all see."

"What will you do now? Where will you go?" Christie asked.

Bill felt it was time to intervene. "Hon . . ."

"Right. Sorry. Nothing that will breach secrecy and confidentiality," Christie yielded.

"Miss, anything else you might want to know about us?" Bill asked.

"Yes," Lori said. "About discipline. God knows every child needs discipline. But it's all in the way it's done. I mean, some fathers—" She tried to find the words to say what she wanted to say rather than what she really felt. "What I mean is, some fathers are too—too severe. Once a child does something wrong, they never forget, never forgive. I wouldn't want my son or daughter to carry that burden—to be—to always be afraid."

Bill and Christie both instinctively realized that the young mother was speaking out of her own painful experience.

"I can promise you that won't happen to your child," Christie said. "It will be loved, cared for, corrected when it needs it, but always with great concern for its feelings and its inner strength. In our house we do not live by fear. But by understanding."

Lori was thoughtful for a long, long moment, during which Christie and Bill exchanged several concerned glances, betraying their shared anxiety about her final decision. Had they passed inspection? Had they been approved?

Lori rose, indicating that the interview was over. Both Salems rose at the same time.

"Thank you," Lori said softly.

Slowly she turned toward the door. In so doing she had to pass close to the Salems. In that instant both women instinctively felt the bond that had been created between them. Without a word they embraced, clinging for a moment as if that symbolized passing the child from one to the other.

# Chapter 13

"Can I see him?" Lori asked, the sweat of labor still glistening on her pale face.

Patting Lori's cheeks dry with a gauze pad, the delivery-room nurse nodded. She took the infant from the hands of the doctor to hold him up for his mother to see. He was a small, red, squirming thing, with eyes clenched against the sudden light after nine months in the comforting warm darkness of his mother's body.

Lori reached out to touch him, then did not dare. For fear of something she had heard or read about touching and bonding between mother and infant. A right to which she was no longer entitled by virtue of her decision to give him up for adoption.

She yearned to hold him in her arms but dared not ask.

Hours later she did ask one thing.

"Just once more," Lori begged of Ms. Heckinger. "I would feel better if I could speak to them just once more."

"They'll be here tomorrow to pick him up. I'll see if I can arrange it."

"Christie! We'll be late," Bill Salem called from the door to the garage.

"Just a moment. I have to check the nursery," she called down.

"Again?" Bill called back. "We went over everything last night."

"I'll be right down," she called, then proceeded to check the new bassinette, the new supply of diapers, shirts, blankets, after-bath oil, liquid soap, bottle warmer, everything new and fresh for a new and fresh start.

"Christie!" Bill called again. "We have to pick up Dr. Whitmore, and you know how careless doctors are about being on time."

Christie came down the stairs hurriedly and raced into the kitchen. She grasped the thermal bag from Bill's hand, zipped it open, and began to take inventory.

"Christie? Please?"

"I better warm up another bottle of formula," she decided.

"Honey, there are three bottles in there now. And it's a two-hour drive. How many times in two hours can any infant eat?"

"There's no such thing as having too much. Not when a new-born is involved," she insisted.

Because there was no other way to do it, Bill took the bag from her hands, zipped it shut, pointed to the garage, and said, "Go!"

"We can't be too—" she started to protest.

Bill interrupted. "Honey, remember what you promised?"

"Right," she agreed. "I won't overdo. I won't use this child to make up for little Billy. All that is past. This is a new life. For us and for him. I can't wait to see what he looks like."

On the way to pick up the doctor, she asked suddenly, "Do you think he'll have her blond hair?"

"Who knows? Besides, we don't know what the father looked like," Bill said.

"Of course," Christie replied, determined not to raise such questions on the way.

By late afternoon Christie and Bill Salem arrived at the hospital.

In the company of Dr. Whitmore they pulled into the Patients Only parking lot, piling out of the car in such a hurry that Whitmore had to go back for his bag.

Preparations had been made in the nursery for their arrival. The nurse led them to a bassinette in the corner of the room. Alongside was a small table on which Whitmore could make his examination.

Christie stared down at the little red face of the sleeping infant. She reached out very tentatively to touch his cheek. She moved the coverlet back to reveal wisps of his hair.

"Blond," she said softly to Bill. "And very, very handsome. They'll all say he looks like you."

She glanced at the nurse, who understood that look.

"Go on. Pick him up," she urged.

Very carefully Christie reached into the bassinette, slid her right hand under the warm little bundle, and picked him up. Supporting his head, she cradled him in her arms.

"Fits," she said to Bill. "He fits."

She passed him to Whitmore.

With Christie and Bill hovering over him, Dr. Whitmore did a very careful and intensive examination of this thirty-six-hour-old male infant.

*Let him be perfect,* Christie prayed. *Let him be the one. He looks so helpless, yet so active, and hungry, the way his lips are pursed for sucking. Oh, God, I never thought. . . . Did they permit her to nurse him? Is that a good thing? Especially since I can't. I'll have to bottle-feed him, and if he became used to her breast—*

Her thoughts and fears were interrupted by Whitmore announcing, "Perfect. As far as anyone can tell, he is a perfect baby. You're both very, very lucky."

Relieved, Bill grasped Christie's hand to share his moment of joy with her.

"What do we do? What happens now?" she asked.

Her question was answered when Ms. Heckinger entered the room.

"Anything more we have to sign?" Bill asked.

"Not *sign. Do,*" Heckinger said. "She wants to talk to you."

"But we've been investigated and approved," Christie protested. "Our home, our references—"

"The birth mother still wants to talk to you."

"She's changed her mind," Christie assumed at once.

"She only said she wanted to talk to you," Heckinger reiterated.

"Christie," Bill said, "she does have a right."

They were shown into the small private room where Lori Adams was just giving a social-services clerk the last information necessary before the hospital could file the infant's birth certificate.

"And the name of the father?" the woman had just asked when she was interrupted by the appearance of the Salems. In deference to the required anonymity, the clerk handed the pen to Lori, suggesting, "Just print it in this space."

Once Lori had done that, the woman retired, leaving Lori alone with the Salems.

"You . . . you wanted to see us?" Christie asked.

"Yes."

"You're not . . . not changing your mind, are you?" Christie asked.

"No," Lori assured her at once. "But I wanted to say some things. . . ."

"Of course," Christie encouraged, now that she was herself reassured.

"Someday, I don't know when, you are going to tell him. I would want him to know that I did not give him *away*. There is a great difference between giving him *up* and giving him *away*. Tell him I gave him up only after a great deal of thought—and prayer. . . . I gave him to the two best people among all those who wanted him. It wasn't easy. But I did it for him. So he could have the best life possible. And I want your promise that he *will* have the best, the best care, the most love. . . . The opportunities that I wouldn't be able to give him . . ."

"I give you my word," Christie assured her. "We will treat him with all the love, kindness, and care any child has ever had."

She leaned over and kissed the young pale-blond stranger.

With the infant wrapped in a white blanket, and enough formula in warmly protected bottles for the careful return journey, Christie and Bill Salem started home.

In the social-services office at the hospital Ms. Heckinger was going over the final paperwork of the adoption of Baby X. Though months later, when the adoption was finalized, a new birth certificate would be recorded that would identify him as the son of Christine and William Salem, for now a birth certificate had to be filled out by the hospital.

Ms. Heckinger scanned the document until her eye fell on the space denoted "father's name." There appeared the name *Higgins, Henry.*

It did not trouble her then, but later that afternoon as she was working on another case, the name *Higgins, Henry* came back to provoke her.

*Higgins, Henry . . . Higgins, Henry . . . why does that name sound so familiar? Higgins, Henry . . . Henry Higgins . . . Henry Higgins. Of course! Henry Higgins, the professor in* My Fair Lady. *Having worked in the theater, what would be more natural for Lori, if she wanted to conceal the father's identity, than to choose the name of a theatrical character?*

*Well, she isn't the first young woman to use a fictitious name for the father of her child. And, by law, we can't insist that she reveal the true name. All the law requires is that the father be notified.*

*Which is no longer my duty or the duty of this hospital but of the Godmothers' League Adoption Agency, which now assumes the obligation of formalizing this procedure.*

# Chapter 14

It was the longest, slowest, most cautious eighty miles Bill Salem would ever drive. He stayed in the right lane of the Interstate while drivers going forty and fifty passed on his left. Some honked at him impatiently. Others gave him the middle-finger salute once they pulled into the lane ahead of him.

Meanwhile, Christie sat in the backseat, cradling in her arms the infant who slept through it all. She kept easing the blanket aside to catch a glimpse of the little scrunched red face. Trying to determine what he would look like. His young, pretty blond mother? Or that unknown father whom they would never see?

From time to time Bill glanced in his rearview mirror to catch sight of his wife and their new infant son. He strained upward in his seat to see if he could catch a glimpse of the infant's face.

"Bill! Keep your eyes on the road!" Christie reprimanded. "This is a precious little human being we have here. We don't want to take any chances."

When they arrived home, two of Christie's neighbors were there, waiting to greet them and lend any help. They did the inevitable oohing and ahhing over the tiny infant, offering all kinds of assistance, from warming up his bottles to changing him.

Until one of them rebuked, "Sue, it isn't as if this is Christie's first child."

A moment of embarrassed silence followed. Jennie Holt, who

spoke the words that recalled the tragedy of little Billy, flushed a deep red. Christie tried to put her at ease.

"Let's not stand around talking. We've got things to do." She was determined not to cry in their presence.

It took almost two hours before Christie and Bill Salem were left alone to enjoy their new status as a family.

The infant having been fed and changed and now asleep, and breathing freely, Christie and Bill stood over the new bassinette and watched.

Christie whispered, "Do you think he has any sense at all of what happened today? They say infants sense things."

"All I know is when you adopt, the earlier the better. Infants need a sense of security from their first days," Bill said. "It affects them all their lives."

"Bill, do you think I was foolish?"

"About adopting? How can you even ask such a question?"

"Keep your voice down," Christie whispered. "I meant about giving away Billy's—the old bassinette. And wanting a new one."

"No, no," he assured her at once. "New life, new everything."

"It isn't as if we would be forgetting Billy. We could never do that."

"Never," Bill agreed.

"About the name?" she asked.

"Not Billy."

"Of course not," Christie agreed. "With all the waiting, the interviews, and the questionnaires, the uncertainties, I didn't give much thought to a name."

"I was afraid choosing a name would put a hex on," Bill confessed. "Do you have any ideas?"

"From the earliest times I can remember I kept hearing Gramma talk about my uncle Scott. He died in Vietnam, so I never knew him. But from what everyone says, he must have been a terrific young man. So I was thinking, if you don't mind, I would like to name him Scott. I know Gramma would have liked it."

"Scott," Bill tried it out. "Scott . . . Scott Salem. Scotty Salem. Sounds perfect to me."

"And we *will* have him christened, won't we?" Christie asked.

"You'll never get over thinking that if I had agreed to have Billy christened, that never would have happened."

"No, it's just that in my family *all* infants have always been christened," Christie said.

"Okay. Sure. Then maybe your dad will forgive me *my* early upbringing," Bill agreed.

Christie kissed him, then straightened their new son's blanket for the hundredth time. They tiptoed out of the room.

Shortly before midnight Bill Salem came awake with that sudden feeling that he was alone. He reached back. Christie's side of the bed was empty. And cold. She had been gone a long time. He rolled out of bed. Slid his feet into his slippers, which were in their usual familiar place. He crossed the hall to the nursery.

In the dim glow from the night-light in the floor outlet he found Christie standing at the bassinette staring down. He put his arms around her. She shivered, partly from the cold, partly from his sudden, unexpected touch.

"I'm just watching him breathe," she explained.

"You can't keep reliving things, hon. You have to let go."

"I wasn't reliving anything," she protested. "He woke, was hungry. I gave him his bottle. That's all. Then I just watched until he fell asleep again."

Feeling her cold arms, Bill said, "That was an hour ago. Longer. Come. Back to bed."

She leaned close enough to the infant to whisper very softly, "Good night, Scotty, darling. Sleep well. Wake well."

She kissed her son on the cheek and started from the room.

An hour later Christie slipped back into the nursery. In the dim glow she found Bill standing at the bassinette staring down. Embarrassed to be discovered after he had chided his wife, he admitted, "Just watching him sleep. He's a good sleeper. A real good sleeper."

"I think we both better get back to bed. Catch some sleep ourselves before his next feeding."

"Yeah. I think we better," Bill agreed, taking her hand. They started back to the bedroom.

Neither of them could fall asleep before the infant's next feeding.

With each passing night, Christie gained more confidence that her new son was thriving. She spent less time hovering over him, though she enjoyed every moment she spent bathing him, changing him, feeding him, putting him down to nap, lifting him once he woke. She played with him, repeating over and over, "Scotty . . . Scotty . . . Scott . . ." searching his tiny face for some sign that he was responding to his name.

Like all new mothers, she found reactions, responses, and wisdom that no weeks-old child could possibly exhibit.

The small party for family and neighbors that followed Scotty's christening was a very happy event.

More than one guest, on leaving, remarked quietly, "She couldn't be happier if Scotty were her very own."

At the time determined by state law, the adoption of an eight-month-old infant named in the petition as "Scott Salem" was finalized and duly signed by a judge of the family court. Presiding at the time was Judge Peter Palmer.

He insisted that the event be an official function to be attended by the adoptive parents and the infant. He never treated this event so perfunctorily as to be executed by simply signing a court order.

Before he actually put his signature to the final adoption order, Judge Palmer delivered a brief but very sincere talk on the lifelong duties of adoptive parents.

When they returned home, the first thing Christie did was feed little Scotty his bottle. As she held him in her arms, she looked up at Bill and confessed, "Until today I always had a terrible feeling that at the last moment something would go wrong—something."

"Christie, darling, we agreed . . . no more looking back."

"No more," she echoed. She admired her infant son, who

sucked at his bottle with lusty hunger. "God, he's got a healthy appetite."

It was several months before Bill could coax Christie to take a night out. Dinner and a movie at a theater not too far from town.

During dinner, she called home twice to inquire of the baby nurse how Scotty was doing.

During the film she slipped out and called three more times. Finally Bill whispered, "Sweetheart, we'd better go. You're disturbing all the people around us."

On the way home she apologized, "Sorry. We'll try again next week."

# Chapter 15

❧

Ten months after she had signed the final papers to complete the adoption of her infant son, Lori Adams was summoned to the office of the medical director of the hospital.

On her way up to the executive floor she recounted every event of recent weeks that might have called for such official attention. When she arrived at Dr. Cordes's office, she found him beaming in the way a man does when he is about to unwrap a great and pleasing surprise.

"Lori," Cordes began, while gesturing her to a chair, "we have been going over all employee performance records. And we—when I say we, I mean Ms. Berryman and I—have come to the conclusion that you are not making the most of your abilities."

"I do the best I can," Lori started to protest.

"The best you can within the limits of your training. What Ms. Berryman and I have decided is that the hospital will provide you with a four-year scholarship to Northwestern to study nursing."

Before Lori could react, Cordes continued, "Mind you, we are not being charitable about this. In fact, we are being very selfish. If you do take advantage of this opportunity, we expect you to return here and serve as a nurse for at least five years. With the hope that you will take graduate courses leading to a degree in hospital administration."

"Dr. Cordes . . . I . . . I don't know what to say. . . ."

"Of course not," he agreed at once. "Think it over. This is the opportunity of a lifetime. A career. A future of satisfying work in health care, the fastest-expanding field in American life. Your opportunities would be unlimited."

Lori nodded but could not quite bring herself to speak.

Cordes smiled even more warmly.

"Now, you think about it. I know you'll come to the right decision. Meantime, just remember that we love you here and we appreciate your fine work these last two years."

In all her time at the hospital Lori had made many friends, but none so close and intimate as to encourage her to share her inner thoughts with them.

In the late hours of night, after she came off duty, Lori returned to her small apartment. Made herself a snack and tried to concentrate on Cordes's generous offer.

The work itself, yes, she enjoyed that. She liked helping people. The look of relief and gratitude, of reassurance and hope, that appeared in the eyes of the patients she ministered to was extremely satisfying. The nurses did the medical work, the treatment, administering IVs and medication, drawing blood. But they were far too busy to stop and talk, to encourage the patient, to see to the little amenities, a newspaper, a magazine, tuning in the right television station, reading the cards that came with the flowers. The little things that made the process of healing or surviving less difficult, and so, in the end, helped patients recover who might have given up otherwise.

That was good work. Satisfying work. And if Dr. Cordes and Ms. Berryman had noticed that she enjoyed doing it, they were right.

But . . . but to spend the rest of her life . . .

That she had stayed on as long as she had was out of gratitude for how well the hospital had seen her through her pregnancy and the adoption procedure. She had paid that debt.

Now . . . Now, she realized, Dr. Cordes was saying, "It is time to plan the rest of your life. Either commit yourself to medicine, or . . ."

By the end of a week of great internal conflict, Lori Adams realized that her original career choice still remained the theater.

Go back to New York? She could not face that. At least not yet. But there were other active theater centers. Chicago was the nearest and the most promising. Many actors, writers, and directors had gone from Chicago to New York to Hollywood, and achieved great success in all those places.

Perhaps, she considered, it was possible to combine the two. Go to Northwestern during the day and work in one of the theater companies at night. Most of the young people who worked in those productions usually had other jobs to support themselves.

But no, that would not be honest. The hospital's offer was made in good faith, with a view to a lifetime career. She had no right to take advantage of that and then change careers.

One thing became quite clear. The time had come to end one career and resume another.

At the end of the week Lori Adams reported to Dr. Cordes. He was disappointed to hear her decision, but also quite understanding.

"Looking at me, Lori, you'd never guess that while I was going to college, I was first trumpet with a jazz outfit called the Purple People Eaters. We took our name from the fact that at Northwestern our school colors were purple and white. We worked our way through college, playing fraternity dances, weddings, graduation parties. Until came time for our own graduation. When *we* had to decide. Two of us went on to law school. Chuck Aaronoff and I were accepted at medical school. Of course, we all vowed that we would never lose touch. At first we had an annual jam session. Then various duties made that impossible. So we just . . . just dispersed . . . gone with the winds of necessity.

"But to this day I can't hear a jazz band, even a few bars of jazz, without feeling that urge, that desire to be part of it again. Mind you, Lori, that was almost forty years ago, but it's still part of me. So, if you've had a taste of the theater and loved it, do what you have to do."

"Thanks, Dr. Cordes."

"If . . . well, I know how uncertain the arts can be . . . if things don't work out, as long as I'm the medical director here, the offer stands."

"I'll remember that," Lori promised.

She started for the door. But at the instant she touched the knob, Cordes said, "Lori, is it possible this place can never be comfortable for you?"

She turned to dispute him. "Oh, no, I'm treated well here, very well."

"I meant, my dear, this will always be the place where you gave up your child for adoption."

Cordes had touched the nerve that she had not dared.

Yes, it would be good to get away from here.

Best to forget the past. Start a new life. With no ties, no encumbrances. The next time one of those envelopes from Brett arrived, with his well-intentioned if small contribution, she would simply mark the envelope ADDRESSEE MOVED, NO FORWARDING ADDRESS.

That chapter of her life, too, would be closed.

Three times before she left for Chicago such envelopes arrived. Three times, with determination, she printed the message across her address to conceal her handwriting.

When his third letter was returned, Brett Mann phoned the hospital only to be told that Lori Adams no longer worked there. She had gone, leaving no address, no phone number.

*She must have taken the baby back home,* he was sure. When he called her parents' home, her father answered.

"Lori? We don't have any Lori here anymore."

"But you must know where she is!" Brett protested.

"Don't know. Don't care."

Brett was sure that from the background he heard a woman call out, "*I care!*"

When Brett insisted, "Let me talk to Lori's mother!" he heard a click and found himself holding a dead phone.

Gone. Lori was gone. And their child with her.

His initial reaction was one of anger. *She had no right . . . no right at all to do this to me,* he protested.

But once his anger passed, he was forced to admit, *When she needed me, I had nothing to offer her but love. Which in this real,*

*everyday world is not much. She had every right. I'm the one who had*
*no right. But someday, man . . . someday . . .*

Lori arrived in Chicago by Greyhound bus. Her two pieces of
luggage in hand, she went to the newsstand, bought a copy of the
*Tribune,* and went to the coffee shop just outside the bus terminal.
Over a sandwich and coffee she studied the want ads and circled
the few promising opportunities. Then she turned to the theatrical
section and made a list of the minor theatrical companies to which
she was determined to apply.

Within the first three weeks Lori had found a job at a small
restaurant in the market area of Chicago, where before dawn
trucks carrying all sorts of produce rolled in and unloaded.

Those early-morning hours left her free after the lunch trade,
making it possible for her to visit the theaters and seek an opportunity to read for plays about to go into production.

During her fifth week she caught the fancy of a young director
who asked her to become standby for the actress who would play
the lead.

It wasn't much of a chance. Lori had to be at every rehearsal,
constantly making notes in her script to reflect every change in
lines or moves that evolved in the process of finding a new role
and a new play. So that, should an emergency make it impossible
for the leading actress to appear, Lori could step in knowing every
line, every move, without any interruption in the continuity of
the performance.

Unfortunately for Lori, during the entire run of the play the
leading actress did not fail to appear for a single performance. Lori
did not become a star overnight. Or even get a chance to show what
she could do. So much for show-business legends, she thought.

One thing the experience did accomplish for her. It gave her
access to the one copy of weekly *Variety* to which the company
subscribed. She searched it eagerly for all news of the Broadway
theater. Without realizing it, she was searching for news of an
actor named Brett Mann.

She found none.

The only sign of him, and she was not too sure about that,

was in a men's fragrance commercial on television. One of those commercials shot in dim light and shadow. A young man in the background *looked* like Brett. Had the same strong, lean upper body Brett had. She watched television as often as she could but was able to catch that commercial only twice more. And she was still not sure it was Brett.

June 12, 1995, fell on a Sunday, which was fortunate for Lori Adams. Since there were always two performances on Sundays.

She now had a small role in another new play. So she was thankful to be involved during both the afternoon and the evening. For June 12 was a most important and painful day for her. As would every June 12 be for the rest of her life.

It was on that day that her son was born. This was his first birthday. Though she had personally interviewed and approved her son's new parents, she could never feel quite sure. If it had been possible to discover who they were, where they were, she would have found them. To make sure that her son was safe and secure in a good home environment.

That's all she wanted, just to make sure.

But even in the hospital where she had worked, she'd never had access to those confidential files.

She barely made it through the Sunday matinee. She was constantly on edge, constantly fearing that in the middle of her scene she would start to cry, though the scene did not call for it.

At the end of the performance, as she came off, the director, who had been standing in the wings watching, said, "Terrific! What dramatic energy! What tension. I never saw that in rehearsal. You must have been saving it up for the performance."

"Yes, yes," Lori agreed. "I . . . I was holding back during rehearsal."

She couldn't escape fast enough to make it into the alley outside the stage door and start sobbing.

*What a way,* she thought, *to celebrate my son's first birthday. I must stop thinking of him as my son, I must.*

But she never would.

# This Child Is Mine

On that same Sunday afternoon, hundreds of miles west of Chicago, at the home of William and Christine Salem, an outdoor barbecue was being attended by neighbors, friends, and all relatives who lived within half a day's drive.

This was a very special barbecue. The celebration of the first birthday of Scotty Salem. While Bill presided over the double-wide grill and Christie hustled from kitchen to outdoor table attending to all the other details of food and drink, little Scotty engaged all the guests with his efforts at walking.

He would take a few steps, quickly, as if to cram in as many as he could before falling on the soft grass. The guests applauded his efforts. He reveled in their cheers. He would smile up from his all-fours crouch, his blond hair a halo around his handsome face. Then, avoiding their help, he would get to his feet to make another run at it.

From his place at the grill Bill Salem watched and beamed. As he loaded hamburgers onto buns and dispensed ribs onto paper plates, he was aware and proud of everything about his young son. His physical efforts, his smile, his ability to attract people and endear himself. People loved him, and he loved people.

Christie interrupted little Scotty's antics by sweeping him up in her arms and saying, "Show-off! Time for your nap!" She took him upstairs and sang to him until he fell asleep.

Once she covered him with a very light blanket, she rejoined her guests and relatives. They were still talking about Scotty, his personality, his effect on people. And how mature he seemed for a child of only one year.

Bill went up to wake him for the presentation of the birthday cake. Scotty blew out the two candles, one for this year and one to grow on. But it took him three breaths to do it.

"After all," Christie's mother, a proud grandmother, protested, "it's the first time he's ever done it. Wait till next year."

The gifts were so many, the wrappings so colorful, that little Scotty ended up sitting on the lawn surrounded by brilliant colors and more gifts and toys than anyone could count.

As dusk began to set in, guests with long trips home started leaving.

Christie's mother embraced her little grandson and kissed him with such enthusiasm that he could not wriggle out of her hug soon enough.

She drew her daughter aside to whisper, "What you and Bill have gone through in the last few years, it's all worth it. He's a fantastic child. Your uncle would have been real proud for him to be remembered in such a little boy."

It was past ten. With the help of neighbors, Christie and Bill had cleared up the residue of the party. They were left alone, with only the fragments of the birthday cake to remind them of the day.

Bill was licking some of the frosting off his forefinger as Christie said, "He's really ours. And best of all, he's healthy and alive."

Bill embraced her, whispering, "He's terrific. And a real ham. He just loves to have people love him."

"I hope that means that we've given him all the security and love that we promised his birth mother."

"Could any parents have given him more?" Bill asked.

"No."

"Then why are you so . . . ?"

"So *what*?" she challenged.

"There's a sadness, something—a sadness when there should be only joy," Bill tried to explain.

"I was thinking of her, that desperate young girl. . . ."

"Let's go up and make sure he's tucked in," Bill said, to change the subject.

# Chapter 16

In New York, outside the stage door of the Booth Theater, on Forty-fifth Street just off Broadway, seven young men stood mulling over two pages of a new play with which they had to familiarize themselves to audition for a minor role.

All seven were in their mid-twenties, all tall, all blond, all well-built—the physical requirements for the role. Each of them had selected his corner of the area to try out several approaches to the scene. Some worked silently, some whispered their lines.

As each candidate came out, one or another of the waiting men asked, "How'd it go?"

Each departing candidate shook his head, admitting defeat. Only one responded, "They asked me to come back and read again."

One by one the seven men were called in. Each walked out onto the stage, which was dark except for the single work light that stood to the side. Out of the darkness, the stage manager read the other lines in the scene while the young man responded with the lines of his character.

In the dark auditorium the director, the author, one of the producers, and the lady who had been charged with casting the play sat in a row like a jury at a murder trial. This had been a long, fruitless session. The role that had seemed simple to cast had made this a day of pure frustration.

At one point the producer exploded in disgust. "Christ! There must be *one* actor in this city who understands this role!" He turned to the young casting agent. "Judy! Where the hell did you find these klutzes? Don't know how to make an entrance. Can't hear them beyond the third row. Clint Eastwood shows more emotion than these loxes. Let's call it off for the day!"

Accustomed to his rantings, no one demurred, but neither did anyone change the schedule, for the director called, "Next!"

Stepping out of the darkness into the dimly lighted work area came yet another tall, blond, good-looking young man who announced himself:

"Brett Mann."

In response to the stage manager's opening speech, Brett read his lines. After four exchanges between them, the producer called out impatiently, "Thank you," dismissing him.

"But I haven't finished," Brett protested.

"Oh, yes, you have!" the producer shouted back.

"I was building to the climax of the scene," Brett tried to explain. "It would be wrong for the character to unload everything in his first few lines."

"Young man," the impatient producer called back from the darkness, "you are not auditioning for the role of the director. We already have one. As for the role of Ben, you are definitely not right."

"But, Mr. Kimmel . . ."

"If I said 'Thank you,' I retract that. Just get the hell out. We have no time to waste."

Brett Mann crumpled his two pages, tossed them into the dark backstage area, and marched out. When he passed through the stage-door area, the others asked, "How'd it go?" He did not reply but strode blindly through Shubert Alley. He had just turned onto Forty-fourth Street when he heard his name called.

"Brett Mann!"

Impatiently, angrily, he turned back in a combatant attitude to discover a woman in her late twenties beckoning to him to return. A total stranger, yet she knew his name? He ventured back.

The closer they drew, the more familiar she appeared. He had seen her before. But where? When?

She read the puzzlement on his face and explained, "Calley Ransome. Bordman-Levitt Casting."

He recognized her now. She had interviewed him once and promised to call him in for readings on roles for which he might be suited. It was thanks to her that he had been called in for today's reading.

"What did I do wrong?" he asked. "I couldn't explode into the scene. The character is shy, making an entrance into an unfamiliar place to meet an older woman he has never met before. Naturally he's going to be shy, soft-spoken, waiting to see what she's like."

"Naturally," Calley Ransome agreed.

"Then what did I do wrong?" Brett persisted.

Calley smiled. "It's been a long, tough day. And Kimmel's never been known for patience under the best of circumstances. He would have turned down a young Marlon Brando today. But I may have something else for you. Our agency is casting for a new part in *Time of Our Youth.*"

"You mean that soap?" Brett asked.

"Don't knock it! If your character works, there's good money. And good experience. Quite a few actors have gone from soaps to features."

"And to the stage?" Brett challenged.

"If you want to waste your life, and your youth, working for the kind of money they pay Off Broadway, or Off-Off Broadway, you're welcome to it. But if you want my advice, take a shot at that soap."

She handed him a note.

"Give this to Esther Finn, NBC Studio 8A."

"Gee, thanks!"

"I've got to get back," she said crisply, and headed for the lobby of the Booth.

Brett Mann was confronted by a uniformed guard outside Studio 8A. He asked for Esther Finn and sent in the note he'd been handed. Fifteen minutes later the guard reappeared and escorted him into the studio, which was set up, as it was five days a week, to rehearse and shoot the daily episodes of *Time of Our Youth*. From the control room he heard a woman's voice:

"Brett Mann! Hit the mark on the floor."

He stepped into the light to find the chalk mark on the floor that placed him in the range of the one camera that was lit up.

The voice from the control room came to him again over the loudspeaker.

"Turn right, please."

He did and held the position.

"Now left!"

He turned left and held that position, feeling like a prize bull in a cattle show.

"Now full face!"

He turned to face the camera and held that position for what seemed hours. Actually it was twelve long, agonizing minutes. He knew that during all that time a heated discussion was going on in the control room. The director, the producer, the head writer, the woman from the advertising agency, the man from the network, were comparing their reactions to this specimen of young manhood who appeared on the six different monitors on the wall just above them.

Once more came the woman's disembodied voice: "Right profile again, please."

Once more Brett complied. This time he was forced to hold that position for a longer time than previously.

"Left profile, please!"

Again he complied.

Finally the voice called, "Thank you!"

He turned to face the camera. "No lines? Don't you want to hear me read?"

"Not yet," the voice replied. "Do you have any tape?"

"Tape?"

"Tape of yourself in anything you've done."

"I did a commercial . . . one of those men's cologne ads. But I'm just in the background there."

There followed a long silence. More discussion. Finally the woman's voice called, "Tomorrow. Two-fifteen. And wear something casual. Sport jacket. If you have one."

"Same studio?"

"Same studio," the voice confirmed, ending the interview.

Brett arranged to have someone fill in for him at Orso's, where he had been working as a waiter for some months. The manager, quite used to dealing with the exigencies of show business, acquiesced. So Brett was free all that morning to arrange his wardrobe, get a light hair trim, wash and iron a fresh shirt, and pose before his cracked mirror to determine how he looked his best.

At 2:10 he presented himself at Studio 8A. Half an hour later he was called in. But not before another young man, attired in roughly the same manner, had departed. Obviously his competition.

Brett was put through the same camera angles as the day before. Right profile, left profile, full face.

"Turn up the collar." When he appeared puzzled, the woman explained with a bit of impatience, "The collar of your sport jacket. Give us an informal feel. Turn up the collar. Like Christopher Reeve would do it."

Brett turned up his collar, looked right, looked left, looked into the camera. Suddenly someone slipped into the scene to hand him several pages of script.

"Read!" the woman ordered.

"Don't I get a chance to look it over?" Brett asked.

"Just wing it! We want to see how you react to emergencies. Of which we have more than our share in our business!"

He read his lines. There was another long silence.

"Now look into the camera. We're going to move in for a tight close-up. Read those lines again."

Brett faced the camera, waiting as the camera moved in and the focus was changed. He read his lines. This time from the beginning to the end of the scene. He considered that a hopeful sign.

After another long silence that disembodied voice came at him again.

"Thank you. We'll be in touch."

Four days later he received a call from the production office. Would he come in for costume measurements, and what was the name of his agent?

The very next day his agent called him with the news. They were offering a firm deal for thirteen weeks at one thousand dollars a week. With options and escalating fees for the next five years.

When Brett responded with a diffident "Uh-huh," his agent, Sally Brownell, a seasoned veteran in dealing with young actors, spoke up very sharply, "Young man! You come down to my office at once! I want to talk to you!"

Within half an hour Brett was pacing the waiting room outside Brownell's office. When she opened her door, she dismissed her secretary with a curt, "I will buzz you as soon as I am done with Mr. Mann."

It was the first time Brownell had spoken of him in such a formal manner. She stood aside, saying briskly, "Come in here, mister!"

She remained standing but pointed him to a chair. Once he was seated, the little woman stood opposite him and reprimanded, "Don't you ever—ever—belittle an honest offer of employment as an actor with such an offhand response as 'Uh-huh.' This is a chance, an opportunity that a thousand other young actors would give their right arms for."

"Yes, Ms. Brownell, but it's—"

She never gave him the chance to complete the thought. For she pounced on his last words. "But it's only television. Well, young man, it's 'only television' if that's what *you* make it. But if you work at it, it's weeks of experience working before a camera. It's a chance to be seen by other directors and producers. It's a chance to improve your technique not in the rehearsal hall but in actual day-to-day performance. This may be the chance of your lifetime, young man!

"Or you can screw it up. Become just another actor who blew his big chance by treating it like dirt because 'it's only television.' To a good actor, a dedicated actor, any acting is important acting. Now, if I hear that you are just walking through it, I will personally recommend to those producers a dozen other young actors I represent who would give anything for the chance. Clear?"

"Yes, ma'am," a chastened Brett Mann replied with due humility.

"Now, let's become realistic." Brownell continued, "This thirteen weeks is only a test period. They want to see how the audience—that means the women in the audience—respond to you. If they like you, if the ratings on the show go up, then we're in the driver's seat."

"They want options on me for the next five years," Brett pointed out.

"And they'll pay for them," Brownell warned. "But not with the figures in their offer. Art for art's sake is fine. But getting paid for it is even finer."

Brett realized that his agent had serious and long-range plans for him.

"Well, young man, that's all for today. Go along. Get measured for wardrobe, meet the other cast members." She smiled for the first time as she asked, "Well, how does it feel to be on the verge?"

"Feels . . . feels great . . . Terrific! Feels . . ." Then he relented and admitted, "Feels kind of scary, and empty. . . ."

"Of course," she replied with complete understanding. "Since my husband died, I know the feeling. Everything is empty without someone to share it."

"Yeah, that's it. No one to share it with," Brett admitted.

"A young man like you . . . good-looking . . . " She had no need to be more specific.

"Oh, there've been women."

"But not that *one* woman," Brownell assumed. "Maybe now, with your new status in the business—"

"I don't even know where she is," Brett admitted. "All my letters come back 'Address Unknown.' "

"With the kind of money you'll be making now, you can afford to find her," Brownell suggested. "Meantime, career, young man, career." She had barely gotten the last word out when she remembered: "Oh, by the way, they would like you to change your name."

"Change my name? Why? What for? I like my name," Brett protested.

"They think it sounds fake."

"It's my real name!" Brett insisted.

"I know. But they say it sounds like you took the name Mann to sound like a hunk."

"What's wrong with that?"

"Too obvious. They would rather you had a name like Manning. Has class and can still sound like a hunk. So what'll I tell them?" Brownell asked.

Brett considered the change. Only the hope that this role might enable him to find Lori made him say, "Brett Manning? Sounds all right, I guess. Okay. Brett Manning."

# Chapter 17

For thirteen weeks Brett Manning's days consisted of presenting himself early in the morning at the studio, lines learned, ready to rehearse, do the run-through, and go on air.

At the end of each show he received his pages for the next day. Dutifully he went back to the little apartment he shared with a young aspiring playwright who supported himself by walking the dogs of women who worked at day jobs and could not provide their pets with exercise. There Brett studied his pages faithfully, learning his lines, trying different readings until he hit them perfectly.

Only to receive a call on most evenings that there had been a last-minute change in lines of entire scenes due to some persistence on the part of the star.

Since this was his first thirteen weeks, his test period, he did not enjoy the privilege of longtime cast members, who rarely worked every one of the five weekdays. He rarely had long scenes. But he was visually prominent each day, so the women in the audience would have a chance to react to him, positively or negatively.

For those thirteen weeks he conducted himself like an athlete in training. He devoted himself to his work with religious dedication.

He never forgot Sally Brownell's lecture. She was reputed to be the wisest and most experienced agent in show business. The list of young men she started in the business who had become Hollywood stars was impressive. Brett was determined to become one of them.

On the day the ratings were due to come out, a sense of anxiety pervaded the studio at every level. In the control room the director and the producer, whose jobs depended on continued favorable ratings, were attuned to every ring of the telephone. Out on the floor the cast members ran through their scenes with the usual interruptions and suggestions from the control room. But each member of the cast had his or her own reasons for being anxious about the new ratings. Camilla Storm, the leading lady, was up for contract renewal for her twelfth year. There was no danger of her being canceled. But the raise her agent was planning to ask for needed a strong bounce in the ratings to give him clout. One of the older men in the cast, a dignified white-haired actor with a long list of Broadway credits, lived in fear of a ratings drop. For he always suspected the producer was waiting for some pretext to write him out of the show for all time. With the New York theater shrinking so badly, what was there for an old actor to do?

During a break in rehearsal Brett went into a corner of the studio to run his lines once again. He was almost through with the scene when he heard the voice from the control room over the intercom.

"Well, folks, we did it! Not fantastic. But we did more than hold our own," the producer crowed.

A small cheer went up from the cast and crew on the studio floor. Brett took a deep breath and felt what during this thirteen-week test had become a permanent knot of tension in his stomach slowly start to dissolve. It was only half of the crucial verdict as far as he was concerned. He would learn the other half soon.

His first clue came near the end of rehearsal. The producer's assistant came onto the floor with the new tentative pages for the ensuing week. When she reached Brett, she passed him by with a soft "Buzz wants to see you in the control room after air." She continued handing out batches of pages to the rest of the cast, including the old actor, who accepted them with a grateful smile.

Brett was quite nervous throughout his performance. He hoped the camera did not catch it. He smiled his best. He did the scene in which he had to strip to the waist with a sense of animal bravado. He hoped that would impress not only the women in the audience but the people in the control room. For a young man who was not a workout freak, he was muscularly well endowed. He used it to the utmost in that scene that day.

Finally the show was over. There was the usual relief combined with the assurance that the series would continue with a minimum of problems. Everyone felt secure and sure. Except for Brett Manning, who awaited his summons to the control room.

It came when the director's voice called, "Brett-baby? Got a minute?"

*A minute?* Brett thought. *Bad news never takes long. There's nothing to celebrate or dwell on. One thing I can tell Brownell, I did my damndest. She won't believe me, but it's the God's honest truth. Nobody could have worked harder. Never blew a line. Always hit my mark. Always on time with my cue.*

Thus preparing his defenses, Brett Manning pushed open the control-room door.

With enforced casualness he asked, "You wanted to see me, Buzz?"

"Sure did," Buzz Blair, the director, said, while penciling his notes on the next day's script. Something in the script annoyed him, for he ripped out the page. "Damn it, if I told those writers once, I told them a thousand times, no poetry. I don't give a damn if it's a quote from Shakespeare, no poetry. Camilla can't handle poetry. We're lucky she can even say her own lines. Poetry!"

With that he flung the crumpled page toward the far corner of the control room, then turned to Brett.

As if taken by surprise, he stared at Brett. "Oh, oh yeah. Kid, I have lived in dark control rooms so long, some days I feel I should show up in a miner's cap with a light on it. So when I come across someone like you, young, just starting out . . ."

*Uh-oh,* Brett thought, *here it comes. The well-meant consolation speech.*

". . . young, ambitious. Working tables, department stores at

Christmas, delivering documents by bicycle maybe, while waiting for his big chance. Kid, I know the routine. I was an aspiring young actor myself long ago. Couldn't cut it. That's how I became a director."

*Of course he failed, so it's not so bad that I failed. It's not the end of the line. There are always other things to do in show business,* Brett thought impatiently. He wanted to scream, *Just get it over with, Buzz! I'm fired. Right?*

But with the show secure for the next thirteen weeks, Buzz Blair took this opportunity to luxuriate in his position as elder statesman and sage.

"Know what's the biggest mistake in this business, kid? Greed! That one-syllable word has destroyed more careers than anything except maybe that other one-syllable word, sex. Of course these days with AIDS, sex is not so loose as it was. But it can still ruin a career. Still the worst thing is greed. It can kill you. Remember that!"

The last was spoken with such finality that Brett realized Buzz had just ended the brief meeting. Brett started out of that control room as much confused as depressed.

That heavy feeling grew until he arrived at his small apartment, where Harvey Kline looked up from his word processor to inform him, "Brownell called. Wants to see you. Right away."

"She say anything?"

"Just wants to see you. So haul ass, kid."

When Brett arrived at Sally Brownell's office, he had to wait through three visitors who had preceded him. Finally it was his turn.

Brownell was just finishing up on the phone as Brett slipped into her office. She gestured him to a seat, ended the conversation, and looked at him, saying, "Well, young man, what did they tell you?"

"Not they. Buzz."

"What did he say?"

"Sounds stupid. But he said—"

Brownell usurped Brett's answer, "The worst mistake a young actor can make is to be greedy."

"Yeah. How'd you know?"

"He always gives that little speech before signing a long-term deal. Buzz has a piece of the show. He likes to keep costs down. Mainly where salaries are concerned. They want you, Brett. They really want you. They are hungry. Not only the new ratings but the special survey they did on you proves why. So I have to figure out a new deal for you. I will be tough. But not greedy." She smiled and added, "Of course, Buzz will scream, rant, rave, and finally say yes to everything. Now, young man, you have a career!"

"I thought he was getting ready to fire me," Brett admitted.

"Part of his strategy. Shake your confidence so you would plead with me to go easy on him. Well, I will craft a deal that will make everyone happy. Mainly you."

Brownell rose from her chair and extended her hand across the desk for Brett to shake. Then, in a softer, more personal tone, she said, "That girl, that one girl, don't let her get away, son."

# Chapter 18

✣

Christie Salem zipped up her son's snowsuit to protect him from the seventeen-degree temperature of the Midwestern early winter frost. She would have preferred not to take Scott with her on this particular day, but her baby-sitter had been forced to disappoint her. Today's visit was one she always liked to make alone. To face the moment, and the usual disappointment, alone. The last two times, after it was over, she had sat in her car and wept. She hoped, with little Scotty along, she would retain control. He had never seen her weep. And, young as he was, he was a very sensitive child.

While she dressed him, she talked to him in words he did not comprehend. But it was a source of great comfort to her since she could express her thoughts without later having to confess her disappointment.

"Scotty, how would you like to have a little sister?" she asked as she fixed the navy-blue hood around his blond head so that only his cheeks would be exposed to the freezing prairie winds that swept across the area on the outskirts of the small city where their home was located.

"Scotty—a pretty little sister?" she suggested.

She had read in several books on infant and child care that if there was a possibility that a new child was to be introduced into the family, then, by whatever means, the present child or children should be prepared in advance of the event. Thus the new infant would be anticipated and welcomed rather than feared and resented. Having just missed her second period, she thought maybe this time . . . maybe.

As much out of hope for herself as preparation for her son, she continued talking as she dressed herself for the outdoors.

"Of course, it's nice to have a baby brother. Especially since you would be the older one. Imagine the fun you could have with a brother. Showing him how to do things. Teaching him how to kick a football on the back lawn. Or pitching to him while you teach him to catch a baseball. Or tennis? Your daddy, he likes tennis. The three of you could play together. And if Dad was busy, he gets so busy these days, why you'd have a partner right in the family. Wouldn't that be neat, Scotty?"

She looked down at his handsome if puzzled face, framed by the fake furry trim of his hood. She had to smile at the way he had become a bundle of snowsuit. So round and padded, he looked like the Pillsbury Doughboy.

"Okay, darling, let's go. Let's find out: Is Mommy having another pipe dream? Or could it really happen this time?"

Dr. Moncrief's waiting room was full, as always on the mornings when she was seeing patients, instead of attending a delivery or performing surgery at the hospital.

Christie recognized two of the women. Nice-looking. Nicely dressed. Nicely mannered. Pleasant. Each smiled at little Scotty and his impatient antics.

Christie felt an obligation to explain. "My baby-sitter couldn't make it today." They both nodded in complete understanding, continuing to smile at little Scotty.

But just underneath their smiles, apparent to a woman like Christie who suspected she was in the same situation, was that slightly tense attitude that betrayed that both women were here on a mission in which they had failed more than once before.

Moncrief's waiting room was usually full of women of three types. The ones who hoped they were pregnant. The ones who hoped they were not. The third group who hoped the doctor would find them free of diseases, malignant or otherwise.

These two were of the first type. Christie could diagnose that from the jealousy they tried to camouflage by being unusually solicitous and admiring of little Scotty. They seemed to be saying, *If I had a handsome little son like your son, I'd be satisfied. I wouldn't want for any more.*

Christie knew the feeling, knew it well. But she also knew that one little one like Scotty, dear as he was, was not enough. She wanted a family, a big family.

Time was dragging. Not only was Scotty more restless, she herself had grown impatient. Either Dr. Moncrief was slower than usual or else her cases this morning were more complex, demanding more time. As for Scotty, was he more active and hard to control? Or was Christie more tense? She could not face another failure. She was also racked by a special guilt that had arisen since Scotty's adoption.

Was she being less a loyal and devoted mother to Scotty by desiring to have another child? A child who would be Bill and herself joined in one human being?

This morning, as at all other times when the thought plagued her, she reminded herself, if it was to happen, if Moncrief confirmed what she hoped, she must never, never show any favoritism to a second child. She was still too new at being an adoptive mother to know that time would take care of that. The time would come when she would have to be reminded by other people that one of her children was adopted.

If any child in this world had no need to fear taking second place to anyone, it was Scotty. By his warmth, his openness, his need to embrace and be embraced, sung to, his ready, friendly smile, his eagerness to be part of everything that took place around him, he had become so much a part of their lives they would feel empty, if not desolate, without him.

Of course, Christie realized if that . . . that . . . she had never found a proper word for it . . . hadn't happened to little Billy, by this time he'd be almost four and ready for nursery school.

People urged, "Put all that behind you. You have a child now, a lovely, bright, healthy little boy. Forget the sad past about which you can do nothing."

Part of her rebelled, insisting, *I will never forget little Billy. He was my son. A human being in his own right. Deserving to be remembered. And I will remember him always. Always.*

When a woman is forced to sit in a doctor's waiting room for what seems hours, when she is anticipating a diagnosis that could change her life, she has little else to do but think of many things.

By the time the nurse came out to call "Mrs. Salem?" Christie was taken by surprise. Hurriedly she asked the woman sitting alongside, "Would you?"

The woman was delighted to lift little Scotty into her lap, though the boy strained to follow his mother as she disappeared into the doctor's private office.

Moncrief, a disarming woman in her mid-forties, had the strong face of her pioneer ancestors. But she had the slight body of a woman about whom they would have said in those olden days, "She ain't hardly got enough flesh on her bones to make it through a real stiff winter."

What Moncrief lacked in physical bulk, she more than made up for in strength of character, of which honesty was her most important attribute. Whatever the diagnosis, she delivered it with tactful forthrightness. Four times now, in the past year alone, she had been forced to tell Christie, "Sorry, Christine, but no. No chance you are pregnant."

"But," Christie always protested, "I missed my period."

"Sorry, Christie."

While she lay on the table, her legs in the stirrups, with Moncrief carrying out her examination, Christie Salem was resigned to hearing the usual, "Sorry, Christine—"

This time Moncrief was taking more time than usual. Why? Had she found something else? Something that—At once Christie recalled the unfortunate case of Marjorie Newman. One day she went for a routine check, and the doctor discovered something in her ovaries. It turned out to be malignant. Seven months later Marjorie was dead—at only thirty-two, leaving a husband and three children, and all without any warning, any symptoms. Just during a routine exam.

*God, please, no,* Christie protested. *I can't leave Bill, little Scotty. They need me. I will even . . . even give up wanting another child if You just let me go on. . . .*

"Christie," Dr. Moncrief interrupted her fantasies, "I wanted to make sure, absolutely sure, before I said a word. But *you* are pregnant. You really *are* pregnant."

Christie started to smile in relief but began to cry instead.

"Go on, Christie, enjoy it," Moncrief said, beaming.

Christie sat up, crying and smiling.

"Would you like to call your husband?"

"This . . . this is too good to say over the phone. I want to see his face when I tell him."

She dressed hurriedly, went out to the waiting room, bundled up her little son, and carried him out into the parking lot.

All the way to Bill's shop she kept thinking: *Scotty, you really are going to have a baby sister or brother. We'll have to change things at the house. Don't worry, sweetheart, we are not taking your room. That's yours until the day you go off to college. But we will have to make plans. Perhaps your little sister will be in our room until we get a new addition built on the house. Your daddy will have to work that in with the rest of his business, but he'll manage . . . he'll manage. He's got nine months, no, wait, I forgot to ask Moncrief when I can expect. No, that can wait. The important thing now, drive carefully, very carefully, tell Bill, and then . . . then . . . God, what a wonderful world! I can almost feel the changes going on inside me right now. Scotty, I really can . . . I really can. . . .*

Bill Salem was on the phone, the instrument cradled between his shoulder and his ear to free his hands to encode into his computer the figures for a job he was estimating. At sight of Christie and Scotty he smiled apologetically for being too involved to lavish on them the warm greeting he would have loved to give them. Finally he brought the conversation to an end with a pleasant "Mr. Simonson, did we do a good job for you last time? We'll do it again. Trust me."

He hung up the phone, starting for Christie while saying to

his son, "Scotty, boy, by the time you take over this company, we'll be so computerized all you'll have to do is think, and the machine will do the rest."

He kissed Christie on the lips, and at the moment of contact he stopped. He sensed something different.

"Hon?" he asked.

"Yes. Moncrief said yes."

Yielding to his instant impulse, he lifted his wife off her feet and started to whirl her around the office when he realized, "Oh, my God, I can't do that to you anymore." Cautiously he set her down, then insisted, "Sit down. Sit right here. In my chair."

"Bill, honey, there's no need. No special instructions. Everything goes on as usual. It's just that everything is—well—different now."

"You bet. We have to start another college fund. Another room, we have to have another room and . . . and first, I have to get control of myself. Wow!"

# Chapter 19

Brett Manning, naked to the waist again, had just embraced his leading lady, Melanie Caine. He kissed her with all the passion he could command at eleven-thirty in the morning. He held that kiss for as long as it took the camera to move in for a tight close-up until the director called, "And blackout! Thanks, kids. See you Monday as usual. Your new pages will be delivered to you by noon tomorrow."

Brett rose from the bed. Without a word to his co-star he started for his dressing room.

Melanie called after him, "Brett? Busy tonight?"

He half-turned, interrupted in his haste. "Gee, love to. But I've got to be in Chicago by evening."

"Chicago?" Melanie asked, surprised.

"Uh, one of those publicity things," he improvised.

He continued to his dressing room thinking, *Melanie's a terrific woman, and a joy to work with, but as for anything serious . . . it wouldn't be fair to her.*

He entered his dressing room to find his agent, Sally Brownell, waiting.

He reacted in surprise. "Sally?"

She handed him the airline envelope. "Your tickets. To *Chicago*," she emphasized.

"You didn't have to *bring* them. All I asked your secretary was to *get* them," Brett replied, somewhat aggressive since he felt quite guilty.

"Brett, two things you must never do. First, endanger a career I have taken the trouble to structure very carefully. Especially don't endanger it now. I am getting ready for your next move. To feature films. I have my eye on two different roles in new and important scripts. I am working on having you meet the directors when they come to New York. Meantime, I have sent both of them cassettes of your best work."

"Terrific!" Brett said, sounding more cautious than enthusiastic. "And the second thing I must never do?"

"Lie to *me*. I never want to be caught misleading the press or anyone in the business because you lied to me. I can withhold information. I can play cozy as well as anyone in this industry. But for myself I insist on knowing the truth. Now, what's this about having to go to Chicago in such a hurry?"

"For God's sake!" Brett exploded. "I'm entitled to a life of my own! Isn't it enough I work my ass off seven days a week? Yes, seven days a week, even though we only shoot five. The other two I'm learning new lines. So I can forget them on Monday to learn rewritten lines. Christ, Sally, give me a break. Permit me a little privacy, a life of my own."

Since he had avoided her real question, Brownell decided to come straight to the point.

"Brett, who is Lori Adams?"

"Lori . . . How did you know?" Brett started to ask, then decided to say no more for fear of adding to what the woman already knew.

"Several weeks ago when you were on a heavy schedule, doing publicity appearances in addition to your regular shooting schedule, you asked my bookkeeper to pay a handful of your bills."

"She does it for some of your other clients," Brett countered.

"I was delighted to have her do it. She'll do it all the time if you want."

"Then what's the problem?" Brett demanded, as he started wiping his makeup off.

"One of the bills she paid was to a private-investigating agency, Hanrahan Associates."

Brett looked up at her through the mirror of his makeup table.

"Brett, I knew Johnny Hanrahan when he was a mounted cop on Forty-fifth Street years ago and I was just starting out. He knows I wouldn't do anything to hurt you."

"He told you," Brett realized. "Okay. I paid him. He found her. I am going to Chicago to see her."

"Is she *that* girl?" Brett nodded. "Does she know?"

"No. I want to surprise her," Brett said.

"Men! What makes you think she wants to be surprised? Maybe by now she has a life of her own. Doesn't want to ever see you again. Maybe there's another man—a husband. What right do you have to just ride into her life again and take over?"

"I didn't say anything about taking over," Brett protested.

"If that isn't what you have in mind, why bother?"

Brett finally conceded, nodding, turning from the mirror to face her.

"Yes, I do want to take over. As for her being married, nothing Hanrahan's man could find indicated that. So most likely that isn't true."

"At least you're hoping it isn't true," Brownell surmised.

"Yes. I'm hoping it isn't true," Brett admitted.

"Are you sure she's the one?" Brownell asked.

"There've been others. As I guess you know. She's the one I keep coming back to. If that's love, then this is it. Besides—" But he thought better of it and returned to removing the last traces of his makeup.

"Besides *what*?" Brownell persisted.

Brett studied his face in the mirror, then glanced up at the little graying woman who hovered over his shoulder staring into his mirror and his eyes.

"The last time we talked or wrote, she was pregnant, and pretty far along."

"And?" Brownell insisted.

"That's the part I don't know. She never wrote, never called.

Nothing. Letters I sent to her were all returned. No forwarding address."

"Then it's obvious she doesn't want anything further to do with you," Brownell pointed out.

"That's what I have to find out," Brett replied.

"You're 'assuring' yourself she may have turned down a young unknown actor like Brett Mann. But she will welcome with open arms big daytime star Brett Manning. I've seen too many surprises in my long life to bet on anything a hurt woman is capable of."

"I have to find out," he insisted.

Brownell handed him his airline tickets, with a warning: "Whatever you do, don't get any bad publicity. Former lover. Child out of wedlock. Brett Manning, daytime idol, gets turned down by a waitress or a secretary in some plastics factory in Chicago. Don't jeopardize your career, Brett!"

"I'll remember that," Brett said, hoping to be left alone.

Brownell started for the door, stopped, then turned to him to confess, "You know, Eric and I, we broke up four times before we finally got married. So I know what you mean about the only one. I wish you luck. Just be careful. For your public image."

He taxied directly from O'Hare to the address mentioned in the report from Hanrahan Associates. It turned out to be a deserted store in a row of deserted stores in the South End of Chicago. From the outside it seemed just another long-ago abandoned store plastered over with layers of posters.

He searched for a door. And found it at a break in the old posters. He opened it. He slipped in. He could hear voices but saw nothing until he rounded a partition that separated him from the rest of the place. At the far end of the store, in the glow of a work light, four actors and a director were working out a scene.

Brett scanned the two women in the cast, seeking Lori. She was not one of them. But when the woman director turned from the raised rehearsal platform, Brett realized *she* was Lori. Pretty as always, despite her unkempt working hairdo. And . . . and something else. She seemed stronger than he remembered. More mature. Of course. The last time he had seen her face-to-face she was a frightened young woman, pregnant and unsure.

Now she was directing a play and, from what he could observe, had the respect and obedience of her cast.

Brownell's warning came back to him in a rush. In the dark he searched out a folding chair. It squeaked slightly as he sat down. Everyone glanced back but only momentarily, then continued with their work.

He listened intently, thinking, what a luxury to be able to rehearse a scene until you knew it, felt it, and were really part of it. Instead of running through a time or two, being told where your floor marks were, then going out and winging it.

He also admired how meticulous Lori was with the actors. Solicitous of their feelings but very firm as well. She *had* changed, he was forced to admit.

They had been rehearsing for more than an hour when one of the young actresses in the cast reminded the director, "Lori, rules."

"Oh, sorry," Lori replied. "Of course. Let's break for fifteen minutes."

The actors were relieved to put their scripts aside. One of them lit up the cigarette she had craved for the last hour. The men just dropped onto their chairs and relaxed. The young actress who had reminded Lori of the Equity rules drew her aside. An intense discussion followed, Lori doing most of the talking and the young actress nodding, nodding, nodding. She left Lori's side and started toward a corner of the work area to try out what Lori had suggested.

Lori stepped down, needing a break of her own.

Out of the darkness she heard a voice call softly, "Lori?"

She froze, turned slowly in the direction of that voice, and whispered, "Oh, God . . ."

Brett approached her, reached for her hand, tried to draw her close.

"No, Brett. Not here. Not now."

"It has to be here. It has to be now. I don't have much time."

"I can meet you later. After my rehearsal."

"What time? Where?"

Lori hesitated, as if debating whether to tell him.

"Lori? Please? I wouldn't have come all this way if what I have to say wasn't important. To me. And I hope to you."

"I'll meet you at five. In the cocktail lounge of the Drake."

"Such a public place," Brett protested.

"I don't trust private places. Not at a time like this. I need all the defenses I can muster," she replied, unashamed to admit she still loved him.

"Okay. The Drake. Five o'clock. Be there," he urged.

"Did you think I wouldn't?"

"I don't know. You're not . . . not the Lori I expected."

"Funny," she said, smiling that impish smile he had always loved.

"What's funny about it?"

"I'm not the Lori you expected. You're the Brett Manning I see on television. But never expected. Five. The Drake."

# Chapter 20

❧

For the tenth time Brett Manning looked at his eighteen-karat-gold Rolex watch, a gift from Camilla Storm. Ostensibly it was a token of her admiration for his work on the soap. Actually Sally Brownell had warned Brett, "Stay away. She's deadly on young leading men." As always, he had heeded Mother Brownell's advice, a title he had conferred on her since she guided his career so successfully. Told him what to do, warned him what not to do. Her advice had proved always correct, as witness his thriving career.

He glanced at his costly watch once more. Lori was twenty-two minutes late. Or, to avoid him, had she promised to meet him at the Drake, never intending to appear? Well, he knew where he could find her. Forced to do so, he would.

He had to admit, once timid and unsure, Lori was different now. Could a woman, or any person, change this much in only three years? Maybe it began when, unmarried and pregnant, she had chosen to go it alone.

*Not my fault,* Brett protested. *I wanted to be with her. Offered to leave New York and get a regular job. Didn't I send her what little money I could at the time? Then suddenly my letters were all returned. No forwarding address. She just disappeared. With my child.*

*Was she punishing me because she blames me? She didn't say it.*

*Didn't have to. I could see it in her eyes. Okay, if it takes accepting the blame, I'll accept it. Anything to make her know that I still love her. Of course, if she turns out to be unreasonable, and women can be stubborn, sometimes for the most peculiar of reasons. . . . Of course, if she turns out to be too stubborn. . . . Well, I have certain rights.*

His hostility continued to build as he began to ascribe to her motives for which he had no ground but his own guilt. Until he saw her enter the lobby. He tried to read her state of mind from her physical attitude. She entered, a woman in haste. She glanced around the lobby with that swift, anxious look that revealed she was afraid he had grown impatient and left. Only when she spied him did she seem to relax. She started across the lobby toward him.

He had always admired the graceful way she moved. He had noticed that even before he met her. She had added confidence to that easy, graceful walk.

He rose to greet her. As naturally as if they had parted only yesterday, he kissed her. She appeared aloof. Or was she merely taken aback?

He suddenly felt ill at ease, like a high school sophomore on a first date.

"Shall we . . . ?" he invited her to be seated.

She chose a chair across the small round cocktail table from him.

"Lori," he began at once, "sorry I took you by surprise. I should have called ahead or written. But I thought it would be more . . . more—"

"Romantic?" she asked wryly. "Like one of those corny episodes you do every afternoon?"

"Don't knock it, Lori!" he rebutted. "It's good, hard, honest work. And it gives a man a chance to sharpen his skills."

"That's like practicing how to burn down houses," she replied.

Abandoning his resolve to be conciliatory and gracious, he replied, "It beats directing a group of would-be actors in a cold, abandoned store!"

He was sorry the instant he heard his own angry words.

"I . . . I didn't mean that. What I meant was, acting on a soap gives you a chance to try different things, to stretch your abilities where it counts—in front of an audience."

"That's what I mean. . . ." She stopped abruptly because in the natural flow of her language she would have called him "darling." Resuming, she phrased her response more deliberately. "What I was trying to say, whenever I can, I watch your show."

"You do?" He was pleased.

"Lately I've noticed that you're beginning to repeat yourself."

"Repeat myself?" he asked, indignant that she chose to criticize him. People no longer did these days. "Repeat myself? How?"

"Certain moves, facial gestures in your close-ups. Particularly your delivery on certain lines."

"That's not me!" he protested. "It's those damn scripts they give me. Those hack writers run out of new ways to say things. Sometimes I feel like I'm doing the same scene that I did two weeks ago, a week ago, a day ago."

"I would think," Lori said, "that would make it more challenging. To keep your character alive, keep the lines sounding fresh precisely because they're not. Brett, I think you've wasted a terrific chance this last year and a half."

Touched though he was that she had followed his career so closely, he was more resentful that she had chosen to reveal that fact through criticism.

"Since when have you become such an expert, such a hotshot director?" he demanded.

She smiled. A condescending smile that made him feel she considered herself his superior where acting was involved.

"Sorry," he continued, "I didn't mean that."

"Oh, yes, you did," she replied. "But I didn't meet you here to discuss views on acting. You came all the way from New York. Why?"

"I love you is why."

"You could have written that. Or left it on my answering machine," she replied coolly.

"After my letters all came back 'No Forwarding Address,' I

gave up writing. Once you disappeared, I didn't have your phone number."

"Still, you found me," she countered.

"I paid a private investigator good money for four months to track you down."

"You hired a private detective to find me?" She was more touched than she wanted to admit.

"Once the network picked up my option, I could afford it. So I hired them. I figured by then the baby would be about a year old. I wanted to see him, or is it a her?"

"Him," Lori said.

"I want to see him," Brett insisted.

"I'm afraid you can't."

"Lori, I came here to ask you to marry me. To become a family now. So don't play games with me."

" 'Games'? You think all this time I've been playing games?" she demanded angrily.

"If it isn't marriage, what *do* you want to let me see my son?"

"What do I want? What do I—" she struggled to say, as her anger turned to tears.

"Lori . . . Lori? Please, not here. Right in the middle of this place . . . all these people . . . Lori?"

She was weeping openly. She started across the lounge through the lobby in such haste that everyone turned to watch her. Brett raced after her. He had to brush aside two women who recognized him and begged for his autograph.

He caught up with Lori halfway down the street. He seized her arm, turned her to him, embraced her.

"Lori . . . darling . . . please. If I said anything to hurt you, I'm sorry. Forgive me. But there's no need to cry. I don't mean any harm. To you or to my son. All I want to do is see him. Make sure he's okay. After that, if you don't want me to see him again, I won't bother you. I swear. I just want to make sure he's okay. And now that I'm able, that he's well cared for. Good schools. A nice place to live. A lot of the things I never had. Is that too much for a father to want?"

Still weeping, she tried to avoid him, but he held her tightly.

"Lori? Lori!" he persisted. "All I want to do is see him."

"You . . . you can't . . ."

"Can't? I have rights! I'm his father! I'll take a DNA test to prove it. I'll go to court if I have to. Or we can do this peacefully. Just let me see him."

"I can't," she reiterated.

"Can't? Or won't?"

She paused, wiped away her tears with her palms, and braced herself to say, "Not won't. Can't."

"Why not? Has something—has something happened to my son?" he demanded.

"He's not your son, Brett. Not any longer."

He seized her by the shoulders. "What do you mean 'not my son any longer'?"

"He's . . . I . . . he's been adopted."

"Adopted? Why? How? By whom?"

"I never knew their names. Or where they were from. I was not allowed to know. But they seemed like nice people, good people."

"Adopted, without my knowing . . . without . . . No, that can't be."

"I had no choice, no home . . . my father wouldn't even let me stay there until my baby was born. I had to do what was best for my son."

"He's my son, too," Brett protested.

"I know, I know," Lori admitted softly. "That's why I was so startled to see you today. For a long time I've been fantasizing the scene in my mind. One day we would meet again. And you would ask about your son. I rehearsed a thousand ways to tell you. But never found a right one. Well, now you know. And you must hate me."

"I don't hate you," he insisted, embracing her more tightly despite the turned-head looks of curious passersby.

"I hate myself. For giving him up. But it was the only way. Not a day goes by that I don't think of him. I say to myself, if I hadn't seen him just that once, maybe it wouldn't be so hard. But no, I feel that pain all the time. Sometimes . . ."

She faltered until Brett coaxed gently, "Lori . . . darling . . . please?"

"Sometimes . . . no, *every* time I see a headline in the papers or hear a news item on the radio or television about some child abused or even killed by adoptive parents, I pray, 'Dear God, I hope the people who have my son aren't like that.' Even though they seemed like such good people, I can't help but feel the pain each time. And the guilt. No matter how difficult it would have been, at least I would have kept him safe and alive."

"Lori," Brett said, lifting her face by a firm finger under her quivering chin, "Lori, I make big money now. I'll be making lots more. I can afford the best lawyers in New York or anywhere. I will start legal proceedings to get your son back . . . *our* son. If I do, will you marry me?"

"Yes," she agreed.

# Chapter 21

Lee Curry had been Brett's attorney ever since he drew up the papers for his renegotiated contract. Curry sat back in his swivel chair pondering the request Brett had just made.

"Brett, I appreciate your confidence. But I couldn't, in good conscience, handle such a case. Especially in another state. I'm not up on their Family-Relations law. And even if I were, I'm not familiar with their Rules of Practice. Which could be a fatal handicap if this went to trial."

"Then find me a lawyer in that state to represent me!" Brett insisted.

"That I can do," Lee conceded. "But first, talk this over with Brownie. I think before you do anything she should know."

"She's a terrific agent," Brett conceded. "And nobody respects her more than I do. But this has to do with getting an adoption annulled. Or whatever they call it. It has nothing to do with business!"

"In show business *everything* has to do with business. Talk to her. If, after that, you want me to find you a lawyer, I'll find you the best there is in that state," Lee promised.

Behind her desk, in a chair that made her seem even smaller than she was, Sally Brownell looked like Whistler's mother minus the cap.

She had listened without interruption. When Brett finished, she said, "I think this calls for a full-scale meeting."

"Of whom?" he demanded.

"Your producer, your director, the public-relations people of the network, and the sponsor."

"For God's sake, Brownie, I am talking about getting my son back. That is my own private business! I'm not asking anyone else to get involved. Tell them to stay the hell out!" Brett protested.

"Brett . . . Brett . . ." Brownell tried to calm him. "At this stage in your career, and from now on, you *have* no private business. You are Brett Manning. Any time you get into a courtroom for any reason, it becomes everybody's business. Especially the sponsor's business. Let's have that meeting," she insisted.

"Okay, but it won't change my mind!" he warned.

The meeting was held in one of the small conference rooms at the network. Brett, Brownell, Lee Curry, were on one side of the long table. Opposite them, ranged as if they were adversaries, were the producer of *Time of Our Youth,* the director, a network executive, the network attorney, an account executive from the advertising agency, a representative of the sponsor, and a thin dark-haired woman whose age Brett could not discern, as she was entrenched behind large-framed, thick-lensed glasses.

The matter was put before them by Brownell. A brief history of the affair with Lori, the pregnancy, her running off, Brett's desire to find the child and do the right thing. Then the shocking discovery that the child had been given up for adoption. Hence the need now for a legal proceeding to reclaim custody.

To present the matter in a light most favorable to her client, Brownell ended by saying, "Because of Brett's high regard for the show, the people who do it, the network, and the sponsor, he wants your input before he does anything."

With the issue before them, the first man to speak up was Buzz Blair, the director.

"If Brett is so concerned about us, and this show, the best thing he can do is nothing!"

"Buzz, Buzz," the producer intruded, "let's not go ballistic.

Our young man has a problem. A serious problem. Let's see if we can help him solve it." He turned to the sponsor's representative. "Ward, we're all in this together. We want your input. What do you think Cincinnati will say?"

"Cincinnati" being a euphemism for the sponsoring company, their representative now had the floor. Ward Russell was paid to protect the public image of the sponsor. In any case in which there was even the slightest question of good taste or adverse public reaction, it was Russell's duty to be diplomatically but firmly negative.

In this instance that was easier than usual.

He began slowly, with almost judicial weightiness. "Let's review what we have before us. The young male star of a very costly and successful daytime show wants to go public with the news that he had an affair with a young actress. That he fathered a son. That he did nothing to aid in the birth."

"I did all I could! I took an extra job to send her money. She refused it!" Brett justified himself.

"Brett, Brett," Brownell cautioned. "Let the man speak."

"I am not judging you, my boy," Ward replied. "Any man around this table might be in the same predicament. I am only anticipating public reaction. Brett Manning, whom we have spent more than a year building up to be a clean-cut, right-thinking, beyond-reproach young hero, suddenly becomes the father of an illegitimate child. I don't know."

"Ward, let's not go overboard," Buzz said. "I don't like this any more than you do. But having kids out of wedlock is routine in Hollywood these days."

"But not on our soap opera!" the sponsor's representative protested. "Our audience, our customers, do not look with favor on such conduct. They are straitlaced, Middle America. They won't like it! So I think I can speak for Cincinnati. If Brett goes ahead with this, his tenure on this show will be, shall we say, limited, very, very limited."

The network representative kicked Ward Russell under the table.

"What the hell!" Ward exclaimed.

"Damn it, Ward! I told you before we ever walked into this room. No threats. No ultimatums."

"I'm sorry. But that's the way we see it in Cincinnati!" Russell persisted. "If he goes ahead with this lawsuit, he can finish out his thirteen weeks, and that's it."

Since Brett had become a key factor in their rising ratings, the producer and the director both blanched at Ward Russell's threat.

Attorney Lee Curry jumped in. "Ward, don't forget we have a firm two-year deal with eighteen months still to go!"

"We'd rather pay him and keep him off the air for eighteen months!" Ward Russell responded.

"Boys, boys!" Brownell took command. And she was old enough to call them boys. "I think we're all becoming a little too emotional. We are much too smart for that. Now, we've got a great show. With fat ratings which are continuing to grow. Let's not do anything foolish."

At having his declaration described in such terms, Ward Russell crossed his arms and sat back from the table as if withdrawing from the entire process.

"Mr. Russell . . ." Brett sought to bring him back into the discussions, "if that child was your son, what would *you* do?"

"Young man, the point is, I would not have got myself into this predicament in the first place!"

"If that's the only answer you can give me, then I feel sorry for you. But I'm the father of a son I have never seen. I owe it to him to find him and get him back. And if it costs me this role, so be it. Other men have sacrificed a hell of a lot more for their sons!"

With that, Brett pushed back from the table so furiously that his chair tipped over. He slammed out of the room.

The echo of the door slam had not subsided before Brownell brought her skill at damage control into play.

"Well, at least we know the young man is sincere."

"Which, unfortunately, does not help the situation," Ward Russell declared adamantly.

Seeking allies wherever she could find them, Brownell addressed the young woman at the end of the table, who had been a silent observer throughout.

"Charlotte? You haven't said a word."

The dark-haired woman readjusted her thick-lensed glasses. "I've been thinking."

"Sweetie, that's your job as a spin doctor," Brownell said. "Think. And come up with the right spin on this situation."

Then, as if she were not suggesting but only inquiring, Brownell continued:

"Let me guess what you've been thinking. Here is this young actor, with a great career ahead of him. Right? Does he do what so many other young actors do in a situation like this? Avoid responsibility? Brush off the mother of his child? Try to deny paternity of the child? Not Brett Manning. He is the same hero in real life that he is on television. Honorable, forthright. He doesn't shirk or avoid responsibility. He embraces it. He doesn't avoid the mother of his child, he goes looking for her. Spends a fortune and months of time to find her. He offers to marry her. And when he finds that his son has been adopted, he fights to get him back. Is that what you were thinking, Charlotte?"

"Close, very close," Charlotte Dunham was relieved to agree.

"God, with spin like that," Brownell predicted, "your ratings will go through the roof. Charlotte, where did you figure to break the story? The checkout-counter rags?"

"Either that or *Inside Story, Doheny* . . . With a story like this we can pick our spots."

"Terrific!" Brownell said, to wrap up the meeting before Ward Russell could introduce any new hurdles. "Let's get on the ball, boys!"

# Chapter 22

On Saturday morning, two weeks after that network meeting, Brett Manning and Lori Adams flew to the Midwest to confer with attorney Henry Clement.

Clement, in his late forties, the slightest touch of gray at the temples of his well-coiffed head, had the distinguished look of a thoughtful, benign, fatherly attorney. However, Lee Curry had not selected him for that reason, but because those members of the bar who had opposed Clement in a courtroom called him "The Shark." At his specialty, family-relations cases, he was considered the best man in the state. The best, and the worst, that could be said of Henry Clement was that he won more than 80 percent of his cases.

He started the consultation with an affable, "Well, Mr. Manning, Mrs. Manning . . ." At the same time he cast a glance at Lori's left hand to note there was no wedding ring there.

Professionally trained to read reactions, Brett responded at once. "We're planning on getting married as soon as we settle this matter."

"If you want my advice, get married now. For the record. It will make a good impression on the judge, which makes my job less difficult."

"Lori promised, if we get our son back . . ."

Lori interrupted. "Mr. Clement, are you saying it would make

119

it more sure to get our son back if we were married?"

"Yes, young woman, it surely would."

"Okay, then," she agreed. "Now, what's the next thing we do to get our son back?"

"Mrs. Manning—I want to get used to using that term so I do it easily and naturally—Mrs. Manning, in cases like this I feel compelled to be utterly frank at the outset. If my own daughter were seeking my advice now, I would warn her that this kind of litigation is, if I may borrow a phrase, the kind that tries men's souls. And especially women's souls. It is bitterly fought. It is usually protracted. It can become quite vicious at times. So it takes a strong stomach."

"I want my baby back," Lori said softly, but with convincing firmness.

"Okay, Mrs. Manning. As long as you feel that way. But I want you to know what you're getting into. What it takes to see this through. Six months from now, a year from now, I don't want you saying to me, 'I can't take it anymore. Let's call it off.' "

"Mr. Clement," Brett explained, "if my attorney in New York didn't tell you, let me say it now. We will not back off. Lori and I have our hearts set on getting our son back."

"If I could be sure of that, despite the problems I see from what little I know about the facts, I might be convinced to take this on."

"If you need some assurance, I will write you a check right now for ten thousand dollars," Brett offered.

"You would?" Clement pretended to be interested.

Brett reached for his inside pocket and presented his checkbook.

"Mr. Manning, if you think a dramatic gesture like that would convince me, you've come to the wrong lawyer. Why, ten thousand dollars would just about pay for the services of my investigators."

"Investigators?" Lori asked.

"We have to discover the identity of the adoptive parents. Closely guarded secret. We need access to many other state records not open to the public. Then we also have to research the background of the adoptive parents."

"Their background?" Lori asked.

"Ammunition. This will become a nasty fight. We have to be prepared to be as nasty as they are."

Lori glanced at Brett. Already this impending litigation loomed more ominous than she had anticipated.

Clement caught that glance and took the moment to instruct them. "Mrs. Manning, or Lori, if I may, adoption cases and divorce cases are the most vicious matters that ever come into a courtroom. Because emotion is the essence of the conflict. In divorce, people who once loved now hate with even greater passion. In adoption cases, a mother who was forced to give up her child now desperately wants him back. Which can be the most powerful emotion of all.

"So, no matter what promises you make to me now, before this is done, your emotions will have been put through a meat grinder. Just remember, you are paying me *not* to be emotional. Feel all you want, but leave the thinking to me. At times you may think I am being too tough. On you. On the opposing parties. But that's exactly what you are paying me for.

"Getting back to the work of digging up the relevant facts, there is also the matter of—" Clement rubbed his thumb and forefinger together, indicating that payoffs were necessary. "State and court clerks can be very helpful. And don't let the ethics trouble you. The other side will be doing the same thing."

Again assuming Clement was angling for a stiffer fee, Brett volunteered, "Would twenty thousand up front do it?"

"Mr. Manning, I'm not running an auction here. I am giving this matter the kind of preparation necessary to develop a case solid enough to impress Judson Hart."

"Judson Hart?" Lori repeated, trying to recall if at any stage of the birth or adoption of her son such a person was involved.

"The strictest and most exacting Family Court judge in the state," Clement explained. "But not for long. There's talk of his being moved up to the State Supreme Court. Fortunately he'll hear your case before that happens."

" 'Fortunately'?" Lori asked. "Why?"

"Hart is a strict constructionist. Goes by the book. The letter of the law. Not one of those judges who goes off on his own and creates new law. That's what the governor likes about him. And since the Family Reunification Act favors us . . ."

"What's that?" Brett asked.

"Federal Law. Title Four E of the Social Security Act. Provides that . . . as I recall the language . . . 'Wherever practicable all reasonable efforts should be made to reunite a child with the family.' "

"Social Security Act?" Brett questioned. "What's that to do with my son?"

"Because to conform with federal guidelines, this state, like almost all states, has passed its own Family Reunification Act. Otherwise they can lose federal funding for social services," Clement explained. "Result? Wherever possible, families must be reunified. Blood counts more than any other factor. There is some language in there about 'the best interests of the child,' but that's mainly to protect a child who's been subject to abuse. Which is no factor here. If we build a case that's legally sound and emotionally appealing, Hart should rule in our favor."

" 'Should' rule, is that all?" Lori asked.

"I can't give you any guarantees," Clement said, "but backed up by the Family Reunification Statute of this state, we have an excellent chance."

"I want my son back!" Lori insisted. "I will do whatever you say, Mr. Clement."

"That's all I need to hear," Clement said, "because this is the kind of case that will draw considerable media attention."

"I don't want to hurt Brett's career."

"I've discussed all that with Lee Curry. The opening shot is being handled in New York. After that we coordinate our public-relations activities. When we are done, Brett Manning comes out smelling like a rose. The women who watch soap operas will come rushing to his support."

"As long as it doesn't hurt his career."

"Young lady, all you have to remember, speak to the media only when I permit. I will very carefully prepare you for what you are to say. Understood?"

"Yes, Mr. Clement," Lori agreed.

"Good! Now, let's get the primary facts. Where did you give birth? Exactly when? Meaning date and time of day. Which doctor delivered your child? And, if you can recall, which members of the delivery-room staff were present?"

"Is it necessary to remember all that?" Lori asked.

"In a case like this you never know who will come up with some bit of helpful information," Clement pointed out. "For example, it would be very valuable if one of the nurses who saw you at the time of the birth or immediately thereafter could recall your mental or emotional condition. It would enable us to prove that your decision to surrender the child was not a carefully considered act."

"But it was—" Lori started to contradict.

"Young woman, please! Let me develop this picture the way I think will impress Judge Hart. It might turn out that it is best for me to question your state of mind at the time."

Having disposed of Lori's objection, Clement then asked, "Did you know anything about the adoptive parents before you gave your consent?"

"*Know* about them? I met them."

"You did?" Clement was startled. "How did that happen?"

After Lori explained about her insistence, Clement just shook his head.

"Is that going to hurt our case?" Lori asked. "That I gave my approval?"

"No, no, no, Mrs. Manning. Not 'approval.' You were 'led to believe' that it would be best for your child. But you never 'approved' in the sense that you met the couple, they impressed you, so you approved of them. Understand?" Clement instructed.

Lori nodded, then asked, "Do you think you will be able to find that couple now?"

"I told you. We have ways. Now, one more thing. Mr. Manning, when you were notified that the child was up for adoption—"

123

"I was never notified," Brett informed him. "Didn't Mr. Curry mention that to you?"

"It's not in my notes of the conversation," Clement said. He pondered. "So you were never . . . Are you absolutely sure you never received notice of any kind?"

"Of course I'm sure. You don't think I'd forget something as important as that?"

"Well, a very telling point," Clement said, then smiled. "Mr. and Mrs. Manning, your case has just improved. Yes, improved remarkably."

Instinctively Lori raised her hand to interrupt, then lowered it quickly.

"Yes, Mrs. Manning?" Clement asked.

"The reason, I mean the reason Brett was never notified—"

"*What* reason?" Clement asked sharply, dropping all pretense at politeness.

"When it came time . . . time to fill out the birth certificate—" Lori started to explain.

"Yes! When it came time, what about it?" Clement demanded.

"I gave the name of the father as Higgins . . . Henry Higgins," she admitted.

"You gave a fictitious name!" Clement exploded. "Well, now . . ."

"Does that . . . does that destroy our case?" Brett asked.

"It's not a fatal flaw. But it surely won't help. And I will no longer be able to sue in both your names."

"What does that mean?" Brett asked.

"Well, if I sue in your name and Lori's, then the other side will attack us on the ground of fraud. That Lori's false statement on the birth certificate misled everyone, mostly the adoptive parents," Clement explained.

"And if you leave her name out of it?" Brett asked.

"Then you are an innocent party, as much a victim of the false statement as everyone else," Clement pointed out. "And in that way we maintain your image as a young man fighting to right a wrong and get his young son back. It helps all around."

"I'm sorry," Lori apologized. "At the time I did it to protect Brett."

"Don't worry, we'll handle it," Clement assured her, but Lori thought she detected a slight reservation in the attorney's tone.

"And now, my dear, Mr. Manning and I have a little private business to attend to."

With a troubled look toward Brett, Lori slipped out of the office.

"Mr. Clement, how much—"

"That's not what I wish to discuss," Clement said, then very briskly asked, "Manning, you know this young woman. Level with me. Because I have a reputation to maintain. I do not wish to be embarrassed in public. Has she the stamina to see this through?"

"Enough to go off on her own. Support herself until she had her child. Refuse any help from me. I call that stamina. Don't you?"

"Very well," Clement said, leaning back in his costly leather swivel chair. "Now, about you. My fees run into big numbers. Six figures. Possibly more. Can you stand it?"

"It's as important to me as it is to Lori to have our son back. I'm good for the money. If you like, I can provide you with a certified statement from my accountant."

"Your word is good enough," Clement said, sealing their relationship. "I'll go to work on tracking down those adoptive people first thing Monday."

# Chapter 23

✤

The first week of the eighth month of Christie Salem's pregnancy coincided with the second birthday of little Scotty Salem. But nothing could stand in the way of her son's birthday party.

In addition to her son's friends from the neighborhood with whom he enjoyed the sandbox in the community playground, Christie had invited her parents and Bill's mother, who had been widowed during the past year, along with other relatives and friends.

Every time someone protested or suggested that a woman in her eighth month might do better with a smaller, more intimate party, Christie responded, "My son is going to have the best and biggest birthday party it is possible to have. Besides, these days there isn't anything you can't have made up and delivered to your door from the supermarket, the gift shop, or the village bakery."

This last had led to an uncomfortable situation with Bill's mother. She had insisted on baking that birthday cake herself. Having been exposed to the products of her mother-in-law's oven during past Thanksgivings and Christmases, Christie decided to rely on the local bakery. She had given them precise instructions as to the icing: Red and blue—Scotty's favorite colors. And the inscription, *To Scotty, Happy Birthday, A Gift from God.*

She could hardly have expected her mother-in-law to master that in red icing.

Christie had asked for the help of her one-day-a-week cleaning woman to hang the streamers and the decorations on the dining-room sconces. She herself had affixed the WELCOME TO SCOTTY'S PARTY sign on the front door.

She was standing back to judge if it was at the proper height and well centered when the first car pulled up, and Maryanne Purcell called, "Ready or not, here we come!" Maryanne piled out of her station wagon, picked up the brightly wrapped gift, and took her little daughter Sharon by the hand as they started up the walk.

"Sorry to be early," Maryanne apologized, "but you know kids. They get so excited they have no sense of time. Everything is 'Now, Mommy, now!' "

"Come on in," Christie insisted. "You can help me lay out the dishes and the party favors."

The others began to arrive soon thereafter. Except for Sean Grantham, whose mother called to report that her son had awakened in the middle of the night whoopsing and was running a slight fever, so it was not wise to expose the other children.

Everything was in order and on time, with the exception of the birthday cake. Even Bill's mother arrived on time, if a bit breathless, explaining, "Never again will I take the bus. Even if I have to drive myself all the way, no more bus. They just dump you at the station like you were a load of hay."

Christie glanced at Bill, who, in a slight nod, acknowledged that Christie had been right. He should have driven all the way out to pick his mother up and bring her. Next time he would.

After the children had played all the games Christie could think of, and having stalled as long as she could for the cake to arrive, she decided to call the children to the table. At the same time she dispatched Bill to go pick up the cake and to hell with the delivery.

But when Bill called before leaving, he was assured by the bakery that the cake was already on the way.

At table, each child delivered, not quite faultlessly, the little speech Mother had rehearsed him or her to make. Each then presented Scotty with a gift. The look in his blue eyes grew wider with each colorful package and each large toy that appeared when he unwrapped them.

One of the little girls, Sharon, not only presented her gift, but kissed Scotty on the cheek, to the amusement and delight of the adults.

Christie's mother beamed, declaring, "That little girl has excellent taste."

Everyone laughed. Except Christie, who stared at the grandfather clock in the corner of the dining room. The cake was already more than an hour late.

Bill's mother said nothing. But Christie could read her indignant glare, which practically shouted, *If you'd let me bake it like I offered to, it would have been here on time.*

When all the speeches had been heard and gifts unwrapped, Bill rose and said, "And now for my son's special gift. One he has wanted since he was able to say the words."

He went to the kitchen closet. He reappeared wheeling in a little tricycle festooned with blue and red ribbons on the handlebars.

With a yelp of delight, Scotty jumped up from his seat, ran to the tricycle, and knelt down beside it to hug it.

"Daddy . . . Daddy . . ." Little Scotty beamed.

"And don't forget Mommy. This was her idea," Bill coached.

"Mommy, when the baby comes, I let her ride my bike, too."

He rubbed his hand on Christie's bulging belly as she had taught him to do so he would be familiar with the event that was soon to come.

Christie's mother betrayed both embarrassment and disapproval of such contact. But her father was quite pleased.

It remained for Bill's mother to add the blessing of her approval when she exclaimed, "My, isn't that nice! What a lovely idea. You know, Bill, when your sister, Patsy, was born, you sulked for a whole year." She turned to the other mothers. "The time I had with him you wouldn't believe. Well, it's good to see my grandson won't take after his dad. Yes, Christie, you can take pride in that."

The laughter was interrupted by the sound of the doorbell.

"Thank God! The cake!"

As Christie started from her chair, Bill intervened, "No, I'll get it."

The bell rang quickly a second time and a third. Bill called out, "We waited an hour for you, you can at least wait ten seconds for me!"

He yanked open the door. Instead of the delivery man carrying a huge box with the birthday cake, there was a stranger, a short man who seemed in his early fifties.

"Mr. Salem?" he asked.

"Yes," Bill replied irritably, since he had no time now for door-to-door salesmen.

"Mr. William Salem?" the man persisted.

"Yes! What the hell is this about? We're having my son's birthday party and—"

The man reached into his inner coat pocket to bring out a thin blue-backed document.

"What's this?" Bill demanded.

"Sorry, sir. My job is only to serve it."

As the man started away, Bill called after him, "Serve what? What the hell is this all about?"

But, used to such reactions in his line of work, the man never turned back.

From the dining room Christie called, "Bill, Bill, bring it into the kitchen. I have the candles in there!"

Bill Salem stared down at the blue-backed document that read *Brett Manning* v. *William & Christine Salem.*

"What the hell—" He opened the papers and scanned them quickly to get some idea of what this mysterious litigation was all about.

Once he read the words *that said child be restored to his natural parent,* his hands began to tremble.

From the kitchen came the voice of his wife. "Bill! The kids are getting restless!"

He had to decide, show this to Christie now or wait until the party was over?

He headed for the kitchen, determined to face it now. But as he pushed open the swinging door, he shoved the paper into his pocket and apologized, "Honey, it wasn't the cake."

"Then who?"

"Some . . . some stranger. He lost his way. Was asking directions."

"Then where *is* that cake?" Christie demanded.

Before Bill could respond, the doorbell did it for him. This time it was the cake.

Fortunately it was exactly what Christie had ordered. So the two candles, one blue, one red, matched the icing. The one to grow on was white. As soon as they were inserted, Christie carried the cake while Bill swung the kitchen door open for her.

She swept into the dining room to the outcries of the children, who greeted the cake with exclamations of delight.

With Christie holding him up, little Scotty was able to blow out the candles on his first try. She guided his hand so he could make the first cut into the cake. After that she carved and distributed the pieces as quickly as she could while Bill poured milk for the children and coffee for the adults.

During the banter that followed, Bill reached into his pocket from time to time to touch the legal document that seemed to burn against his thigh. Later. He would tell her later. After the festivities.

After everyone had left and the house settled down, Christie put Scotty to bed at once, since he had missed his afternoon nap.

*Now,* Bill realized, *now is the time.* But at the last moment fear of the confrontation forced him to consider: *Why upset Christie if there's nothing to be concerned about? I'd better check it out with Paul Henderson first. Tomorrow. Tomorrow morning first thing.*

Before nine in the morning Bill Salem was at the law offices of Paul Henderson, his counsel and the man who had guided him in his brief business career from the incorporation of Handyman through all the legal problems such a business confronts.

Paul settled into his chair behind a desk that was always in such disorder it amazed Bill that he could find anything there.

The aging lawyer opened the document, scanned it quickly,

looked up at Bill, then started to study the paper very, very slowly.

"Bill, you tell Christie?"

"No. Not yet."

"I thought so," Henderson remarked. "Well, you better tell her. Right now. She has a right to know."

"You mean it's that serious?"

"It's that serious," Henderson replied. "It would be a mistake to protect Christie from the truth."

Bill drove home from Henderson's office very slowly, in his mind composing his words, then reframing them.

*There is no good way, no easy way to say it. No way that will not hurt Christie worse than she's ever been hurt before. Except for that time, that terrible time, of little Billy's sudden, unexplained death.*

*What if I went back to the adoption agency? What if I talked to that woman at the hospital where Scotty was born, the one who introduced us to the mother. What if . . .*

*No. As Paul insisted, Christie has a right to know. Now.*

She was surprised to see him come back home so soon. Usually he was too busy even to come back for a hasty lunch. Maybe he wasn't feeling well.

"Hon?" she asked solicitously.

"Christie . . . we have to talk."

"Talk? About what? What's wrong?" she asked, unaware that her hand instinctively crept to her bulging belly.

"Yesterday. That man at the door. He served me with legal papers."

"Something wrong with the business," she assumed. "Don't worry. Paul will take care of it. He always does."

"Not about the business. About . . . about Scotty."

"Scotty? What are you talking about? How can anyone sue a two-year-old infant?"

"They're not suing *him*. They're suing *us*."

"Suing us? About Scotty? You mean someone is accusing us of abusing our son? What's this world coming to? Has everyone gone crazy?" she demanded, furious.

"Christie, please. Just simmer down and listen. The father,

Scotty's natural father, he's suing to get him back."

"Back? They want to take Scotty away from us? They can't! They have no right. Scotty is ours, has been from the day he was born. He's our son. It was all legal. We did everything right . . . we did . . ."

At that moment a surge of pain made her gasp. She gripped her belly. Bill could see the stain of her water begin to discolor her stockings.

"The hospital. We better get to the hospital . . ." she said in a breathy whisper.

Less than six hours later Christie Salem was delivered of a six-pound, four-ounce boy. From the Apgar tests administered in the delivery room the infant was perfectly healthy, despite being slightly premature.

# Chapter 24

❧

Christie's sudden and premature delivery caused Attorney Paul Henderson to call Henry Clement, attorney for Lori and Brett Manning, to ask for time to respond to the summons and complaint that he had served on the Salems.

Since they had both practiced in the same small city for some years, their paths had crossed. Not only at Bar Association functions but as adversaries in the course of their legal work. They had never become friends, but neither did they harbor any animosity for one another.

When, as in such cases as *Manning* v. *Salem,* they became adversaries, they maintained the casually cool attitude of lawyers devoted to the cause of their clients, but with no sense of personal involvement or animus. In the course of lengthy litigation there were always occasions when small favors such as delays in filing of papers or postponing hearings or examinations before trial were granted as a matter of course, as long as it did not affect the interests of their clients.

Such favors usually being reciprocal, Paul Henderson had not hesitated to call Henry Clement.

"Henry, on the Salem matter, could you see your way clear to granting us an extension of time to file our reply?"

"Well, my clients have instructed me to move things along as quickly as possible," Clement hedged.

"My client has just experienced a premature delivery," Henderson explained, "and she's not quite up to giving me all the time and information I need to frame a proper response. So if you can see your way clear . . ."

This new piece of information, imparted to him by Henderson in good faith, suddenly loomed large in Clement's mind. To have heard it was worth the fifteen days' delay, which was actually of benefit to Clement as well, since he had a crowded calendar of court appearances.

"Sorry to hear that, Paul. Of course you can have another fifteen days. More, if it will ease things for your client."

"Thanks, Henry. Talk to you soon."

After he had hung up the phone, Henry Clement thought for a long moment, then pressed down his office intercom. "Hazel, mark my calendar. The day after we receive the answer in the Manning matter, we are to request an examination before trial of Mrs. Christine Salem."

Clement felt that he had made what might prove an important strategic move in the Manning case. No telling what he might unearth in such an examination.

"I don't need a wheelchair," Christie Salem protested. Still, the nurse insisted that she could not leave under her own power. Hospital rules.

So, with her newest and youngest son in her arms, Christie permitted Bill to wheel her out to the car. Once she was safely in the backseat and securely belted in, with her little son in her arms, she joked, "Home, James!" After they rolled out of the circular driveway, she asked, "Scotty . . . What did he say? Did he ask why Mommy was away for four days?"

"He missed you. More than a little. But I kept him happy with the thought that when you came home, you'd be bringing that baby brother you promised."

"I wonder . . ."

"What?"

"You know what they say about the jealousy when an older child is forced to confront a new addition to the family."

"I think that only works when the older child feels insecure to begin with," Bill assured her.

No more was said. But both Salems had the same sense of concern about that first meeting.

To prepare the way, Bill called from out in the garage, "Scotty! Mom's home. Come see your new baby brother!"

Instead of the expected rush of his active little feet, they were greeted with silence. They looked at each other with considerable concern.

"Scotty?" Bill called again.

Eve Young, the neighbor who had volunteered to baby-sit Scotty when Bill went to bring Christie home, came to greet them in the hallway between the kitchen and the dining room.

"He's up in his room. Playing," Eve said. "Now, let me see!"

Christie held up the baby, moving the blanket from his face.

"My, but that's one handsome boy," Eve said. "You can tell by the eyes and the color of his hair he's a real Salem."

Christie's reaction flustered her. "Oh, I didn't mean that," she protested. "I would never mean that. I just meant he has your coloring and Bill's eyes."

"Of course," Christie pretended to agree to ease Eve's discomfort. "Now, we'd better go see the older of the Salem boys. Scotty! Scotty! Mommy's home!"

They heard him start down from the top of the stairs. He came down slowly, haltingly, staring cautiously.

When he reached the foyer, he looked up at his mother.

"Mommy . . . See?"

Christie sat down on the third step so that the infant would be at Scotty's eye level. He leaned back, not daring to look, much as he wanted to. Christie held aside the flap of blanket that obscured his view. Scotty stared at the little stranger.

To him it seemed too small, too motionless in its sleepy state, to constitute a threat. He was reassured.

"Hold him?" Scotty asked.

Eve interposed, "Do you think that's wise?"

But by that time Christie was very carefully easing the blanketed infant into Scotty's arms, subtly supporting the infant so that Scotty felt he had him in his sole charge. He looked down at his tiny brother, studied his wrinkled red face, then looked up at his mother and smiled. He was reassured and at ease once again.

The first moment of transition from a one-child family to a two-child family had just been accomplished.

For the next several days, every time Scotty passed his new brother's bassinette, he stopped to look at him, sometimes to pat him gently on the head.

The only time he displayed any sign of jealousy or displacement was when, for several days, he refused to go to the playschool that he had become accustomed to attending in recent weeks.

The only change for Christie, and no small one, was that she fed this child at her breast. She wondered if, when he watched, little Scotty had any recollection that he had not been nursed by his mother. Could an infant days old or weeks old or months old have memories of such things?

In the excitement of giving birth to her new son and the attendant readjustment of bringing him home and integrating his requirements into the family's life, Christine Salem had been able to eliminate from her mind all concerns of that lawsuit that was threatening to take from her her oldest son, now just past two years of age.

She was rudely forced to face that issue by an unexpected phone call from Paul Henderson.

"Christie, something has come up in relation to the lawsuit."

"What?" she demanded.

"Henry Clement, the attorney for the Mannings, would like to take your deposition."

"What's a deposition?"

"He wants to examine you before trial. It's a very routine procedure. Since we're not concealing anything or making any false statements in our reply, there's nothing to be afraid of."

"What's he want to examine me about?" Christie demanded.

"Naturally he's not going to tip his hand by telling me," Henderson replied, "but I'll be there. If he asks any questions I don't think you should answer, I won't let you respond."

"But what's he want to know?" Christie persisted.

"We will only discover that at the time of the examination."

"What if I refuse?" Christie demanded.

"He'll go to Judge Hart and ask for an order *compelling* you to appear."

"Can he do that?"

"Yes, he can. And if I know Clement, he will. He's a very cantankerous bird when he wants to be. And in this case, where his client's a television star and there's the chance for lots of publicity, he will be."

"In other words, you're telling me I'd better agree," Christie realized.

"We don't want to give Judge Hart the impression that you're a difficult person," Henderson advised. "We may have to be asking a favor or two later and will need his help."

"When, and where, and how long will it take? After all, I'm a nursing mother. My time is not my own."

"I'll make sure this won't interfere," Henderson replied. "Why don't I say a week from Monday. Would ten in the morning be convenient?"

"A week from Monday. Ten o'clock," Christie agreed reluctantly.

When Henderson called Clement, he tried once more to avoid the entire procedure by arguing, "Henry, what in the world do you expect to learn from Mrs. Salem that I can't give you if you just ask?"

"There are things, details, that you probably are not familiar with. I promise not to take too long. And I'll go easy with her. If at any time she feels uncomfortable, just request a break or a postponement."

At nine-thirty the following Monday morning, Christie finished nursing her infant son, kissed her older son good-bye, and started out. But not before Scotty clung to her, still remembering that the last time she left she did not return for four days that seemed endless. He clung to her and asked, "Mommy—comin' back?"

"Of course, darling, I'll be back in time to have lunch with you."

Thus reassured, Scotty slowly released her.

When she arrived at Clement's office, Henderson was waiting. They were ushered into the library, where a stenographer was setting up her machine to record the proceedings.

Clement came bustling into the room and stopped abruptly to admire her. "My, are you Mrs. Salem? Why, you don't look a day over eighteen." In an aside to Henderson he said, "And so pretty, too. Well, I know your time is limited, so let's get right to it. Miss Egleston?"

The stenographer turned to Christie. "Mrs. Salem, raise your right hand."

Christie was puzzled. She looked at Henderson.

"Part of the procedure, my dear. You will be giving testimony under oath."

It dawned on Christie that for the first time in her life she was being put under oath. She felt awesomely uncomfortable as she heard the words, "Do you solemnly swear that the testimony you are about to give is the truth and nothing but the truth?"

"I do," Christie replied in a whisper.

This preamble by itself had made her quite tense.

Clement's first questions were perfunctory. Name? Address? Married? Age? First marriage?

He then settled down to questions more specifically related to Scotty and how he had come into their lives.

"How long had you been childless before you decided to adopt?"

Since she felt the burden of the oath and wished to comply with it to the fullest, she felt that his question was in such form that her answer might later be deemed to be less than the whole truth. She looked to Henderson for advice.

He misinterpreted her look. Thinking she was asking if it were a proper question, he replied, "It's all right, Christie, you may answer."

Tentatively, she ventured, "I . . . I . . . had already had one child. . . ."

Clement seized on that, but for quite another reason. "Mrs.

138

Salem, when you applied for the adoption procedure, you stated that you had no other children. Was that simply a lie to get another child?"

"It was no lie!" Christie insisted. "I had had a child. He was four months old."

"*Was,* Mrs. Salem?"

"He . . . he died. From Sudden Infant Death Syndrome," she was forced to explain.

Clement pretended great compassion. "What a terrible thing. You have my deepest sympathy."

To himself he thought, What a gem. *Like striking oil in my own backyard. I can do wonders with that at the right time.*

Clement continued with routine questions, none of which were of great consequence. He was simply testing Christie's endurance under questioning. He observed her facial expressions, her hands, which betrayed her nervousness, and the number of times she glanced at her attorney for his help.

When Clement had made his expert appraisal of her performance under cross-examination, he pretended to be suddenly reminded, "Oh, Mrs. Salem, I'm so sorry. I've kept you a little longer than I intended. You must be getting home to your new little one. So let's terminate right now."

Appearing gracious and solicitous, he escorted both Christie and Paul Henderson to the elevator, apologizing all the way, "I'm sorry I had to insist on this meeting. Believe me, I don't enjoy this kind of thing."

Christie was glad to see the elevator doors close and block out his smiling face.

As the elevator car descended, Christie asked, "How did I do? Was I all right?"

"You were fine, my dear, first rate," Henderson reassured her.

But he was distressed by the way in which the sudden death of the Salems' first child had emerged. He had had his own strategy for revealing that in a manner that would make Christie more sympathetic. Something he was sure Clement would not do.

This case was becoming even tougher than Paul Henderson had anticipated.

# Chapter 25

❧

Several weeks later the Salems' day started with an early-morning call from Attorney Henderson. Christie had just fallen back to sleep after David's seven o'clock nursing.

Bill answered from the kitchen extension.

"Bill . . . Paul. Sorry to call so early. But I think Christie should be prepared."

"Prepared for *what*?" Bill asked protectively.

"Until now this has been a private matter. But last evening Clement called. Now that my answer is in, he is filing the papers with the court."

"Is that the thing to do?" Bill asked.

"It's mandated by law."

"Then what's the problem?"

"Once papers are filed, they become open to anyone who wishes to inspect them."

Bill realized, "Meaning the media?"

"Yes. And the way I figure, this is Clement's first shot in an active campaign to influence public opinion. Say what they will, there is no such thing as a jury not influenced by what they read and hear. And I find the same goes for judges. They preside with a keen awareness of the effect their decisions have on the public at large. Judges being human, they like to be loved and popular like everyone else."

"And in this case, with Manning being a television star and loved by millions of women . . ." Bill considered. "What can we do, Paul?"

"Tell Christie to be very careful in answering the phone or the door. Tell her to refuse to talk to any newsperson. Man or woman. With cameras and recorders or without. In fact, tell her not to talk about this to any person whom she does not know."

Paul Henderson had been correct in his appraisal of Clement's campaign. He was wrong only in his estimate of the size of the media response. It was even heavier than he had anticipated.

Obeying instructions, Christie hung up the phone every time she was greeted by an unfamiliar voice. Two different television crews arrived on the Salems' front lawn and began setting up. She called the local police. Within fifteen minutes the TV crews began to disassemble their equipment and were soon gone.

That did not stop local television stations from picking up the feed from the networks, which featured an interview with Brett Manning in which he declared that all he wanted was justice and the return of his son.

At the end of each local replay of the interview the reporter made pointed mention that the Salems, who held the disputed child against the will of his natural parents, had been offered the opportunity to respond but chose not to.

By the end of the second day the furor created by breaking the story in the national media died down. Paul Henderson was relieved that it had subsided so quickly. He assessed the damage as consequential but felt sure he could rebut all adverse publicity in court at the proper time.

A man who had been practicing law for forty-six years, he had little tolerance for the newfangled manipulation of justice via the media.

Since the first volley had been fired in the publicity campaign, Henderson decided it was time to educate his clients in the legalities of their case.

For purposes of privacy and to keep the meeting more confidential, he called on the Salems in the evening at their home.

"Christine . . . Bill . . . In a strange way this really constitutes two cases. First, there is the situation as it relates to Mrs. Manning. Hers will be the usual story of a young mother who had a change of heart after giving up her child. She will plead that she was the victim of unfortunate circumstances. She was too confused and upset at the time to fully appreciate what she was doing. She was given bad advice by those who befriended her. She was penniless at the time and feared she would not be able to care for her child. A very usual and ofttimes effective story.

"However, Brett Manning's story confronts us wth a more imposing legal challenge. He was a father who had been deprived of his legal rights."

"Legal rights?" Bill challenged. "They weren't even married!"

"Yes. But under the law, married father or not, he was entitled to be informed before any adoption. He never received any notification. So his lawyer will claim he's been deprived of his legal rights to make or affect any decision or control over his son's future."

"But that wasn't our fault," Bill protested.

"Of course not," Henderson agreed. "But in a certain sense this is like dealing in stolen property. No matter the good intentions of a buyer, the seller of stolen goods cannot pass good title even to an innocent buyer."

"You mean," Christie began to realize, "that because Lori Manning gave a false name as the father, we could lose Scotty? No! No! I don't think any court would be so—so brutal."

She had to stop breathing for an instant to keep from crying.

Henderson took charge. "Christine, I didn't say our case hung on that. I only said it was a complication in our defending it. Now, I am sure that Judge Hart will take our good faith and innocent action into consideration at the proper time."

"He'd better!" Christie said, resorting to determination to conceal her fear.

"Paul," Bill asked, "do you think it would do any good to examine the birth mother like Clement examined Chris?"

"I'm considering that. But the advantages do not yet outweigh the damage that could result if I examine her and we uncover nothing. Then it becomes a fishing expedition. A move dictated by desperation. We have weathered the first barrage of publicity without severe damage. And that's good. But our plan remains the same. We just go about our daily routine. We do not talk to the media. If they want to snoop or grab a news photo of Chris out walking the boys, we can't stop them. But that's all."

For the next several days Christie followed her routine as recommended by Henderson. She did her marketing. She walked in the fresh air. She paid no attention to photographers and TV camera crews. She studiously avoided answering all the questions that were shouted to her by various news reporters.

Her first painful shock came when she was checking out at the supermarket with a cartload of groceries, household supplies, and baby needs. As she waited in the slow-moving line of overloaded carts, she glanced to her left. She was startled by a rack of magazines, the headlines of which read TV HERO FIGHTS TO RANSOM ADOPTED SON. Below it was a still shot of Brett Manning in a scene from his soap opera. Christie had just started to read the text when it was her turn to check out. She seized the magazine and stashed it in with her groceries.

After she arrived home, put away her purchases, nursed her newborn son, and before Scotty was delivered home from playschool, she sat down at the kitchen table to read the gossip sheet.

*Taking time from his hectic schedule as one of daytime's leading leading men, Brett Manning sat in his dressing room, almost in tears as he pleaded, "All I want is my son, my own flesh and blood. Any father in this world would want the same thing. To have his son back, to be able to hold him in his arms. Know that he is safe from harm. Well-fed and cared for. Those people . . . Salem . . . or whatever their name . . . they are strangers to my boy. Whatever they intend, no one can replace a real father. No one can love a child as well as the mother who gave birth to him. If these Salems are decent people, they would realize that. Or maybe they are just money-grubbers who are really holding my son for ransom. And if I meet their price, they'll give him back. There have been hints. . . ."*

"Why, you lying son of a bitch!" Christie exploded to no one in particular. She went to her phone and called Paul Henderson to read to him the contents of the article.

"Paul, what are we going to do about these terrible lies?" she demanded.

"Absolutely nothing," Henderson replied. "And when it gets worse, we are still going to do nothing. My hope is that they will overdo it. Then the tide of public sentiment will turn in our direction."

"And if it doesn't?" Christie asked.

"We'll have our day in court," was all the consolation Henderson had to offer.

By day's end four neighbors and several mothers of Scotty's playschool-mates as well as Bill's mother called. All calling about the same thing. That article in "that scandal sheet." Though they all used the term with contempt, they were all evidently habitual readers.

By the time Bill arrived home for a late dinner, having to work longer hours to make up for the time he lost during and after the birth of his youngest son, he found Christie in a fury.

"We have to do something! Even our friends are asking questions."

"I got two calls at the shop myself," Bill admitted, then confessed, "I talked to Paul. He said to lay low and not try to reply."

"But if we let them get away with such lies—" Christie started to protest.

"Paul said . . ."

" 'Paul said,' " Christie interrupted. "Bill, maybe Paul is too much of an old-school gentleman to go up against someone like Henry Clement!" Immediately she retracted her accusation. "I'm sorry, darling. I didn't mean that. He has been a good friend and a good adviser to you through some tough times."

"I never could have started Handyman or built it into the business it is without his help. So I say we go along with his advice."

\* \* \*

The wedding of Brett Manning and Lori Adams was far more public than either of them had planned. The cast of the show gave them a party right on the set where the television show was shot. The producers provided a very lavish catered wedding supper. There were telegrams and gifts from the network, the sponsor, and the public-relations agency that handled *Time of Our Youth*.

But it was Brett's agent, old lady Brownell, who, in her straightforward acerbic manner took the young couple aside during the festivities to instruct, "If you two kids who've been through so much for each other ever let this marriage slip through your fingers, I will never forgive you. All this . . . the music, the champagne, the caviar, the hilarity, the gifts, the congratulations, they only last until dawn. Marriage lasts, or should last, a lifetime. I know. Yes, kiddies, I know."

Brownell kissed Lori, then stood on tiptoe to kiss Brett.

Brett and Lori left long before the partying was over. They slipped out the back door of the studio to the deserted late-night Manhattan street. Lori was surprised to find an open sightseeing horse and carriage waiting.

"Brett?"

"Remember we used to say if we ever had the money, a nighttime ride around Central Park in an open carriage? Well, we have the money. Mrs. Manning . . . may I assist you?"

"Please do, Mr. Manning, please do."

The carriage started slowly up Avenue of the Americas toward Central Park. Lori nestled into Brett's arm around her.

"Brett, darling, you ever think . . . like I think . . . maybe we should have done this long ago?"

"More times than I can tell you. I used to stay awake nights figuring all the ways we could have got along on the little we had. Even with a baby. Of course, by morning when reality set in, it was all impossible again. I can promise you one thing. The hell you've been through, I'll spend the rest of my life making it up to you."

"No, darling . . . no 'making it up to me.' I don't want you to ever do anything for me because you feel guilty. Whatever we do, one for the other, it has to be done out of love. I think your old

145

lady Brownell is on to the secret. Life begins when the celebrating is over."

"Our life begins when I make good on my promise. We are going to be not just a couple, but a family. Our life really begins when we get our son back," Brett declared.

The carriage had reached deep into the park. The only sound on this mild night was the slow clip-clop of the horse. And then the soft sound of Lori's voice.

"Brett . . . honey . . . what do you think he looks like?"

The sudden question took him by surprise.

"What who looks . . . oh! Little Brett? He looks like all the Manns. That sounds like bad grammar. But it isn't. He'll be a Mann. With some Adams added to the mix, so he can smile the way you smile. And pout the way you pout."

"I don't pout!" Lori denied.

"Whatever you call it, looks awful cute when you do it."

"And that's another thing. I'm a twenty-four-year-old woman. Too old to be cute. And I am now a married woman. A married woman. Just the sound of it makes me feel more mature. And when I have my baby back in my arms . . . we will get him back, won't we, Brett?"

"Clement says we have the law on our side. I promise we'll get him back."

He kissed her, and they held each other close, barely aware of the lonely sound of hoofbeats in the still early Manhattan dawn.

In pursuit of his promise, at his first weekend break in shooting, Brett Manning and his wife, Lori, asked to fly out to meet Henry Clement.

Clement would much rather have gone off on a golfing weekend, but because of the notoriety the case had already achieved, and therefore the risk to his public image if it collapsed, he acceded to the Saturday-morning meeting.

"Now, what's this big emergency that couldn't be handled on the phone?" he began.

Lori blurted out a single word: "Libel!"

"Libel? What in the world are you talking about?"

In a more controlled attitude, but no less serious, Brett assumed the task of explaining.

"One of the attorneys at the network . . . He came across that article in that scandal sheet."

"And damn good it was. You said everything I wanted you to say," Clement protested.

"Well, the part where I said the Salems might be holding little Brett for ransom? This network attorney said it could be considered libel."

"Oh, that," Clement said dismissively. "Pay no attention. First of all, it's phrased as a guess, an opinion, not a fact. Second, libel cases are hard to win. You've got nothing to worry about."

"He said the sponsor of my show wouldn't like the idea of my being publicly accused of libel. It might hurt my public image."

Lori added her reservations: "Didn't I hear somewhere that truth is a defense against a libel suit?"

"Yes," Clement confirmed.

"Well," Lori continued, "what you had Brett hint at *isn't* the truth. The Salems have never said anything to us at all. And certainly not anything about paying to get Junior back."

Clement smiled, a sad, indulgent smile. He reached for her hand. "Now you just let Daddy take care of things. Be a good little girl. Go back to New York, and I will keep you apprised of how things go, and when the date for the trial is set."

At such condescension Brett could see the blush of anger rise into Lori's cheeks. His eyes pleaded, *Don't say a word. He may be obnoxious. But he's the best lawyer in this state. So if we want little Brett back, just let it go.*

In response to Brett's plea, Lori regained control of her resentment. Slowly the blush in her cheeks dissolved.

# Chapter 26

❧

Henry Clement having spurred the publicity war into high gear, it was inevitable that media interest would elevate accordingly. Especially interest in the hitherto-unknown Salems. And in a little two-year-old boy whom one television reporter had named "Baby Brett." Within two days all the media, print and electronic, were using it.

The phone at the Salem house rang so frequently that Bill applied to the phone company for a change of number. Though the new number was unlisted, somehow members of the media succeeded in ferreting it out.

Despite that, Christie and Bill Salem were determined to protect the sanctity of their home and the privacy of their son. Each morning, when Sylvia now came to clean, Christie would drive little Scotty off to playschool. Just before Sylvia left, Christie would pick him up to bring him home for lunch and the rest of the day.

The week following the Brett Manning interview, Christie took Scotty to the door leading from the kitchen into the garage. She called back, "Sylvia, we're on our way. I have to pick up some things at the market, so I'll be back in half an hour. Three quarters at the most."

She watched little Scotty climb into the station wagon, belted him securely into his safety seat. She pressed the remote control to lift the garage door. She started to back out.

She was halfway down the driveway when she looked into her rearview mirror to discover that her driveway was blocked by not one but three remote trucks from three different television networks.

Angrily she blew her horn to signal them to clear a path for her. Instead, the camera crews surrounded her wagon, to begin shooting tape of her and little Scotty, who had become a frightened prisoner in his safety seat behind his mother.

"Mommy!" he cried. "Mommy!"

Herself a prisoner, she was tempted to back out swiftly even if it meant engaging in a collision with the television trucks. But she took only a moment to calm herself and pursue the most sane course. She put the wagon into drive and pulled back into the garage. At once she activated the electronic control, bringing the garage door down. Even that did not discourage the cameramen, who got down on their knees to catch as much film as they could until the descending door shut them out.

Shaken by the experience, she recovered sufficiently to call Bill and tell him what had occurred. He called Henderson, who in turn called Christie back.

"Unfortunately, my dear, this kind of thing will go on from now on."

"But what about Scotty? He loves playschool."

"I'm afraid now that he's a so-called celebrity, he will have to suffer the limitations that go with that status. I would advise keeping him home. At least until we can see if the media interest in this case dies down."

"He won't like it. And I can't explain it to him. I will not do anything to shake his security. He's ours. He's always been ours. And he's going to stay ours! I see no reason to frighten him by telling him all the gruesome details of this lawsuit."

That evening, on the news, both local television stations and the town's only newspaper featured what they all called "exclusive first photos of Baby Brett."

None of the photographs, television action photos, or still shots on the front page of the newspaper were quite clear, having been shot through the car windows. But they were close enough to anger and frighten both Christie and Bill Salem.

"Damn it, there must be some law that protects a two-year-old boy from this kind of thing! I'll call Paul!"

But he realized at once there was no law that protected anyone of any age from the intrusive news media of our time.

Christie worked out her own strategy for outwitting the hungry newshawks and -hens. Each morning she would slip Scotty out the back door, walk him through the alley to the Gottfried house, whose backyard adjoined their own. Anita Gottfried then drove Scotty to playschool.

With that change in routine, things at the Salem house settled down. Through it all, six-week-old David slept peacefully, nursed hungrily at his mother's breast, and thrived as a healthy newborn should. The threat to his family had made no inroads into his peaceful life.

Several weeks after the confrontation in the driveway, Christie was summoned from David's bassinette by the front doorbell. She tucked him back in and went to answer.

Cautiously she opened the door. A woman in her mid-thirties asked, "Mrs. Salem?"

"Yes."

"Patricia Chatman. State Social Services," she announced.

"Social Services?" Christie was puzzled. "What can I do for you?"

"All this recent publicity has naturally come to the attention of Social Services. We feel we have an obligation to make sure that infant we entrusted to you two years ago is safe and well cared for."

"You can be damn sure that he is!" Christie replied indignantly.

"For our records I have to ask certain questions and have a look around," Ms. Chatman announced.

"We have nothing to hide," Christie declared. "Come right in. Ask anything you want."

Christie stood aside, welcoming Ms. Chatman into her home. The woman stood in the center of the foyer and looked around, noting, "Living room. Den. Dining room. May I see the kitchen?"

"Of course," Christie said. "I just started a lamb stew for dinner when little David started crying. I was nursing him when you rang. So the kitchen may seem a little untidy."

"Untidy does not trouble Social Services as much as unclean."

"Oh, you can examine my kitchen with a magnifying glass. It is clean!" Christie insisted proudly.

Ms. Chatman did not reply but entered the kitchen. She looked around at the cut-up potatoes, the carrots and peas ready to be added to the stew pot bubbling on the stove.

"It certainly is clean," Ms. Chatman was forced to concede. "Now, about Scott's living and sleeping conditions."

"Right this way," Christie said, leading the way up the stairs. When they reached the landing, she explained, "This is our room, the main bedroom. And there on the right is the nursery. We have a second son, David."

"Yes, we have a record of that," Patricia Chatman replied. "Now, where does Scott sleep?"

"He has his own room. His own playthings. His own everything."

"May I see for myself?"

"Yes, of course. Right across the hall."

Chatman stood in the doorway to Scotty's room. She surveyed it in a slow, critical gaze. Christie tried to study her reactions without becoming too obvious. What, she wondered, could this woman possibly find wrong with this room?

Chatman leaned on the bed to test the mattress. She looked around at the various playthings, toys, and educational games that had accumulated in the two years of Scotty's life.

"Well," Chatman observed in a noncommittal way. Then she added, "So far, so good. But I've been ordered to make a complete report. Would you mind if I took a few Polaroid shots of the room? I'm sure that will satisfy my supervisor."

"Photograph anything you want. We have nothing to hide."

The woman produced the smallest version of a Polaroid camera. She shot the room from every angle. Scotty's bed. His clothes closet. Most of his toys and games.

"Of course the best way," Christie said, "is this. This gives you Scotty's whole life. From the time he was only two days old."

She took from the top shelf of Scotty's toy cabinet a photo album with a leather cover into which had been stamped in gold SCOTT W. SALEM, HIS STORY.

She opened the volume to reveal page after page of small five-by-seven color photographs, which she proceeded to identify.

"This is Scotty the day we brought him home. Those hands holding him are Bill's. And here is Scotty the first time I ever diapered him. And this one is Bill trying to diaper him."

She turned the heavy page to the next set.

"This is Scotty asleep in his bassinette. I think this was his second week. And here he is, Bill feeding him his bottle. He seems to know me by then. And here he is in his bath. You can see, by the look on his face, he loves warm water. Except when the shampoo gets in his eyes."

Christie turned the heavy page to reveal the next set.

"By this time we weren't photographing every moment. Here he is starting to learn to turn over. Notice Bill in the background? He's like a coach. Trying to give him that extra effort. And this one," Christie said as she turned the page, "this one is Scotty beginning to crawl. And notice that by now he's a regular camera ham. See how he's looking up into the camera. And smiling. And here he is with his first tooth."

"And now," Christie announced before turning the page, "now the big moment. Scotty walking. On his own! My, how proud he is! You can see it on his face.

"I don't like to say this, makes people think we're either vain or boastful, but he does photograph well. Doesn't he?"

"He does indeed," Ms. Chatman agreed. "I wonder would it be possible for me to have some of those? They would surely prove how well he's developing."

"Oh, I couldn't let you have these," Christie protested. "But I have some duplicates."

She looked in the back of the leather album to find some extra prints.

"Here's one of Scotty with his alphabet book. He's extremely bright. Knows all his letters. And here's one the first day he started eating with a spoon. And this one here . . . This one on Bill's lap watching the Super Bowl. And here, I love this one, Scotty last Thanksgiving at my mother's house. Someone, I think it was Bill's sister, bought him that little checked cowboy shirt. He looked just fantastic, didn't he?"

"He is a very handsome young man," Chatman agreed, slipping the duplicate photographs into her briefcase. "I think that should do it."

"I hope so. God knows, we've had enough intrusions into our lives since that damn lawsuit started."

"You know television people. No regard for people's feelings," Chatman concurred. "Shoving a microphone and a camera into the face of a woman who has just lost her child and asking, 'Madam, how do you feel?' Disgusting!"

"It damn well is," Christie agreed.

"Well, I've got to be going."

"Would you like a cup of coffee before you go?"     .

"Thanks. But I do have to get on. These days we have such a heavy caseload that minutes count. Thanks so much for your help today. Makes my life a little easier."

Christie saw her to the front door.

"I trust you'll give us a good report," Christie said in farewell.

"The best!" Chatman promised.

The next morning at quarter to seven the phone rang in the Salem residence. Christie was just finishing nursing David. Bill was coming out of the shower. He reached the bedroom phone just before she did.

"Hello?" Bill called with some irritation. "Who is . . . ? Oh, Mother! What's wrong?"

"Have you seen the morning paper?"

"Not yet. Why?"

"Well, get it! Look at that front page!" his mother urged. "Terrible. Simply terrible!"

153

"What, Mother, what?" he yelled in frustration.

"Go to your front door. Get the paper. You'll see!"

Towel wrapped around his midriff, Bill Salem went down the stairs two steps at a time. He opened the front door. The paper was not on the doormat. He had to venture out in his condition to find it on the edge of the walk.

He slipped back into the house. He opened the paper to read the banner headline: TV REPORTER SNARES EXCLUSIVE PHOTOS BABY BRETT. Below the headline a layout of photos. Scotty's room. His bed. One of his toys. Four shots of him at various ages.

"Christie!!!" Bill shouted.

She came racing down the stairs. Bill held out the front page to her.

"How the hell . . . ?" he demanded.

"That woman! That . . ."

"What woman?"

"Chatman. The woman from Social Ser—" Christie interrupted herself when she realized. "She wasn't from Social Services at all. She was from *The Dispatch*. And I . . ."

Christie started to cry. Bill took her in his arms to comfort her.

" 'S' okay, hon. You didn't know. We'll just have to learn how to live in this new world we're in now. We can't say a word. Or treat anyone we don't know with simple courtesy. We're marked people now. We have no life of our own any longer."

With considerable anger he uttered the words, " 'Baby Brett.' Who the hell thought that one up? Bastards!"

# Chapter 27

❧

"And here is a photo of Lori and Brett on the day of their wedding," Rick Doheny, host of *The Doheny Show,* identified as the picture flashed on television screens across the nation.

"Now, to join in our guest panel of 'Mothers Who Gave Up Their Children for Adoption' is Lori Manning herself."

Lori stepped out of the wings onto the studio stage to join three other women who qualified for today's show. She was vigorously greeted by the audience. Modestly she acknowledged their applause with a slight smile and a head nod and took her seat onstage.

White-haired, well-groomed, smiling incessantly, Doheny roamed the aisles of the studio asking his questions, preparatory to inviting the audience to ask questions of their own. He started things off with what was calculated to sound like a hostile question. Actually it was intended to make his audience defensive on behalf of his guest. It was one of his techniques that always worked.

"Now, Mrs. Manning, or would you object if I just called you Lori?"

"Lori is fine," she replied.

"All right then, Lori . . . Since you're an actress and should be able to speak up more readily than the other mothers on the stage, let me ask you, point-blank"—and here his smile changed subtly

155

to a malevolent sneer—"after having given up your child, your only child, to two total strangers, the most selfish action any mother can perform, how do you have the nerve—the chutzpah—to come before this audience and all America, and defend yourself?"

From the audience came a mixture of boos for Doheny. Inwardly he beamed. For, with that single question, he had hooked his audience for the rest of the hour.

Lori's presence here had not only been agreed to by attorney Henry Clement, he had actually urged it. "Lori, my dear, judges always deny they are influenced by public opinion. Don't you believe it. They are as vulnerable as the rest of us. Especially to talk shows like Doheny's. So you go out and tell the country your story. It can only help. Even with a tough stone-face like Judge Hart."

Lori had come prepared with answers and explanations to questions she assumed Doheny would ask. But his first question and his attitude were far more harsh than she had expected, catching her by surprise.

"Mr. Doheny, you may think it's selfish to give up a child. But you've never been a woman or a mother. Never had to face a future with no prospects. Never had to ask yourself, 'What kind of life can I offer my child? Poverty? Living off welfare for the rest of his days?' I was helpless and alone. I had to do what I thought best for my child.

"As for giving him up to strangers, that's not true. I wouldn't do that. I wanted to know as much about them as the agency was allowed to tell me. I insisted on seeing them, talking to them, before I signed those papers."

There was a torrent of applause from the audience. One of the other mothers on the panel joined in, defiantly, "Men think it's easy to give up one of your own. . . ."

Aware who was the only newsworthy person on the panel, Doheny cut short the intrusion with a sharp question to Lori.

"So you exercised considerable care in selecting and approving those adoptive parents. I believe their name is Salem. William and Christine Salem. Right?"

"Right," Lori agreed.

"Tell my audience, what happened?"

"Happened?" Lori asked, puzzled.

Having taken time out of his heavy schedule to watch his client on television, Henry Clement was beginning to have second thoughts about having given his approval. Doheny was being tougher on her than he'd expected. His client appeared less secure and glib than he had hoped.

"Mrs. Manning—Lori . . . What happened?" Doheny persisted, feeling he was on the verge of the kill.

"What happened to what?" she asked.

"One day you talk to the Salems. They seem like nice people, good people. People able to give your newborn son a good home. Then, two years later, you change your mind. And, if we're to believe all the public fuss about this case, the Salems turn into two terrible people not fit to continue to be parents to little Baby Brett. How come?" Doheny thundered as he raced down the aisle to the stage as if to confront her physically as well.

"I've never said a word against the Salems. I just want to hold my baby in my arms again. I want to feed him. And bathe him. And sing him to sleep. I want to be by his side when he is sick, when he needs a mother to comfort him. I want to help him grow up like only his real mother can."

By that time, not through artifice but through honest emotion, Lori began to weep. Doheny could not have been more delighted.

Nor could a relieved Harry Clement. "Terrific," he whispered to himself. "That girl will be worth her weight in gold. I can't wait to put her on the stand."

At that same time Christie Salem sat in the den of her home watching the show, which had had considerable advance publicity since Baby Brett was national news.

When Lori started to cry, Christie started to cry. Not in sympathy but because she could foresee the impact Lori's words would have once this case came to trial.

In the television studio Doheny was pressing his headset to his ear, receiving word from the control room.

"Okay, okay," he replied, then addressed the audience, "Folks,

157

our telephones are flooded with calls. Let's take one of them now. Come in, caller, let's hear from you."

A voice, shrill from tension, echoed through the studio. "Mr. Doheny, you lay off that poor girl! All you men! You don't know what it feels like to have a child. And then to have to give it up. I know how she feels. And I say, go for it, Lori! Go for it! Get your baby back where he belongs!"

The audience cheered. The other mothers onstage comforted Lori, who was still in tears.

From that point on Doheny roamed the studio giving audience members their chance to ask questions. All of which were directed to Lori. Once past her initial breakdown, she handled all questions, hostile and friendly, with considerable grace.

With the usual numerous breaks for commercials, the hour went by more swiftly than Lori had anticipated. When it was over, and the final credits were rolling on the screen, many women rose to give Lori a standing ovation.

Finally the voice from the control room came over the speaker: "And out!"

Smiling, Doheny took off his earpiece and passed it, along with his hand microphone, to his stage manager, then hopped onto the stage to catch Lori before she reached the wings. He drew her aside.

"We gave them one hell of a show, kid. You were terrific. Terrific!" Doheny beamed. "I don't know why you never made it as an actress. That bit with the tears? Inspired is the only word for it. I bet that gets you a dozen offers for parts on television. In fact, while you were in the middle of that speech, I thought, hey, what an idea. Lori Manning appearing opposite Brett Manning on *Time of Our Youth*. I don't think that's ever been done before. Real-life husband and wife playing opposite each other on a soap. Just don't forget, it all started here on *The Doheny Show*."

"You son of a bitch!" Lori replied.

Stunned, Doheny was almost speechless. "Why . . . what the . . . what are you talking about? . . ."

"You've been trading on people's emotions so long, you don't know anymore what's real and what's phony. I didn't come on your damned show to give a performance. I came here because I want my son back! And my lawyer said this would help. Now I'm sorry I did it!"

With that, Lori Manning stalked out of the studio, and Doheny turned to his producer. "What did I do? What did I say?"

His producer, a woman who liked her high-paying job, replied, "High-strung, that's all. She's high-strung."

"I can bet you now when she gets her kid back, she won't thank us. We never get the appreciation we deserve."

"No, no, we don't," the producer agreed, keeping her own opinion of Doheny to herself.

The phone in the Salem household started ringing even before the final credits rolled on *The Doheny Show.*

"Christie." She recognized Bill's mother by her ascending "Christie," in which the second syllable ended up almost an octave higher than the first. It was always the prelude to a declaration that the woman considered of extreme importance. "Christie, I'm coming over."

"Really, Mom, there's no need."

"Oh, yes, there is. You saw that show. Don't deny it. You saw it. And you shouldn't be alone at a time like this. You need someone to talk to. Someone to confide in. Someone to cry with if you feel like it. So I'm coming over!"

By that time the doorbell was ringing. Christie begged off to answer it. Anita Gottfried and two other neighbors were there, Eve Young carrying a coffee cake.

They were here, as Anita announced, "To have a coffee klatch."

Nothing was said about *The Doheny Show.* But Christie knew they had all seen it, all figured she needed company at a time like this. She was doubly thankful. For their company. And for the fact that she could return to the phone.

"Mother, that's Eve and Anita and Claire. And Eve brought a coffee cake. I won't be alone. So thanks. But I'll be fine. Just fine."

"Good." Then Mother Salem lowered her voice. "Chris . . . I never said anything to you . . . or to Bill . . . but in the beginning I had my doubts."

"Doubts, Mother?" Christie asked, puzzled.

"About . . . about the adoption. We'd never had an adoption in the family before. So I . . . I just . . . had doubts. Reservations. But that little angel has changed my mind. I'm with you and Bill all the way. You tell Bill that Dad left me pretty well fixed. If you two need money for legal expenses, I am ready, willing, and able. Even if it means putting a mortgage on the house again."

"Thanks, Mother."

"Nobody . . . nobody takes my grandson from us!"

The ripples and reverberations from Lori Manning's appearance on *The Doheny Show* were far wider than either Christie or Bill suspected.

Christie became aware three days later when, on her way upstairs to the linen closet, she passed the nursery and found Scotty at the head of David's bassinette, talking to his four-month-old brother.

Curious and amused, Christie stopped to eavesdrop. What she heard chilled her.

"Baby Brett, Baby Brett," Scotty was saying.

In as calm a voice as she could muster, careful not to betray her anxiety, she called, "Scotty, darling."

Her little blond-haired son turned to her. Pointing his forefinger at his sibling, he said, "Baby Brett . . ."

"Scotty . . ." She gestured him to come to her. She knelt down on one knee, to hold him close.

"Scotty, how do you know about Baby Brett?"

"Lady . . ."

"Which lady?" Christie asked.

"School . . ."

"Lady in school? Your teacher?"

"Lady," Scotty repeated, indicating that not a teacher but some other woman, possibly one of the other mothers, had used that term in his presence.

"Darling, what did the lady say?"

"She say . . ." He gestured as the lady must have done by pointing his little forefinger accusingly.

"She was pointing? At who?"

Scotty turned his forefinger against his own chest.

"And then she said?"

"This Baby Brett?"

"She asked someone if you are Baby Brett?"

"Uh-huh. She said, 'This Baby Brett from television.'"

Christie pressed her son against her breast so forcefully that he protested in fear, "*Mommy?*"

She relaxed her sudden embrace to say, "And you just called David Baby Brett."

"He the baby. I Daddy's boy. Daddy's big boy," he explained in his own naive way.

Looking into his blue eyes, Christie instructed, "Darling, you are never to use the words 'Baby Brett' again."

"Why, Mommy?"

"One day when you're older, Mommy will explain. But for now just do as Mommy says. Never say those words again."

"Never?" the baffled child asked.

"Never!"

"Yes, Mommy," her son agreed. But he remained puzzled and somewhat fearful. Fearful of those words that had frightened his mother so.

Several times during that afternoon, when no one was within earshot, in the rebellious manner of two-year-olds, Scotty approached David's bassinette to pat his infant brother on the head and whisper, "Baby Brett."

He did so daring whatever fate his mother had so vaguely hinted at. But nothing happened. Leaving Scotty more puzzled than ever.

It was shortly past midnight. Having nursed David, changed him, and put him down until his four o'clock feeding, Christie checked his bassinette, made sure the protective towels had him securely in place. She went back to bed, where Bill interrupted his deep sleep to murmur a faint "Hon . . ." before he slipped off to sleep again.

She climbed into bed and pulled the blanket around her. With the facility for resuming sleep quickly, developed through Scotty's infancy, she was soon deep enough asleep to experience a disturbing dream. Scotty was missing. She spent the night racing down dark streets calling him by name but getting no response.

She woke suddenly, thinking it was the dream. But she felt a small warm presence in bed with her, curled up and pressing against her belly.

"Scotty?" she whispered.

"Can't sleep," he apologized.

It had been almost a year since Scotty had climbed out of his bed and sought refuge with Mommy and Daddy in the middle of the night. Christie's first impulse was to send him back to his bed. Instead, she put her arm around him and drew him even closer to her warm body.

Because he had had a disturbed night, Christie allowed Scotty to sleep late, even if it meant missing playschool.

When she came down to the kitchen, Bill already had the coffee going and was making himself some eggs and toast.

"Hon . . . how did Scotty wind up in our bed last night? I thought we got him over that months ago," Bill said.

Christie related to him the conversation of yesterday about being called Baby Brett.

"God, you would think adults would have more sense!" Bill exploded.

"And we have no way of knowing what else that woman said to him." Christie revealed her own concern. "All that publicity . . . Must be something we can do."

"If I was a big television star, maybe. But I'm just an ordinary, hardworking, taxpaying citizen. I don't stand a chance," he complained. "Unless . . . I'm going to talk to Paul. Maybe there's something he can do. Meantime, we have to be very careful what we let Scotty hear. And he can't watch or even overhear television."

"Honey, we can't disrupt his life completely. That might be the worst thing. Maybe we should—" She broke off her thought abruptly.

"Should do what?" he insisted.

"Maybe he should have treatment," Christie ventured to suggest.

"Treatment? You mean take a two-and-a-half-year-old kid to a psychiatrist? Not my son! He is as normal a boy as I've ever seen!"

"But he's not in a normal situation," Christie pointed out.

Bill had to admit, "True." But he made no concession to her suggestion.

"I know," he admitted, "you're thinking what I'm thinking. This may just be the beginning. Will it be this way the next few months, the next few years? Like other cases we've read about?"

In the days that followed, the manifestations of Scotty's disturbed state were evidenced when he resumed a habit he had long overcome. He began to wet his bed at night.

# Chapter 28

Judge Judson Hart appeared older than his forty-eight years. He was tall, wiry in build from a rigorous exercise regimen that was a remnant from his college days as a cross-country runner. He had deliberately resorted to cross-country as an antidote to the hours he had spent in libraries in pursuit of his studies. That habit of long hours of intensive study deepened when he entered law school, where he had excelled. He was top man in his class in his first year and was named to *Law Review*. By his senior year he was editor.

He was sought after by a number of large law firms in Washington and New York but chose practice in a small city in the Middle West. To him the law, and its principles and practice, was more important than the financial size of his clients.

He was named to the bench at the age of thirty-one. When the Family Court system of the state fell into disrepute, the governor appointed him to that court to reorganize it and bring improved stature to it.

Among the lawyers who practiced before him he was known as a strict constructionist, adhering to the law except in the most unusual cases. He was zealous in enforcing courtroom procedure. And he was wise to all the tricks of the lawyer trade.

Any attorney who appeared before Judge Judson Hart knew that he had better be prepared with all the applicable law, and present only honest witnesses. For he was quick to hold any lawyer who did otherwise personally responsible.

Dour as he appeared in the courtroom, or in the lectures he was often called upon to give at law schools and Bar Association meetings, in his private life he was a warm, relaxed man with a wife he had married in his early forties, after many of his friends had given up on him as husband material. Even the wives of his friends had surrendered, no longer inviting him to dinner with their unmarried, divorced, or widowed friends.

When he finally met the woman he did marry, it was, no surprise to anyone who knew him, a woman he had met in the course of his pursuit of the law.

It was one of the first cases over which he had presided after ascending to the Family Court bench. The case involved a child who had suffered a brain disease. Doctors at Children's Hospital were urging surgical intervention. But the parents, fearful of the risks involved in such a procedure, resisted adamantly.

The doctors had appealed to the court for an order permitting them to perform surgery, even if the parents refused to sign the informed consent.

During the course of the emergency trial, since time was a crucial factor, much expert testimony was introduced. Among those experts was a woman surgeon. Dr. Karen Craig.

When she took the stand, Judge Hart assumed she was a woman in her mid-thirties. Long accustomed to experts who were chosen for their age as well as their credentials in order to impress juries, Hart was surprised to find an expert so young. And also so . . . so—he allowed himself the word—pretty. As her testimony continued, he conceded she was attractive in a mature way that made the word "pretty" seem insufficient. She was . . . was—though it was an unusual word to apply to a woman—she was handsome.

By the time she had withstood the fierce attacks of opposing counsel, Judge Hart had again revised his estimate. This Dr. Craig was a damn good-looking woman who appeared to be handsome only because she was strong as well. For most of an afternoon she withstood the battering from the lawyer for the parents. She continued to insist that surgery was the only treatment, not only indicated but mandated, by this child's condition.

Her testimony reached its climax when she rose from the witness chair and turned to the bench: "Your Honor, I have never testified in a trial before. So I don't know the first thing about courtroom procedure. And, what's more, I don't give a damn. All I care about is the child I examined two days ago. Her life depends on surgical intervention. Now! So, whatever you have to do to make that happen, for God's sake, do it!"

After that outburst there was a momentary hush in the courtroom before the opposing counsel exploded with a host of objections.

Once Judge Hart had gaveled the courtroom to order and silenced the irate attorney, he addressed the witness.

"Dr. Craig, just as you have certain protocol in surgery, we have our rules, too," he chided. "We have a way of asking and eliciting expert testimony. Questions have to be framed in a certain way. And answered in a certain way."

"Which seems to take endless unnecessary time," she commented.

Offended by her intervention as well as the demeaning nature of her remark, Judson Hart resorted to a bit of judicial sarcasm.

"Fortunately, Doctor, in the interest of justice, our rules of practice afford us that time. However, if, in your opinion, those rules should be changed, this Court is willing to entertain any suggestions you have to make."

There was a snicker of laughter from among the lawyers in the courtroom, as well as from many of the spectators.

"You could start by cutting short all this nonsense when a child of seven is dying," the doctor shot back.

Judge Hart had to resort to his gavel to restore order. Gravely he ordered, "The witness will join me in my robing room!"

In the small office just behind the bench Judge Hart confronted the witness.

"Doctor, you have put me in a very embarrassing position. Your conduct calls for an official reprimand."

"I'm sorry about that, Your Honor. But I thought as a witness it was my *duty* to tell the truth. And as a citizen it was my *right*," Karen Craig replied.

166

Instead of starting to lecture her on the difference between life inside the courtroom and out, he could only think, *Violet, her eyes are violet. And when she gets angry, they shine with conviction.*

He had to banish all such thoughts to face the issue of the moment.

"Now, Doctor, in the privacy of this room, with the formality of the rules of evidence suspended, give me your frank medical opinion of this case."

"That little girl needs surgery. Needs it now. Or she will suffer permanent damage to her brain stem. Which would mean death. That's the truth, the whole truth, and nothing but the truth. Sign that order. Or the life of this child will be on your conscience for a long, long time."

"Doctor, I assure you I will give your opinion great weight in my decision," Judge Hart promised.

By eight o'clock that evening Judge Judson Hart had considered all the testimony he had heard in the last two days. He signed the order authorizing surgery on the little girl.

Three days later when he came off the bench during the lunch recess, Judge Hart found a message waiting.

Please call Dr. Craig at the hospital.

He called at once. Since Craig was busy, their conversation was brief.

"Dr. Craig, you called me?"

"Yes, Your Honor, I wanted you to know. Surgery was completed this morning. It went just fine. That little girl is going to be all right."

"Thank you, Doctor. Thank you very much. Thoughtful of you to call."

For the rest of that week he was pursued by thoughts of Dr. Craig. On Monday he called the hospital. She was off duty for the day. He called again on Tuesday.

"Doctor, do you have any idea what judges do in their spare time?"

"Not the slightest," she responded.

"Would you like to find out?"

"If it's as time-consuming and dry as what you do *in* the courtroom, no," she replied.

"Do you run? Cross-country, I mean."

"Jog. City streets, I'm afraid."

"There must be something we can do together," he urged.

"Why don't we start with a drink?" she suggested, then had second thoughts. "Or don't you drink? From what I heard . . ."

"You heard? About me?" Judge Hart asked. "What have you heard?"

"That you run your courtroom by the book. That you have a higher regard for statute law than for people."

"Who said that?" he interrupted to demand.

"Everyone," she replied without hesitation. "Everyone I talked to."

"You took the liberty of discussing me with other people?"

"Yes, I did."

"May I ask why?" he demanded indignantly.

"For the same reason you just called me," she admitted frankly.

Their courtship was brief. They decided at her age, thirty-seven, and his age, forty-two, they were both mature enough to know their own feelings. And, unless they married now, most likely both of them were fated to end up single forever.

That had been six years ago. During those six years they blended their heavy professional obligations in a manner that gave them sufficient time to enjoy life together.

On occasion Karen might mention an unusual case she had at the hospital or some run-in with some of the medical hierarchy. Not unusual for a woman so feisty. Jud Hart made it a point never to discuss legal problems that came before him. Since his cases were yet to be decided, he zealously guarded his intentions as to his final disposition. Since he often brooded over his cases, and they usually involved sensitive family matters concerning children and women, Karen granted him his privacy in that regard.

# Chapter 29

A stickler for the rules and for promptness, Judge Judson Hart did not easily grant delays, as he was ever conscious of the cases piling up on the calendar.

To him the old legal maxim "Justice delayed is justice denied" had very special meaning because of the litigants and subjects that came before him. He was especially stringent with counsel when the case involved young children. A delay of months might be of only dollar consequence in a commercial case. But such a delay could have serious impact on the life of an infant or a two-year-old, as was the case in *Manning* v. *Salem*. To allow such a trial to drag on would only complicate the outcome. Especially when it seemed the child would have to be taken from one family and transferred to another.

Thus Judson Hart was in no mood for indulging counsel on either side in *Manning* v. *Salem* when he summoned them to one of the early-morning pretrial meetings in chambers for which he was noted.

He made only one concession to such circumstances. He was noted for serving excellent coffee, which he took pride in brewing himself.

Henry Clement and Paul Henderson had settled down, each with a cup of steaming coffee, when Judge Hart opened the conference.

"Gentlemen, as we approach the trial date, I wish to arrive at an agreement. That neither of you will attempt to try this case in the media. A case like this has a compelling emotional appeal to the public. Who can be immune to the fate of a child of two who has become the pawn or prize in such a struggle? So the less this matter is fought out in public, the better."

"Of course," Clement agreed heartily.

Henderson appeared more reserved but equally amenable.

It was then that Judge Hart reached into his desk drawer. He held out to Clement a television cassette.

"Then how do you explain this, Mr. Clement?" Hart demanded, his lean face set in a prosecutorial mode.

Clement knew that look, had seen it before. Very gingerly he reached for the cassette.

One glance told him this was a film of *The Doheny Show*, "Mothers Who Gave Up Their Children for Adoption."

"Mr. Clement?" Judge Hart persisted.

"My client was invited to appear, and *she* decided to do so," Clement explained.

Irritated that Clement had chosen to avoid blame by shifting it to his client, Hart demanded, "You mean your client didn't clear this with you?"

"Well, when she mentioned it, I had no idea what it would lead to."

"You were not aware of Doheny's technique of using important problems as grist for his shoddy mill?"

"Well, I . . . of course I've heard about Doheny and his way of doing things. But I never expected that in a case like this, so touchy and sensitive, he would go this far. It is very regrettable."

"Counselor, if you want to know the *true* meaning of regrettable, just let this happen once more. I will hold you in contempt. Clear?"

"Clear," Clement acquiesced, relieved to get off with only a warning.

The judge turned to Paul Henderson. "Mr. Henderson, I wish I could say that your client has behaved much better."

"If Your Honor is referring to that picture story about little

Scotty, my client was not a participant, she was a victim. She was completely taken in by a newspaperwoman who claimed to represent the State Department of Social Services."

"Instruct your client to be alert and on guard in the future," Hart reproved. "Also, I forbid both of you to make any public statements about this case from now on. The same holds for your clients. And if you can't maintain control of your clients, I will. Warn them that not only will they be subject to contempt of court, but it may have an effect on the outcome of this case. So much for that.

"Now to the main reason I called you together. Neither of you has yet filed notice of a demand for a jury trial. Do you intend to? Or do you wish this to be heard by me alone?"

Clement responded at once, "I prefer to have this heard by Your Honor alone."

*And well you might,* Paul Henderson thought, *since this judge is known as a stickler for adherence to the statutes. And in this case both federal and state statutes on Family Reunification favor natural parents over foster or adoptive ones.*

Judge Hart turned to Henderson. Ordinarily Paul would have chosen a jury trial. In this case he had to consider the effectiveness of witnesses like Brett Manning and Lori Manning, both experienced actors. He might exclude from a jury some candidates who admitted being habitual watchers of soap operas. But he knew he could not exclude them all. It would better serve the interests of his clients to have the judge decide the outcome. Especially since he had appeared so highly critical of Clement over the Doheny interview.

"Your Honor, in the interest of a speedy and efficient trial, I would prefer to have the matter decided by the bench."

"So be it," Hart said. "The date for trial will be April seventeenth, putting us beyond the Easter holiday, thus minimizing the need for delays and interruptions."

"April seventeenth," Clement agreed.

"The seventeenth it is," Henderson confirmed.

"Okay, gentlemen!" the judge said crisply, indicating they were being dismissed.

As both counsel were rising, Clement pretended to be reminded, "Oh, by the way, Your Honor, I am about to make a motion for the right to have a psychiatric examination of the child presently known as Scott Salem. It would save us all a great deal of time and paperwork if we could agree to that now."

The matter was addressed more to Henderson than to the judge.

"Mr. Henderson?" Judge Hart asked.

"It was my hope to carry on this trial with the least possible interference with Scott's life. He's already been the subject of intense attention from the media," Henderson protested.

"Your Honor," Clement replied, "one of the key issues in this trial is the mental and physical welfare of this child. It would be impossible for me to contest any assertion the defendants make on that issue unless we have access to the child in order to have an impartial professional assessment of his condition."

Judge Hart glared at Henderson, his granite-gray eyes transmitting a message that said, *I am about to grant Clement permission, so anything you say will be of no avail.*

In view of that Henderson replied, "We will need proof of the credentials and expertise of the psychiatrist Mr. Clement has in mind. If he is qualified, we will interpose no objection."

The very next day Clement's secretary submitted to Paul Henderson a list of three psychiatrists from which he was free to choose one. Henderson was familiar with all three names. Each was an experienced, well-known forensic psychiatrist long accustomed to testifying in legal matters.

He selected the woman on the list.

Knowing this would be a highly sensitive issue with the Salems, Henderson called on them in person that evening.

"No, no, no!" Christie protested. "Once they get their hands on Scotty, they'll kidnap him. They'll take him out of the country. We'll never see him again!"

Realizing she was starting to sound irrational, Christie calmed and asked, "Paul, do we *have* to?"

"Yes, my dear, we *have* to," he advised.

"What will they do to him?" she asked.

"First of all, Dr. Finch is a very experienced psychiatrist. She has worked with children for years. I am sure all she will do is question him in a very calm, casual way. If he talks freely, we have nothing to worry about."

Bill had kept his own curiosity and suspicions under control for fear of inciting Christie. But he interceded now. "Is it possible that this doctor might in some way influence Scotty? Kids are very impressionable. She might try to hypnotize him. Or give him some kind of drug like that pentothal I used to read about—you know, truth serum."

"We're all becoming too overwrought and suspicious about this. If I were in Clement's position, I would ask for exactly the same right. And would be entitled to it. The more cooperative we are with Judge Hart's orders, the better for us in the long run."

Christie looked to Bill. She shrugged, then nodded.

"All right, Paul," Christie said. "Just tell me when and where. I will have Scotty there."

The next afternoon Christie Salem received a call from Mr. Clement's secretary.

"Mrs. Salem, will you please have Scotty at Dr. Finch's office three o'clock on Tuesday? The address is Suite Three-oh-four, Langston Towers."

Christie picked Scotty up at playschool just before noontime. She brought him home, fed him lunch, took him up to his room to change him from his school clothes into the blue sailor suit she had bought for his appearance at Christmas dinner at Mother Salem's. The suit was a bit snugger than four months ago. But still it made him look the handsome, properly dressed young boy everyone had admired.

During the time she dressed him, she tried to prepare him for the event.

"Scotty, remember how we went downtown to Blecher's Department Store where you saw Santa Claus? Well, we are going to that same street. To a tall building. And we are going to ride in the elevator. Remember the time we went to see Dr. Driscoll about your ears? His office was in a tall building, too. Well, this time you are going to see a lady doctor. Dr. Finch."

At once Scotty's hand went to his right ear in memory of that pain.

"Dr. Finch won't do anything to you except talk."

"Talk?" Scotty repeated, suspicious now.

"Just talk. She will ask you some questions. You just tell her anything she wants to know."

"Why?" he asked.

"Well, you have to." He did not seem convinced. So she repeated, "Just take Mommy's word for it. You have to."

Scotty said no more until they were in the station wagon on the way downtown, when he suddenly asked, "I do something wrong?"

"Of course not, darling," Christie was quick to reassure him.

"Why you takin' me there?"

"Well," Christie began, "the judge—" She stopped at once. He must never have even a hint of the fact that he was the object of a lawsuit that might take him from his family.

"Mommy?" he persisted.

"We just have to go there. You have to talk to Dr. Finch. She . . . uh . . . she's a very nice woman. You will like her."

"Why, Mommy?"

"Please, Scotty, we're getting into the downtown traffic. Mommy has to concentrate on her driving."

They continued in silence, but every once in a while she glanced furtively at her little son, handsome, blond-haired, but now with a very troubled look on his face.

Christie had found an empty metered parking space across from the Towers. Waiting out the light, with Scotty's hand in hers, she crossed the street. As she entered Langston Towers, she noticed a slight blond woman standing against the right wall of the lobby. After a quick glance Christie paid her no mind. But as they approached the elevator Christie suddenly stopped, then looked back to discover the young woman had followed them halfway to the elevator.

Suddenly it came to Christie. She had seen that blond young

woman before. By God, she was Lori Manning! Betrayed as she felt, Christie dared not give vent to her anger, for fear of upsetting Scotty. Instead, she tightened her grip on his hand and waited for the elevator.

They found the door with a bronze plaque announcing DR. HAZEL FINCH. Christie pushed it open. They were greeted by a secretary who asked, "Mrs. Salem?"

"Yes. I insist on talking to Dr. Finch myself first!" she declared.

"I'm afraid the doctor's time is too closely scheduled to allow for impromptu conferences."

"If she wants to see my son, she had better see me first!" Christie insisted.

"Just a moment," the flustered secretary said. She retreated into the private office. Some minutes later she reappeared. "Dr. Finch will see you now . . . alone."

"Scotty, darling, you wait right here."

Christie entered Dr. Finch's office, which was outfitted more as a children's playroom than an office.

A tall woman with graying hair, Hazel Finch was on her feet to greet Christie. "Mrs. Salem, I know exactly how you feel."

"The hell you do!" Christie interrupted.

"Mrs. Salem . . ." a surprised and resentful Dr. Finch tried to intrude.

"Doctor, you're not going to get away with this! Using your office and your position as a psychiatrist to allow that woman to spy on my son."

"What are you talking about?"

"She was down there in the lobby waiting for us!" Christie said. "And don't say I am mistaken. I know her. I remember her from the day she interviewed us before she gave up her baby. And I saw her again on *The Doheny Show*."

"Mrs. Salem, if what you say is true, then I agree with you."

"You do?" Christie asked in surprise.

Finch went to her desk, lifted her phone. "Get me Henry Clement at once!"

In moments she had him on the line.

"Henry, what are you up to this time?" she demanded. In

response to his plea of ignorance she relayed Christie's complaint to him. The conversation ended with Finch saying, "Well, make sure such a thing never happens again! Not as long as I'm involved in this case!"

Finch hung up the phone.

"Satisfied, Ms. Salem?"

"Until this terrible lawsuit is over . . . until Scotty is ours for all time, I will *never* be satisfied," Christie declared.

With her practiced diagnostic eye Finch observed the rapid throbbing of the blue vein in Christie's pale neck. This was indeed a tense and highly vulnerable woman, the doctor concluded.

The matter settled, Christie brought in Scotty and introduced him.

"Dr. Finch, this is my son Scott. *Scott Salem.*"

Finch greeted the lad with a smile and an outstretched hand, which he shook in quite manly fashion. Once assured that he was at ease, Christie withdrew.

Finch beckoned Scott to the play table, where she had prepared some toys that would appeal to a young boy. Mostly they were miniature cars and trucks.

At once he picked up a red sports model. He started to race its wheels across the table, accompanying it with appropriate roaring sounds.

Dr. Finch proceeded to ask Scotty a number of seemingly innocuous questions about his mommy, his daddy, his new little brother, his playschool, his home. All of which he responded to in an offhand manner while engrossed in the other toys he had selected from the great variety.

After an hour of such questioning and play, Dr. Finch said, "Okay, Scotty. Time to go."

After they left, Dr. Finch dictated her findings in a memorandum to Henry Clement:

*Re: Subject SCOTT SALEM:*
*He seems a well-adjusted two-and-a-half-year-old. He appeared somewhat tense at the outset but was quite at ease when he left.*
*His original tension may have been a reflection of his mother's*

*state of mind when she appeared here, due to the unfortunate confrontation with your client in the lobby of this building.*

*If you are seeking to make a legal point of the boy's condition as a means of attacking the adoption, I cannot honestly testify on your behalf. However, if you feel an attack along psychiatric lines is necessary, in this case the boy's mother seems unusually sensitive.*

Henry Clement made a note of that last sentence. But he also arranged that young Scott Salem be tested by four other, more amenable, psychiatrists.

# Chapter 30

Paul Henderson waited in the anteroom to Judge Judson Hart's private chambers. Impatient, he paced back and forth until the judge's secretary felt compelled to apologize. "Sorry, Counselor, but the judge is detained on the argument of an important and complicated notice to amend a complaint. He'll be off the bench any moment."

After far longer than a moment Judge Hart burst into the room, his black robe flying. As he passed Henderson, he ordered, "Come on, come on, let's go! This is one of those days!"

Henderson followed the judge into chambers, where, while he slipped out of his judicial robe, he asked, "What is it this time? These damn high-profile cases take more time than all the others put together. Why this sudden call for a meeting and without your adversary being present?"

"Harassment," Henderson replied.

"Good God, how can sexual harassment possibly enter a case like this?" the judge demanded, starting to pour a cup of coffee. "Want a cup?"

"No, thanks. I was not referring to sexual harassment. But to one party to a lawsuit harassing another. I would like a cease-and-desist order to keep the wife of the plaintiff in this case from harassing the defendant."

Stirring his steaming coffee, Hart demanded, "Exactly what are you referring to?"

"You granted the plaintiffs the right to a psychiatric examination of the Salem boy. Clement named the doctor and the time. Lori Manning showed up there. At the appointed hour. To spy on Mrs. Salem and little Scott. I'm sure Your Honor can appreciate the emotional strain Mrs. Salem was under, having to surrender her son to such an examination, without the added trauma of having that other woman there to confront her."

"I'm sure it wasn't easy for either one of them," the judge replied.

From his attaché case Henderson produced the blue-backed document. "Then I ask you to sign this document."

The judge raised his reading glasses, which hung from his neck by a gold chain. He scanned the order and sipped his coffee before replying.

"Mr. Henderson, before I take such a formal step, I would like to speak to each of the participants."

"Without attorneys present?" Henderson asked, an edge of resentment in his demeanor.

"Without attorneys present," the judge replied. "Cases in Family Court are not subject to the same rules and practices as other courts in this state."

"I know that," Henderson argued. "Still . . ."

The judge cut him short with a curt "Counselor, are you questioning my judgment in this matter?"

"No, no, of course not," the elderly attorney replied, though if he did not question it, he surely resented it.

"Since your client is the complaining party, I would like to see her first. Tomorrow during my lunch recess. One o'clock."

Having arranged with Anita Gottfried to feed Scotty lunch after his return from playschool and to baby-sit David, Christie Salem arrived at the judge's chambers at eight minutes after one.

She was most profuse in her apologies.

"I'm sorry, Your Honor, but there was David to nurse . . . and

I had to make sure Scotty was home safe. If you were a mother, you'd understand."

"I've never been a mother, but just assume that I do understand," the judge comforted her, smiling. "Now, you just relax. In fact, why not have a cup of coffee? I brew this myself. From a special hazelnut-flavored mix that I buy in that little shop down the street. Like a cup?"

"Yes, yes, I would . . ." Christie replied with considerable hesitation.

"You would . . . *but*. Am I right?" the judge asked.

"Ever since this . . . this trouble . . . started, the case, I mean, my doctor says caffeine is not good for my nerves."

"I understand," the judge replied. "Now tell me what happened that caused your lawyer to ask for a cease-and-desist order."

"Well, Your Honor, it had been a difficult day. Started out that way. David seemed a little—I don't know the exact word for it. But when I was nursing him, he was somehow hard to handle. He was not content to just nurse and then fall asleep. You know how babies are."

The judge nodded merely to urge Christie along in telling her story.

"That was just the beginning. Things got worse. Scotty—he's used to dressing himself. Mostly. I do the finishing touches. But not that day. He seemed to take longer. He dawdled. Finally I had to dress him. And I didn't dare say anything. You see, Your Honor—"

Christie shook her head, then confessed, "I was worried that if I said anything—even just corrected him—he would tell that psychiatrist, and she might think I was not a fit mother. Children sometimes say the strangest things. . . ."

"Indeed they do," the judge agreed. "I've heard them here in my chambers."

"Anyhow, by the time I got Scotty dressed and into the wagon, I was a bundle of nerves. But I was determined to see it through. If that was one of the steps we had to go through to protect Scotty from those Mannings, I would do it. I would do anything to keep Scotty. He's part of us. Without him this wouldn't be the family we've become in the last two years. Yet there I was delivering him into the hands of . . . of the enemy. After all, she was *their* doctor. *Their* psychiatrist. So she would be looking for any clue at all to take Scotty away from us. And if that happened—Bill, my husband—he would never get over it. You have no idea how much he loves that boy. And the plans he's made. Our whole life, what we do, what we plan, it all revolves around Scotty."

"I understand there *is* a second child," the judge reminded her.

"Of course, David. He rounds out our family. Unless maybe a few years from now we have a girl. Bill's always had his heart set on a little girl. He loves children."

Returning to her recall of that day, Christie continued, "Yet there I was delivering his son . . . our son . . . into the hands of the enemy. If anything went wrong, if someone—you, Your Honor—took Scotty away from us, Bill would blame me forever."

It was a confession she had never made, even to herself.

She started to weep. "Sorry . . ."

She sniffled back her tears, forced herself to continue. "With all that on my mind, with Scotty's hand in mine, I started into the Towers. And what was the first thing I saw? That young woman, that blond young woman. Two and a half years ago when I saw her I felt two things: First, I was sorry for her. She seemed so young. So helpless. Second, that we would never see her again.

"Yet there she was. Staring at Scotty. I thought being ordered to see that psychiatrist was only a trap. So that woman could get a look at Scotty. The two of them, that woman and the psychiatrist, they were scheming to take our son from us. I was so terrified that I almost took Scotty by the hand and ran. I didn't. But it took all the courage and willpower I had."

"And now?" the judge asked.

"I don't want that woman following us, spying on us, harassing us. I don't want her to see Scotty or Scotty to see her. My attorney says it is possible for you to issue such an order."

"Yes, it is possible," Judge Hart confirmed. "But harassment has to be considerably more persistent and threatening than you describe. However, I won't reject your petition. I shall hold my decision in abeyance."

"Does that mean—"

"It means what I said. I shall decide on this later," the judge replied.

"I see. Is . . . Is that all . . . Your Honor?"

"Yes, that's all for today," the judge agreed.

Christie started toward the door. Then, with the desperation of a litigant who feels this may be the only chance she will ever have to plead her cause, she turned back to say, "Your Honor . . . you must know what this means to us, having little Scotty from the age of only three days—feeding him, bathing him, holding him when he is well, and when he is ill—every day he has become more and more a part of us. He is ours, and we are his. We're the only family he's ever known. You must understand that, being a father yourself."

"Mrs. Salem," the judge replied, as gently as he could, "I think I understand. But not because I am a father. . . . You see, I have no children."

Christie Salem left the judge's chambers rebuking herself. *Idiot! What have I done now? Whatever chance we had of winning this case is gone . . . lost. . . . Bill will never forgive me now.*

The following day, at five minutes to one, Judge Hart glanced at the desk clock on his bench.

He interrupted the attorney who was questioning a woman complaining of lack of child support by a husband who could well afford to pay.

"Counselor, would you mind holding over this witness until two o'clock? I have an important matter waiting for me in chambers."

"No problem, Your Honor," the attorney replied.

The judge had left instructions with his secretary that when Lori Manning arrived, she was to be shown into chambers instead of having to wait in the anteroom.

When the judge opened the door, he found Lori standing at

the window. With the daylight bright behind her, it was difficult to see her face. But as he came toward her, the judge found her to be even prettier than she appeared in her photographs in the newspapers and on the television news.

She seemed in full possession of herself, but the tense lines around her mouth betrayed her.

"Do sit down, Mrs. Manning. And would you like a cup of coffee? Fresh brewed."

To put the young woman at ease, the judge pretended to ramble on. "I do all the fixings, then at ten minutes to one my secretary just plugs in the machine. By one o'clock, lo and behold, fresh coffee. Just the fragrance keeps me going for the rest of the day."

But he sensed that Lori's tension, instead of abating, had actually intensified. Better get to the matter at once.

"Mrs. Manning . . . did your attorney tell you why you're here?"

"Yes . . . Your Honor."

The judge recognized that belated "Your Honor" that lay people felt compelled to use, in accord with strict instructions from their attorneys.

"Is it true that you did confront Mrs. Salem at Langston Towers that day?"

Lori looked down at her hands in her lap, her active fingers looking like a tangle of small snakes. Color rose into her pale cheeks.

Finally she admitted, "Yes . . . Your Honor."

"In order to do that, you would have had to know when and why Mrs. Salem would arrive there."

"Yes, Your Honor."

"*How* did you know that?"

"Mr. Clement."

"He told you?"

"No. His secretary let it slip. I called there one day to find out how things were going. She said . . . I guess to cheer me up . . . that a meeting with our psychiatrist had been arranged for that afternoon," Lori explained. "I only wanted—"

The judge cut her explanation with a curt, "Tell me, did you make an effort to contact Dr. Finch?"

"No," Lori replied.

"Not before? And not after Mrs. Salem's visit?" the judge asked crisply.

"No. I swear," Lori replied.

"Then why *did* you go there?" the judge asked.

Slowly the color rose into her cheeks. She rubbed her hands against her thighs to conceal her trembling.

"Why, Mrs. Manning?" Judge Hart insisted.

"I . . . I wanted to see him."

"Who?"

"My son. I wanted to see what he really looked like. Not those smudged pictures taken through the windows of a station wagon. But how he really looked. Oh, he's handsome. Very handsome. And blond. Like Brett. And he looks so good in blue. Light blue. Though he would look good in any color. With that blond hair."

"That's all? You just wanted to see him?" Judge Hart asked.

"I didn't say a word. I didn't do a thing. I just looked. Stared, I guess. God, I have a right, don't I? I'm his mother! I carried him for nine months. I gave birth to him. He's really mine. I have a right to look! I have a right—"

She broke down and started to cry.

"Mrs. Manning . . . Lori . . ." the judge said softly. "Can you understand that I have to ask you never to do that again?"

Lori did not reply. She was too busy wiping away her tears with the palms of her hands.

"It isn't fair to Mrs. Salem. And not even to little Scotty."

"Brett," Lori Manning corrected. "In my mind he's Brett."

"Whatever name you choose to use, it isn't fair to add to this stressful situation by such unexpected confrontations. Unfortunately there'll be enough of that during the trial."

"Why does there have to be a trial? He's our son. Brett's and mine. There's no legal or scientific question about it. Any blood test will prove it! We can take good care of him now. We'll give him everything he could want. Especially love. Lots and lots of . . ."

"Ms. Manning!" Judge Hart interrupted. Once she was silent, he continued soberly, "The question before the Court is not whether you gave birth to this child but whether to undo an adoption. An adoption to which you consented. You gave up your son, signed the requisite papers."

Lori could not control herself. This time she interrupted, "You don't understand. Yes, I signed those papers. But I didn't know what I was doing."

"Ms. Manning, are you telling me that no one explained to you the effect of what you were signing?"

"Oh, they explained it. But nobody . . . nobody except a woman in that situation knows how . . . how confused . . . how frightened . . . how . . . how out of my mind I was at the time. I didn't know what I was doing!"

"You were not aware you were giving up your child for adoption?" Judge Hart asked sharply.

"Yes, I . . . I knew that . . . but I didn't know what it would mean. I was too frightened to know . . . I had no one to turn to. . . ."

"Did anyone coerce you?"

"No . . . but they shouldn't have let me do it . . . they shouldn't . . . so now it's up to you to give me back my child. Please, Your Honor . . . please . . ."

On her last word she broke down and began to weep.

Very softly the judge replied, "Ms. Manning, I assure you that I appreciate your feelings at that time, and now. But this issue must proceed to trial. You may be sure Mr. Clement will present your husband's case very vigorously."

Once she recovered, Lori Manning departed Judge Hart's chambers, leaving the judge feeling, *God, I wish I didn't have to preside over cases like this.*

# Chapter 31

❧

With the trial date set, Henry Clement had to prepare his clients for the ordeal of testifying. Mainly for making the proper impression on Judge Hart.

"Now, Lori," Clement lectured, "each time you appear in this courtroom is like walking onstage. You are playing a character. And that character is an ingenuous, innocent, naive young woman. The opposite of everything people here in the sticks think a young actress is like.

"Watch every word you say. On the stand. And off. Even when you think no one is listening. You never can tell when there's an open microphone around. So watch your every word."

Lori nodded, casting a glance at Brett, as if to ask, *Does he think I'm an idiot that I don't know all that?*

"Now, as to your wardrobe," Clement continued, "I want you to go to Sears or Penney or Wal-Mart. Buy a few simple dresses. Nothing that looks like it came from Fifth Avenue or Rodeo Drive. And no fancy makeup. No eye shadow. A little pale lipstick maybe. I want you to be a typical young American woman from any small town in this country. That is especially important when I put you on the stand. Got it?"

Lori felt a mixture of resentment and pain as tears rushed to her eyes.

"Mr. Clement, to *you* I may be playing a part. But I am a

186

mother whose only purpose in being here is to recapture her son. And I will do anything to get my child back. But as for playing a typical young American woman from a little town, that's not a role. That *is* me. Who do you think I am? Tammy Faye Bakker?"

Not accustomed to having his advice or judgment questioned by clients, Clement declared testily, "I am only trying to put you in the best light in the eyes of Judge Hart."

Before Lori could respond, as she was poised to do, Brett intervened, "Honey, just do as Mr. Clement says. Think of him as our director all through this trial."

Stifling her impulse, Lori replied, "Yes, of course. Anything you say, Mr. Clement."

"My dear, follow my advice, and we'll win this thing," Clement assured her. He patted her hand indulgently, as if she were a petulant schoolgirl. A gesture Brett could read in her eyes she resented.

Nevertheless, the day before the trial, wearing dark glasses and a scarf over her blond hair to disguise her identity, Lori went shopping in the local mall as Clement had advised.

Later at the hotel she modeled her purchases for Brett. He was sure Clement would approve.

As she tried to slip out of the simple periwinkle-blue dress she had bought for her first appearance on the stand, she was so nervous she started to fumble with the buttons. Finally Brett had to help her. She was clad only in her bra and her briefs. He drew her close and kissed her. He slid his hand under her bra, reaching for her bare breast when she slipped out of his embrace.

"Lori?"

"No. Not now . . . not yet. Not till this is over . . ." she said softly. "I want him back—that's all I can think of—I want my son back more than . . . more than I want you right now."

Respecting her feelings, he kissed her lightly on the lips and said, "I understand how you feel. And I love you for it. I want him back, too."

It was late. The quiet of the night was disturbed by the far-off sound of a church bell several streets away. Bill Salem counted them. Ten . . . eleven . . . twelve . . . Midnight. The last time the bells were set to sound until six in the morning. He reached behind him to find that Christie was no longer there. He slipped out of bed.

With the trial due to start in the morning, he had an inkling of where he would find her. He was right.

She stood at the foot of Scotty's bed staring down at him as he slept peacefully.

It gave Bill a sudden chill. This was a painfully familiar scene. It was the way Christie used to stand at Scotty's bassinette when they first brought him home. She had stood there watching, to make sure he continued to breathe. The tragic fate of little Billy would be part of their lives forever.

He put his arms around her, whispering, "Come back to bed. We have to be fresh and alert for tomorrow."

"I have the most terrible feeling . . . they're going to take him away from us."

"No, they won't," he refuted, more strongly than he intended, for Scotty stirred in his sleep, opening one eye. Then, reassured since both his parents were there, he was asleep again.

Bill led Christie back to their bedroom. She would not get into bed but insisted on sitting on the side.

"Hon . . . please . . ." Bill urged.

"He's going to take him away. . . ."

"What makes you so sure?"

"After I explained to him what Scotty means to us, what we mean to him, that judge should have said right then and there that he belonged to us forever. But he didn't."

"Chris . . . darling . . . He couldn't decide before the trial."

"He could if he wanted to," she continued to insist. Suddenly she asked, "You think it was a mistake?"

"We don't have any choice. We're being sued," he pointed out.

"I mean Paul. You think he's too old? That maybe he made a mistake not asking for jury?"

"Chris . . . we can't be having second thoughts about that now. The trial starts in the morning. Now come to bed."

When she did not move, he very gently took her by the arms and put her to bed. He climbed in alongside her. He embraced her cold body until she finally started breathing in the regular shallow rhythm that revealed she was asleep.

Across the street from the courthouse where Family Court held its sessions was a hotel that preceded that legal edifice by some years. Though there were newer and more modern hotels in the city, the proximity to the courthouse had made Brett Manning choose that one.

In the best suite on the top floor of the old five-story building, Lori Manning had left their bed. When Brett woke, he spied her rooting around the cart that had brought their room-service dinner earlier that night.

She discovered only some soft rolls turned rock hard. And some coffee left in the large thermos.

She tapped the roll on the edge of one of the plates to see if she dared try to bite into it. She decided no. She poured herself some coffee. It was less than lukewarm. Nevertheless, she sipped it.

Brett found her there, perched on the arm of the overstuffed armchair, sipping cold coffee for want of something to do to pass the time until dawn, when she would shower and dress for her courtroom appearance.

Now, she sat dressed only in a silk nightgown that covered her slender body. It was not sufficient protection against the draft from the primitive air conditioner perched in the window that rhythmically pumped cool air into the room.

Brett took the coffee cup from her hands.

"You don't need any more of that," he said.

Strangely she replied, "How would you know?"

"You had three cups with dinner," he replied.

"You can't know. You've never seen him. Pictures, maybe. But you never saw him, never held him."

"Brett . . . are you talking about little Brett?" he asked.

"Who else would I be talking about?" she demanded impatiently. "When I saw him that day . . . he's everything I imagined . . . so blond, and his face. . . . He is a very handsome little boy. He doesn't look like them. He looks like me, like you. He belongs with us. He's part of us. Part of me. For nine months he was part of me. I want him back, Brett. I want him back."

"So do I, darling. Don't worry. Mr. Clement said the law is on our side. Family Reunification. And Judge Hart is a stickler for the law."

"I wish I could be sure," Lori said.

"Lori . . . darling . . . Take one of those sedatives Dr. Mallory prescribed for just such times. Please?"

"No! I don't want to dull the pain. It would be like running away . . . like deserting my child a second time. If pain is part of this, then I want to feel the pain, all of it."

"At least come back to bed. Get some rest," Brett pleaded.

She shook her head, adamant. When he put his arms around her, she resisted. Until she broke down and cried.

"Lori, baby, starting tomorrow we take the first step toward getting our son back. I want you to be ready for it."

That convinced her to relent and start back to bed.

# Chapter 32

"Bill . . . your mother here yet?" Christie Salem called from David's room, where she had just finished nursing him.

"She'll be here, she'll be here," Bill assured her from the kitchen, where he was serving Scotty his breakfast.

"This is one day and one occasion I don't want to be late for!" Christie called back as she walked her months-old son to burp him before she put him down for his nap.

"I know, I know," Bill agreed.

As soon as he had served Scotty's breakfast, he picked up the phone and punched in the number hurriedly.

"Sis? Where's Mom? On the way? Okay. Good. We don't want to be late. Not today. Thanks, darling. We'll need all the good luck we can get. Okay, we'll call you soon as we come back from court. Scotty? Can't say. I'd rather not . . . not right now. Right, Sis, you got it. In the kitchen having breakfast. Yes, yes, call you."

He hung up and came back to the table to discover that Scotty, usually hungry for his breakfast, had left his food untouched. His son was staring up at him.

"Come on, Scotty-boy, eat up. I want to see that plate clean before we leave."

The boy picked up a triangle of toast, but instead of starting to eat, he asked, "Why Gramma comin' today?"

"She's going to stay with you and David while Mommy and Daddy are away."

"You and Mommy goin' away?" Scotty asked, his young face screwing up in the manner that usually preceded crying.

"No, no, Son, we're not 'going away.' We're just going to be out for a few hours. Meantime, Gramma'll be here to take care of you."

"She take me to school?" the boy asked.

"Not today, Son. You'll be staying home. Gramma'll be reading to you and going over your alphabet. . . ."

"Today a holiday?"

"Son, please, just eat your breakfast." Bill took the toast from his son's hand to spread a layer of jam over it, in the hope of tempting him into eating.

But the boy's mind was still troubled, puzzled by an unfamiliar word he had overheard.

He took one bite and while chewing asked, "Daddy? You an' Mommy caught?"

"Caught?" Bill repeated, startled. "Who said anything about being caught?"

"You said . . . Mommy 'n' you comin' from caught."

"Oh, that," Bill realized. Very gingerly he tried to explain. "Son, 'caught' is a word that sounds like another word. Caught is when I throw the softball to you. After you catch it, it is caught. What we call past tense . . ."

He knew he was getting into areas deeper than his two-and-a-half-year-old son could understand.

"Anyhow, once ·   · catch the ball, it is caught." Bill was relieved to terminate the discussion.

Until, just before taking a second bite, Scotty asked, "Daddy . . . other word . . . ?"

"What other word?"

"Caught," Scotty reminded. "You said, Daddy, you said."

"That word, that other word is . . . court."

" 'Court'?" the boy repeated, puzzled, since both words sounded as one and the same.

"Court," Bill repeated. "Someday, Son, when you're older, I'll explain what the difference is."

"Daddy . . ." But before Scotty could ask another question, the doorbell rang. Bill was relieved to say, "That's Gramma now."

Scotty raced from the table to precede his father to the door to greet his grandmother. As soon as Bill opened the door, the boy threw his arms around his grandmother, saying, "Mommy and Daddy are court."

Mrs. Salem glared at her son, demanding, *Have you told him about the lawsuit? I thought we all agreed it was not to be mentioned in his presence.*

Bill whispered, "I'll explain later."

"There may not be any need," his mother said, with the superior attitude of someone possessing special knowledge.

"Mom?" he demanded.

"I promised not to say anything," she revealed. "But things are . . . are . . . I don't want to make any promises, Christie being so tense as she is, but just . . . just don't worry."

"Ma, please!" Bill pressed.

But Christie came down the stairs to detail for her mother-in-law David's routine, needs, and habits, though the woman was quite familiar with them.

Bill and Christie Salem were ready to set out for court.

When he took her hand, it felt cold. But no colder than his own.

Bill Salem had to circle the courthouse in his effort to find a parking place. The ones designated for litigants and attorneys were filled with television trucks.

Parking a block away forced Christie and Bill to run a gauntlet of cameras and reporters who surrounded and pursued them, bombarding them with questions to which, following Henderson's instructions, Bill replied, "No comment, no comment."

They were rescued from their tormentors only when someone cried out, "Brett Manning!" At once the entire wolf pack deserted the Salems to surround Brett and Lori Manning, who had just emerged from the hotel. They escorted the noted couple across the plaza to the courthouse and up the steps. There, special uniformed court employees barred the door to them, announcing, "Only those with press passes will be admitted!"

Those so empowered lined up to be checked and admitted, giving the Mannings a chance to proceed to the courtroom unhindered.

As spectators and media people filed in, the courtroom was filled with a buzz that grew to a torrent. At their respective counsel tables Paul Henderson and Henry Clement pored over their notes and files. Their clients sat beside them, silent, nervous, daring from time to time to cast a furtive glance at their adversaries.

Experienced as he was with the media and their attentions, Brett Manning was no more at ease than Bill Salem. His public image could not avail him now. For he had been warned by Clement that Judson Hart was not one of those fawning judges who was dazzled or influenced by the fame of a litigant.

Paul Henderson was beginning to feel the familiar tension and eagerness to commence the formalities that always preceded the opening of a trial. No matter how many years he had done so, and the many trials in which he had taken part, that excitement was always part of it for him. Without it, he would have felt naked.

Today the proceedings were delayed. Perhaps, Henderson thought, other attorneys had managed to corner Judge Hart in his chambers with some issue that demanded an immediate ruling. But it was not usual, even in such circumstances, to keep Hart from assuming the bench for this long.

At forty-five minutes after ten o'clock, the judge's secretary, appearing quite agitated, emerged from the door to the judge's robing room. She approached Paul Henderson. "His Honor would like to see you. At once!"

Since it was most unusual for a judge to dispatch his secretary on such a mission, Paul Henderson realized that this was the summons to a conference of great gravity.

As he rose, he heard the same instruction being issued to Henry Clement. By the baffled look on Clement's face Henderson realized that this was a shock to Clement as well.

They found Judge Hart on his feet in an angry and defiant stance. Impatiently he beckoned both counsel into the room, then brusquely gestured his secretary to close the door.

Though he remained standing, he motioned both lawyers to

chairs. He paced back and forth, marshaling his opening volley.

"It's not only the personal insult involved," Hart began. "It's the inference that *any* judge on the bench of this Court is amenable to such underhanded tactics. Since I assumed the position of chief judge of the Family Court, I have rooted out every judge even rumored to be subject to outside influence. Yet now I find myself the target of just such an attempt."

He wheeled suddenly on Paul Henderson. "Counselor, do you have anything to say at this point?"

Confused, yet the object of this serious attack, Henderson found himself unable to respond. "Your Honor . . . I . . . I have no idea . . ."

"Early this morning," Hart resumed, "I received a phone call from one of the leading political figures in this state. I will not disclose his name, since this matter may go before the grand jury. But the hint was . . . it was more than a hint, it was a virtual offer . . . that if I decided this case in favor of your clients, Mr. Henderson, it would greatly facilitate my elevation to the Supreme Court of this state."

"Your Honor, I give you my word—"

Before Henderson could complete his assurances, Hart continued, "I was led to believe that the governor himself was behind this offer."

"Your Honor, I take an oath, as an officer of the court, as a member of the bar for forty-two years, I know nothing about this."

Meantime, Henry Clement did his best to appear to commiserate with his unfortunate colleague. Actually this development was a gratuitous event he might use to advantage later in the trial.

"Mr. Henderson, do you know a person named George Archer?"

"No, Your Honor," Henderson replied forthrightly.

"Never had any conversation or communication with such a person?" Hart pursued.

"No, Your Honor."

"Do you know a person named Eloise Salem?" the Judge demanded.

"No, sir. The only Salems I know are William and Christine. My clients," Henderson replied. Then a sudden and troubled look clouded the face of the aging lawyer.

"Yes, Mr. Henderson?" the judge demanded.

"I seem to recall . . . I don't want to be held to this. . . . But I think I do have a memory of the name Eloise Salem. I believe she is the sister or the cousin of my client."

"Henderson," Judge Hart dropped all formalities, "if I discover that you are not honest with me on my next question, I promise you now you will be disbarred!"

Henderson nodded gravely, admitting his awareness that this could bring a shameful end to his long and honorable career.

"Henderson, did you ever have any conversation with your client leading to the idea that if he could, by some means, bring pressure to bear on me, I would lean in his direction?"

"Absolutely not, Your Honor!"

"I accept your word. But I cannot promise the matter will stop here."

The tone and the words let both attorneys know that this unhappy meeting was over. As they rose to leave, Judge Hart had one last volley to fire.

"And, Mr. Clement, before you delude yourself into thinking that this unfortunate event will figure in my ultimate decision, I would like to remind you that, while I do not implicate you, I have been the subject of inquiries from a certain television network with a slimy hint that they could *advance* my public image if Brett Manning should prevail in this litigation. Since their 'hints' were so obvious, I did not think to blame someone as subtle as you. See you both in court in ten minutes!"

By the time Judge Judson Hart ascended the bench, Paul Henderson had informed his clients that any further interference in this case by either family or friends would cause him to resign from their defense.

Once on the bench, Judge Hart warned, "Any interference by any of the media in the orderly progress of this trial will result in a ban of *all* the media. You may then accuse me of stifling freedom of the press and pillory me in your editorials. Nevertheless, this trial will be conducted in fair and legal fashion. Since the life of a child is an issue here."

The case of *Manning* v. *Salem* was ready to begin.

# Chapter 33

❧

"Will the attorney for the plaintiffs make his opening statement?"

Henry Clement rose at his counsel table and picked up his sheaf of notes. A single glance to refresh his memory, and he began.

"Your Honor, my client, the natural father of the child involved in this proceeding, claims the right to have that child returned to him. The adoption involved in this case was irregular and illegal, as we will prove."

Sitting side by side at the defense table, Christine Salem tugged at her counsel's arm, demanding he object.

"Christie," Henderson whispered, "it's only an opening statement. We'll have our turn."

Irritated by the exchange, Judge Hart interrupted Clement to ask, "Mr. Henderson? Can you control your client so that Mr. Clement can complete his opening?"

"Sorry, Your Honor. There will be no further interruptions."

Clement resumed. Since part of his strategy involved creating a strong anxiety in Christine Salem, he repeated his previous charge: "The fact that this adoption was faulty in the inception opens the entire question of whether the child was ever in the proper hands to begin with!"

This time when Christie reacted, Bill gripped her arm strongly enough to force her to restrain her emotions.

"There is also," Clement continued, "the matter of statute law that governs here. The law of this state provides that, failing clear and convincing proof to the contrary, every child belongs with its blood parents. As we will prove, there are many valid reasons why this would benefit this particular child. Thank you, Your Honor."

Judge Hart nodded in Henderson's direction. The older man rose and cleared his throat before beginning.

"Your Honor, my clients' position is very clear. Scotty Salem is their son by legal adoption. He is an integral and inseparable part of their family, and has been since he was three days old. To change that status would do irreparable harm to him and to the only family he has ever known."

With that the old attorney slipped back into his chair.

"Mr. Clement," Judge Hart ordered, "your first witness."

In line with his legal strategy to treat Brett Manning's legal rights as the foundation of his case, Clement announced, "I call Brett Manning, the plaintiff, to the stand."

There was a great stir among the media people and the spectators as the television star came forward. Women in the spectators' section strained forward, rising halfway up to get a glimpse of him.

Once he was sworn and seated, Henry Clement proceeded to ask basic questions to establish his background, his early years before arriving in New York.

Then Clement asked the question he had been leading up to: "So, Brett, is it correct to say that you came out of a warm and loving family?"

"Yes, sir."

"So that family is an important part of your life," Clement commented.

Henderson cleared his throat instead of making an objection.

Clement continued, "Brett, during your early struggles to become an actor, what sort of work did you do to sustain yourself?"

"Anything and everything," Brett replied.

"Such as?"

"I waited tables. I did windows. Once I did a few months as a painter."

"You're an artist?" Clement pretended surprise though fully aware of Brett's response.

Brett smiled in his most amused and ingratiating way. "No, sir. A housepainter. Had to give it up. I discovered I was allergic to paint."

"Any other jobs you did?" Clement continued.

"Bicycle messenger. Oh, yes, and I delivered pizzas. What a rough winter that was. Seems every time there was a blizzard, all of New York craved pizza. Delivered to the office or the house. I damn near . . . sorry, I almost froze to death that winter."

Brett chuckled, and Clement joined him. Then the attorney turned more serious.

"Brett, tell this Court what happened on the day Lori told you she was pregnant."

"Yes, sir. I . . . I was . . . I'll be honest about it . . . I was scared. There we were, two young kids, hardly making enough to get along on. Even when we both worked. And suddenly I'm confronted with this news that there was going to be a baby. I'm going to be a father. Man! Was I scared!"

"Did you turn and run?"

"No, sir! I wasn't brought up to run from obligations. I offered to marry Lori. To leave New York, get a regular job. You have to understand, I love Lori. I always have and always will. Why would I turn and run from her?"

Anticipating that if he didn't ask the question, Henderson surely would, Clement challenged, "Yet we know that you *didn't* get married, did you?"

"No, sir. But that wasn't my decision. It was Lori. She said she was doing it for my sake. When I thought back over it, it was like that O. Henry story. 'The Gift of the Magi.' This poor young husband and wife so in love were buying Christmas gifts for each other. Because she had such long, beautiful hair, he sold his most precious possessions to buy a tortoiseshell comb for her. While she, without being aware of that, cut off and sold her beautiful hair to buy a gift for him. It was that way with Lori and me. For her I was willing to leave the theater and get a job selling tires. While she insisted on going back home so as not to hinder my career. We were each willing to sacrifice for the other."

"Brett, during the time Lori was out there in the Middle West, did you make any attempt to keep in touch with her?"

"Continuously, sir. I wrote regularly. And almost always I would enclose five, ten, twenty dollars. Whatever I could. It wasn't the amount. I wanted her to know that I still loved her. That I was helping in every way I could. Then suddenly my letters started coming back. With no forwarding address."

"And what did you do then, Brett?"

"There was nothing I could do then. But as soon as I was financially able, I hired a private investigator to find her."

"Once they found her, what did you do?"

"I flew out to Chicago. I wanted to see Lori. I wanted to see my child."

"So that at the time you had no idea your child was a boy."

"No, sir."

"Or that he had been given up for adoption?"

"No, sir."

"Brett, answer very carefully. Did you ever receive any notice, written or oral, by mail or otherwise, of that adoption?"

"No, sir! No notice in any form, sir, none."

"Are you telling this Court that until that day in Chicago when Lori told you, you had absolutely no knowledge of the fact that your child, your son, had been given up for adoption?"

"Yes, sir."

"Brett, if you had been notified, what would you—"

"Objection!" Paul Henderson called out.

Before Judge Hart could rule, Henderson continued, "Your Honor, that is a purely hypothetical question. The answer to which we have no way of evaluating for its truth. The plaintiff claims he was not notified. End of story. Let's leave it to O. Henry to deal with the 'ifs.'"

"Mr. Clement, counsel has a valid point," Judge Hart ruled.

Clement turned back to his client. "Brett, what is your plan now if your son is returned to you by this Court?"

"To become a family. A real family. Like I was used to in my childhood. Lori and I've already picked out a house up in Connecticut. A place where a boy can grow up with a feeling for the outdoors. Where he can run and play. A fine community with excellent schools. And a place near enough to New York so after my show I can be home every evening for supper. A family supper like we used to have when I was a kid. A real home. And as I said, a real family. That's all we live for, Lori and I. But all our plans, all our hopes, are built around little Brett. Because without him, my success means nothing."

"Thank you, Brett. Your witness, Mr. Henderson."

Paul Henderson had only a moment to decide. This young man was not only a most ingratiating and appealing witness. He was also telling the truth. Not likely to be trapped by any shrewd questions.

Discretion being the better part of courtroom valor, Henderson replied, "No questions, Your Honor."

"Mr. Clement," Judge Hart ordered, "your next witness."

Having established the legal foundation to his case, Clement now was ready to launch into the emotional side of it. Culminating in Lori's testimony.

So he announced, "I call Ms. Rose Berryman to the stand."

Sworn and identified for the record, Rose Berryman, supervisor of the hospital where Lori worked during her pregnancy, took the stand.

She smiled warmly at Lori to assure her that she was here as a friend and supporter and would do her best for her.

Once Clement had identified Berryman's relationship to the case and established her credentials and her position at the hospital, he proceeded with his questions.

"Ms. Berryman, describe for His Honor how you came to know Lori Manning."

The woman described the manner in which they met, her early association with Lori, ending up with, "I secretly had great ambitions for her in nursing. She was so intelligent and caring. But, of course, I could see that being pregnant would have great bearing on her future plans."

"Ms. Berryman, as her pregnancy advanced, did you at any time have any discussions with her as to what she would do about the infant once it was born?" Clement continued.

"Oh, yes, we talked about that at great length."

"Can you summarize for His Honor the nature of those conversations?"

"She had enormous concern for the father of her child. She did not want to do anything to damage his career. Which left her little choice. Since she could not continue to work and raise an infant at the same time."

"What would you say was her attitude about the situation?"

"She desperately wanted to hold on to the child, raise him herself. But failing that, she was determined to make sure that if he was adopted, it would be by a family of which she approved."

"Is that usual, Ms. Berryman? For the natural mother to have approval of the adoptive parents?" Clement asked.

"No, it definitely is not."

"So would you say that in this instance Lori Manning, then Lori Adams, displayed *more* concern about her infant son than unwed mothers usually do?"

"Considerably more concern. She not only wanted to, but insisted on meeting all possible adoptive parents. Talking to them herself. She had turned down four couples prior to approving the Salems. In fact, I think that the only reason—"

"Object!" Henderson called out. "We are not interested in what the witness thinks, only in the facts she observed."

"Sustained," the judge ruled.

"I was only going to say—"

"Objection sustained!" the judge ruled once more.

To sum up her testimony, Clement asked, "Ms. Berryman, is it possible that the reason the plaintiff approved the Salems was that she was tired, worn down, emotionally exhausted by the process of those previous interviews?"

This time Judge Hart did not wait for Henderson's objection. "Mr. Clement, please, don't try the patience of this Court. And don't put words in the mouth of the witness."

"Your witness," Clement conceded to his adversary.

Henderson advanced toward Rose Berryman so slowly that she thought he was afflicted by senility. The manner in which he shuffled his notes led her to suspect he might also have trouble with his memory. She did not realize that taking advantage of his age was a tactic he employed when it suited him, while his faculties remained as sharp as ever.

"Uh . . . Ms. . . ." He consulted his notes for her name. "Ah, yes, Ms. Berryman. Ms. Berryman, as a hospital administrator, how many times in the last dozen years have you had to confront such a situation?"

"Sir?" Berryman asked, puzzled.

"Where one of your employees was pregnant out of wedlock, as the saying goes."

"In the last dozen years . . ." Berryman pondered. "There were two other cases."

"What was the disposition of those cases?"

"Object. Lack of relevance!" Clement called out.

"Mr. Henderson?" Judge Hart inquired.

"Ms. Berryman made a statement comparing Mrs. Manning's conduct with other unmarried women in the same situation. In response to Mr. Clement's question about how much concern she showed, I believe her words were, 'Mrs. Manning showed considerably more concern.' Well, what I would like this Court to know is how many other women the witness used as her basis for comparison. And what happened to those other women. I think that is a reasonable and relevant area to explore."

"Proceed, Mr. Henderson."

"Ms. Berryman, I believe you said two other women. What was the outcome in those cases?"

"One woman took her child and moved back to her family's home in Montana. Or it could have been Wyoming."

"And the other?" Henderson continued.

"She married the father, and I don't know what happened after that."

"So that neither of the other two women gave up her child for adoption?" Henderson concluded.

"No, neither did," Ms. Berryman admitted.

"Now, did I hear you testify that Mrs. Manning was especially meticulous about the family to which she was giving her child?"

"As I said, she interviewed five families in all."

"Then she must have thought very highly of the Salems to give up her child to—"

"Object! We have already had a ruling that this witness is not to testify as to what *she* 'thought' the plaintiff thought. But only as to the facts she observed," Clement called out.

"Yes, Mr. Henderson, as you yourself pointed out," Judge Hart reminded.

"I stand corrected, Your Honor," Henderson conceded. Facing the witness, he asked, "Ms. Berryman, if a woman were choosing from five of anything—dresses, shoes, kitchen utensils, furniture, fabric—and she rejected four of them but chose the fifth, what would that indicate to you?"

To Henderson's surprise Ms. Berryman replied, "It would indicate to me that she was probably tired and made her decision out of sheer fatigue."

"Not that she found that fifth one to be superior to the other four?" Henderson asked.

"Not necessarily," Ms. Berryman disputed, out of loyalty to Lori's cause. "Fatigue, impatience, possibly fear that there might not be a suitable alternative."

Since Berryman had gone on the attack, and seemed quite sure of herself, Henderson decided he had better cut his losses and try to repair the damage by asking a concluding question.

"However, Ms. Berryman, the fact remains that the plaintiff did, after interviewing the Salems, decide that they were a proper family to whom to give up her child."

"That was her judgment," Ms. Berryman said, bristling. She added, "at that time."

Henderson turned back to his counsel table, where Christie and Bill Salem sat, staring at him. The disappointment on their faces moved him to glance at his notes once more. He half-turned to the witness.

"Ms. Berryman, before you go, just one last question. During your conversation with Mrs. Manning did the question ever come up of her marrying the father of her child? As happened with one of the other two couples?"

"Yes," she admitted.

"Did she ever say to you why she *didn't* choose that alternative?" Henderson asked.

"She did not want to force him into marrying her and thus giving up the career he was determined to pursue," the witness responded.

"Therefore, would it be correct to say Lori Adams gave up her child in exchange for her boyfriend's career?"

"Object!" came the strong intervention from Clement, who rose swiftly to his feet to fight the issue if it became necessary.

Judge Hart saved him the trouble. "Objection sustained."

"I have no more questions for the witness," Henderson conceded.

He returned to his seat alongside Christie Salem. She said nothing, but the fear of defeat was written on her face.

Having won this last skirmish, Clement availed himself of the final question. "Ms. Berryman, at any time during her pregnancy, or after, did you ever detect in Lori Adams any sign of a less than totally devoted, loyal, loving mother?"

"No, sir, I did not."

"Thank you, Ms. Berryman."

# Chapter 34

Henry Clement proceeded to introduce and question two witnesses involved in Lori's pregnancy and the delivery of her son.

The first was a nurse practitioner who saw Lori through the latter stages of her pregnancy. She testified to the conscientious manner in which Lori observed all the rules and practices prescribed for her and for the benefit of her unborn child. She also testified that Lori's attitude throughout the pregnancy was optimistic and upbeat. The witness quoted Lori as saying, "I want my son to be born with the right attitude. I want him to be a happy child and an optimistic person."

Clement concluded, "So that from what you were able to hear and observe, you concluded that Lori Adams was devoted to her child and his future even before he was born?"

"Object!" Henderson called. "It is up to His Honor to draw such conclusions rather than the witness."

"Withdrawn," Clement concluded. "Your witness."

"No questions," Henderson replied, to the chagrin of both Bill and Christie Salem.

Clement then introduced the doctor who had presided at the actual delivery of Scotty Salem. He testified to the birth as uneventful. The patient was calm and in control, though suffering the usual birth pains. She did not require the use of any drugs to minimize pain. Nor did she require an episiotomy, since her perineum expanded quite normally and did not obstruct the delivery. In all, an uncomplicated birth.

"Doctor," Clement continued, "in your examination of the mother and the child, did you find any evidence that during the pregnancy the mother had indulged in smoking?"

"No, sir."

"Excessive ingestion of coffee or other caffeine-containing beverages?"

"No, sir."

"And as to alcohol?"

"Neither she, nor the infant, showed any effects of alcohol use during pregnancy."

"Is it fair to say that Mrs. Manning, then Ms. Adams, was an ideal mother even *before* her child was born?"

"Object!" Henderson called from his place at the table.

"I will allow the question," Judge Hart ruled.

"Her record, and all tests, reveal that she took care of herself and her baby all through the pregnancy. As a result, she gave birth to a perfectly healthy infant of six pounds twelve ounces. Whose Apgar results at birth were better than average."

"Your witness, Mr. Henderson."

Since he had plans to counter that testimony with later testimony of his own, Henderson passed with, "No questions."

Clement introduced several other witnesses who had taken part in the adoption procedure itself. The officials of the Godmothers' League Adoption Agency, especially the woman who had cooperated with Rose Heckinger in arranging the meetings between Lori and potential adopting families.

Emily Daniels, a woman in her early forties, had devoted the past eleven years of her life to the Godmothers' League as an unpaid public service. She was well versed in appearing as a witness, having been called to testify in a number of adoption disputes in recent years.

On the stand she was in full control of herself and gave brief and direct answers to Clement's questions.

"Ms. Daniels, at what stage of the adoption procedure did you become involved in this case?"

"As soon as the hospital notified our agency that Lori—Ms. Adams—had decided adoption was her chosen course. I took charge of her case."

"For the benefit of the Court would you explain what 'taking charge' of such a case entails?"

"Counseling the mother as to the emotional and other consequences of adoption. At times it involves recommending psychiatric help. The main purpose is to educate the mother fully in all the factors to consider before finally committing to adoption."

"Ms. Daniels, would you say that Ms. Adams was delighted at the prospect of having to give up her child to complete strangers?"

"Of course not!"

"How *would* you characterize her attitude?" Clement asked.

"Objection!" Henderson interposed.

"On what ground?" Judge Hart asked.

"The witness is not a psychiatrist or a psychoanalyst but a social-services caseworker. Therefore not professionally qualified to give opinion testimony as to the plaintiff's state of mind at a crucial time in her life."

The judge considered that for a moment, then ruled, "The witness may answer the question."

"Lori Adams resisted the idea of adoption. But decided that, under the circumstances, it was the only path open to her at that time. It is my opinion that she accepted that with great reluctance."

"Thank you, Ms. Daniels. Your witness."

Henderson approached the witness with the air of a troubled man baffled by what he had just heard.

"Ms. Daniels, did you suggest to this particular mother that she have psychiatric help?"

"Once she and I had gone into all aspects of adoption and she had made up her mind, I saw no need for psychiatric intervention."

"Do you think such intervention would have made any difference?"

"If I thought so, I would have insisted on it."

"Based on your conversations with Ms. Adams, would you say

she was of sound and mature mind when she made her decision?" Henderson asked.

"Yes, I would say so."

"She knew what she wanted to do, and she did it," Henderson summed up. He started back toward the table when a thought seemed to have occurred to him.

"Ms. Daniels, is it the policy of your agency to contact the father in cases of adoption?"

"Wherever possible, we do that. After all, the father does have legal rights. If he chooses to exercise them."

"Therefore we must assume that Mr. Manning did not choose to do so," Henderson concluded.

"Oh, no, sir," Ms. Daniels contradicted.

"No? If he didn't object—"

"He had no *opportunity* to object."

As if this came to him as a surprise, Henderson pretended shock. "Are you telling this Court that your agency's negligence is responsible for this unfortunate situation?"

"No, sir."

"If the father in this case did not have the opportunity to object and if it was your duty to inform him, who else *could* be responsible?" Henderson asked.

Aware of the impact of her response on these proceedings, Ms. Daniels paused before replying, very carefully, "Our failure to notify the father was not due to negligence, but to the fact that we were unable to locate him."

"Meaning that your agency tried but was unable to reach him?" Henderson pretended to assume. "A young man who lived in New York and was listed in the Manhattan phone book. Who was listed on the rolls of Actors Equity. Which also has a listing of his agent. And you had no way of reaching him?" Henderson demanded.

"Based on—" Ms. Daniels began, then broke off to start anew. "The name we were looking for was not Brett Mann, as he was then known."

"What name *were* you looking for?" Henderson demanded.

"The name listed on the baby's birth certificate."

"Which was?"

"Higgins."

"Higgins is quite a common name in New York City," Henderson commented. "How many Higginses did you contact?"

"Forty-two," she admitted.

"Surely there are more than forty-two Higginses in New York. Likely a hundred in Manhattan alone. Why did you stop at forty-two?"

"Because . . . because someone in our office realized that the name Higgins, *Henry* Higgins, was the name of the leading character in *My Fair Lady*."

"I see. And having discovered that, you, of course, confronted Lori Adams and demanded the correct name of the father of her child," Henderson remarked, quite aware of what the response had to be.

"No, sir."

"You didn't? Why not?" he asked, pretending ignorance.

"Because under the law we have no way to force a mother to reveal the name of the father."

"Aha! So what really happened here was that Lori Adams, knowing she could not be forced to do so, refused to reveal the correct name of the father of her child. She resorted to a fictitious name to mislead you and everyone. And now she is trying to take advantage of her own deliberate lie to tear that child from the arms of the only mother he knows!"

The courtroom erupted in an uproar, which Judge Hart quelled by vigorous use of his gavel.

Once quiet was restored, the judge asked, "Mr. Henderson? Any further questions for this witness?"

"Your Honor, I think we've heard quite enough from this witness."

"Your next witness, Mr. Clement?"

Relieved to change the nature of the testimony, Henry Clement announced, "We call to the stand Dr. Rosa Dietrich."

A small, almost diminutive woman in her early forties, one of Clement's chosen psychiatric experts, came forward from the first spectators' row to take the oath and ascend the stand.

After qualifying her through her educational training and professional experience as a practicing child psychiatrist, Clement proceeded to have her recount her sessions with Scott Salem and her conclusions as to his condition.

Dr. Dietrich had found him to be a reasonably well-adjusted two-and-a-half-year-old. Though in her opinion he would become better adjusted under the loving care of his natural parents. Clement did not press too hard for her reasons. He was saving that for his prime witness yet to come.

Aware of Clement's strategy, Henderson, for the same reason, did not pursue Dietrich with any sharp questions.

From the bench Judge Judson Hart watched this charade being played out with well-controlled impatience.

Like the attorneys he, too, was awaiting the arrival of Clement's star witness, Dr. Walter Blessing.

After two more psychiatric witnesses, Clement asked for a lunch recess so that Dr. Blessing's testimony would not be interrupted.

Both Paul Henderson and Judge Hart were wise to Henry Clement's tactics. They knew that Clement did not wish to give Henderson a clue to Dr. Blessing's impending attack before the lunch break. Thus depriving the old lawyer of that precious time to formulate his counterattack.

Nevertheless, Judge Hart recessed the trial until two o'clock.

# Chapter 35

Promptly at two Judge Hart reappeared on the bench to open the proceedings with a sharp "Mr. Clement?"

Clement started up the aisle to the courtroom door. He disappeared for a moment, then returned accompanied by a tall, portly man in his mid-sixties. He had a flowing white mustache and a blushing bald head that gleamed in the reflected overhead lights as if it had been waxed and polished for this occasion. Alongside Blessing, even Clement seemed to shrink in size and stature.

An experienced courtroom practitioner, Dr. Blessing strode directly to the witness stand. Waited to take the oath. When asked his name, he replied in a voice so deep and impressive that Christie reached to Bill's hand for support. This was a witness to be feared.

Clement led Blessing slowly through his impressive record: University of Chicago, Harvard Medical School, four years at the Mayo Clinic in Minnesota. And finally, many years as clinical professor and chief of psychiatry at a leading New York medical center.

Before proceeding with his other questions, Clement took a moment to observe, "Professor, we thank you for coming all the way from New York to testify here today."

Blessing dismissed that with a slight wave of the hand that testified to his modesty.

"Now, then, Doctor, have you ever examined the child now named Scott Salem, who is the subject of this lawsuit?"

"I have."

"And what did you find, Doctor?"

"He seems a reasonably normal child, for two and a half. At that time when children are beginning to fight for their own identity and hence tend to become rebellious," Blessing declared.

As prearranged, Clement asked, "Doctor, you used the term, if I remember correctly, 'reasonably normal.' Could you elaborate on that for the Court?"

Blessing swung his considerable presence around in the witness chair to address Judge Hart directly.

"I used the descriptive 'reasonably' because I detected beneath his normal responses a certain *un*certainty, if you will pardon the use of that phrase. Something is lurking there. Something a keen observer would detect, which one cannot ascribe to any particular act or word from the subject child. But enough to give one pause."

"Doctor," Clement continued, "what significance would you attribute to such a conclusion?"

"Well, now, if we were dealing with a child secure in the family framework of his natural parents and siblings, emotionally supported by grandparents, aunts, uncles, etcetera, I would not be concerned. However, as I am aware, in this case, where a child is an adopted child, at least for the time being . . ."

At this point Bill felt Christie's hand stiffen in his.

". . . such an adopted child, who already betrays a sense of insecurity, will doubtless be under severe strain in the years to come."

"Why do you say that, Doctor?"

"Oh, there are many reasons," Blessing replied, as if there were too many too well known to need recounting here.

Which, of course, gave Clement the opening he needed. "Doctor, for the edification of this Court, would you enumerate some of those reasons?"

"Of course." Once more Blessing addressed the bench. "Adopted children, under the best of circumstances, face a lifetime of problems. Take the most immediately apparent. Lack of a personal history. A medical history. There come times in many a person's life when he desperately needs medical treatment which may, in some crucial measure, depend on his family history. I am sure, Your Honor, you, like all of us, read in the papers or hear on television news of how family histories aid in the diagnosis and treatment of ailments as serious as cancer. Also, when that adoptive child becomes an adult and contemplates having children of his own, knowing little or nothing of his family history and how it might affect a child of his, how is he to protect that unborn child from such diseases? Or, indeed, decide to have any children at all."

As if there were an infinite number of reasons, Blessing concluded, "Many reasons, too many reasons."

"Doctor," Clement pursued, "for purposes of the record, may I prevail on you to continue?"

"Well, intensive research done at Bellevue Hospital in New York proves that adopted children have a higher crime rate than natural children. And when they end up in the justice system, they receive longer sentences and have higher recidivism rates."

"How do you account for that, Doctor?"

"Mr. Clement, I did not do the research, so I have no answer for that. And the doctor who did that research could only speculate on the reasons. However, if I were pressed to supply my own theory, it would be this: Somehow, parents of adopted children, quite unconsciously, transmit to the child a feeling different from what they would extend to a natural child. There have even been cases where adoptive parents have gone to Court to, if I may coin a word, 'unadopt' an unruly child. Suffice it to say, the facts prove that adopted children have such an unfortunate record."

"Dr. Blessing, based on your own extensive experience treating children, natural and adopted, what would you say is the principal difference?" Clement asked.

"The process of growing up for any child is a difficult and evolving journey. The stresses and strains of the changing relationship between parent and child through the years demands a rock-solid base of mutual love, plus the child's ability to rely on the parents' love despite those stresses and strains. Now, if a child knows he is adopted, there is never quite that degree of trust and dependence. There is always the unspoken, perhaps even unconscious fear, 'If I argue or disagree or fight to become a person in my own right, they will throw me out. After all, they have no obligation to take care of me. I am just someone they took in and can just as easily throw out.' It is like a lifelong wound that never quite heals."

"Doctor, based on your long experience with children, young and old, based on your observation of the child in question here, have you formed an opinion as to the proper disposition of the child currently named Scott William Salem?"

"I have indeed, Mr. Clement."

"What is your opinion, Doctor?"

"There is no question in my mind that this child would be best served by being returned to his natural parents."

"Thank you, Dr. Blessing. Your witness, Mr. Henderson."

Aware of the tension this testimony had created in the two clients who sat by his side, Paul Henderson reached under the table to pat Christie Salem on her cold hand. Then, taking every advantage of his age, he rose slowly. He approached the witness giving evidence of being a tired and troubled man.

He consulted his notes. "Ah, yes, Dr. Blessing. This—this study you refer to, concerning the experience of adopted children who get into trouble with the law—you said that was done by a psychiatrist in New York?"

"Yes, a very reputable woman, long experience in the field. Excellent record," Blessing volunteered.

"I'm glad to hear that," Henderson remarked. "Just one thing troubles me. Did she do a corresponding study of adopted young people who do *not* get into trouble with the law?"

Blessing smiled in a most condescending manner. "My dear man, the purpose of her study was to investigate and codify the experience of adopted young men in the criminal justice system."

"Then may I ask what relevance it has to this case? Since we are dealing with a two-and-a-half-year-old boy with no criminal tendencies that anyone has yet observed! Unless by some chance *you* detected such tendencies in your study of the boy."

Blessing's bald head blushed to an even deeper shade of red, but before he could respond, Henderson continued, "Now, Doctor, do I recall correctly that you found some . . . some undefined and mysterious something that, though Scott Salem has all the characteristics of a normal two-and-a-half-year-old, 'disturbed' you?"

"Yes, that reflects what I found. And I so stated."

" 'Disturbed' being such a general term, can we perhaps qualify that? Would you say it disturbed you merely a little?"

"Much more than a little," Blessing corrected.

" 'Much more than a little,' " Henderson echoed. "Then would you say it disturbed you a lot?"

" 'A lot' is hardly a proper designation for the kind of reservations I felt," Blessing said with disdain. "Professionally it disturbed me to such a degree that I felt it was highly material to arriving at my opinion."

"I see," Henderson remarked gravely, then continued, "Doctor, I must say I was deeply impressed by your long and distinguished record in the field of pediatric psychiatry. But, like that certain 'disturbed' intuition *you* had about Scotty Salem, I have a similar 'disturbing' intuition about *you*."

"I beg your pardon," Blessing exclaimed, looking to the bench for some reprimand for this old lawyer who dared attack his record.

"Once I heard you say you drew that conclusion about Scotty, I asked myself, as I now ask you: In your long career, how many boys of two and a half have you examined who have been the subject of such a media-intensive lawsuit? How many such boys have you examined who have been pursued by the press, photographed by television, been forced to be secreted out of their homes up a back alley to be taken to playschool in order to avoid the hounds of hell, known to us as the media? How many, Doctor?"

"Not many," Blessing was forced to concede, then started to add, "However, that does not—"

But Henderson was quicker with his next question: "And, Doctor, how many two-and-a-half-year-olds have you had experience with who have, in close succession, been tested and examined by six different psychiatrists?"

216

"Not . . . not many," Blessing conceded.

"Doctor, I ask you now, in your professional opinion, might a child of two and a half, subjected to all these intrusive and unusual assaults upon his tender young consciousness, react in such a way as to give you that 'disturbed' feeling you tell us you experienced, which formed a major part of your opinion?"

"Mr. Henderson, that is a far-fetched conclusion. Shall we say, an exercise in laymen's psychiatry," Blessing replied with a sad shake of the head and a demeaning smile.

"Then are you now prepared to state without reservation that my supposition is completely wrong?" Henderson demanded. "Because if you are, I would like, and I am sure this Court would like, such a firm statement from you."

Blessing flushed slightly. The witness chair seemed too small for his bulk as he shifted nervously.

"In a science like psychiatry, such questions cannot be answered with absolutes," he replied.

"Yet you did not hesitate to express an 'absolute' opinion as to the proper disposition of the child involved in this lawsuit!" Henderson thundered back.

With that, and before Blessing could respond, Henderson turned away and shuffled back to his table.

Clement rose in his place to ask a single question. "Dr. Blessing, did anything which occurred in this cross-examination lead you to change your opinion that the best interests of this child demand that he be returned to his natural parents?"

"No, sir, it did not!" Blessing affirmed strongly.

Clement's next witness was an elderly woman whom, at great expense to Brett, he had brought in by ambulette from a seniors' home.

She steered herself into the courtroom in a mechanized wheelchair. And was given permission to testify from that vantage point.

She identified herself as Belle Werner. She gave as her address the Senior Care Home allied with the hospital where Lori Adams had worked during her pregnancy and where she was delivered of her infant son.

Clement approached this witness with considerable warmth and indulgence.

"Now, I must ask you just a few questions. And you take all the time you need to answer."

"Ask me anything except my age," the woman responded dryly.

Clement chuckled to humor the old woman, who did not appear to enjoy it.

"Now, Ms. Werner . . ."

"*Mrs.* Werner," she corrected. "Werner and me, we didn't just live together like they do today. We were married."

"Yes, of course," Clement agreed, to get on with her testimony. "Mrs. Werner, tell His Honor when you first met Lori Manning and under what circumstances."

Old, shriveled, her white hair so fine one could see her pink scalp, the feisty woman swung her chair around to look up at Judge Hart.

"Well, Your Honor, I was in the geriatric wing of the hospital. They were trying to figure out if I just suffered loss of memory or had that—you know—that Alzheimer's disease that's going around these days."

To coax her into the testimony he was after, Clement reminded her, "Mrs. Werner, when and how did you meet Lori Manning?"

She half-turned in Clement's direction. "Young man, I'm talking to the judge. Don't interrupt! Now, Your Honor, it turns out that I didn't have—"

Once more Clement interrupted. "Mrs. Werner . . . Lori Manning?"

To which Judge Hart responded, "Mr. Clement, the witness is addressing the bench. Go on, Mrs. Werner."

"Well, as I was saying, they were trying to figure it out. Loss of memory? Or this here Alzheimer's? And that's when Lori came on the scene. Why she was like a breath of spring in that wing of the hospital. Here she was, nineteen, maybe twenty, so pretty and blond, and—and young—just young. She was like, well, like my granddaughter. She was everyone's granddaughter. We all waited

218

for her to come on the floor every morning. She was so cheery. And so helpful. More than one man and woman on that floor used to say, 'I wish my own grandchildren were so nice and loving.' "

Belle Werner looked up at the judge, studied his face, then decided, "No, Your Honor, I guess you're too young to have grandchildren. Children, maybe?"

"I'm afraid not, Mrs. Werner," Judge Hart responded.

"Too bad. Then again, maybe not too bad. You have no idea the headache kids can be in these times."

Fearing she was wandering off the subject, Clement suggested, "Mrs. Werner—When Lori became pregnant . . ."

"I was getting to that," she reprimanded. She turned back to the judge. "Mr. Clement was wrong about that. Lori didn't *become* pregnant while she was at the hospital. She *was* pregnant before she ever got there. Of course, we didn't know the man was a big television star. Not that he was at the time. That came later. But once we knew she was pregnant, we all started to—to root for her. As if when she had her baby, we would become grandparents all over again. We went through her whole pregnancy with her. When we heard she gave birth to a boy, you shoulda seen the excitement and the happiness there was in that wing. It was like we were all family. And she was a big part of it. She was the most considerate and kind person we ever met. None of us will ever forget her."

This time Clement waited to make sure Mrs. Werner had finished before he asked, "Mrs. Werner, based on your long observation of Lori Manning over the months of her pregnancy, did you come to any conclusions as to what kind of mother she would make?"

"I certainly did," Mrs. Werner declared. "Any young woman so sweet and kind and considerate would be a wonderful mother. Just wonderful." She turned back to Judge Hart. "The best, Your Honor, the very best!"

"Thank you, Mrs. Werner," Clement said. Then, with a slight smile, he invited sweetly, "Mr. Henderson, your witness."

Henderson sat at his table rubbing his fingers across his cheek as if trying to determine if he needed a shave. Then he replied, "No questions. Excuse the witness."

Disappointed, Mrs. Werner swung her mechanized chair about to rebuke Clement. "You said this old man was going to ask me a lot of nasty questions."

Judge Hart intervened. "Mrs. Werner, it's up to Mr. Henderson to decide whether to cross-examine you."

"And I had so many good answers," she said mournfully.

"Now," the judge continued, "you are free to go. Except I would like to ask you a question."

"Anything, Your Honor."

"Did the doctors ever come to any conclusion?"

"About what?"

"Was it loss of memory or Alzheimer's?" Judge Hart asked.

"Neither," she replied. "Seems I just got bored. Lost interest. Didn't have *reason* to remember anything. Which all changed once Lori came into our wing. She gave us all something to care about. To be interested in. Something besides Oprah and Geraldo and all that stuff."

"Thank you, Mrs. Werner, for taking the time and trouble to come here and testify."

"Wasn't much trouble, Your Honor. And as for time, it's all I got. Though I don't have too much of that left," she replied. She started to wheel herself through the gate of the railing up the aisle where the uniformed attendants held the double doors open for her.

"Your next witness, Mr. Clement!"

"Your Honor, since the hour is late, and the testimony and cross-examination of my next witness are certain to be quite lengthy, I would like a recess until ten o'clock tomorrow."

"Mr. Henderson?" the judge sought his approval.

"Who is that witness?" Henderson asked.

"Lori Manning," Clement informed him.

Since to anticipate testifying would give Lori Manning a long, stressful, sleepless night, Henderson was quite amenable. "Ten o'clock tomorrow will be fine with me."

"So ordered," Hart announced, and rapped his gavel to end the session.

# Chapter 36

That evening was one of the rare times that Dr. Karen Craig arrived home before her husband, Judge Hart.

Their housekeeper, Hilda, took that to be a bad sign.

"You're not feeling well, Doctor," Hilda concluded.

"I'm fine. Just fine," Karen reassured her.

"But so early . . ." Hilda commented to explain her assumption.

"The surgery we had scheduled was delayed," Karen explained.

"Oh, I see," Hilda said. Then, ever curious, she asked, "Is that a good delay? Or a bad delay? I mean, sometimes they find out the patient doesn't need it. But other times they find out it wouldn't do any good anyhow. Which kind was this?"

*One of these days Hilda will be asking to see the MRI results,* Karen thought. *But she means well, and she wants so much to be part of the family.*

"Neither, Hilda. It wasn't an emergency, so we simply decided to hold the patient over until tomorrow."

"Very good," Hilda agreed, adding her expertise to the decision. Then, as long as they seemed to be on common ground, Hilda took the opportunity to observe, "He . . . he has a great deal on his mind these days."

"Does he?"

"In the morning he has no time for a real breakfast. And in the evening he has no appetite. Is he all right?"

Though annoyed at Hilda's presumption as to her husband's condition, Karen explained, "He's presiding over a very difficult case right now."

"Oh, don't I know," Hilda lamented. "All you hear on the radio and television these days—Baby Brett this and Baby Brett that. And who should be his real mother? This one is blond and pretty. And that one is dark and pretty. And both are—"

The sound of the door from the garage interrupted. In a hushed voice Hilda said, "That's him. We better not talk anymore."

Stifling her amusement at Hilda's attitude of intimacy, Karen agreed, "Yes. We'd better not."

To the surprise of both of them, Judge Hart entered in a rather cheerful mood. Smiling, he set down his bulky briefcase to lift the cover of the cast-iron pot on the stove. One sniff was enough.

"Beef stew! With onions and those small potatoes! Hilda, how do you always know exactly what I crave for supper?"

"I try, Your Honor, I try," she responded modestly, blushing at the compliment.

As they left the kitchen, Karen whispered, "You've made her day. Only problem, now we'll get beef stew every week until Christmas."

"Wouldn't upset me," Jud Hart said.

"The way you feel tonight, it seems nothing would upset you," she remarked. "I thought you resisted cases like this."

"I do. But today there walked into my courtroom—I should say there *rode* into my courtroom—no, that's not exactly right either. There *wheeled* into my courtroom a refreshingly delightful old lady. Gave me something to look forward to when *we* get old. Doctor, may I amend that statement? When *I* get old. Because *you* are never going to get old."

He set down his briefcase to take her by the arms and kiss her on her pert nose.

"You *are* in a good mood tonight," she said.

By the time he finished describing to her the appearance and attitude of Mrs. Belle Werner, she, too, was chuckling. But not for long.

He broke the mood by remarking, "Of course, tomorrow it starts."

"What?" she asked, curious about the mysterious and depressing "it."

"The bloodletting."

"The what?"

"Bloodletting," he reiterated. "In cases like this each couple is determined to prove that the other couple is unfit to be the parents of the child. First, they introduce character witnesses on their own behalf. Followed by psychiatric testimony. But the real down-and-dirty fighting comes when each party attacks the character of the other. That, I'm afraid, will start tomorrow."

"Can't you prevent that? Rule it out of order or something?"

"Since the issue is between two parties as to who are the legal parents of little Scott, character is of the utmost relevance. So the attorney representing the Mannings has a right to attack the character of the Salems. And their lawyer has a right to fight back by attacking the character of the Mannings. That usually happens when each lawyer cross-examines the other mother. It is a nasty, demeaning spectacle. A bloodletting. Let's have a drink."

Later that evening Dr. Karen Craig studied the scans and the MRIs in preparation for her surgery the next day. Judge Judson Hart was refining the notes he had made during the day's testimony in *Manning* v. *Salem*. Until Karen suddenly exclaimed, "I know what's wrong!"

"You discovered the source of that tumor?" he assumed.

"I discovered what troubles me so about your case."

"Angel, please . . ."

Undismayed, Karen persevered, "It's like modern warfare. The battle rages between two opposing armies, but it's the poor civilians who get killed."

Jud Hart looked up from his notes. "I think you've been watching too many Sunday-morning discussion shows on television."

"Your Family Reunification Law. Isn't that the same one that gives abused children back to their parents?"

"Under certain circumstances, yes," he conceded with considerable irritation. "The purpose of the law is to rehabilitate broken families. Wherever possible. Since there *is* such a law, we must apply it to *all* cases."

"Crazy," was all she said.

"Holding the family unit together is a very sound sociological concept!" he insisted.

"Even when abused kids given back to their families end up dead?"

"Unfortunately such things have happened," he granted. "But they have nothing to do with *my* case!"

"There *is* a common thread . . ." she suggested.

"There is no issue of child abuse here. None!" he pointed out with considerable exasperation.

"Not yet," Karen observed.

Jud Hart slapped down his legal pad on his desk.

"What does that mean? 'Not yet'?"

"The bloodletting. That vicious battle between two sets of parents with conflicting rights. When all the time the real party whose rights should be protected sits there in the middle like an innocent civilian in a war zone. And nobody, nobody, speaks up for him. I consider that abuse of the child's rights," Karen argued.

"The problem is they are *both* speaking up for him!" Jud argued back. "That's what this lawsuit is about."

"From your description they'll both be too busy attacking each other to speak for him, what he needs. . . ."

"Karrie . . ." he interrupted.

"I know," she acknowledged his reproach.

"This is exactly the reason I refuse to discuss pending cases with you. You take one side or the other. And if I don't agree, suddenly I'm the villain."

He turned back to his notes, which he now scribbled with a vengeance.

She resumed her study of those MRIs.

This time he broke the silence.

Intended as both explanation and justification, he proclaimed it as doctrine: "Our law does not make provision for the child to be represented by counsel in such cases!"

Applying herself to her scans to avoid any appearance of taking issue with him, she observed softly, "Does it provide that he *can't* have a lawyer?"

"It is *my* obligation to protect his rights!" Jud Hart said, putting a cap on any further discussion.

After some moments of silence Karen observed, "Sometimes in surgery, by accident, we sever an artery and get spattered with blood when we least expect it."

"And what does that have to do with anything?" he demanded.

"With all that bloodletting you talked about, how can that little boy's rights escape getting some blood spattered on them? You can call it *Manning* v. *Salem* and pretend there are only two parties. But there are three. And the third is an innocent two-and-a-half-year-old boy, a civilian in a war zone, helpless."

"Karen! I refuse to discuss this any further! I will apply the law to this case as I do in all other cases. It is public policy that families be kept together, and, if apart, they be reunited. And that's that!"

No more was said that night.

# Chapter 37

✤

Lori Manning rose from her place at the counsel table. Brett pressed her hand warmly to encourage her. She was attired in her simple periwinkle-blue dress, trimmed only by a modest white lace collar. Her blond hair was in a simple loose arrangement that made her look even younger than her twenty-four years.

As Clement had instructed, she came forward to the foot of the witness box and raised her right hand as the clerk administered the oath. Once she had replied, "I do so swear," the clerk asked her her name and address for the court record.

Henry Clement guided her through a number of routine questions: place of birth, early years, schooling, family background, leading up to the time she left home to go to New York to pursue an acting career.

His questions and Lori's answers were all intended to establish her as an innocent, well-intentioned young woman whose predicament was the result of misfortune rather than wrongdoing.

"Now, Lori, tell Judge Hart in your own words about your relationship with Brett Manning, who is now your husband."

"We were both in acting class together, just starting out. He was working at Joe Allen's."

"Joe Allen's?" Clement asked for clarification.

"A restaurant in New York. In the theater district. He hires young actors and actresses as waiters so they can continue with their training and keep looking for acting jobs. Joe is very good that way."

"I see," Clement said. "Go on, please."

"Well . . . Brett and I . . . we worked there at the same time, and studied in the same acting classes. So we kind of—"

"You fell in love?" Clement assisted.

"Yes. Then, having so little money, we figured it would make sense, economically, to move in together," Lori admitted.

"Tell me, Lori, at that time, in New York, among young actors and actresses, was that a usual thing?"

"You mean, was it the thing to do?"

Clement would have preferred she had phrased it differently, but he agreed, "Yes, yes. Was what you did usual, accepted conduct among young people?"

Irritated by the spin Clement was trying to put on every one of Lori's statements, Judge Hart intervened.

"Mr. Clement, you may assume that this Court takes judicial notice that in these times young people do live together out of wedlock in New York. In Chillicothe. And in Spokane. Just let the witness tell her own story."

He looked down from the bench. "Mrs. Manning, you are doing fine. Just continue."

The judge having eased the situation for her, Lori continued, more briskly, "We'd been living together for five and a half months when I discovered I was pregnant."

"What did you do then, Lori?" Clement asked.

"I told Brett."

"And what did he say?"

"He wanted us to get married right away," Lori replied.

"But you *didn't* get married. Why not?"

"For us to get married, for me to have the baby, would have meant he would have to take a job with one of his relations who ran a tire business."

As he had warned her he would, Clement asked, "Lori, that is good, honest work, isn't it?"

"Yes, sir," Lori replied.

"Then why did you refuse?" Clement asked, anticipating that if he did not, Henderson surely would.

"Because . . . because I know how it was in my family. Early in my mother and father's marriage he wanted to risk everything they had to go into business with a partner. My mother was pregnant with my brother, my older brother, and she wouldn't let my father take the risk. But his friend scrounged around among family and friends and put together enough money to buy one of the early McDonald's franchises. That man became a millionaire. My father never forgave my mother. All my life I heard him blame her, saying, 'If not for you, I'd be a rich man. Not a hired hand slaving away for a miserable bastard of a boss.' All my life, until the day I left home to come to New York, I heard that."

"And, my dear?" Clement urged.

"I didn't want Brett to feel that way about me. I didn't want my child to be brought up in a house where he would hear such bitterness every day of his life."

Lori ended in tears. Honest tears.

Clement pressed on. "Under those circumstances did it occur to you to have an abortion?"

"We . . . we talked about it," she admitted.

"And?"

"I couldn't do it. Once I decided that, I didn't want to be a burden to Brett or stand in the way of his career. So I went back home."

"And what happened then?"

"My father, bitter as always, made that impossible."

"So there you were, a young woman, pregnant and alone, no one to fall back on, desperate—"

"Mr. Clement," Judge Hart intervened, "we get the picture without your dramatic embellishments. The witness will continue."

Lori proceeded to relate her experiences during her pregnancy, her work at the hospital, her meticulous care as to diet and exercise to make sure her baby would be born healthy.

"Lori, tell the Court. During the time of your pregnancy, did you ever hear from the father of your child?"

"Yes. He would send me letters. Sometimes with money. Ten, fifteen dollars. I don't know how he could have afforded even that little."

"Lori, tell His Honor how you decided to give up your baby for adoption."

"It wasn't easy . . ." Lori began. "But I couldn't see any other way. If I kept him, I'd have no way to work to support him and still take care of him, and I promised myself he would never become a welfare baby. I wanted him to have a real chance at a good life. Oh, there were times I would think I could do it all. That was at night. But by dawn I knew how impossible that was in the real world. . . ."

"So, Lori, is it fair to say that you were desperate, in fear and turmoil?"

"Mind you, Your Honor," Henderson called out, "I have no objection to Mr. Clement testifying. Provided he takes the oath and is subject to cross-examination."

"Mr. Henderson, your objection is sustained, but your sarcasm is not."

"Lori," Clement resumed, "in your own words, tell His Honor your state of mind at the time you were forced to decide on the adoption."

"I was frightened and desperate," she echoed his words. "Yet I knew I had to do something. And do it quickly. Because . . ."

When she faltered, Clement coaxed, "Because?"

"If I didn't do it quickly, I would never be able to do it. Then I would be facing all the things I had come to fear. So, for my baby's own good, I did what I had to."

"Exactly how did you go about it, Lori?"

"First, I determined that my baby would not be given to just any family who happened to be next on some adoption agency's list. I wanted to see them for myself."

"And did you actually, shall we call it, interview such families?"

"Yes, sir," Lori replied. "The first four . . . I just didn't have a right feeling about them. But the fifth couple—"

"The man and woman seated at that counsel table?" Clement asked to identify them.

"Yes, sir."

"You, shall we say, 'accepted' them?"

"Yes, sir."

Anticipating Henderson's line of attack on Lori's most vulnerable area, Clement asked, "Lori, since in your own words you have told this Court that you personally accepted the Salems as adoptive parents for your infant, when and why did you change your mind about them?"

"Soon," Lori replied.

"Soon?" Clement pretended to be surprised. "Why?"

"The first time I saw on the television news the story of an adopted baby who had been abused . . . abused to the point of death . . . I began to ask myself, what have I done? I saw those people only twice for maybe an hour. Yes, they seemed like nice people. But how could I be sure? I didn't know who they were. Had no way of finding them. They might be doing anything to my baby . . . anything. That's how my fear started. Then with each story on the television news or in the papers about another adopted baby or foster baby abused, killed, I would start to cry and couldn't stop. I would have nightmares for weeks after, I was so tormented. I would think, how do I know that baby wasn't *my* baby, *my* son? I can't rest until he is back in my arms again. Safe. I want him back. I must have him back. . . . I thought that feeling would grow less strong with time. And that eventually it would go away."

"And did it?" Clement asked.

"No. It grew stronger and stronger every day. Especially after what's been in the newspapers and on television this last year."

As he had prearranged, Clement asked, "Exactly what do you mean by that, Lori?"

"I kept reading and hearing about all kinds of diseases being discovered in children. And the only hope they have is to get blood or bone marrow that only a close blood relative can give them. And I think, my God, what if my son develops such an illness and I'm the only one . . . or Brett's the only one . . . who is compatible, is able to save him? When I think of that, I know that no one can love him or help him like his own mother. His blood says he's mine. The law says he's mine. I want him back. I want him back. . . ."

She broke down and wept.

Softly Clement said, "Your witness, Mr. Henderson."

Not disposed to cross-examine a witness already in tears, Henderson addressed the bench: "Your Honor, for the sake of the witness, may we have a fifteen-minute recess?"

"This Court will stand in recess for half an hour so the witness may compose herself." Judge Hart emphasized that with a sharp rap of his gavel.

Just as Judge Hart was stepping down from the bench, there was a flurry of excitement outside the courtroom.

He ordered the uniformed courtroom attendant to investigate the nature of the outburst. But before he reached the door, it burst open. A chunky woman, with straggling hair and carrying a large poster, entered to cry out, "Every child has only one true mother! And no damn judge can say otherwise!"

The attendant looked to the judge, who signaled him to remove the woman. Once the door was closed, once quiet had been restored, Clement jumped up to say, "Your Honor, I wish to assure you that neither the plaintiff nor anyone connected with him had anything to do with that shameful display."

"I understand, Mr. Clement," the judge assured him. "This case has stirred up considerable public emotion. On both sides."

# Chapter 38

❖

Once court had reconvened, a dry-eyed Lori Manning resumed the witness stand. Paul Henderson came forward shuffling a number of sheets of notes in his fumbling manner.

Christie and Bill Salem exchanged nervous glances, concerned that they had indeed retained a lawyer who was too elderly for the difficult task ahead.

Henderson cleared his throat and began:

"Mrs. Manning, would you describe for me the characteristics you found in Christine and William Salem that induced you to believe that they would be proper, loving, and supportive parents for your infant son?"

"Describe . . ." Lori temporized.

"What did they look like? What did they say? What was your impression? What convinced you, 'Yes, here are the two people to whom I would entrust my son for the rest of his life'?"

"They . . . they were nice looking, nicely dressed, clean, neat. They told me about their home, the nursery for my baby, the plans they had if they adopted him. All those things made me feel they could be good adoptive parents."

"Mrs. Manning, Lori, tell me, has anything happened in the last two and a half years that has led you to believe that they are *not* 'nicely dressed, clean, neat, have a home with a room for the

232

child, with plans for his future'? Do they look any different now than they did that day?"

Lori hesitated, then had to admit, "No, sir, they do not."

"Lori, do you know that the child who is the subject of this lawsuit has been seen and tested by six—mind you, six—different psychiatrists, four retained by your husband, and all six have found him to be a well-adjusted two-and-a-half-year-old?"

"Yes, yes, sir. I've been told that," Lori admitted.

"So, Lori, as far as you know, have the Salems lived up to every promise, every expectation, that convinced you that they would be proper parents for the child?"

Lori glanced toward Clement, then had to admit, "Yes, sir."

"Lori, are you aware that as part of the adoption William and Christine Salem agreed to pay all the medical expenses you incurred during your pregnancy and the birth?"

"Yes, sir," Lori admitted.

"Yet you come into court and say these good people, who lived up to all their promises, are now not proper people to continue being the parents of that child?"

"He's ours! He always was. He always will be. No matter what name he bears, no matter where he lives, he is ours! Brett's and mine. And no one can change that!" Lori protested.

"And that is the only reason we are in this courtroom today?"

"Yes!" Lori said defiantly.

"May I suggest a different possibility? Having found these two fine, hardworking people with a good home, with a need to have and love a baby, you thought, what a wonderful place to store my child for safekeeping while I and my boyfriend get on with our lives. Then, when we are able, we will return and take our child back. Isn't that the truth, Mrs. Manning?" Henderson thundered.

"That's a lie!" Lori protested, and began to cry.

The stir in the first two spectator rows reserved for the media told Judge Hart what would be the banner lead on the evening television news and in the morning newspapers.

He gaveled the courtroom to silence.

"Mr. Henderson?" he asked.

"Just a few more questions, Your Honor."

"Mrs. Manning, do you wish another recess?" the judge asked.

Through her tears Lori replied, "No, Your Honor."

Henderson continued, "Mrs. Manning, do you know the meaning of the word 'fraud'?"

"Fraud? Stealing . . ." Lori replied.

"According to *Webster's Unabridged Dictionary*, fraud is defined as—now follow me closely, Lori—'fraud, an instance and an act of trickery and deceit especially when involving misrepresentation, an act of deluding—"

"Your Honor," Clement rose to protest, "this line of questioning is not only irrelevant but intended to obfuscate this issue for lack of more substantial arguments."

"Your Honor, I ask leave to continue subject to connection," Henderson replied.

Judge Hart considered Henderson's request, then ruled, "You may continue."

"Lori, Webster defines 'fraud in fact' in the following terms. I quote: 'an intentional misrepresentation, concealment or nondisclosure for the purpose of inducing another, in reliance upon it, to part with some valuable thing or surrender a legal right.' And Webster continues: 'a false—'"

"Your Honor," Clement interrupted with an air of bored impatience.

"Continue, Mr. Henderson, but don't subject us to reading the entire unabridged dictionary."

"Webster continues: 'a false representation of a matter of fact by words or conduct, by false or misleading allegations or by the concealment' . . . mind you, Lori, *'concealment of what should have been disclosed, that deceives or is intended to deceive another so he shall act upon it to his legal injury.'* Do you understand what that means, Lori?"

"Yes, I think I do," Lori admitted tentatively, for she could not discern the old lawyer's purpose.

"Isn't that why we're here in this courtroom today, Lori?" Henderson thundered like a righteous prophet of old.

"Sorry . . . I . . . I don't understand," Lori protested, looking to Clement for help.

As Clement started to rise, Judge Hart anticipated him by calling, "Mr. Clement, sit down!"

Henderson glared at Lori Manning, demanding a direct response. When none was forthcoming, the old lawyer continued, "Fraud, Lori, *'concealment of what should have been disclosed.'* Lori? Well, Lori?"

Lori did not respond but only shook her head in tense puzzlement.

"Fraud!" Henderson shouted. "False representation of a matter of fact. Henry Higgins, Lori! Naming Henry Higgins as the father of your child! False representation of a matter of fact intended to deceive another. Intended to deceive these decent people who in all innocence, with only love and honest intentions, took into their home, into their lives, into their hearts, a three-day-old infant. Yet now, two and a half years later, you come into court to claim him. Have you no shame, woman? By God, you have given the word 'fraud' a new and more disgraceful definition!"

By the time he was finished, Lori Manning was sobbing loudly.

Henderson turned back to his table, where Christine waited to plead in a painful whisper, "Mr. Henderson, please, she's suffered enough. Just . . . just leave her alone."

"Christie, do you want to keep Scotty?" Henderson whispered in turn.

"You know I do."

"Then let me do what I have to do," the old lawyer replied.

Henderson withheld further questions until Lori had sniffled back to a calmer state. Then he resumed, "Mrs. Manning, would you say that a woman who was guilty of such misrepresentation, who was so calculating as to plan such a devious strategy—"

"Your Honor," Clement intervened, "there is no basis for counsel to impute to the witness *any* strategy, much less a *devious* strategy."

"Oh, no?" Henderson demanded, wheeling on Clement. "What do *you* call it, Counselor? A young woman who deliberately poisons the adoption of an innocent child, who misleads these honest defendants by deliberately misstating the father's name. Thereby creating a legal loophole through which they both now conspire to take that child from these two good people? What do you call that, Counselor? I call it fraud in the inception. A very devious strategy. And if you need proof of that, what are we doing here in this courtroom today?"

The media representatives reacted so loudly in Henderson's support that Judge Hart threatened to clear the courtroom.

"Gentlemen, approach the bench!" When both counsel stood before him, he spoke in a whisper, an authoritative whisper, "You will both refrain from such arguments until the time for your summations. This case is fraught with enough emotion without trying to stir up more. We are dealing here not simply with legal questions or witnesses who can be cross-examined without regard for their feelings, but with the deepest and most painful of human emotions."

Both men nodded gravely.

"Mr. Henderson, do you have any further questions for this witness?"

"No, Your Honor."

"Mr. Clement?"

"Just one."

"Ask it, and let's get on," Judge Hart ordered.

Henry Clement turned back to his witness, who was twisting her damp handkerchief and rocking pathetically in her chair.

In a voice deliberately intended to calm her, Clement asked, "Lori, at the time you used a fictitious name for the father of your child, did you have any knowledge of the law, knowledge that would later enable your husband to reopen the adoption of your son?"

"No, sir, I did not," Lori Manning responded in all honesty.

"Thank you," Clement said with an air of finality, as if the curtain were descending on her appearance in this trial.

As she was about to rise, Paul Henderson asked, "If Your Honor will permit . . ."

Judge Hart nodded his consent.

The old lawyer turned to the witness.

"Mrs. Manning—Lori—let us suppose that three years from now, four, five, ten years from now, one of those genetic illnesses you mentioned were to strike Scott Salem, and his survival, his very life, depended on your willingness to give up part of your blood or your bone marrow, or even one of your kidneys, would you refuse?"

"Your Honor!" Clement rose to protest loudly. "That question is not only hypothetical but grossly unfair. An obvious trick which has no relevance, no legal bearing on this trial. I demand that it be withdrawn!"

Judge Hart looked to Paul Henderson. "Counselor?"

"Your Honor, I did not raise the question of blood compatibility or genetic homogeneity. Counsel and counsel's witness introduced that subject. And I was so fascinated by it that I decided to pursue it to its logical end. I withdraw nothing. And I urge the Court to instruct the witness to respond."

"So ordered," Judge Hart ruled.

At a loss to answer, Lori looked to her counsel, who dared not make an obvious attempt to coach her since the judge was staring at him.

Finally, on her own, and despite realizing that it could weaken her chance of regaining her son, Lori Manning responded, "I would do whatever I could to save him. After all, he is my son."

# Chapter 39

Angered as he was, this time Judge Hart dispensed with such amenities as serving coffee. Instead, he came to his point at once and quite succinctly.

"Gentlemen, I'm well aware that in this case, very much like lawsuits for libel, an attorney is tempted into expeditions of character assassination."

Sensitive to the fact that the judge's criticism was aimed at his particularly hostile cross-examination of Lori Manning, Paul Henderson was quick to reply.

"Your Honor, you may object to my characterization of Mrs. Manning's part in this unfortunate situation. But I don't think you can quarrel with the substance. This entire heartwrenching dilemma could have been avoided for my clients, and also for Mrs. Manning, if she had been forthcoming and truthful about the correct identity of the natural father of little Scott Salem."

Clement argued in return, "Let's keep the record straight, Paul. It's not Lori Manning who is asserting the right to reopen this adoption. It is the father. Who, by any test, was innocent and unaware of any name but his own being used at the time."

"That argument is specious! As phony as the name Henry Higgins! Whether it is the husband or the wife who claims the child, they should both be barred from such a remedy by virtue of gross fraud in the inception! I would hate to think that any court would even consider taking a child from decent, honorable, unsuspecting people like the Salems to give him to a couple who would practice such deceit."

"Now, hold on, Paul!" Clement exploded. "Your clients don't come into court with such clean hands!"

"What the hell do you mean by that?" Henderson demanded. "In all innocence and good faith they took that infant in, gave him a good, clean, warm, loving home. You want to deny the parents who gave him all that the right to consider him their son? How cruel and heartless can you be?"

"The law doesn't look at it that way, as you damn well know!" Clement shot back. "God knows, you've been in practice long enough! Or has it been *too* long?"

A flush of anger rose into the pale, wrinkled cheeks of Paul Henderson. "In my day attorneys were a hell of a lot more ethical than what I see going on around me now!"

"Gentlemen, gentlemen!" Judge Hart intervened to prevent the confrontation becoming even more bitter. "I know these cases generate the strongest of emotions. And the bitterness that goes with that. Now, you will both go out and make your points in a civil manner. And in accord with the rules of examination and cross-examination. Save your comments for your summations. Mr. Clement, am I correct that you have finished with the presentation of your case?"

"Yes, Your Honor."

"Mr. Henderson, I assume your first witnesses are present and ready to testify. See you in the courtroom in fifteen minutes!"

Both attorneys withdrew, leaving Judge Hart to ponder what he had just witnessed.

*If only such cases could be decided on submitted briefs,* Judge Hart thought, *with no need to face the warring parties. Or to give attorneys the opportunity to attack the character of the opposing parties. But it was ever thus, as the phrase runs, and will continue to be in these cases.*

*Each attorney trying to prove the other woman is so lacking in character as to be unfit to be a proper mother. If I were to believe them both, I would take the child away and give it to some stranger.*

*I would take the child away and give it to some stranger,* Judge Hart repeated silently.

*Not that I would contemplate doing such a thing. But it makes me realize that in the turmoil, the harsh and angry sounds of battle drown out the voice of the most important party to this dispute. Clement argues, and well, for the natural mother. Henderson in his way is equally zealous on behalf of the adoptive mother.*

*But for a little two-and-a-half-year-old boy presently named Scott Salem there is no one to speak. As Karen said.*

Much as he had resented her intrusion, she was right when she argued on behalf of the child. The trouble with spending a lifetime in the law, one's mind could become encrusted with the statute law and the endless cases flowing from it. While the human values faded into the background.

He pondered for a moment, trying to recall a particular name. When he could not, he buzzed his secretary on the phone.

"Evelyn, remember that young lawyer, rather pretty, the kind of pretty that makes men assume she hasn't got a brain in her head? You know the one I mean?"

"I'm afraid I don't. Not from that description."

"You must!" the judge insisted.

Seeking some more definitive clue, Evelyn asked, "Maybe if you remember—blond or brunette?"

"Sort of, sort of brownish hair . . ."

That detail did not aid in Evelyn's attempt to recall.

Frustrated, the judge insisted, "You must remember! The one I threatened to hold in contempt."

"Oh, *that* one! The lawyer who had what we used to call a big mouth," Evelyn remarked.

"I assume by that you mean she was vigorous and articulate on behalf of her client," the judge corrected.

"Your Honor, where I come from, same thing," Evelyn explained, then reminded him, "But, if you recall, you decided to drop contempt charges."

"I don't want to charge her. I want to retain her."

At that, Evelyn ceased communicating by telephone and came

bursting into his office. "*You* need a lawyer? Good God, what for?"

"Calm down, Evelyn. Relax. I wish to appoint her to represent an unrepresented party in interest in *Manning* v. *Salem*."

"Unrepresented party in interest?" Evelyn questioned. Then, startled, she asked, "You mean there's someone *else* claiming that child?"

"I mean that child is the unrepresented party. I want that young woman in my office by four o'clock when I get off the bench!"

Instead of leaving at once to carry out the judge's order, as she usually did, this time Evelyn lingered in the open doorway.

"Evelyn, something troubling you?"

"Well . . . Are you allowed to do that? I mean, that's never done in custody cases in this state. Leastways in all the time I've been here. It's always two attorneys representing the two parents. But an attorney for the child . . . Your Honor, I don't know."

"Evelyn, if you're concerned about my being appointed to the State Supreme Court . . ."

"Governor Brady does not favor judges who make new law," Evelyn reminded him.

"Governor Brady is not sitting on this case! So let's get cracking. And if there are any consequences—well, then there will just be . . . consequences."

"I've always wanted to be secretary to a Supreme Court judge. It would be the perfect climax to my career."

"Evelyn, I'm late getting back on the bench. Just do it!"

Paul Henderson had made it a rule when presenting a case: The hard facts first. Only after he had established a solid base did he introduce witnesses whose testimony would supply the emotional values.

He did not vary from his strategy in *Manning* v. *Salem*.

To the surprise of both his adversary and Judge Hart, Henderson called to the stand as the first witness George Hinckley, CPA. As the accountant for William Salem and Handyman, Inc., he testified and produced records that proved beyond doubt that the Salems were financially solid and perfectly able to give their son Scott a comfortable life, assuring him a good education and the opportunity that went with that.

Clement chose not to cross-examine. His manner of refusing was one of disdain for Henderson's tactics.

But the old lawyer plodded on with witnesses who testified to the character of their neighbors. Followed by Dr. Whitmore, the pediatrician who had cared for Scott from the day he was brought home to the Salem family.

Since Henry Clement chose not to cross-examine, by the end of the afternoon Paul Henderson had established that, by any test, Christine and William Salem were well qualified to continue as the parents of two-and-a-half-year-old Scott.

As soon as Judge Hart recessed the trial until ten the next morning, he hurried up to his chambers. Evelyn rose to intercept him before he could reach the door to his private office.

"She's in there," Evelyn whispered.

When he seemed puzzled for the instant, Evelyn reminded him, "That young lawyer you asked me to find."

"Oh, yes, what's her name again?"

"Brook. Nancy Brook. State University Law School. With honors. Twenty-seven. Unmarried." Evelyn added in a lower tone of voice, "Just broke up with her boyfriend. Frankly I think they were living together."

"Evelyn, how in the world . . ." the judge started to ask.

Evelyn anticipated him, "While she was waiting, we just . . . just chatted a little."

" 'Just chatted a little.' Evelyn, you could give lessons to the CIA," Judge Hart said as he started for his private office.

Hart opened the door to find Nancy Brook looking out the window down at the traffic below in Courthouse Plaza. The young woman turned quickly to greet him.

"Your Honor—" she began, "if it's about the Nemery case, we've worked out a visitation schedule. So there is no need for further judicial action."

"This is not about the Nemery case," Hart pointed out.

"Oh . . ." Nancy Brook realized. "Then it must be about that matter of . . . of contempt of court. I can only say, if zeal on behalf of a client is contempt, I plead guilty. And I am willing to face the consequences."

Judge Hart stared across his desk at the attractive young attorney, wondering, was her choice of words by chance or by clever design?

"Young woman, sit down!" he replied. Once she had, he continued, "That was a very noble-sounding speech."

With a hint of a smile that dimpled her pretty face, Nancy Brook replied, "It was also noble-sounding when *you* made it. Twelve years ago."

Startled, Hart asked, "How could you know that?"

"I was in the courtroom that day," Nancy Brook said.

"That day? Why, you couldn't have been more than fifteen years old."

"Our guidance counselor took a group from our high school to the court. To give us a realistic view of the practice of law. Those of us who were thinking of choosing that as a career. I liked the way you stood up and spoke out fearlessly for a client and a cause you believed in. I said to myself, 'I want to be like him.' "

"Ms. Brook, if you're telling me this to escape a contempt charge, you've just wasted a very good argument. You're here because I wish to assign you to represent a client who needs an especially strong, bold attorney. Since he cannot speak up for himself."

"Can't speak up for himself?" Nancy Brook considered. "Does he have a handicap of some kind?"

"According to the practice of this state, yes," Judge Hart replied. "He suffers from being only two and a half years old. The law makes no provision for him to be represented by counsel in what is the most important legal proceeding of his life."

"And you want me to . . ." the young attorney realized.

"Give him the same diligent, outspoken representation you gave Ethel Nemery in that custody case."

"Even if the judge accuses me of contempt?" she asked, not quite smiling.

"*Especially* if the judge accuses you of contempt," Hart replied. "This has already turned into a bitter legal battle. And, I'm afraid, will grow worse. So I want that little boy's rights protected by someone whose sole responsibility is to him."

"I understand, Your Honor," Nancy Brook replied.

"This being an assigned case, your fee won't be large. But I think that little boy is as much entitled to legal representation as some indigent murderer. I'll find the money in the court budget somehow."

# Chapter 40

❧

Though Henry Clement and Paul Henderson both considered the introduction of additional counsel into the case an unwelcome intrusion, neither thought it wise tactics to object.

It fell to Paul Henderson to explain the situation to Christie and Bill.

"We're protecting Scotty's rights!" Christie protested. "Why does he need a lawyer? Isn't that what you're supposed to be doing?"

"Christie," the elderly lawyer replied, "I am your lawyer. Bill's lawyer. Until now Scotty hasn't had a lawyer. For that matter neither has any other child in this state in his situation. But if Hart says he's to have one, we have to go along."

"What does that mean, 'go along'?" Bill asked.

"When this Ms. Brook shows up, welcome her into your home. Give her every opportunity to spend time with Scotty. The one thing you won't do is make her feel she is the enemy."

"It won't be easy," Christie said. "I'll never forget that news-paperwoman who got in here under false pretenses."

"Christie, I want your word," Paul insisted, "no matter how you feel, you will extend to Ms. Brook a friendly welcome. And do nothing to intrude on her contact with your son. Promise?"

Reluctantly, but in good faith, Christie replied, "Promise."

* * *

On Saturday afternoon, a time convenient to the Salems since court was not in session, attorney Nancy Brook paid her first visit to her young client.

When she asked to see Scotty alone, Christie's first impulse was to refuse. But with Paul Henderson's warning in mind she relented.

"Careful going past the nursery. David is asleep," Christie warned.

Although Scott's door was slightly open, Nancy Brook knocked lightly.

"Mommy?" Scott called in a voice that revealed that he was preoccupied.

Nancy pushed the door open wider to discover him sitting on the floor working on an intricate structure of red and white Lego parts. It was an imaginative free-form object.

"Scotty?" she called softly.

At this strange voice the boy looked around. When he had confirmed it was a stranger, he rose to hover protectively over his work in progress.

"Mommy!" he called for help and protection.

At the foot of the stairs Christie started up, until Bill reached out to catch her arm. He shook his head.

"I know. Paul," she said, relenting.

Up in Scotty's room Nancy reassured him. "Mommy is here. Right downstairs. But I came here to see *you*. I want to be your friend."

She could read in his frank blue eyes a curiosity shadowed by fear as well. He drew back from her.

She slipped down to the floor so she was no longer a large strange person looming over him but a companion on his own level.

"Scott, what's this?" she asked, indicating the project.

"Mall . . ." he said, still reluctant to come to her side.

"Of course, I should have recognized it," Nancy said. "It's very nice . . . like the Beaver Mall." It being the closest to the Salems' home and most likely the one with which Scotty would be familiar.

Her recognition of his work induced him to come forward hesitantly to finally join her at his project. He studied the jumbled mass of unused plastic Lego pieces. Finally he selected one. She noticed that his little fingers were very precise in handling the piece. Suddenly, for no reason discernible to her, Scotty put aside the white piece to select a red one of exactly the same size and form.

"Much better," Nancy agreed.

Scotty looked at her. She smiled. He seemed uncertain, until slowly his handsome face seemed to relax. He smiled. A slight smile, unsurely, as if accepting her but only tentatively. Encouraged, she selected a piece to add to his work. He considered it. Then took it to carefully integrate it into his work in progress.

For a few minutes they continued in silence. Scotty carefully selecting a piece, fixing it into place. Then waiting for Nancy to add her piece. Until gradually it became a pleasant collaboration between the two.

Without prologue Scotty asked, "What's your name?"

"Nancy."

The name being new to him, he repeated it.

"But you can call me Nan, if you like. If I can call you Scotty."

"Nan . . ." He spoke it several times and found it suited him better than Nancy.

As they continued working, she gradually asked him about his mommy, his daddy, his new little brother, playschool, friends.

In time as they worked she had him talking freely.

Gradually, Nancy Brook formed certain opinions about her new young client. Shy at first, even fearful, once put at ease he was outgoing. Warm. Friendly. He had good manual dexterity. An eye for structure. He could work diligently and with concentration. For a two-and-a-half-year-old he was not nearly as difficult as two-year-olds were reputed to be. Was that a good sign? Or bad? She would need some professional expertise on that.

"Scotty, I have to leave now," Nancy said.

He did not appear distressed, but he did ask, "Comin' back?"

"Yes, yes. I'll be back," she promised.

Assured, he returned to his work. As she went out the door, he called, "Bye-bye, Nan."

Christie was waiting at the foot of the stairs.

"Well?" she asked, defiant, daring the young attorney to find some fault with her young son.

"He's a delightful child. And when he relaxes, very friendly."

"Make sure you report that to Judge Hart!" Christie insisted.

"Mrs. Salem, I'm not here as a spy for Judge Hart. I've been appointed to protect Scotty's rights in a lawsuit which will determine the rest of his life."

"He belongs *here*! For the rest of his life. With *us*. His mother and his father!" Christie Salem insisted.

"Judge Hart will decide that."

"But you can help."

"Mrs. Salem, I can't discuss this with you. I am Scotty's lawyer, not yours."

Every day Nancy Brook would appear in court, sitting at a small counsel table added to the well of the courtroom. She listened to all the testimony, made her notes, and only occasionally took the opportunity to examine witnesses.

But her main activity was to call on her young client every afternoon after court sessions. With only one thought in mind.

*How can I achieve for him what is in his best interest and conforms with desires he is too young to appreciate and articulate?*

Each day he talked more freely. Showed and shared with her his many toys. One day he took her by the hand into the nursery.

"David," he said. "Brother."

# Chapter 41

Having presented the factual part of his case, Paul Henderson used the intervening weekend to prepare his clients for the crucial part of his defense.

He gathered Bill and Christie in his private office, a room cluttered with files and dusty case books with old state and federal court decisions. Christie and Bill exchanged uneasy glances. Despite his performance when he cross-examined Lori Manning, they still had not achieved complete confidence in his vigor or the surprisingly swift working of his mind when necessary.

"Bill, after a few more character witnesses and Dr. Frank's crucial psychiatric testimony, I will put you on the stand. To lay a foundation for Christie's testimony. From you I will elicit the sequence of events. The tragic death of your first child . . ."

"Must you do that?" Bill asked.

"If *we* don't, Clement *will*," Henderson pointed out. "I'll only touch on it lightly, but I don't want it to appear we're hiding anything. Then we continue with basics. How you learned of the Godmothers' League Adoption Agency. What the agreement was. How you carried out your end of things by submitting financial statements, opening your home to inspection, giving references, your friends, your minister, etcetera. Then, of course, the payment you made to cover the expenses of Mrs. Manning's pregnancy. So much for the factual side of things. And then . . ." Here the old attorney turned to Christie. "I put you on the stand to supply the emotional side, or the crucial side, of our case."

"I thought you didn't *want* me to become emotional," Christie reminded him.

"No matter what Clement says to provoke you, you are to remain calm, answer honestly, and in as few words as necessary. All without losing your temper. Emotion? Yes. But of the right kind. Honest feelings, of course, tears. But not anger. Don't give in to the urge to fight back. Remember, you are trying to impress a judge. A tough, rule-by-the-book judge who holds your son's fate in his hands. So you testify with dignity and control, far above anger and provocation. And yet as a woman of deep feelings and honest emotion."

He then reviewed with her the questions he would ask and listened to her answers, criticizing her when she went on too long or volunteered information Clement could seize on in his cross-examination. At the end of four long hours Christie had learned to modify and control her responses. Brief. Honest. To the point of the question and not beyond.

"My dear, I think you will do very well," Henderson assured her.

But later in the afternoon he phoned Bill.

"William . . . you alone?"

"No, Christie's here. Scotty, of course. And a few neighbors who dropped by to wish us well and offer to baby-sit, cook, or do anything else Christie needs."

"I meant, are you alone on this line?" Henderson asked.

"Yes. Why?"

"Call your doctor. Get a prescription for a sedative for Christie."

"Sedative?"

"After my years in practice I know when a witness is starting to show nerves. They'll get worse over the weekend. By Monday she could be a wreck. Let's head that off. A light sedative. Your doctor will know."

"Okay, sir, anything you say," Bill agreed.

\* \* \*

Monday morning, quite unusual for him, Judge Judson Hart was a little late ascending the bench.

He apologized. "Sorry. Urgent business required my immediate attention."

He did not consider it necessary or appropriate to reveal that the "urgent business" was a lengthy and heated discussion with Karen at breakfast. He was already sufficiently troubled by this case. Her unusual interest only served to add to his discomfort. Without even knowing what his decision would be, she seemed to have him on the defensive about it.

Hart opened the proceedings by announcing, "Mr. Henderson, you may proceed with your case."

The old lawyer presented several character witnesses who testified to the excellent reputation of the Salems in the community, in the church, and among Bill's business associates.

Though throughout the morning his witnesses were performing as well as he had expected, Henderson had been proceeding with an air of caution and hesitation, constantly glancing at the clock on the courtroom wall. Twice he asked for a brief recess to call his office.

Both times he was frustrated. Dr. Grover Frank, the psychiatrist whom Henderson considered a crucial witness, would not be available as arranged. So Henderson carried on with the few witnesses still available to him.

Finally, when he had no alternative, and though it disrupted his original plan, he announced, "I call William Salem to the stand."

Bill held up his right hand to swear the oath, then assumed the chair.

Henderson touched lightly on the unfortunate sudden death of young Billy Salem. From there he led Bill through the various steps leading up to and through the adoption procedure.

"And is it true, William, that on the twenty-fourth of June a judge of this court did sign the order making legally final the adoption of your son Scott?"

"Yes, sir."

"Since that day has he been your son, and been treated in all respects as your son and the son of your wife, Christine?"

"Yes, sir."

"Thank you, William. Your witness, Mr. Clement."

Since Bill's testimony was limited to the facts, and he had testified to them honestly, Clement saw no value in cross-examination. It would only serve to allow Bill to reaffirm his previous testimony. So Clement waived that right.

"I call Mrs. Christine Salem to the stand," Henderson was forced to announce.

With an encouraging press of his hand on hers, Bill sent her on her way to the stand. As she took the oath, Henry Clement watched her closely, trying to assess her state of mind. She appeared to be more composed than he expected from a woman about to testify on so emotional a matter. But, bearing in mind the note Dr. Finch had included in her report on Scotty, Clement was content to seek his opportunities.

Henderson began by asking, "Mrs. Salem, Christine, how many children do you have?"

"Two. Scott—we call him Scotty—and David."

"How old is Scotty?"

"Two years, nine months."

"Has he been your son during all that time?"

"From the first three days of his life, yes."

"Why do you say, 'from the first three days of his life'?"

"Because he was an adopted child," Christine explained.

"Tell His Honor, did you and your husband enter into this relationship with no reservations and with the full and honest intention of treating Scotty as your natural-born son?"

"Yes, sir."

"And have you done so?"

"Yes, sir."

"Seen him through health and sickness, from the third day of his life until the present?"

"Yes, sir. As any doctor can tell you, he is now a healthy child. Anything that woman said, about worrying that Scotty is being abused or in danger, is nothing but—"

The look in old Henderson's moist eyes rebuked her. She had

gone too far, exceeded answering the question as she had been instructed.

"Tell the Court, Christine, when you and your husband entered this relationship, did you intend to devote yourselves to bringing up Scotty to the best of your ability for the rest of your lives?"

"Yes, sir, we did."

"And in doing so, did you rely on the good faith of the child's birth mother, Lori Adams?"

"Yes, sir. When we saw her face-to-face, and gave her a chance to approve us, we had no idea that more than two years later she would be suing us to take away our son. Because"—and she turned to the bench—"because he *is* our son. Just as we are his daddy and mommy."

"Christine, if you had had any hint that one day Lori Adams, under any name, would try to take your son from you, would you and Bill have adopted him?"

"Knowing the pain that has been involved for us, and for Scotty, no, we would not have adopted him."

Her response had opened an avenue of opportunity, and Henderson proceeded to exploit it.

"When you say the pain inflicted on Scotty, exactly what do you mean?"

"A child, even as young as two and a half, has a sense of things. He knows when there is tension in his home. And he reacts."

"Exactly how does he react?"

"He is restless at his usual nap time. Sometimes is more difficult to discipline. He tends to wet his bed, which he had stopped doing before. And at night, sometimes, he slips out of his room and climbs in with us. As if he is afraid."

"Afraid of what?"

Clement raised his hand sharply. "Object!"

"Let's hear the response first, Counselor," Judge Hart ruled.

"Christine?" Henderson coaxed.

"He is afraid that he will be taken from us, from the only home he has ever known."

"Thank you, Christine," Henderson completed his examination.

Clement rose, appearing to respectfully give way to his older colleague as Henderson crossed to his table. Clement then addressed himself to the witness.

"Christine," he began, subtly mocking Henderson's more gentle use of the name, "tell us, has Scotty ever said to you, 'Mommy, I'm afraid they're going to take me away'?"

"In so many words?"

"Or in similar words. Has Scotty ever expressed to you the thought that he is afraid he will be taken away?"

"No, but—"

"Is that your answer, 'No,' Christine?" Clement demanded.

"Yes. But—"

"Christine, as a matter of courtroom procedure, we do not embellish our answers with 'buts' or 'howevers.' When the answer is no, we simply say 'no,'" Clement instructed, with mocking indulgence. "Now, isn't it true that at the age of about two children change? They become more assertive. Hasn't it been said that at the age of two they learn the word 'no' and use it frequently, perhaps too frequently?"

"That's what the books say," Christie was forced to agree.

"Then isn't it possible that a child of two and a half, asserting himself for the first time, could feel that by defying his parents he might invoke reprisals and thus threaten his own security?" Clement asked.

"I wouldn't know. I'm not a child psychiatrist," Christie replied impulsively.

"Exactly. And *not* being a child psychiatrist, how would you know the cause of his recent conduct, such as bed-wetting and other changes you describe?"

"I know my child," Christie declared.

Clement shrugged slightly, as if treating her response as unsatisfactory and unconvincing. He now consulted his notes to pursue his planned cross-examination.

"Tell me, Christine, does the term SIDS mean anything to you?"

"Object!" Henderson rose to his feet.

"Grounds, Counselor?" Judge Hart challenged.

"Irrelevant and immaterial to the issue!"

"Your Honor," Clement insisted, "this subject has already been introduced in the direct testimony of one of the defendants. As to the question now raised by counsel, this line of questioning is *highly* relevant to the crux of this lawsuit."

"Your Honor, there is no need to open up old and painful wounds which have no bearing on the outcome of this case!" Henderson protested.

"May I proceed subject to connection?" Clement pleaded.

Judge Hart took a moment to consider the request before ruling, "Proceed. Subject to connection."

Clement turned his attention to the witness once more and repeated his question.

"Christine, are you familiar with the term SIDS?"

She had tensed so stiffly that by now her knuckles had turned white as her hands gripped the arms of the chair. Both Bill and Henderson automatically leaned in her direction to lend her support.

"Yes, of course I know the term."

"Would you enlighten the Court as to *how* you came to know that term?" Clement asked.

She hesitated, then, urged on by the moist old eyes of Henderson and a slight nod of his gray head, she responded, "As my husband said, my child—my first child—was a victim of SIDS."

"Would you tell the Court what that means?" Clement persisted.

"Sudden Infant Death Syndrome. An infant dies from no cause that the doctors can discover."

"And your child was the unfortunate victim of that syndrome?"

"Yes, yes, he was."

"I am sure everyone in this courtroom sympathizes with you, my dear," Clement said. "Christine, would you tell us how a woman *feels* when something like that happens?"

Henderson was on his feet a good deal faster than anyone

would expect. "Objection! Not only is the question an invasion of deep personal feeling, but this painful subject is neither relevant nor material to this trial!"

"Mr. Clement?" Judge Hart invited his reply.

"Your Honor, first I apologize for being forced to delve into such tragic matters. But, as I will prove, they are not only relevant but vital to this case."

Before Judge Hart could rule on the question, Paul Henderson was interrupted when his secretary came hurrying down the aisle to hand him a note.

He scanned it briefly, then asked, "Your Honor, may I approach?"

At once Henry Clement joined Henderson at the bench.

"Your Honor, I have just received word that Dr. Grover Frank, the psychiatrist I had intended to call this morning but who was not available, can be free to attend at this time. I would like permission to—"

"Hold on, Paul!" Clement interrupted. "Are you asking this Court to prevent me from cross-examining your witness at such a crucial time?"

"I'm not asking the Court to prevent you from doing anything. Except allow me to introduce a witness who may not be available otherwise. After that you have total freedom to continue at your leisure."

"Your Honor, this is only a tactic to vitiate the effect of my cross-examination. I object. I object very strenuously!" Clement protested.

"Mr. Henderson, do I have your word that your expert witness can only be available at this time?"

"Yes, Your Honor." He proffered the note that had been handed to him.

Hart read it and held on to it before ruling, "We will take a short recess. Counselor, get your expert on the phone. Tell him to be here within twenty minutes!"

"But, Your Honor," Clement started to protest.

"Twenty minutes!" Judge Hart reiterated. But he kept the note that Henderson had presented.

# Chapter 42

❧

Paul Henderson riffled through his notes and glanced at his watch, then looked back to the doors of the courtroom. Beside him, Christine and Bill Salem kept a nervous eye on their attorney.

They were called to attention with the courtroom attendant's sharp "All rise!" Judge Hart swept into the courtroom obviously in a hurry and just as obviously quite irritated by something that had occurred just before he entered. "Be seated," he announced, followed at once by a brisk "Mr. Henderson, your witness!"

"Your Honor, Dr. Frank should be here at any moment."

"Mr. Henderson, I permitted you to take this witness out of sequence to accommodate his schedule. But now you tell me that he is late?" Judge Hart demanded.

To his own ears Hart sounded uncharacteristically harsh. He wondered why this case had come to involve him so personally. He moderated his attitude to suggest, "Mr. Henderson, call the doctor! Then let's get on with other business."

"Yes, Your Honor," Henderson agreed. He was on his way to the courtroom doors when they were flung open.

A portly middle-aged man, his face flushed and damp from perspiration, raced in, carrying a heavy briefcase.

Halfway down the aisle he called to Henderson, "Sorry, very sorry. Couldn't be helped."

Judge Hart leaned forward to study the man. "Dr. Frank?"

"Yes, Your Honor," he replied. "I apologize to the Court for being late, but I am in the middle of an emergency. A young patient who—" Realizing that he was about to make public a matter of confidence, he stopped abruptly.

Judge Hart summoned him to the bench with a single sharp forefinger.

"Now, then, Doctor?"

In a hushed voice Frank replied, "Your Honor, since early this morning I have been confronted by an emergency. A young child of seven who tried to commit suicide."

"At only age seven?" Hart was shocked.

"His parents are divorcing. Seems he overheard them argue over his upbringing, so he thinks he's the reason for the divorce. The guilt was too much for him."

"How was he when you left him?" Judge Hart asked.

"In hospital. Sedated. Fortunately the wound in his wrist turned out to be superficial. But I have to be back when he wakes."

"Of course!" Hart agreed. "Now, Doctor, if you need some time to compose yourself . . ."

"No, thank you, Your Honor. I am ready to testify."

Dr. Frank having been sworn, Paul Henderson led him through his curriculum vitae from his college education up to his present status as professor of pediatric psychiatry at University Hospital and Medical School.

"Doctor, have you examined Scott Salem?"

"On two occasions. For two hours each time."

"And what did you find, Doctor?"

"The subject is a child of two and a half, with the usual characteristics common to boys of that age. He is an active child. Well-spoken when he wants to be. Although he tends to be more taken with what he is doing than with responding to questions."

"And how do you interpret that?" Henderson asked.

"There is no deep interpretation necessary. He is simply at an age when he values his own interests more than the questions of others."

"Did you, in your observations, reach any conclusion as to his relationship to his mother and father?"

"He has a strong tie to them, more to his mother than his father. Which is normal. Since his father is a busy man and leaves the house early and sometimes returns late, after Scotty has been put to bed. But he does look forward to weekends when they play games together, go for walks, trips to the mall. And when he watches television with his father, mainly ball games, he likes to climb up onto Daddy's lap so they can watch together."

"Doctor, did you notice any sense of unease, of insecurity, during your sessions with him?"

"I detect an underlying tension, slight but evident. Which I attribute to the intrusive forces he's been subjected to during this legal situation."

"Did he manifest this in any particular way?"

"He did make reference several times to 'Baby Brett,'" Dr. Frank reported.

"Did he indicate how he had come to use those words?"

"He was not aware that he was using them. They came out at times when he was busy playing with some of his toys."

"Do *you* have any idea how he came to use them or even know them, Doctor?"

"Children of that age are all ears. They soak up everything around them. From discussions between adults. From phone conversations. From television. From what their peers overhear and repeat. He could have come upon that name in a hundred different ways. But the *way* it happened is less important than the fact that he did hear it. And, I suspect that, in some way, he connects *himself* with it."

"Doctor, do you mean he is aware that he is the subject of this lawsuit?" Henderson asked.

"Without being aware of the true nature of it, and the legal possibilities inherent in it, yes. I think at a certain level he is disturbed by it."

"Doctor, do you think it may become a serious problem for him?"

"It is impossible to say at this time," Dr. Frank replied, adding, "What it has done, from my observations, is to make him more suspicious of strangers. The first problem I had to overcome. And it has made him more dependent on his mother and father. Since both times, when they had to leave him alone with me, they had to literally disengage his hand from theirs. He clung more tightly than a child of his personality should have."

"Doctor, based on your observation of Scott Salem, can you state with a reasonable degree of certainty what would be the effect of a complete and total separation from his parents?"

"Object!" Clement called from his defense table.

"On what ground, Mr. Clement?" Judge Hart asked.

"Dr. Frank may have excellent credentials, but I doubt that any psychiatrist, with even the best credentials, can respond credibly to the question Mr. Henderson was about to pose."

"You object to the form of the question?" the judge asked.

"I do indeed, Your Honor. To limit the question to 'complete and total separation from his parents' is improper. The question must contain the part which Mr. Henderson omitted, unwittingly, I am sure," Clement jibed. "The question Dr. Frank *should* be asked must include the fact that the child will be returned to his natural parents. Who have demonstrated their love for him by the very existence of this lawsuit."

"Mr. Henderson?" the judge invited his rebuttal.

Before Henderson could respond, Nancy Brook rose to intercede. "Your Honor, representing Scott Salem, I demand that *both* questions be asked. And answered. The effect of separation. And the possible countereffect of being joined with his natural parents."

"A reasonable request, Counselor," the judge agreed. "Mr. Henderson?"

Henderson put his first question once more, ending with "complete and total separation from his parents?"

"Based on the child's sensitivity to the turmoil going on around him, with no hint to him of an impending separation, I would have to conclude that such a separation would be devastating. It would do long-lasting if not lifetime damage to his emotional structure," Dr. Frank testified.

"And would your answer be the same if that separation was

accompanied by being given into the care of other parents?"

"His natural parents!" Clement called out to correct.

"Mr. Clement, make your objection in the usual way!" the judge remonstrated.

"Sorry, Your Honor, but I do object to the phrase 'other parents,' as if my clients, Lori and Brett Manning, are just two faceless strangers with no natural claim to their own son. In fact, I object to the use of the words 'separation' and 'being given into the care of other parents.' This child is finally being *returned home*. To his *rightful* parents. According to the law of this state."

Henderson turned on Clement. "According to the law of this state, Scott Salem was duly and legally adopted by Christine and William Salem! And will remain so, if I have anything to say about it!" the old lawyer thundered.

Lori Manning started to rise to her feet to join in, but Clement's firm hand on her shoulder prevented it. Brett whispered something into her ear. She settled back in her chair. Her dimpled chin quivered. It seemed she might start to weep. Brett offered her his pocket handkerchief, but she brushed it aside, determined not to cry.

"Gentlemen, gentlemen—" the judge continued. "Mr. Henderson?"

The old lawyer resumed with his witness. "Doctor, which is the more crucial factor, being separated from the only parents he has known, or being given to his natural parents?"

"Separation is the defining fact. The formative years, from a few weeks up to two and a half years, are the time of greatest and most enduring bonding between child and parent. As to a child being given to its natural parents? Children do not have any awareness of who their natural parents are. There are some species of animals in which smell or some other sense designates natural mother and offspring. The human animal has no such ability. Under these circumstances, to a child of two and a half, his natural parents would be total strangers."

"Thank you, Doctor," Henderson said. "Your witness, Mr. Clement."

"Doctor," Clement started to ask as he came forward, "have you ever had a case in which a child's parents were, by some act of fate, removed from the picture?"

"You mean killed, or died?" Dr. Frank asked.

"Say, in a plane crash or an automobile accident?" Clement added.

"Yes, I have. Several cases, actually," the doctor granted.

"What happened to those children?" Clement asked.

"In one case the boy, he passed into the care of his grandmother and a single aunt. The girl was adopted by her mother's sister and brother-in-law. Her aunt and uncle."

"Did those children survive?" Clement asked.

"Yes, of course."

"Did they thrive?"

"If by thrive you mean that they eventually carried on with their lives, yes."

"So that a sudden, and in those cases tragic, separation did not prove to be so damaging after all, did it?" Clement pursued.

"Mr. Clement, the way in which those cases came to my attention is significant. They were brought to me for treatment some time long after the sudden separation. These things are not without their emotional toll," Frank pointed out.

"Doctor, are you comparing their tragic situations with a calm, orderly transition from one set of parents to the child's natural parents? Come, come, Doctor," Clement chided.

"Mr. Clement, whether by accident or court decree, separation is separation and, to the child, sudden and traumatic," Frank insisted.

"But by your own words they survive, they thrive and live good lives!" Clement shouted. "That is all we have to know, Doctor!"

# Chapter 43

Once Dr. Frank was excused, all eyes focused once more on Christie Salem. Before she resumed the stand, Bill insisted she take another of the sedative pills her doctor had prescribed. She refused, wishing to be as alert as possible for the attack Henry Clement was poised to level against her.

With Judge Hart's permission she did go out to the women's rest room to freshen up. She stood at the washbasin staring into the mirror. She thought her hair was a mess. Her makeup, light as it was, appeared to her to be smudged. A mother fighting for her son should not appear weak, distraught in attitude or appearance. She determined to project a strong image on the stand.

She washed her face vigorously with cold, stimulating water. She touched up her makeup. She undid and recombed her hair. She studied herself in the mirror once more and felt encouraged.

As a last-minute means of strengthening her determination, she held her hands under the hot water until they no longer felt so icy cold.

*Let Clement do his damnedest, I'm ready for him!*

Clement was even more eager to prove he was ready to face her.

He began gently enough. "Christie . . . when we were forced to recess, you were about to tell us, and the Court, how a woman feels when she has become the victim of such a tragedy as losing a child to SIDS. Do you feel able to tell us now?"

"What would you like to know?" Christie countered.

"How does a woman *feel*? What does she *do*? After such a soul-shaking and tragic event?"

"She . . . she cries a lot. She keeps asking why—why? Of course there's no answer. She . . . she spends a great deal of time in the room. . . ."

"Room?" Clement asked.

"Where it happened," Christie explained. "She keeps asking, *How* did it happen? And always *why*?"

"And do you find out why?" Clement asked, the soul of sympathy.

"Eventually you realize there are no answers. But the crying, the pain, never stop. And then . . ." Christie hesitated, and abandoned answering the question.

"And *then*?" Clement urged, a bit less gently now.

"You realize that though the pain will be with you forever, you must carry on with your life."

"Tell the Court, Christie. During that time, or at any time thereafter, did you find the need for psychiatric help?" Clement asked.

Henderson was on his feet at once. "Object! Such a question, and any answer, are not germane to this proceeding!"

"If Your Honor please, this question is extremely probative of the issue at stake in this case. I insist on the right to an answer."

Judge Hart drummed his fingers lightly on the desk before deciding. "Mr. Clement, you may continue. At the Court's discretion."

"Tell the Court, Christine, at such a time would a woman feel the need for psychiatric intervention?"

"Object!" Henderson called out.

"Overruled," Judge Hart declared.

"Christine?" Clement coaxed.

"Well, there . . . there came a time . . . it had to do with . . ." She turned to the bench. "Your Honor, do I have to?"

"It would be of help to the Court if you would," Judge Hart

responded. "But take your time, and if you feel need of a recess, just ask."

"Thank you, Your Honor," Christie said, then proceeded. "After a while we decided, Bill and I, that the best thing was for us to have another child."

"But that proved difficult, did it?" Clement anticipated.

"Yes. So after a time Dr. Moncrief, my obstetrician—"

"Your Honor," Henderson objected, "we are getting into confidential matters between doctor and patient."

Clement addressed the bench. "Your Honor, confidentiality binds only the physician. The patient is under no such restriction."

"True, Mr. Clement. You may continue. But, again, at the discretion of the bench."

Clement continued: "Christie, you were telling about your obstetrician. Continue, please."

"Dr. Moncrief thought the problem might be psychological, in view of what happened," Christie admitted.

"So, may I assume that *she* referred you to a psychiatrist?"

"Yes. And . . . and . . ." Despite herself she began to weep, but regained sufficient control to continue, "and she made me relive the entire . . . the whole thing . . . all over again. She said that might release me from my guilt feelings."

"Guilt feelings?" Clement seized on the phrase. "Everyone knows that medical science has never discovered the cause of SIDS. Why would you have guilt feelings?"

"She said that I . . . that for some reason I felt guilty, that maybe I felt that I had *done* something or *didn't* do something I should have done. And that caused . . . that was what caused Billy's—his SIDS."

"And that was the reason you couldn't conceive after that?" Clement asked.

Her face buried in her handkerchief, Christie sobbed.

Gently Judge Hart urged, "Please, Mrs. Salem, we will need a response."

"Yes, yes, she said that."

Clement paused, but only briefly before he asked, "Did your

psychiatrist also say that sometimes a woman who has been unable to conceive somehow is able to conceive after she has *adopted* a child?"

"Yes, yes, she did mention that," Christie conceded.

"And isn't it a fact that after you had adopted the infant you call Scotty, you did indeed become pregnant and are now the mother of a five-month-old infant, a healthy infant, from what I hear?"

"Yes, yes," Christie replied.

"So that your adopting the son of Lori and Brett Manning was really a form of therapy," Clement commented.

"Object!" Henderson rose to challenge. "Mr. Clement has exceeded the bounds of cross-examination with his unfounded, and I daresay vicious, attribution of evil motives to the witness. That three-day-old infant was taken into their home and into their hearts with the best of intentions and with a love that all good parents feel for their children."

"And *I* say," Clement shot back, "the boy having served his purpose, the Salems now have a healthy son of their own. And it is time to give Scott back to his rightful parents as the law of this state provides!"

Judge Hart brought the argument to an abrupt halt with five measured raps of his gavel. Thereafter, the only sound in the courtroom was the sobbing of a distraught and shattered Christie Salem and her protest, "That's not true! Not true! We love Scotty, and he is ours . . . ours!"

"Mr. Clement, are you finished with the witness?" Judge Hart asked.

"No, Your Honor. I have several areas yet to probe," Clement responded.

The judge considered his statement for a moment, then ruled, "The witness is obviously unable to continue at this time. We will stand in recess until ten o'clock tomorrow."

"But, Your Honor—" Clement started to protest.

Judge Hart declared, "Ten o'clock tomorrow."

He rapped his gavel with such finality that Clement could only yield with a curt nod of his head.

# Chapter 44

❧

As Bill pulled the station wagon into their driveway, Christie Salem was still trembling, part in rage, part in fear. To compound her anguish, the front lawn and the street, clear down to the gutter, were cluttered by television cameras accompanied by a host of reporters and technicians.

Because some of them crowded the driveway, Bill was forced to slow to a stop. The media men and women instantly surrounded them. Through the windows they assaulted Christie with shouted overlapping questions.

"Mrs. Salem, how did it feel on the stand?"

"Christie, did you expect such a vicious attack from Mr. Clement?"

"Bill," Christie pleaded, "get into the garage! Lock them out!"

"Christie, I can't just mow them down."

But he did start the wagon, moving very slowly so that the media people were finally forced to give way. Using the remote control to raise the garage door, he eased the wagon in.

The garage door down again, Christie drew her first pain-free breath since she had ascended the witness stand. Bill put his arm around her to comfort her. Not a moment too soon. She went limp in his arms.

When she came to, she was on the living room couch. Little Scotty was asking, "Mommy? Daddy?"

"Scotty," she called.

He rushed to her side. She lifted him up to lie on top of her.

"Chris? You okay now?" Bill asked. "Or do you want me to call the doctor?"

"I'm okay . . ." and because she was not, she insisted, "I'm fine, terrific." She cuddled her little son. "Scotty, did you have your supper?"

"Yes, Mommy."

"What did you have?"

"Chicken, carrots, milk—and ice cream," he reported buoyantly.

"That's good, very good, darling. And I'll bet you ate it all."

"All the ice cream," he admitted.

"Now you go upstairs and start getting ready for bed. You can wear your dinosaur pajamas tonight."

With a light pat on the behind she sent him on his way. Once he had left the living room, Christie announced, "I have to call Paul Henderson."

"Not tonight, hon. Anything you want to say can wait until tomorrow. When you're rested and more yourself."

"Why did you say that?" she confronted him.

"Say what?"

"That I'm not myself."

"I only meant you've had a rough day."

"Maybe, but I'm myself right now. I have to talk to him!" she insisted, picking up the phone on the end table. She punched in the number she had come to know quite well in recent months.

"Paul?" she asked; then, in response to his secretary's inquiry, she declared, "Yes, this is Mrs. Salem! And I insist on talking to him. Now!"

"Christie, please?" Bill tried to intercede.

But Henderson had come on the line.

"Paul, was that right? What Mr. Clement said in court today?"

"Clement said a lot of things in court today. Some right. Some very wrong," the old attorney replied.

"What he said, that the state law provides children *must* be given to their blood relatives."

"Christie," the old man reminded her, "I explained at the outset it was our job to *overcome* that law by our testimony and by other proof."

"But the law *is* on *their* side?" Christie tried to pin him down.

"Yes," Henderson admitted.

"Is that the law in *all* states?" Christie asked.

"It doesn't matter what the law is in other states. We're saddled with the law here. Now, Christie, you just get some supper and go to bed. Because between Clement's cross examination and my redirect to rebut some of his lies, you'll have a rough day tomorrow."

"Yes, yes, Paul," Christie replied submissively.

As she hung up the phone, Bill pleaded, "Darling, don't try to second-guess Paul. He's an old experienced attorney. And damned effective in court. As you saw when he cross-examined Lori Manning."

"You refuse to understand, don't you?" she demanded.

"Understand? Understand what?"

"He said there *is* such a law," she said.

"He told us that before. And we have to overcome that," Bill reminded her.

"With testimony, *my* testimony," she said. "And I failed. Don't you see? I failed Scotty today."

"You did no such thing!"

"But I did. Clement said all those terrible things. And all I could do was cry!"

"You were upset, overwrought. As I would be. Anyone would be. With Clement pounding away at them. And Judge Hart realized that. He was very considerate."

"That's not the point!" Christie insisted, her voice becoming shrill. "It was *my* job to overcome that law. And I didn't! I failed Scotty, failed him!"

"Darling, leave the law to Paul. Just take another of those pills."

"No!" she refused adamantly.

"Then let's have a glass of wine with that nice vegetable-beef soup Janice left on the stove."

"Okay." She appeared to relent. "But first, I have to go up and make sure David is safely tucked in."

She had never been able to say those words without both of them remembering that night when their firstborn had suffered that mysterious tragedy.

Neither commented on it, but their eyes exchanged the message. As Christie started for the stairs, Bill called, "I'll heat up the soup and pour the wine!"

She found David lying on his side, safely held in place on both sides by fluffy pillows. His nose and mouth were clear of any bedclothes and of his sleepsuit. He was breathing easily in a deep sleep. She bent over the bassinette and kissed him lightly on the forehead. He felt healthy, cool and dry. From all signs, he was thriving on his midday bottles now that she was in court all day.

She checked Scotty, who had fallen asleep halfway through changing from his clothes into his pajamas. She finished the procedure carefully, so as not to wake him. She succeeded because he woke for only an instant to say, "Mommy . . ." Then, reassured, fell back asleep. She sat by his side and held his little hand. She rested her head alongside his and pressed her cheek to his. Try as she might, she could not control herself and began to weep.

"They . . . they won't, they can't, take you away! Mommy won't let them, darling. Mommy won't fail you again."

It was ten after two by the glowing face of the clock radio on their night table. Christie had fallen asleep three different times, had awakened three times. She was suffering the same pain she sometimes experienced with her menstrual period. But with even more intensity. She was not due for weeks. Why that pain? Why worse than before?

After lying awake for more than an hour, she realized that this particularly sharp pain was related directly to her first genuine acceptance that Scotty was in danger of being taken from them. When Henderson had first explained the law that favored blood parents, Christie had unconsciously brushed his warning aside. She so believed in the righteousness of their cause that she swept aside all impediments.

This Child Is Mine

But in retrospect Henderson's warning was far from reassuring. He never specified what kind of legal proof could overcome the law.

Did he mean testimony like hers that failed to withstand the attacks of a shrewd lawyer like Henry Clement? What more could they offer besides their good faith in entering the adoption and in their loving treatment of Scotty since the first day they took him into their home and into their hearts?

Other of Henderson's words came back to her painfully: *It doesn't matter what the law is in other states. We're saddled with what the law is here.*

And why did Judge Hart suddenly assign a lawyer to represent Scotty? She and Bill were protecting Scotty's rights. Protecting him from two strangers who wanted to take him away through sharp legal tricks like having Brett Manning be the one to sue, instead of Lori.

Was Judge Hart appointing that lawyer actually a sly maneuver to subtly interpose a legal barrier between Scotty and themselves?

It was a conspiracy to steal her son from her. And all under the law of this state.

Christie slipped out of bed stealthily, so as not to waken her husband. She knew what she had to do. She did not want to give Bill the chance to prevent it.

Hastily, working by the night-lights in the hallway and in the children's rooms, she assembled changes of diapers and other clothes for David and made up a small suitcase of Scotty's things. She carried both bags down to the kitchen door to the garage. She went back up. Very quietly she slipped past the open door to her bedroom, where Bill was asleep. She picked up David in her arms. Then, in hushed tones, she woke Scotty and made him follow her.

Halfway down the stairs he asked sleepily, "Mommy, where we goin'?"

"Shhhh! You'll wake Daddy . . ." she cautioned in a whisper.

When she had Scotty strapped into his safety seat and David

271

alongside her, in the special rig that Bill had designed and installed, she raised the garage door with her remote, started the
motor, and slowly backed the wagon out.

At the corner she stopped, looked up and down the empty
street, and turned left in compliance with the arrow that pointed
to I-80.

After seven minutes of cautious driving, she reached the on
ramp of I-80 and started west at high speed.

Two hours later she was relieved to cross the state line. They
were out of the jurisdiction of the court, free of the threat to
her son.

Since both her sons had slept all the way, she knew she could
safely turn on the radio, to pick up the newscast. She listened
through the national news, the local news, the farm news, and the
weather. There was no report of her disappearance. Bill had not
yet wakened and discovered her flight.

Soon, in her rearview mirror she could see the thin red line
across the landscape behind her. Back home, dawn was breaking.

At the time Christie Salem caught sight of daybreak in her
rearview mirror, Bill Salem came awake with that weary, bruised
feeling football players experience the morning after a grueling
game. His bruises, though, were in his mind, in his emotions.
Through a night of troubled sleep he had relived the turmoil of
watching Christie on the stand being hammered at by Henry
Clement.

Bill had said all he could to encourage her, praising her efforts
beyond their due. Secretly he agreed with her. Her breakdown
had not helped their case. And if they lost Scotty . . . No, they
wouldn't lose Scotty, couldn't lose Scotty. But if they did, it would
be the result of Christie's collapse under Clement's vicious attack.

Bill moved with great care. If Christie was asleep, a sleep she'd
richly earned, he did not want to risk waking her.

Cautiously he sat up on the side of the bed, relieved that he
had not detected any movement from her. Relieved until it struck

him that he heard no breathing either. He looked behind him. The bed was empty.

*Hell,* he thought, *if she's back there in Scotty's room, standing at his bedside staring down at him, as she has done so often since this damn lawsuit started . . . She's got to stop doing that! It doesn't help her, it doesn't help Scotty.*

The instant he discovered Scotty's little bunk bed was empty, he started for the nursery, sure that Christie was there. She was not. Nor was David.

He raced down the stairs, relieved to see the light was on in the kitchen. It would be an early hour to feed the boys, but it was a relief that they were here and in Christie's care.

The kitchen was empty. On the table, propped up against his coffee cup, was a note.

Darling, don't worry about us. We are fine. And safe from any law that will take Scotty away from us. Will call you when we are settled. Love, Christie.

*Safe from any law . . . will call you when we are settled?* Bill protested, *We're due in court this morning. . . . She will be called to testify again. . . .*

He reached for the telephone, punched in a number, waited for a reply, then exploded, "Paul! Sorry to wake you so early."

"Son, when a lawyer is in the midst of a trial, five o'clock in the morning is not early. And don't tell *me, I'll* tell *you.* Your wife woke up in the middle of the night with all the answers she should have given yesterday. Well, don't worry. I'll get them all on re-direct today."

"Paul—" Bill tried to interrupt.

"Never saw it fail. The witness always knows afterward what she should have said the first time. Tell Christie not to—"

"Paul, I can't tell her anything."

"Then *I'll* tell her."

"You don't understand. She's not here."

"Not there? What do you mean?"

"Gone! And both boys with her!"

"Gone?" Henderson echoed, his voice betraying his shock.

Bill read the note to him.

"Foolish, foolish girl," Henderson remarked, as if to himself. "To think she can escape the reach of the court."

"The trial," Bill said. "What do we do?"

"First thing we do is *not* say a word about this to anyone. Absolutely no one is to know what happened."

"But court . . . she's supposed to be in court this morning," Bill protested.

"I'll find some way to handle that. Meantime, call every relative you think she might take refuge with. Swear them to secrecy. Just find out where she is staying."

"What if she isn't with any relative?"

"I'd hate to call in the police on this. That would blow everything wide open," Henderson replied. "We can't risk that. So first make those calls. Let me know. I'll be here until I start for court."

# Chapter 45

❧

Within the next three hours Bill Salem called all their relatives, his and Christine's, who lived outside the state but were close enough to be a logical refuge. After he had exhausted the list of those closer, he started to call those who lived two hundred miles or more away.

All were shocked to hear, all promised not to say a word to anyone. But none could offer any information. By the time he had exhausted his possibilities, Bill was forced to accept the fact that his wife had not sought refuge with any relative. Possibly with a friend, he thought. But he resisted calling for fear of jeopardizing secrecy. Which, in Paul Henderson's mind, was so crucial.

By the time he called the old lawyer, Henderson had already gone. He had left a message for Bill. "Meet me in court."

Bill spotted him hunched over his counsel table, diligently making notes. As Bill drew closer, he discovered the old man was only doodling, intending to give the impression that he was making notes. As Bill slipped into the chair alongside, Henderson demanded, "Well?"

"Nobody has seen or heard from her," Bill whispered.

"We've got to find her. And, if at all possible, before anyone discovers that she was ever gone."

"It was an act of desperation. She's sure her testimony lost the case," Bill tried to justify his wife's behavior.

"If her testimony didn't, this surely will. This is exactly what Clement was trying to prove in his cross-examination. Her emotional instability. Her need to see a psychiatrist. What had prevented her from conceiving. If she has run away with those children to keep Scotty out of the hands of the Court, Judge Hart could consider it not only contempt of court, but also rule them the actions of a woman too unstable to be a mother."

"You think he would do that?" Bill asked.

"Hart does not treat lightly anything that attacks the jurisdiction of his court."

With considerable reluctance Paul Henderson admitted, "Son, we may have lost our case . . . and Scotty besides."

"What do you do when the judge asks her to resume the stand and she's not here?" Bill asked.

That problem loomed more ominously in the old lawyer's mind than Bill realized. For Henderson was now confronted by another dilemma. He had the duty of confidentiality to his client not to reveal her self-defeating action. But he also had the duty to the Court not to lie when the judge asked the tough questions Henderson anticipated.

Within minutes Judge Hart entered the courtroom. All present rose until the judge ended that formality with a crisp gesture. He addressed the attorney:

"When we recessed yesterday, Mr. Clement was about to continue his cross-examination of Mrs. Salem—" He stopped abruptly. "Mr. Henderson, is your client late this morning?"

"If we may approach the bench?"

Hart motioned them forward.

"Your Honor, I'm afraid my client will not be available this morning."

"Look here, Henderson, if this is some trick—" Clement started to accuse, then refrained. "I demand the right to complete my cross-examination of your client!"

"There's no law of evidence that says cross-examination has to be continuous, or even immediately sequential. You'll have your chance."

Henderson said no more, for there was little he could say that would not either endanger his client's rights or risk misleading the Court.

"Counselor," Judge Hart addressed Clement, "considering the unnecessarily harsh treatment you accorded the witness yesterday, it is understandable she might need a day of rest."

Then the judge rebuked Paul Henderson. "Counselor, if your client is not available to testify tomorrow morning, I shall be forced to throw out all her direct testimony and allow Mr. Clement great latitude in commenting on that fact."

"Of course, Your Honor," Henderson appeared to agree, while thinking, *Twenty-four hours, twenty-four hours to find her, bring her back in time and in condition to testify tomorrow. No chance.*

Since he was still presenting the case for the defendants William and Christie Salem, Henderson filled the day by presenting additional character witnesses who swore to the fact that the Salems were people of good moral character, stable and substantial members of the community. Were active in charitable affairs. And in all respects were ideal parents for little Scotty. They testified they had observed the boy with the Salems, and he was perfectly happy, well-adjusted.

It was pleasing, if less than dramatic, courtroom fare. The kind that bores the media merchants to the point of distraction. There was a constant parade of reporters out of the courtroom as well as in, to steal a forbidden smoke, go to the washroom, or just stand around outside the courtroom and exchange gossip.

The only thing of note, and discerned by one reporter, Patricia Chatman, was that Paul Henderson asked for an unusual number of recesses on this morning.

While she considered this normal for a man of his age, since her own father had suffered from bladder frequency in the last years, Patricia Chatman also noted that Henderson did not go to the men's room. He headed instead for the telephone to place a hurried call. Call completed, Henderson headed back to the courtroom.

With her well-developed nose for news, Patricia Chatman fitted that together with an earlier observation. Bill Salem had come into court alone. Conferred with his lawyer. Then departed and

277

had never returned. That, plus those frequent phone calls . . .

Since even in a trial of such public attention, character testimony was bound to be routine and not likely to yield any surprises, Pat Chatman thought her time would be better spent elsewhere.

With a whispered "Hold my place" to a colleague, she slipped out of the courtroom.

Not to betray her suspicions to anyone, she shunned the television-station car and hopped a cab. She gave the driver the address she knew so well from the day she had secured access to the house when this story first broke.

The cab pulled up. Pat Chatman viewed the house through the cab door. The Salem station wagon was parked in the driveway. Someone must be home. She started up the walk, staring into all the windows on the ground level. The living room, the dining room. She stood on tiptoe to peer through the glass inserts high on the front door. She could view the foyer, the stairs leading up to the second floor. No sign of life. She went around back to the kitchen area. She peered through the window. Bill Salem was seated at the kitchen table, portable phone in hand, the family phone book open before him; he was punching in a number with the irritation of a man under great pressure.

Strangely, aside from Bill Salem, no one else was in sight. Not Christine Salem. Not either of the two boys, or someone who would take care of them whenever the Salems were in court.

Pat Chatman climbed back into the cab and ordered the driver back to the courthouse. She arrived as Henderson was putting his last questions to Reverend Edgely.

"Now, Pastor, having observed Christine Salem from the day of christening little Scotty until the present, what is your opinion of her?"

The pastor, tall, heavyset, bald, with penetrating black eyes, responded as if delivering a sermon: "Mr. Henderson, in all respects I have found Christine Salem to be a devoted and caring mother who loves that child with total, complete, and selfless love. In all my years I have never seen a better mother."

After such an accolade, Henderson had only to say, "Your witness, Mr. Clement."

Clement had to consider; attacking a man of the cloth was not calculated to make the judge or the media feel friendly toward him. Or he could allow the testimony to stand and trust that the judge would accept it for what it was, testimony by a friend about a friend and thus of little probative value. Clement chose the latter course.

Meantime, Henderson kept half an eye toward the courtroom doors, hoping that Bill Salem would arrive with some news of his wife. Instead, all Henderson saw was Pat Chatman make her way down the aisle and slide into her seat in the first row, to resume making notes in her usual way.

The rest of the morning passed with additional character testimony from Salem friends.

At the lunch recess, while the other two television crews did their usual reportage from the courthouse steps, Pat Chatman and her crew confronted Paul Henderson in the rotunda of the courthouse. To avoid her, he pretended to be engrossed in his thoughts about the case. But Pat succeeded in cornering him. With the portable television lights full on them, she asked, "Mr. Henderson, your clients have been in the courtroom every moment of this trial. Until today. When neither of them is here. Would you explain why?"

"Mrs. Salem had a particularly difficult day yesterday. So I thought it better for her to rest today," he replied, starting out of the bright-lights TV to head for the telephone booth.

Pat pursued him, gesturing her crew to follow.

"Mr. Henderson, Mrs. Salem is not here. Neither is she at home."

Henderson turned on her. She continued, "Nor is there any sign of either child. Would you care to explain that to our audience?"

Henderson ignored her question to slip into the phone booth, insert a coin, and punch in his call.

With Pat right outside the booth, Henderson turned his head away as he asked, "William! Any word?"

"Not yet," Bill Salem had to confess.

With no other recourse Henderson urged desperately, "Stay with it, son, stay with it."

When court reconvened after lunch, Paul Henderson was startled to find a note waiting on his counsel table.

Mr. Henderson, report to my chambers as soon as you arrive.

Henderson looked across the well of the courtroom to see if Clement had received a similar note. Clement was not present.

Paul Henderson arrived at Judge Hart's chambers to discover that Clement had preceded him.

Judge Hart greeted Henderson with a grim, "Counselor . . . your adversary has reported a very disturbing fact to me. Did you, at the lunch recess, give an interview to Channel Eight?"

"I was cornered by a television reporter. It was not of my own volition, I assure you."

"That is not the point at issue," the judge replied. "But Mr. Clement has some pertinent questions to ask you about what was said, and *not* said, during that interview."

"Henderson," Clement began, "that woman reporter said that Christine Salem is not home. Neither are the children. And you avoided giving confirmation or denial. What is the truth of the matter? I think I am entitled to know."

"And surely this Court is entitled to know," Judge Hart added.

"Your Honor, it is not possible for me to respond to that question without breaching my obligation of confidentiality to my client."

"Do I take it you refuse to respond?" Judge Hart demanded.

"I am *unable* to respond," Henderson replied.

"Oh, are you?" Clement exploded. "Well, I'll tell you what I think. This won't be the first time that a woman in her situation has kidnapped a child and run off somewhere. To keep him out of the jurisdiction of the Court!"

The judge reinforced Clement's accusation. "Mr. Henderson?"

"Your Honor, with all due respect to you and this Court, I am unable to respond," Henderson replied.

"Counselor, that boy is the object of this lawsuit. Hence I must consider him a ward of this court. Since Mrs. Salem has chosen to remove or hide him from the jurisdiction of this Court, I must hold that she is in contempt. And if she and the boy are not here tomorrow when court reconvenes, I will issue a warrant for her arrest. Need I add that her conduct is egregious enough to constitute grounds on which to decide this case?"

# Chapter 46

❧

"Don't move from the house until you hear from her!" an irate Paul Henderson shouted at Bill over the phone.

"Yes, Paul, I understand."

"I am racking my brains to figure out how to counter the effect of this on our case. And frankly, I can't. The least we can do is have Christine in court tomorrow at ten. With Scotty. Failing that, Judge Hart will rule against us right from the bench!"

"I . . . I understand. Now, please, get off the phone so I can have an open line. In case Christine does call."

Henderson hung up at once.

With no choice but to wait, Bill Salem poured himself another cup of coffee. His ninth for the day. He watched the content of the cup as it made little wavelets. His hand was unsteady. Too much caffeine. Nevertheless, he proceeded to drink.

The phone rang. He lurched to pick it up, sending his cup crashing to the floor. To hell with the cup! The phone!

"Hello?" he pleaded.

"Bill . . ."

It was her voice.

"Christie, where in the world are you?"

"Where the law doesn't hold blood more important than love of a child," she defied.

"Tell me. I'll come get you."

"Oh, no! We're here. We're safe from the law. All three of us. The boys are fed and asleep in a nice, clean, comfortable motel. And we are going to *stay* here!"

"Christie, you can't!"

"Oh, yes, I can!"

"Christie," he pleaded, "listen to me. The judge knows you've run off with Scott. He wants you both in court tomorrow at ten. Else he'll take Scotty away from us."

"He can't do that!" she protested.

"Yes, he can."

"We're out of the state, out of his jurisdiction!" Christie declared.

"But he can. And other states' courts will enforce his ruling. Paul said so."

"An empty threat. To make us come back. So he can give Scotty to those people."

"Chris, you can't run forever."

"To keep Scotty, I will if I have to. You may not feel that way, but I do!" she insisted.

"Chris, darling, breaking the law isn't the way. We're not that kind of people."

"A law that is wrong *deserves* to be broken!" Christie said defiantly.

"Christie, where are you?"

"Where we're safe from the law," was all she would say before she hung up.

Dead phone in hand, Bill Salem sat pondering his desperate situation. Christie could be stubborn. But never this stubborn. Never this unreasonable. Never so defiant and determined to fly in the face of reality. And there was Henderson, and Clement, and most of all Judge Hart, demanding she appear in court tomorrow at ten.

His phone intruded, making the rhythmic beeping warning of a phone off the hook. He hung up. Then he snatched it again. He pressed the button marked O. After some half-dozen rings a female voice greeted him, warmly, "This is your operator. Do you need assistance?"

"Operator, I just received a long-distance phone call. It is urgent for me to know where that call originated."

The operator's voice took on a sudden aloofness. "Sorry, sir. You would have to talk to my supervisor about that."

"Well, then, damn it, put me on with your supervisor!" Bill insisted.

A bit aghast, the operator replied, "One moment, sir!" Her words were delivered as a rebuke.

In several minutes an even colder, more aloof voice came over the line.

"Sir, this is the supervisor speaking. What is your problem?"

Without betraying any details, Bill explained his need for that out-of-state telephone number.

"I'm sorry, sir, but I cannot reveal that information," the supervisor said in a tone that indicated that as far as she was concerned, this conversation was ended.

"Now, wait . . ." Bill persisted. "There must be someone in the phone company who has the power to reveal that number. It isn't unlisted. It's a motel!"

"Sir, is this a medical emergency?"

"This is a *legal* emergency!" Bill pointed out.

"Sorry, but we are unable to give out any numbers without authorization."

This time Bill heard a click that meant she had hung up. In anger he slammed down his phone. But a moment later he realized anger was his enemy. Fearing the consequences, he picked up the phone and dialed another number.

"Hello?" the angry voice of a distressed man responded.

"Paul, she just called."

"No matter where she is, go get her! Bring her back!"

Bill Salem was forced to explain to the irate lawyer Christine's refusal to tell him where she was. Except that she was out of the state. The phone company had refused to give him the number.

"Damn it, man, we're no better off!" Henderson exploded, before interrupting himself. "Authorization? They want authorization? There's only one way. We go to the judge. We lay all the facts before him."

"He'll blow his top," Bill pointed out.

"He damn well will. But he's the only hope we have to make that phone company open up. I'll call him."

"Now? At home?" Bill asked.

"Have to. If we want to produce Christie and Scotty tomorrow at ten."

In the judge's home dinner had long been over. The conversation at the table had been confined mainly to the strange disappearance of the defendant in the Salem case, which had been the lead story on the evening news. But for the last hour and a half Karen and Jud had been silent, each engrossed in his or her own duties.

Since *Manning* v. *Salem* was apparently about to come to an abrupt end, the judge was familiarizing himself with the papers in the next case on his docket.

His wife sat across the library in the big old leather easy chair. She studied the history, X rays, MRIs, and neurological findings concerning the patient on whom she would have to operate at six o'clock in the morning.

When the phone rang, Karen reached for it, explaining, "My anesthesiologist. Hello?" She was taken by surprise. "Who shall I say is calling?" She handed the phone across the desk. "Mr. Henderson."

Never wishing to encourage intrusions on his home life, Judge Hart greeted him very coolly, "Mr. Henderson?"

The elderly attorney took the hint. He explained his situation succinctly. As he talked, he also listened very closely, trying to glean from the judge's vocal reactions his response to his clients' predicament.

"Let me understand, Mr. Henderson. You are admitting your client deliberately took the child who is the subject of this lawsuit across state lines to avoid the jurisdiction of my court?" Judge Hart demanded.

"I'm afraid that's true, Your Honor."

"Well!" the judge responded. "A little late with that information, Counselor."

"I have my professional obligations, Your Honor," Henderson reminded him simply.

"Now, what would you have *me* do?" the judge asked.

"Order the phone company to reveal that telephone number so we can find Mrs. Salem, convince her to come back."

"Before I can act, I will have to inform all counsel involved in the case. Be here within the hour."

"Yes, Your Honor."

At quarter past ten Paul Henderson and William Salem reached the home of Judge Judson Hart in a quiet area on the outskirts of the city. A street with huge, towering elms and large houses set back on wide, well-tended lawns.

They were greeted by the judge, who ushered them into the library, where he introduced them to his wife.

"Sorry to be intruding," she apologized. "But I've too many papers to move them all." She resumed her study of her own case.

Within the next quarter-hour Henry Clement and Nancy Brook arrived.

Judge Hart stated the situation directly and briefly.

"I didn't want to take any steps without all counsel fully aware and having a chance to express their views," he concluded. "Ms. Brook?"

"I want it understood that my client is the victim of this latest development. And his rights are to be preserved as if this had never happened," Brook stated her case. "I also think it would be in his best interest to be brought back to this state as soon as possible."

"Mr. Clement?"

"I agree it would serve everyone's interests to have Ms. Salem and especially the boy brought back to this jurisdiction at once."

"Then I shall call the phone company," Judge Hart started to say.

But Henry Clement interposed, "However, Your Honor, the fact that I concur does not mean I forego my contention that Christine Salem's flight is proof that she is emotionally unfit to be the mother of that child."

"I will assume you acquiesce without prejudice," the judge ruled.

He called the phone company, spoke to the supervisor of supervisors, ordered her to reveal the number and location of the motel in question, and threatened he would hold her in contempt.

Judge Hart handed the information to Bill Salem.

"I shall expect all of you in court tomorrow at ten!"

Once they had left, Karen admitted, "Jud, I cheated."

"Cheated?" the judge asked, puzzled.

"All the while I was studying my charts, I also did a little listening. Are you actually going to penalize that woman for giving way to a strong, natural, maternal impulse?"

"Unless you want me to march into surgery tomorrow and tell you how to excise a brain-stem tumor, don't tell me how to handle this case!" he snapped back.

"Sorry," she apologized, and went back to her study.

To soften his sharp response, he explained, "She flouted the jurisdiction of the Court. I can't permit that. Besides, what is it about this particular case that intrigues you so?"

"Not just me," she replied, "the whole country, it seems."

At twenty-four minutes after one o'clock in the morning Bill Salem pulled up at the office of the Wayside Motel in the small city of Middleton, seventy-six miles across the state line.

The office was dark for the night. Even the Vacancy sign was off. Bill pounded on the office door until, from somewhere in the back, a person pulling on an old figured bathrobe came toward the door. It turned out to be a woman in her late sixties. Sleepy-eyed, irritable, she stared at Bill through the glass of the locked door.

After considerable bickering, she finally relented sufficiently to inform, "Room one twenty-two. End of the walk. And don't make no noise. We got others here, you know."

Bill knocked gently on door 122. Sooner than he expected, he heard Christie's tense, defensive voice demand, "Who is it?"

"Hon . . . it's me."

\* \* \*

On the drive home along the Interstate, both boys slept. Christie stayed awake long enough to try to justify what she had done.

"How could I face Scotty later if I didn't do everything I could to keep him? What'll they do to me now? Put me in jail? I don't care!"

Eventually she dozed off, the first sleep she had had since her flight began. Her head rested on Bill's shoulder, and he liked it there.

He kept his eyes on the empty highway. Tired, he had to force himself to stay awake. But at least they were all on their way home.

Christine and Scotty would be in court tomorrow at ten, as ordered.

# Chapter 47

Nancy Brook was giving last-minute instructions to her paralegal assistant before leaving for the courthouse. "And call Mr. Seymour. Tell him the opposition has asked to examine him before trial during the week of—"

The phone interrupted. The young man answered, then handed the phone to her. "Henry Clement."

"Hi, Ms. Brook," Clement greeted her heartily. "Took a chance trying you at the office so early. Especially after last night. Quite a session at the judge's home."

"Quite," Nancy pretended to agree, awaiting the true purpose of Clement's call.

"It made one thing very clear to me," Clement continued. "Our interests are really the same. Yours and mine. We both want what's best for your little client. Can we meet for a cup of coffee to discuss this?"

"If you think it will help my client," Nancy replied.

"The Astor Café?"

"Half an hour?"

"Half an hour," Clement sounded happy to agree.

When she approached the Astor, Nancy Brook discovered through the broad plate-glass window that Henry Clement was not alone.

Seated alongside him was Brett Manning, who was autographing a menu for a waitress who hovered over him, tremulous with delight and anticipation.

*He should have told me,* Nancy protested silently. *If Henry Clement thinks I have stars in my eyes over a soap-opera hero, he is sadly mistaken.*

Nevertheless, she entered the coffee shop that served courthouse personnel, attorneys, and litigants early every morning.

As Nancy approached, Brett Manning rose to greet her.

He held out his hand. From her hesitation Clement knew the moment demanded an explanation.

"When I called this morning, I didn't know Mr. Manning would insist on coming along. But this situation is so vital to him that I couldn't refuse. I hope you understand."

"Yes, of course," Nancy replied, reserving both her judgment and her suspicions.

"Ms. Brook—Nancy, if you don't mind—you being charged with protecting the legal rights of his son, Brett wanted to talk to you face-to-face."

She nodded, indicating she was disposed to listen.

"Ms. Brook, with all the courtroom procedure, lawyers asking questions, witnesses trying to answer, lawyers fighting between themselves and with the judge, one thing gets lost. Never gets a chance to be heard. Feelings. Human feelings. What *I* feel about my son. What *Lori* feels. Do you have children?"

"No."

"Take my word, it is unlike anything else a human being is privileged to experience. That child, that boy, is you. In his eyes, in his smile, you see yourself, your wife. He is the culmination of your life and your love. That's what little Brett means to us. If Judge Hart were to deny him to us, we would be left with a pain that can never heal. Not as long as little Brett is in the hands of strangers.

"You have no idea what it's like. All night you're eaten up, torn apart by the injustice of it. You wake in the morning with a dull pain you can't account for. Until suddenly it becomes sharp and clear. Brett! Little Brett. Where is he now? Is he healthy? Is he sick? Is he happy? Is he sad? What's he doing? Does he need anything?

"You'd like to be sitting across from him at breakfast. Watching his delicate little fingers as he lifts his cup of orange juice. As he plays with his toys. Draws with his crayons. Watch the way he smiles. He's such a beautiful child. Such a handsome little fellow. I've only seen pictures of him. But you've spent time with him. You know. I want to hold him, kiss him, play games with him, read to him, teach him the alphabet, do all the things fathers do with their sons.

"Much as I feel," Brett Manning continued, "the pain Lori feels is even worse."

Manning looked to Henry Clement seeking permission before he continued.

Clement interceded: "Nancy, what Brett is about to tell you must remain confidential. As if you were *his* attorney, too. Agreed?"

"Unless it adversely affects my client's rights," she countered.

"I can assure you it does not," Clement promised.

"All right, then," she consented.

"Ms. Brook, between the time the original papers in this lawsuit were filed and the months before we came here for the trial, Lori became pregnant."

"Well, that's good news," Nancy Brook commented.

"*Would* have been good news . . ."

"*Would*?"

"Four days before we came out here, Lori suffered a miscarriage."

"Oh, I'm sorry to hear that," Nancy commiserated.

"The emotional strain of the impending trial, her doctor said. The fears and anxieties of testifying. Myself, I think it was the fear that if we lose here, we'll have lost our son forever. Evidently Lori couldn't face that. Because she thinks it was her fault. So you see, little Brett means even more to us now that Lori lost the baby.

"Mind you, I'm not saying the Salems are bad people. I only know they are strangers who hold our son and refuse to give him back.

"That's all I have to say. No, one thing more. I never want Lori to know that I told you. She considers her miscarrying a sign of weakness. Now, of all times, she doesn't want to appear weak. Because it might hurt in our fight for little Brett."

With that, his eyes moist, Manning left. Nancy Brook watched as he brushed by a woman who held out a menu for him to autograph.

Nancy turned back to Henry Clement, who started to say, "If you're thinking that was a very good performance—"

"You read my mind exactly," Nancy confirmed.

"He's not that good an actor. Take my word for it. Though you'd never know it from his success on television. And from what Sally Brownell, his agent in New York, tells me. She has sitting on her desk right now three movie offers for Manning, at two-million-plus per film. Which brings me to what I wanted to discuss with you.

"Nancy, as the natural parents of this child, my clients are entitled, by state law, to have him returned. But I say let's not stand on the law alone. It's the child's welfare that should govern. In addition to being his true and natural parents, my clients can give that little boy the most secure and privileged lifestyle any child could want. There is no limit, none at all, to what Lori and Brett Manning can give their son. In education, training, opportunity. I agree with Brett, the Salems are not bad people, but they can't match what my clients can do for that boy."

"Mr. Clement, exactly what are you asking me to do?"

"Since he appointed you to represent the boy, obviously Judge Hart has great respect for your judgment. Join forces with me."

"How?"

"Advise, *urge* Hart, that in the interest of your client, he adhere strictly to the law."

"Surely you don't expect me to instruct Judge Hart on his duty under the law."

"Of course not. But . . ." Clement leaned closer across the table, indicating he was about to speak even more confidentially.

*Hell,* Nancy Brook thought, *after making such a point of Manning's millions, I hope, for his sake and mine, Clement doesn't offer me a bribe. I'll report him if he does.*

"You know, my dear, it wouldn't do you any harm either."

"Harm?" she echoed, thinking, *Here it comes.*

"To have a friend on the Supreme Court in the state capital."

Relieved that no bribe was offered, Nancy Brook replied, "I still don't get it."

"This case, all the media attention. The agitators on both sides. Natural parent groups. Adoptive parent groups. No matter which way Hart decides, there will be groups who object. If he goes with the law as written, the adoptive parents will pillory him, saying he's hiding behind the law. If he decides to make new law, the natural parents and the governor won't like it. So Hart becomes a controversial figure. Too controversial to be appointed to the High Court."

"What can I do to change that?" Nancy asked.

"You're the only one who can provide Hart with the perfect way out. He can uphold the law and still have an unassailable reason."

Nancy Brook played out Clement's scenario for him. "If the child's own lawyer recommended he be returned to his natural mother and father."

"Exactly," Clement confirmed. "You do a great service to your client, assuring him a terrific life. At the same time, you help Judge Hart out of a very nasty predicament. Which is certainly going to stand him in good stead when it comes time for the governor to make his appointment."

"I see what you mean," Nancy said without agreeing.

"My dear, you're young. Still on your way up. There is a rule in politics that works in the law as well. If you want to *get* along, *go* along. You help the judge now. Eventually he'll be in a position to help you later. If you know what I mean."

"A man like Judson Hart?" Nancy replied, openly dubious.

"Even Judson Hart. Nancy, I know men. I know politics. I know men *in* politics. I don't need to know anything else."

To avoid saying what she really thought, she replied, "I'll certainly give this some thought."

"Good. Good! That's all we ask," Clement said, confident of the outcome. He picked up the check and left.

Nancy Brook sat there, a look of deep thought on her slender face. She idly stirred the cold remains in her coffee cup as she tried to assimilate the last hour.

As for Clement's proposal, he was a lawyer trying to achieve a result for his client. By any means.

As for Brett Manning? Yes, she had to concede, he was telling the truth. Since he was, it was natural to feel sorry for his wife, Lori.

But aware of her duty, Nancy Brook could not be guided by sympathy for Lori Manning. Or for Christine Salem. Her flight could be interpreted as the action of an emotionally unstable woman. Or as the heroic action of a mother so devoted to her son that she would defy the law and the courts to keep him.

Either way, Nancy could not allow that to define or influence her duty to her very young client.

She glanced up at the large clock that hung prominently on the wall of the Astor Café for the express purpose of reminding lawyers and litigants when it was time to leave for court.

It was time.

# Chapter 48

❧

When she arrived in the courtroom, Nancy Brook found the other two attorneys already present, as well as their clients. It took only one glimpse of the harried face of Christine Salem for Nancy to see the efforts the distraught woman had made to repair the damage of her long, painful flight. And also how futile those efforts had been. No amount of makeup, even if skillfully applied, could conceal the effects of two sleepless nights ending in tearful self-recrimination.

Judge Hart entered briskly and ascended to the bench. He stared down at the parties and attorneys assembled before him.

In view of the hectic events of the last thirty-six hours, he was most solicitous of the condition of Christine Salem.

He arrived at the same conclusion as Nancy Brook. Instead of ordering Christine to take the stand so Henry Clement could continue his cross-examination, Hart announced, "Counsel will join me in my robing room."

Once assembled, Hart asked, "Clement, what areas do you intend to cover in your cross-examination of Mrs. Salem?"

"Considering what's happened in the last two days, I think that would be self-evident," Clement replied. "I would like the witness to describe for the record what she did, why she did it. Entirely relevant to the issue of whether she can make a good, emotionally supportive mother to a child of two and a half."

"I think your previous cross-examination pretty well covered that," Hart said.

"Not the matter of her fleeing the jurisdiction of this Court," Clement protested.

"If it was necessary for a jury to hear that, yes. But I know all those facts, firsthand. I was part of getting her back here. So there's no need to put on a public spectacle for the media to devour."

"Your Honor?" a baffled Henry Clement asked for clarification.

"Mr. Clement, this Court, this judge, does not see the value in tormenting Ms. Salem with further cross-examination, merely to adduce evidence which can only be cumulative. I think the facts are clear. So I am going to ask you to forego your right to continue this cross-examination. It's up to you, Mr. Clement."

Henry Clement was fully aware, as was Paul Henderson, that when a judge offers a lawyer such a choice, there is only one right response.

"I agree, Your Honor, there is sufficient evidence on the record as to Mrs. Salem's condition and state of mind."

"Since that is your choice, we can now proceed to summation. I shall expect those to start tomorrow at ten."

"Your Honor . . ." Nancy Brook intervened.

"I haven't forgotten you, Counselor," Hart said. "Since you occupy an unusual position in this trial, we shall have to make unusual provision for you. Would you like to sum up before or after counsel for the parties?"

A moment of reflection and Nancy Brook decided, "After, Your Honor."

"So ruled," Hart declared. "Counselors, we will reconvene tomorrow at ten."

Nancy Brook left the courtroom to take her turn at the public telephone booths at the end of the corridor.

She inserted her quarter, referred to a note she held, and punched in the number. At the first response she immediately began to talk but soon realized this was a recorded voice. She was instructed to leave a message and call back after four o'clock, when the doctor would be free.

At her later call, once she explained the urgent nature of her need for consultation, she was granted an appointment.

At six o'clock that evening she was admitted to the office and apartment of Dr. Guy Ludmiller by a woman who greeted her, "My husband will see you soon, Ms. Brook." She showed Nancy into a small waiting room with several comfortable chairs. On the walls were modest watercolors of scenes in London and Vienna.

Soon the door to the inner office opened. A red-eyed girl of thirteen emerged and hastened from the room, relieved to be free.

In the doorway stood a man, tall, erect, his face deeply lined by age, which his white hair confirmed.

When he spoke, he identified his origins by the slight British accent.

"Miss Brook, is it?"

"Yes, Doctor."

"Come in, come in."

He stood aside to give her entrance. He sat down at his desk, offering her the chair opposite. Within the yellow glow of his desk lamp Nancy could study him. If age had marked his face, it had not dulled his eyes, which were sharp and perceptive.

"Now, what is this emergency you pleaded so desperately in your message?" Ludmiller asked.

"Did I say desperately?" Nancy asked, trying to recall her exact words.

"It was your voice, my dear," Ludmiller replied. "Now, then, your child—experiencing some strange difficulties?"

"Not *my* child. I'm here as attorney representing a child. You may be aware of the case referred to in the media as the Baby Brett case."

"Ah, yes, a field day for psychiatrists," Ludmiller said with a tinge of scorn. "Mind you, I do not blame those colleagues who appeared and testified. But the idea of psychiatrists involved in legal proceedings offends me. So, if you have come here to ask me to counter the testimony of the psychiatrists in that case, sorry, I do not attend circuses. Especially in courtrooms."

"I'm not here to ask you to testify. But to help. To help *me*. As the lawyer charged with protecting my little client's interests."

"Ms. Brook, I commend your professional zeal. But I have a

policy. I never become involved in legal matters."

"Not even to give advice to a troubled lawyer?" she asked.

"Advice," Ludmiller considered, as he reached into the mahogany cigar humidor on his desk to extract a slender cigar. At once he apologized, "Don't worry. I shall not light it. I simply enjoy the fragrance and the oral satisfaction. Now, you were saying, 'advice.'"

"I've reviewed all the testimony of those psychiatrists. Some say it is better for the child to be given to its natural parents. Some say leave the child with the parents who have raised him for two and a half years now."

"I daresay they found much to say on both sides," Ludmiller commented.

"As the attorney representing that little boy, I have to take a position on his behalf. I want to be sure I'm not making a mistake. So I have to know, for my own conscience, how much am I to accept of the testimony I read?"

"Such as?"

"One doctor gave considerable weight to the criminal records of adopted children as against natural children. And what happens to them in the justice system. Indicating that possibly adoptive parents were not as loyal to adopted children as natural parents. He testified that a study has been made in New York proving that."

"Ah, that one," Ludmiller replied, indicating that he was familiar with the study. "I don't doubt the genuineness of that New York doctor's findings. However, as with many studies, and even Freud's work itself, one has to be on guard against what other people do with the results. How they may misinterpret them, twist them, sometimes innocently, sometimes for their own purposes.

"*Do* adoptive children have a different experience record than natural children? Some don't. Some do. But take the ones who do, let us trace them back a little. An adopted child may have had a long history *before* he was adopted. Perhaps languished in a hospital until some social-service agency decided what to do with him. Maybe he was lodged in a foster home, then another foster home, and even a third, before he was taken by the adoptive parents.

"That does not instill a sense of stability or security in a child. You cannot bat a child around in some bureaucratic game of badminton before he finally arrives in the one family who takes him permanently. If a child so mishandled turns out to have problems, emotional, criminal, or whatever, we should not be surprised.

"This little Baby Brett, as he is called, when was he adopted?"

"At birth," Nancy informed.

"Good. And his parents, his home surroundings?"

"From personal observation it is a good, comfortable home. Stable, loving parents."

"And so, your question?"

"What do I recommend to the Court?"

"What is your own feeling?" Ludmiller asked.

"I would like him to stay where he is," Nancy said. "But I want to be sure that is the best thing for him."

"So in reality you are asking me to confirm your conclusion," Ludmiller considered.

"No. I want you to tell me what is best for the child," Nancy replied.

"No one can predict how a child will grow up. Natural or adopted. I could show you cases . . ." He waved his hand in the direction of a wall of file cabinets. "Cases of natural children showered with everything money can buy. Cases of adopted children with parents who barely scrape out a living. Both grow up with the same problems. There is no answer to your particular question."

"I need *some* guidance," Nancy insisted.

"I would say, as a general rule, if a child is happy and thriving in a family situation where he has lived since . . . since . . ."

"Since the third day of his life," Nancy supplied.

"Since the third day of his life," Ludmiller continued. "Leave him there. To tear him suddenly from the only security he has known in this short life is brutal. Terrible the damage, the emotional pain, to such a child."

"It sounds to me like performing surgery without anesthesia," Nancy said.

"Exactly," Ludmiller agreed.

"Would you be willing to just . . ."

"Say this in court? I do not believe in practicing psychiatry in courtrooms."

Ludmiller's tone had made it quite clear that he had spoken his irrevocable word on the matter.

Failing to secure the help she had sought, Nancy Brook rose, saying, "Just send me your bill, Doctor."

"You are going away with less than you had hoped for. There is no bill," the old man said.

Early next morning, before court resumed, Nancy Brook was the first visitor to the courthouse library. Using the computer catalog, she searched all cases involving the reopening of adoptions. Actions by mothers and other close relatives seeking to reclaim adopted children.

A review of the cases that had reached the Supreme Court of the state made one thing quite clear. Whatever the law in other states, here consanguinity, blood relationship, took precedence over all other factors.

Except in cases of abuse, where the safety or the life of the child might be endangered. No one had ever claimed, nor could they substantiate, such a charge against Lori and Brett Manning.

In truth, Nancy Brook realized, the one key fact that made this such a highly troubling case was that both parties were good, well-intentioned people. From the inception, all parties had acted in the best interests of little Scott. Or little Brett, as the Mannings would call him if they prevailed.

Nancy Brook glanced up at the clock on the library wall. Nine-fifty. She had to be in the courtroom at ten. Reluctantly she was forced to end her search.

If only Judge Hart could have heard Ludmiller express his opinions from the stand. Failing that, and she had failed, the law would prevail.

# Chapter 49

✤

Judge Judson Hart was in a grim mood when he opened the session curtly. "Mr. Clement, while it is our usual practice for the party who opens a trial to close it, I am taking a judicial privilege by having you sum up first. Are you prepared?"

Though privately he resented the change, Clement replied, "We have no objection, Your Honor. And we are ready."

He approached the lectern, laid out his notes, and began, "We call the Court's attention to the plaintiff in this case. Brett Manning. And his wife, Lori. The natural parents of a boy of two and a half presently named Scott Salem. Mr. Manning is financially, emotionally, and by lifestyle equipped to become the loving father of that child. He is eager and anxious to carry out his paternal duties and is here beseeching this Court to make that possible.

"Now, as to the people who presently have custody of the child in question, Christine and William Salem, we are not going to engage in character assassination, as is often practiced in such cases."

Paul Henderson exhaled in a deep, audible sigh to remind not only the Court but the media of Clement's past attempts to cast nasty aspersions on Christie Salem's motives.

Nevertheless, Clement continued:

"Let us review the facts which have emerged during the course of this trial. The defendants, we learned, were the victims of a

301

tragic event. Sudden Infant Death Syndrome.

"There is no tragedy quite so shocking. And we extend our condolences to them. We are even more in sympathy with Christine Salem, who suffered such anguish, guilt, and self-reproach that she was forced to resort to psychiatric treatment."

*God, Clement, stop the phony sympathy. Get to your vicious attack,* Henderson thought, as he impatiently recrossed his long, lean old legs one more time.

"After the consolation and absolution that psychiatry can offer had failed, Christine Salem's doctor suggested that the best treatment was to become pregnant again, have another child. But after many months Christine Salem failed to become pregnant. So back to the psychiatrist she went. And *this* time . . ."

Clement stepped to the counsel table to take a sip of water. He returned to the lectern to continue:

"*This* time, Your Honor, *this* time her psychiatrist advised, if I may quote from the record: 'Mrs. Salem, did your psychiatrist not advise that in a number of cases a woman who could not become pregnant was able to do so after she had adopted a child?' Answer: 'Yes, yes, she did.' Unquote.

"Your Honor, need I remind you that some months after the adoption of Scott Salem, Christine did indeed become pregnant? Five months ago she did give birth to a healthy baby boy. So that she now has a son. In other words, the adopted child known as Scott Salem had served his purpose."

"That's a lie!" Christine shouted. She would have jumped to her feet had not Henderson on her one side and her husband on the other pinned down her arms.

"Your Honor?" Henderson asked permission of the bench. Granted a moment, the old lawyer gripped Christie's arm and in a hoarse whisper rebuked her. "Christine! Don't say a word or do a thing to antagonize this judge!"

"But that man accused—"

"Don't give Clement any more ammunition than he already has!"

Seething, breathing in deep, exaggerated gasps, Christie finally nodded.

"Sorry, Mr. Clement," the judge said. "You may continue."

"As I was saying," Clement resumed, "little Scott has served his purpose. Perhaps it was all God's divine plan."

Henderson could not resist an impatient sigh and a shake of the head at that.

But Clement redoubled his emphasis. "Yes, God's divine plan. Give this woman, who has suffered so grievously, give her a second chance to have a child of her own by *lending* her this innocent young infant."

"Your Honor," Henderson interrupted, to remind him, "Relevance . . . relevance."

Clement glared at the old lawyer, then turned back to the judge. "Your Honor, Scott has served his purpose, has unlocked the block in Christine Salem's tormented mind. It is time now to send that boy back to his natural mother. Into a good, warm, loving home, safe and secure from all the vicissitudes of life."

Giving every appearance of a man making a heartfelt plea, Clement turned to Christie Salem. "Christine, as a mother who each night suckles her own child at her breast, bathes him, tenderly puts him to bed, kisses him, covers him with great care, sees to him several times through the night, can't you understand how this poor mother feels?"

"Your Honor . . ." Henderson interjected, shaking his head at such maudlin tactics.

"This is summation, Mr. Henderson. Lawyers have great latitude."

"Latitude, Your Honor, is one thing. But this . . ."

"Mr. Clement, continue," Judge Hart ruled.

"All I have yet to say, and then I will be done, is that I wish Mrs. Salem could find it in her heart to do for Lori Manning what Lori Manning did for her."

That odd statement caused everyone in the courtroom to question if they had heard correctly. Or perhaps Henry Clement had misspoken. He deliberately permitted the reaction to linger before he continued, "Your Honor, whether it is due to the emotional strain of these proceedings or some other cause yet to be determined, it is my sad duty to report to this Court that several days before this trial Lori Manning suffered a miscarriage."

There was an immediate uproar in the courtroom. Media people, spectators, the Salems, but mostly Judge Hart on the bench, were shocked by this news.

He gaveled the courtroom to silence, then very grimly announced, "Counsel will approach the bench."

Once they were assembled, Judge Hart attacked, "Mr. Clement, I am aware of your usual dramatic tactics. But to unloose such a startling piece of information during summation! No witness, Mr. Clement? No evidence to serve as a basis?"

"Your Honor, it was only late yesterday that I received Mrs. Manning's permission to make that sad fact known."

"Mr. Clement, do you, as an officer of this Court, and under oath, allege that your client suffered a miscarriage as you stated?"

"I do, Your Honor," Clement replied firmly and without hesitation.

"Mr. Henderson?" the judge asked.

"I accept Mr. Clement's statement," the old lawyer conceded.

"You may continue, Mr. Clement," the judge ruled, adding, "and if I may suggest, briefly."

Clement resumed his place at the lectern.

"What I say now is not said as a legal argument. We are beyond that now. I ask this as an act of sheer human kindness. By one woman who has suffered to another woman who is now suffering. You have your own child now. Is she not entitled to the same?"

Clement pointed to Lori Manning but addressed Christine Salem. "Her son having done for you what no one else could, can't you find it in your heart to say, 'Here, take your child back. Where he belongs. I surrender him into your arms, into your heart?'"

Christie Salem gripped the arms of her chair to maintain her composure. Bill could see the telltale blinking of her eyes that usually preceded tears.

"Clement, you son of a bitch!" Bill Salem started across the courtroom toward the lawyer, who turned to confront him. Fortunately the uniformed courtroom attendant stepped between them. It took all his strength to hold Bill Salem back, allowing Clement to remain at the lectern.

Meantime, Judge Hart pounded his gavel in strong, measured strokes, rebuking, "Mr. Salem! Mr. Salem! Return to your seat!"

Media photographers, forbidden to take shots during the trial, took advantage of the confrontation to steal a few shots of Salem menacing Clement.

"This courtroom will come to order!" Judge Hart ruled angrily. "Any film shot in the last five minutes will be confiscated. Photographers will surrender their cameras at the door before they will be permitted to leave."

"Your Honor, that's censorship!" a voice cried from the media rows.

"I am not preventing the reporting of the events that transpire in this courtroom. Or any expression of opinion about those events. But this trial is not being conducted to afford you photo opportunities. The life of a child is at issue here. And he is entitled to an orderly trial so his fate can be determined in a sober and lawful manner."

He turned to Clement. "Counselor?"

Fully aware of what one of Henderson's main arguments would be, Clement decided to usurp it and disarm the old lawyer.

"Your Honor, much has been made and more will be, I am sure, of the fact that Lori Manning misinformed the authorities that the father was a man named Henry Higgins. I ask you to consider a young woman, frightened, alone, suddenly confronted by that decision. The very man whose career she was trying to protect might be destroyed by placing his name on that certificate. Available to gossipmongers who exist by digging up dirt or manufacturing it where none exists. If they were to discover his name, this now-rising young star, what would they say? That this young woman made an enormous sacrifice for the man she loved? Oh, no. They would say that he *deserted* her in her time of need. Which, as we all know, is not the truth. Your Honor, whatever else her faults, this young woman sought to do two things: protect the father of her child, and give her newborn child what she thought at that time was his best chance at a good life.

"I come now to the essence of this lawsuit. To the real party in interest, the plaintiff in this lawsuit. He is not guilty of any wrongdoing. He stands before this Court with clean hands.

"Your Honor, we ask this Court to return to Mr. Manning the child who is his and was wrongfully denied him by an adoption proceeding that was flawed and illegal in the inception. His rights are validated by the law and by court decisions in this state going back almost a century. We ask no more than that the law be upheld in this case. Thank you."

# Chapter 50

Judge Hart nodded in Paul Henderson's direction, inviting him to the lectern.

"May it please the Court, I would like at once to state for the record that it is not our intention, mine or my clients', to cast aspersions on Lori Manning. She was, as Mr. Clement has so adequately stated, a young woman in turmoil, forced to make a decision based on her conflicting emotions. Torn, shall we say, between loyalties. Her child? Or her lover? No, I withdraw that term. Since it does not do justice to either of them. I would prefer to refer to him as the father of her child, and as we know, her present husband.

"Whatever may be said of her decision at that time, wise or not, the Court is forced to deal with the legal consequences. And those are what I wish to address. First and foremost, a newborn child was given into the care of two very fine people.

"Yes, my client did, in a moment of desperation, take her son and flee across the state line. But she came back. Voluntarily. This Court has been asked to show sympathy and understanding for Lori Manning for using a fictitious name for the father of her child. How much more sympathy should it show for a mother who feared that the child she had nurtured since the third day of his life would be seized and taken from her by this Court?

"When these two issues collide, we must ask this Court to

307

consider, who is the innocent party here? As a matter of equity, to which this Court is dedicated, who is entitled to preference? Innocent people who acted in good faith based on the false representation made in a legal document? Or the party who created this conflict by misleading the adoption authorities?

"Of course, Mr. Clement has argued that his client, Brett Manning, is also innocent. And so he is. But using Mr. Manning as the plaintiff in this action is merely a legal maneuver, a ruse, to shield the real party in interest—Lori Manning.

"So the question comes down to this: Who is entitled to equity in this situation? Parties who come into Court with clean hands? Or parties whose hands are, however unfortunately, soiled by deception?

"In this instance, to follow the law and prior cases in this state would defeat an equitable solution. But there is more here than the matter of equity. Or deciding the rights and limitations of the parties named in this lawsuit. There is the child to consider.

"As to the child, let me refer this Court to the trial record. No witness has appeared here to say a single word of criticism about the manner in which Scott Salem has been raised. Since the day he came into this family, he has been nurtured physically, emotionally, and spiritually. He has grown to be a happy, healthy, two-and-a-half-year-old child. I say this Court cannot, must not, tamper with, or even question, that relationship."

A flush rose into the cheeks of Judge Hart.

Nevertheless, Henderson continued, "The issue here is simple. Which is more holy? A law written years ago by men far removed from this courtroom? Or a happy, loving, unified family here and now? I say Christine, William, Scott, and David Salem are more to be cherished than any law. In these times when American family life is badly threatened and slowly disintegrating into a national crisis, I say this Court dare not use the law to destroy this family!"

Giving no hint of his feelings, save the grim way he drummed his fingers on his desk, Judge Hart looked in the direction of the temporary counsel table where Nancy Brook waited.

"Counselor, your summation?"

"Your Honor, I wish to approach."

At once all three attorneys headed for the bench.

"Your Honor," Nancy Brook began, "what I am about to ask is unusual. But then, this entire case has been unusual. Three crowded rows of media people in the courtroom day after day. A swarm of television cameras on the courthouse steps. This isn't a trial, it's a media event."

Already provoked by Henderson, Hart was now outraged.

"Counselor, are you blaming this Court because this happens to be one of those cases the media loves to exploit? It has what they like to call 'human interest.' But which they treat with *inhuman* exploitation? There is nothing a judge can do about that. I cannot bar the press."

"I only meant to ask for a single exception."

"And that is?"

"I would like to present my summation in chambers."

"That's a deviation from procedure which I object to!" Henry Clement replied in a whisper so loud the judge gestured him to keep it down. "Until now everything in this trial has been open and aboveboard. I see no need for secrecy at this stage."

"Mr. Henderson?" Judge Hart invited his response.

"Your Honor, I'd be inclined to agree with my colleague if I had the media in my hip pocket because I represented a big television star. So that I get the headlines on the five-, six-, and ten-o'clock news every night. But I don't have that advantage. And since I don't know what Ms. Brook has to say that is so sensitive it must be heard *in camera*, curiosity to find out makes me agree to this unorthodox procedure."

"Mr. Henderson," Nancy Brook countered crisply, "I do not intend to have either you or Mr. Clement present."

"Now, wait just one minute, young lady!" Henderson exploded. Then he apologized in a whisper, "Sorry, Your Honor. But this goes beyond anything I've encountered in all my years in practice!"

"And mine!" Clement added.

"Ms. Brook?" Judge Hart challenged her to defend her position.

"Where matters as intimate as this are dealt with, which will determine the future of a young child's life, surely he is entitled to the utmost confidentiality."

"Are you saying this trial has not been conducted with the utmost regard for his welfare? Or that we have unnecessarily invaded his privacy?" Hart demanded.

*Not very bright, this young woman,* Henderson thought. *Now she's antagonized us all. Even the judge.*

"Such unusual secrecy," Judge Hart continued, "can only arouse even more curiosity from the media. There will be all sorts of speculation. I'm afraid I must deny your request."

"Your Honor, if forced to, I will appeal your ruling to a higher court. On the ground that denying my motion may do irreparable harm to my young client."

*Poor girl, does she know the risk she's running?* Paul Henderson thought.

Judge Hart glared at her, thinking his own thoughts.

*Damn this young woman. Brash? She abuses the word. Which, I must confess, is the reason I appointed her. All I need now is an appeal and all the added publicity that will bring. Or is she banking on that? That I won't risk being overruled because of that impending appointment to the Supreme Court. Well, she doesn't know me very well.*

"Counselor, make your motion!"

"I ask for a session in chambers. Excluding all other attorneys."

Before either man could object once again, Judge Hart intervened. "Do I understand you correctly?"

"I ask for a meeting in chambers excluding everyone, except Christine Salem, Lori Manning, and Scott Salem."

"And what do you expect to prove by that, Counselor?"

"Your Honor, I am in a difficult, if not impossible, position. I am appointed to represent a client who can hardly testify for himself. Who has no character witnesses. No witnesses of any kind. Frankly, the one witness I had hoped to call has refused to testify. Says he is not a courtroom psychiatrist. Therefore I am forced to resort to this unusual request. Else my client's rights may be forfeited without any chance to protect them. He is being denied adequate representation. I feel that having earned his trust, I have betrayed it."

Judge Hart could sympathize with her predicament. Then, much as he resisted such an unusual procedure, he ruled, "I will allow such a session first thing tomorrow."

"Your Honor . . ." Clement started to protest.

Hart cut him off with "Gentlemen, you have my word. If anything said in that private session calls for rebuttal from either of you, I will give you every chance to respond. Meantime, I grant counsel's request. To take place immediately after the midday recess."

# Chapter 51

✤

Paul Henderson had just informed the Salems that Christie was required to appear in Judge Hart's chambers and bring her young son Scotty.

"No! Absolutely not!" she responded.

"Christie, please . . ." the old lawyer tried to calm her.

"Once they get Scotty in that courthouse, how do I know we'll get him back?" she protested.

At a signal from Henderson Bill Salem pleaded, "Darling, we can't risk offending the judge again. This may be just the thing that turns him against us."

"He's against us right now," Christie shot back. "I will not let them get their hands on Scotty!"

In his most paternal but firm manner Paul interceded to warn, "Christie, you took Scotty across the state line. If you refuse now, Judge Hart has every legal right to issue an order to take custody of Scotty right now!"

"He . . . he can do that?" Christie asked.

"He can. And I don't doubt for a minute that he will," Henderson confirmed.

"Hon?" Bill pleaded.

After a long silence and very reluctantly Christie started for Scotty's room to dress him for his court appearance.

What to put on? She selected a pair of light blue corduroy

overalls, a color that went so well with his blue eyes and blond hair. And a striped T-shirt, navy and white.

Scotty struggled when Christie tried to slip him into his clothes. With the arrogance of two-year-olds he felt able to dress himself.

"Scotty! Hold still!" his mother instructed, but so sharply that he realized something very critical to adults was happening. Too young to understand exactly what, he did sense the importance of yielding.

As Christie was brushing his silky blond hair with unusual care, he asked, "Mommy? We goin' somewhere?"

"Yes, darling."

"Gramma's?"

"No."

"Playschool?"

"No, Scotty. And hold still."

He allowed his hair to be brushed, then could not resist asking, "Where, Mommy?"

"A place called a courthouse."

"Where you and Daddy go?"

She realized that even at the age of two and a half he had picked up the word and in some way sensed its importance from overhearing adults who assumed he was too engrossed in his toys to hear, or, if he did, to understand.

"Yes, darling, where Daddy and Mommy go every day."

Unable to resist, she embraced her son, holding him tighter than usual. Until, in his concern, he asked, "Mommy?"

She blinked back her tears as she said, "Come, Scotty, we're going to the courthouse."

When they arrived at Judge Hart's chambers, his secretary greeted them, "My God, so this is him. Baby Brett."

Christine tightened her grip on Scotty's hand.

"Judge Hart said you have to wait. But it won't be long." She beamed at Scotty. "My, my, what a big boy you are."

Nancy Brook arrived minutes later. She dropped to one knee to look into Scotty's eyes and kiss him.

"Well, aren't you the handsome little man this morning!"

Nancy rose to find herself staring into the challenging eyes of Christine Salem.

"Mrs. Salem, believe me, for Scotty's sake, this meeting must take place."

Even as she spoke, Nancy Brook could read in Christie's change of expression that something was happening behind her. Nancy turned to the door to discover that Lori Manning had just entered.

"My lawyer never said that *she* was going to be here," Christie said.

"I can assure you this was not *my* idea!" Lori responded.

"Mrs. Salem, Mrs. Manning," Nancy took command, "this is *my* idea. You can both help yourselves and your case by controlling your feelings until it is over. Otherwise you may have a marked negative effect on Judge Hart's decision."

That frank warning accomplished its purpose. Nancy took her little client by the hand.

"Where are you taking him?" Christine demanded.

"To see the judge," Nancy informed her as she headed for the door to the judge's private chambers.

Nancy and Scott disappeared behind the thick walnut-paneled door, leaving the two mothers to stare at each other, each silent, lest she endanger her cause by giving way to anger or accusations.

Within chambers Judge Hart had deliberately removed his black robe to present a less austere image to the young boy. He studied Scotty as Nancy edged the boy forward with a gentle "Go ahead, Scotty. Say hello to Judge Hart."

Scotty took only a single step, then turned back to Nancy, who urged him on with a smile and a reassuring nod.

"Good morning, Scotty," Judge Hart greeted the child, smiling. However, he himself felt ill at ease, still baffled by Nancy Brook's unusual request.

Shy and tense, the boy stared up at Hart as if making his own appraisal. Evidently he was not reassured, for he looked back at Nancy. She reassured him with a nod. He studied the judge once more.

"You the judge Mommy talks about?" Scotty asked suddenly.

"Yes," Hart replied, "and what does Mommy say when she talks about me?"

A glint of humor in her eyes, Nancy interrupted. "Objection, Your Honor. Confidentiality between client and mother."

Smiling, Hart agreed. "Of course. We wouldn't want to prejudice Mommy's case, would we?" Then, in a more formal manner, he asked, "Counselor, exactly what did you have in mind when you requested this . . . this meeting?"

Nancy went to the door. "Mrs. Manning!" she summoned Lori.

Eagerly Lori started for the open door. Christie rose to protest, "No! You can't do that!"

"Mrs. Salem! Please!" Nancy rejected her protest.

Once Lori entered, Nancy closed the door, shutting out Christie Salem. Hart's secretary shook her head in commiseration with Christie's fragile feelings.

Inside chambers, Lori made a slight sign of respectful recognition to Judge Hart. Then she crossed at once to Scotty. She dropped to her knees and held out her arms to him.

"Scotty?" she welcomed him with an eager, ingratiating smile.

Scotty drew back, burrowing against the pedestal of the judge's large desk as if trying to find refuge there.

"Invite him, coax him," Nancy suggested softly.

"Scotty, I'm your—" Lori stopped awkwardly. She realized that the only word she dared not speak for fear of turning the child against her was "mother." "I'm your friend . . . I want to be your friend, Scotty."

Both Nancy and Judge Hart could sense the pain Lori Manning was living through in this moment.

"Hold out your arms to him," Judge Hart whispered.

Her moist eyes fixed on her son, Lori complied. She could not elicit any reaction from the child. He stared at her, then looked to Nancy, asking for reassurance.

Abandoning any hope of drawing him closer, Lori moved to him and picked him up. She carried him to a chair and held him on her lap.

The boy squirmed and twisted until finally, embarrassed and

frustrated, Lori was forced to release him. He slipped from her arms to race to Nancy's side.

"He doesn't know me yet," Lori explained to Judge Hart. "When he does, he'll love me. He will. You'll see."

She insisted, "He will. He will!" until tears prevented her from continuing.

Touched and embarrassed by the pain he had not only witnessed but for which he felt partly to blame, Hart demanded, "Counselor, nothing to say?"

"Mrs. Manning, I'm very sorry," Nancy Brook said. "You're free to go now."

When Lori came out into the waiting room, in tears, even Christie Salem felt sorry for her. As Lori went by, Christie reached out to comfort her until she heard her name called.

As she entered, she was greeted by her frightened little son, who ran to her, calling, "Mommy, Mommy!" He bounded into her outstretched arms and buried his face in her breasts, continuing to say over and over, "Mommy . . . Mommy . . ."

Witnessing this reunion, Judge Hart was more angry than touched. His impatience barely under control, he demanded, "Counselor?"

Nancy Brook knew well what the judge meant, and more, what he intended thereafter. She was ready to face him. "Mrs. Salem, will you and Scotty wait outside?"

"Don't I get to say anything to the judge?" Christie asked.

"That won't be necessary!" Judge Hart replied severely. "Now, please. Because counsel and I have a great deal to discuss."

The moment they were alone, Hart put aside all legal formalities. "Ms. Brook, you asked to deliver your summation in chambers. I consented. But what the hell did you think you were doing with this—this demonstration? Proving what any damn fool would know? That a child who has been calling one woman 'Mommy' all his life is going to prefer her to a stranger? Natural mother though she is, Lori Manning is a stranger to him. You caused her great pain to make a very obvious point. Have you no compassion for that young woman? Brook, I'm surprised and shocked at your conduct!"

"Your Honor—" Nancy tried to plead.

But Judge Hart had no tolerance for argument.

"The emotional factors in this case weigh very heavily on me. But judges must not be swayed by emotion. We interpret and apply the law! And the hard fact is that in this state, by statute, long honored by many decisions, the rights of natural parents take precedence over all others."

Having spoken the last word on the subject, Judge Hart returned to his desk to begin reading the first of a thick stack of legal documents that awaited his signature.

Dismissed, Nancy Brook refused to move. Finally the judge stared up at her, defying her to speak.

"Your Honor, that's precisely the reason for my 'demonstration,' as you chose to call it."

"Precisely *what* reason?" the irate judge demanded.

"The statute . . . the cases . . ." Nancy replied.

"Counselor, you know the law as well as I do!"

"Yes, but Scotty doesn't," Nancy retorted.

"What the hell are you talking about?" Hart demanded.

Despite the flush rising into Hart's lean, angry face, Nancy Brook replied, "I tried to explain the law to him. But he didn't understand. Now, as you saw, he's a bright child. If he didn't understand, I thought it must be my fault. So I decided to give you the opportunity to explain. He's out there right now."

"Don't you dare play such games with me, young woman!"

"Your Honor, when the life of a two-and-a-half-year-old boy is at stake, I do not play games! I need your help to explain to him why one day he has one mother and the next day he will have a different mother. And why for the rest of his life he will keep wondering, who was that first mother he loved? What happened to her? And, in the dark of night, when he cries for her, who is going to be there to explain the law to him? And console him and make him accept this sudden legal surgery, which, without anesthetic, cut away a major part of his young life? I hope you can explain that to him the day you hand down your decision. Do a good job, Your Honor! And that is my summation!"

Without waiting for a response, or a ruling holding her in contempt, Nancy Brook started for the door.

Judge Hart made no effort to call her back. He stared at the closed door, aware that the last word had been spoken. The issue now was his and his alone to decide.

# Chapter 52

When Dr. Karen Craig turned into the driveway to find Jud's car already parked, she suspected something was wrong. Or, if not wrong, at least irregular.

She opened the door of her car and was greeted by sounds from the tennis court behind their house. A ball was being hit with unusual power. Her husband was working off some internal stress through physical exertion. He had done that in the past when wrestling with a difficult decision, but infrequently. *Manning* v. *Salem* was a most troublesome case for him.

She found him in his gray sweats, a basket of tennis balls at his feet, getting set to serve yet another one.

At the top of his swing, when he caught sight of her, he just batted the ball away.

"Concentration," she joked. "You'll never get to the Nationals if you don't concentrate."

"Just practicing for the club doubles. And you should, too."

The end-of-season club tournament was still twelve weeks away, over the Labor Day weekend. But she made no point of it. Instead, she said, "I've had a rough day, too. I'd like a drink."

"I could stand one," he admitted.

While he was scooping up the batted balls from around the court, she asked, "How'd it go?"

"Go?"

"Last evening you said something about an unorthodox form of summation this morning. How'd it work out?" Karen asked.

" 'Bout how you'd expect," he replied.

Meaning he chose not to discuss it.

She said no more. Not after he had showered and joined her for a cocktail. Not even through dinner, though his lengthy silence troubled her.

It was only during coffee that the subject came up again. This time he brought it up.

"How come?" he asked suddenly.

"How come *what*?" she responded.

"How come you *insist* on talking about that case?"

That peculiar accusation confirmed Karen's suspicions. The Manning case troubled him as much as she had suspected.

"Jud, darling, may I point out that it has been almost two hours since I asked anything about that case. Only because last night you made such a point about that young lawyer's unusual request."

He avoided responding by changing the subject.

"For all your complaints, you surgeons have it pretty easy. You know the enemy. You know what you have to do to defeat it. True, sometimes you fail. But *you* don't have to make the choices we judges have to make."

"Oh, we have our choices," Karen refuted. "To operate. Not to operate. Those are life-and-death choices, 'Your Honor,' " she pointed out.

"You only have to figure the odds. Will the patient benefit or not?"

"Will the patient *survive* or not," Karen countered.

He set down his coffee cup so hard it splashed.

"Damn it, Karrie, I'm trying to make a point!" he exploded. "You have the patient, the victim. The disease, the villain. You know who you're for and what you're against. But I have before me two families. Personally I'd like to be for both of them. As judge, I'm going to have to end up being against one of them. That is no easy decision."

"Nobody ever said it was, darling," she sympathized.

"Of course, no matter which way I decide, the media will haul out that old biblical chestnut. About wise old King Solomon. How when two women came before him claiming the same child, he solved it all so simply. Just called for a sword, threatened to cut the child in half and give half to each of them. Until one woman cried out, 'Rather than kill the child, give it to her.' And he knew who the real mother was."

"That was all very well in biblical times because Solomon had it real easy. He didn't have lawyers to contend with. And psychiatrists."

"Besides, if *I* threatened to do that, I'd have a dozen federal, state, and local agencies down on me in a minute."

"You must admit that cutting babies in half *is* child abuse. To say the least." Karen tried to lighten the moment and encourage him to open up and talk more freely.

Instead, he left the table with a half-spoken "'Scuse me."

He went off to the den. This time he closed the door. A signal that he wished to be alone tonight. But she had to make some notes for the speech she was scheduled to deliver to a class of aspiring neurosurgeons at the university on Saturday morning. And her file was in the den. She knocked softly.

He was a bit late in answering. She eased the door open. Except for the lamp behind his armchair the room was unlit. She slipped in, intending to retrieve her file and leave without disturbing him.

But, as if their conversation had been continuous, he argued, "Another thing. When your work is done, either the patient recovers or he does not. If he doesn't, that's too bad. But at least it's over. If he recovers, he's much better off for the rest of his life."

"That's the purpose of the surgery," she pointed out.

"Exactly what I mean!" He seized on it, then exposed the true depth of his confusion. "With surgery the purpose is clear. The result, good or bad, is clear. Not so the law. Certainly not in this case. My decision isn't the *end* of anything. It's the *beginning.* A two-and-a-half-year-old boy has the rest of his life before him. Will the way I decide make his life better or worse?"

Since he had invited her into his dilemma, she settled down

321

on the ottoman at his feet. "What about the *law*?"

"The law is clear. If I hadn't seen that little fellow, I could follow it without great qualms. The statute says, the decisions all confirm, in such cases blood is thicker than anything, even possession. There's good reason for it. Families affect education, public safety, morality, every facet of human life. This nation is composed of families. So wherever possible we should strive to keep them together. And reunite them when they come apart."

"But," Karen pointed out, "there's that little boy."

"Maybe I should never have appointed that young woman," he said in momentary frustration. He relented. "No, the worst I can say about her, she forced me to reconsider the problem."

"Jud, darling," Karen started precipitately, then hesitated before offering, "Does any of this have to do with that appointment to the Supreme Court?"

"You know me better than that," he protested.

"You didn't answer my question," Karen persisted. "And it's important, very important, for me to know."

"Why?"

"Answer my question," she insisted.

Her violet eyes blinked, then grew moist. He realized he had underestimated her deep involvement.

"Yes. I would like that appointment. I've dreamed of it since I decided to give up a lucrative law practice to go on the bench."

Something in her eyes forced him to admit, "Will I shrivel and die if I don't get it? Not as long as I have you, angel. Does that answer your question?"

"Yes, yes, it does."

"Now *you* answer one question for me. Why your deep interest in this particular case? Don't tell me the Supreme Court means that much to *you*."

"I'll take you any way I can have you. Even as a plain old Family Court judge," she tried to joke.

But her tears betrayed her. He leaned forward to embrace her.

"Uh-uh," she refused, but was unable to speak.

"Karrie?" He brushed aside her tears with his forefinger. "Karrie, what is it?"

She slipped from his embrace. She moved to the darkest corner of the den. Without turning to face him, she said, "By your ethics it's wrong for me to influence you. But by mine I have to. I have to say this. And say it now."

"Whatever you—"

She interrupted him brusquely. "Don't say a word. Or you'll make it too difficult."

She paced the room, moving from one wall of bookshelves to the other. He thought, *Whatever this is, it is very painful for her.* So he kept his silence.

"Years ago, during the Vietnam War . . . I was nineteen at the time . . . and I fell in love with a young man. We were going to be married as soon as he graduated from college. Never thinking that graduating made him eligible for the draft. Even before we were engaged, he was called. We decided to wait until he returned.

"What neither of us knew . . . During his last week before he shipped out, I became pregnant."

"Karrie," Jud whispered in pained surprise, "you never told—"

"Please! For the first time in my life I must say this aloud to another person."

He forced himself back in the leather armchair, doing his best to pretend he could listen without reacting.

"I had to decide. Have the baby? Or not? I decided I would have it, and when Charles returned—his name was Charles—Charles Stevenson. . . ."

Despite his resolve, he could not resist. "Chuck Stevenson . . . I knew him. We sometimes teamed up in doubles. Chuck never came back from Nam."

"But by that time I had no choices. I decided when the baby was born, I would give it up for adoption. I told myself it would be best for him, or her, to have a real family. Not a struggling young mother without enough education to support herself, let alone an infant.

"After he was born—yes, he was a boy, I would have named him Charles—I gave him into the hands of a very reputable adoption agency. I thought I had done what was best for my child, and I had closed that chapter of my life.

"But the guilt persisted. The painful second thoughts. Until I had to know, had to make sure he was in good hands. Safe. Secure. Happy. Through various means I discovered who his adoptive parents were. I searched them out. I even planned on going right up to their door and, on some pretext, gaining entrance. Oh, I wouldn't have *done* anything. I just wanted to *see* him. . . ."

"Like Lori Manning . . ." Jud commented in a whisper.

Karen gestured, *Please, please, don't interrupt me now.*

"I waited a little distance from their house. Not once. A number of times. I saw the woman—I could never bring myself to call her his mother—saw her take my son out every day, bring him back. I envied the way he held her hand. The way he looked up at her.

" 'It's my hand he should be holding, me he should be looking up to,' I kept protesting. I had to stifle my impulse to call out, 'I want him back!' "

She hesitated momentarily to brush back her tears and regain her determination.

"You present Lori's case better than Henry Clement ever did."

"I followed them, followed them to the park. Several times. Sat on a bench close enough to the playground to watch him. I saw him run, jump, climb the slide and come down. He was the bravest little boy of the group. This one day he was climbing the monkey bars. He reached the top faster than any of the other boys. He was Charles's son all right. Once up there he clamped his little legs over the top bar and hung head down. He swung there, challenging the others to imitate him. He was a daring little fellow.

"Until . . . until he fell. Before he hit the ground, I was on my feet. He raced toward me in tears, his little hand scraped and bloody. I reached out to embrace him, to comfort him.

"But he ran right by me. To that other woman. She scooped him up into her arms. He pressed his wet little face against her. She lifted his bruised hand and kissed it. Soon . . . soon he stopped crying. Content and reassured to rest in her embrace.

"I realized then, it was a shock, that to *him, she* was his mother.

I no longer had that right. I walked away from that playground in terrible pain. *I would have loved to be the mother comforting him. After all, I gave birth to him. He was mine. Mine.* But I realized that day, the important thing was not what *I* wanted. But that *he* was comforted. *He had his mother."*

Karen turned away, into the darkest corner of that room, to cry more freely. Jud crossed to take her in his arms.

As she pressed against his chest, she said, "What I mean to say, my darling Jud, however painful, as an adult I had to accept the realities of life. Had to live with my own decision. But I had no right to inflict such pain on a four-year-old boy."

He dug into his pocket for his handkerchief. As she wiped her eyes, she said, "That's the only secret I've kept from you. I hope it doesn't change things between us."

Before he could respond, she had slipped from his arms and started from the room.

Leaving him alone to confront his decision in *Manning* v. *Salem.*

# Chapter 53

On all previous court days the media, reporters, photographers, television sound- and cameramen had indulged in their routine intrusive coverage of the parties involved in *Manning* v. *Salem*. They surrounded them when they appeared, escorted them up the courthouse steps, pelted them with questions, all of which went unanswered by attorneys and clients, in accord with Judge Hart's injunction.

On this last day the media people were even more overbearing, shouting, asking questions of both sets of parents such as, "Will you appeal if Judge Hart decides against you?" "If you win, when will you take possession of Baby Brett?" "Mrs. Salem, if the decision goes against you, will you try to leave the country with Scotty?"

Such questions, some even more demanding, were showered on Christie and Bill Salem and on Lori and Brett Manning. Both families could not wait to escape into the rotunda of the courthouse, where Judge Hart's restrictions on the media became effective.

The courtroom was full, with an added row of standees as well. The parties and their attorneys had assembled. The courtroom attendant entered. This usual prologue to the judge's arrival caused an immediate hush in anticipation of what would follow.

But instead of calling, "All rise!" the attendant went first to

Henderson's counsel table, then to Clement's. He delivered a message in hushed tones, and behind his large hand, so that he could neither be overheard nor lip-read.

Paul Henderson and the Salems left their table and exited through the door alongside the bench. Clement and the Mannings followed.

It began to dawn on the media people that to ensure privacy Judge Hart had decided to deliver his decision in chambers. An immediate outcry went up. But since there was no judge to complain to, it settled down into disgruntled grumbling.

In Judge Hart's private chambers, chairs had been arranged in two groups: one before the right side of his large desk, the other group on the left. Once the parties and their attorneys had settled down, Judge Hart entered. When, from habit, the participants started to rise, he motioned them to remain seated.

"No need for such formalities." He reached for his telephone console to contact his secretary and said only a single word: "Now!"

The door opened. His secretary ushered in Nancy Brook. She was not alone. Her little client clung to her hand.

Both sets of parents were startled.

Nancy explained to the Salems, "After you left the house, I took the liberty."

She settled into an armchair alongside Hart's desk.

"Mr. Clement, Mr. Henderson, Mr. and Mrs. Manning, and Mr. and Mrs. Salem, to shield you from the overzealous media at a time of great stress to all of you, I decided this would be a more humane way to make my decision known.

"In reaching it, I have been influenced by many things. First and foremost by the law of this state."

Bill Salem reached to grasp Christie's icy hand to prevent her crying out. Henderson exhibited no reaction save for a slight twitch in his lean and wrinkled left cheek.

Brett Manning permitted himself a slight but reassuring glance at his wife.

Nancy Brook put her arms around her little client, who nestled against her, unaware of the significance of what the judge had said.

"I have also tried to give proper weight to the human factors involved. But this has not been easy."

With that, the judge put on his reading glasses and picked up a two-page opinion he had prepared. He began to read in a very somber voice:

"In the matter of *Manning* v. *Salem* heard before this Court, a copy of the trial record attached to set forth the facts in the case, this Court has decided that the applicable law as cited by the plaintiff shall prevail.

"Section One twenty-one of the Domestic Relations Law, sub-section B titled 'Reunification of Families' does, in the opinion of this Court, govern here."

Henderson shook his gray head in grim disappointment. Christie turned to him, her agonized face begging, *Do something, say something!* He raised his hand slightly, only enough to plead with her to retain her composure.

Judge Hart continued, "It is not only statute law, but also public policy in this state, that, wherever possible, consanguinity prevail. That, even in cases where past child abuse has been proved, families shall be reunited.

"Since in a number of cases that policy has led to subsequent further abuse and, in some cases, even to the death of the child, that section of the law has been amended to contain the following words: 'except in such cases where the Court has reason to feel that the child may be endangered or subject to great pain and suffering.'

"Based on all the evidence before this Court, and on arguments of counsel, this Court finds that this child now named Scott Salem would suffer great pain. It would indeed constitute legal surgery without anesthetic to suddenly separate him from the only family he has ever known.

"Therefore, in the spirit of family reunification, this Court rules in favor of defendants William and Christine Salem, the only family Scott Salem has ever known. It is the hope of this Court that the plaintiff will not prolong the agony for all concerned by appealing this result."

Lori Manning sobbed softly, as Brett put his arm around her to draw her close and console her at a time when she could not be consoled.

"Mr. Clement," Judge Hart said to the Mannings' lawyer, "to avoid the media, I have arranged for your clients to leave by the judges' entrance."

The instant the Mannings were gone, Christie rushed to her son. She dropped to her knees. She embraced him, unleashing all her relief and love. Unaware of the importance of what had just occurred, Scotty said, "Mommy . . . you cryin' again."

Weeping and smiling, Christie Salem said, "Yes, darling. Mommy's crying again. Good crying. Now we have to celebrate. Anything in the world you want, Scotty. Anything. What'll it be?"

"Mommy, can we just go home?"

"Of course we can go home. We'll be happy to go home. Delighted to go home. Won't we, Bill?"

Bill Salem hefted his young son onto his shoulders. "Son, first say thanks to Judge Hart."

His father's request seemed odd, but Scotty complied. "Thanks, Judge."

They started for the door. Scotty looked back. "Bye-bye, Nan."

Waving to him, she called, "Bye, Scotty." Then added softly, "And have a good life."

"Counselor, thank you for your assistance in this case. I trust you won't object too strenuously to my bit of judicial plagiarism. I used your words because, if ever there is an appeal, they will help to uphold me."

"I consider it an honor to be quoted in one of your opinions," Nancy replied.

"Someday . . . someday a woman with your—" Hart sought the proper word.

" 'Brashness,' Your Honor?"

Hart smiled. "Judges are not selected for brashness. Let us say, a woman with your forthrightness. How's that?"

"Very good, Your Honor."

"Yes, someday a woman with your knowledge of the law, your feeling for children, *and* your forthrightness may well be sitting in my place," Hart said.

He was alone now. He picked up the phone, then pressed the first button on his memory panel.

"Dr. Craig, please . . . Oh? Well, when she comes out of surgery would you give her a message? *Little Scott has his mother.* Yes, that's the entire message. Well, you could add: *This evening I'd like to take a long drive out into the country, have a nice leisurely dinner. With appropriate wines, of course. I think we both earned it today.*"